in the world, the stakes are high!' – **Leigh Russell, author of the Geraldine Steel mysteries**

A HIGHER DUTY

'An absorbing read' – *Mystery People*

'A very satisfying read' – *Fiction is Stranger than Fact*

'A gripping page-turner. A compelling and disturbing tale of English law courts, lawyers, and their clients, told with the authenticity that only an insider like Murphy can deliver. The best read I've come across in a long time' – **David Ambrose**

'His racy legal thrillers lift the lid on sex and racial prejudice at the bar' – *Guardian*

'If anyone's looking for the next big courtroom drama… look no further. Murphy is your man' – *ICLR*

'Peter M   o finish and l   *iew*

'This beautifully written book had me captivated from start to finish' – *Old Dogs – New Tricks*

A MATTER FOR THE JURY

'An utterly compelling and harrowing tale of life and death' – **David Ambrose**

'One of the subplots ... delivers a huge and unexpected twist towards the end of the novel, for which I was totally unprepared' – *Fiction is Stranger than Fact*

AND IS THERE HONEY STILL FOR TEA?

'An intelligent amalgam of spy story and legal drama' – **Times**

'A story that captures the zeitgeist of a turbulent time in British history' – **Publishers Weekly**

'A gripping, enjoyable and informative read...Promoting Crime Fiction loves Peter Murphy's *And Is There Honey Still for Tea?*' – **Promoting Crime Fiction**

'Murphy's clever legal thriller revels in the chicanery of the English law courts of the period' – *The Independent*

'The ability of an author to create living characters is always dependent on his knowledge of what they would do and say in any given circumstances – a talent that Peter Murphy possesses in abundance...Arnold Taylor loves *And Is There Honey Still for Tea?*' – *Crime Review UK*

'There's tradecraft of the John le Carré kind, but also a steely authenticity in the legal scenes... gripping' – *ICLR*

'Digby, the real protagonist, will keep you guessing until the very end' – *Kirkus Reviews*

THE HEIRS OF OWAIN GLYNDŴR

'A thought-provoking, intriguing unmasking of courtroom sparring and Welsh nationalism' – *Lovereading*

'After swapping his gavel for a pen, a former Crown court judge has published the fourth book in his popular legal saga' – *The Hunts Post*

'All the details of barristerial life, the rules of ethics and evidence, the social attitudes and the courtroom procedure appropriate for the late 1960s period setting are pitch perfect... the book raises very contemporary questions about the roots of radicalism, the motivations for terrorism and the conduct of the security services in combatting it' – **Paul Magrath**

'The story illustrates and discusses effectively questions of nationalism and national identity, particularly the Welsh language with what is seen by the would-be bombers as English interference in Welsh affairs and culture. As a featured character Schroeder is low-key, clever and determined, but it is Arianwen and the others who hold most interest in this case. It is to the author's credit that this fiction sometimes reads and feels like a dramatic re-telling of a real event' – *Crime Review*

Also by Peter Murphy
Removal (2012)
Test of Resolve (2014)

The Ben Schroeder series
A Higher Duty (2013)
A Matter for the Jury (2014)
And Is There Honey Still for Tea? (2015)
The Heirs of Owain Glyndŵr (2016)

CALLING
DOWN THE
STORM

A BEN SCHROEDER NOVEL

PETER MURPHY

NO EXIT PRESS

First published in 2017 by No Exit Press,
an imprint of Oldcastle Books Ltd,
PO Box 394,
Harpenden, Herts,
AL5 1XJ
noexit.co.uk

ISBN
978-1-84344-673-6 (print)
978-1-84344-674-3 (epub)
978-1-84344-675-0 (kindle)
978-84344-676-7(pdf)

2 4 6 8 10 9 7 5 3 1

Typeset in 11pt Minion
by Avocet Typeset, Somerton, Somerset TA11 6RT
Printed in Great Britain by Clays Ltd, St Ives plc

For further information please visit crimetime.co.uk/@noexitpress
Get FREE crime books and other great offers from No Exit Press

You've got to know when to hold 'em,
Know when to fold 'em,
Know when to walk away,
And know when to run,
You never count your money
When you're sittin' at the table,
There'll be time enough for countin'
When the dealin's done.
— Don Schlitz, *The Gambler*

1

Wednesday 28 April 1971

The man was sitting on the ground, his legs drawn up halfway towards his chest, his hands resting on his knees. In his right hand he held a knife, the blade four or five inches long, the brown plastic handle stained to look like wood. The knife was covered in blood.

The woman was lying directly in front of the man, no more than four feet away from where he sat. She lay on her back, her arms stretched out at her sides, her eyes gazing absently up to the sky. A large pool of blood had formed around her, flowing from her neck and midriff and spreading under her legs. She was dying.

It had started to rain, but neither noticed.

DI Johnny Webb and DS Phil Raymond arrived at the scene within five minutes of the call coming in. The killing took place in Dombey Street, a stone's throw from Holborn Police Station in Lamb's Conduit Street, where the officers were just starting a break in the canteen. Leaving their cups of tea untouched, they commandeered PC Williams, a young uniformed constable who was making a start on a bacon and egg sandwich at the next table. The three of them ran at full speed across Lamb's Conduit Street, turning left into Dombey Street less than a minute after leaving the police station.

One look at the man was enough to tell them that they had a serious problem. They stopped abruptly and desperately tried to evaluate the situation. It didn't look promising. They knew that an ambulance had already been dispatched from Great Ormond Street Hospital, which, like the police station, was only a street or two away. Great Ormond Street is a children's hospital, not a specialist emergency unit; but it was a case of any port in a storm – help was on the way, and that was good. But before the ambulance crew had any chance of helping the woman, something had to be done about the man holding the knife. The woman's body was lying just off Dombey Street at the entrance to a narrow courtyard called Harpur Mews. The man was sitting in the entrance itself, with his back to the street, taking up most of its width and blocking access to her.

There was no time to lose. The officers exchanged several urgent hand signals. Webb took the lead. He approached the entrance quietly, and began to feel his way gingerly towards a position in front of the man, making as wide an arc as he could in the limited space around the man's left side. Raymond, treading as lightly as he could, made a direct approach towards the man's back until he was within touching distance. Williams waited like a sprinter in the blocks for Webb to advance sufficiently to allow him a clear path, and as soon as he saw daylight he raced through the gap on the man's left. When he reached the woman, he knelt protectively by her side between her and the man, a last desperate line of defence in case the man attacked her again.

As Webb approached, he noticed that the man was not responding at all to the activity going on around him. He must have known that the officers were there, but he sat perfectly still, his eyes fixed on the ground, his breathing barely noticeable. Webb turned his attention to the knife. His eyes focused on it and stayed there. He was approaching the point of no return now. He would have to put his body within range of a strike. There was no other way to disarm the man. If he chose to use the knife, Webb had no way of defending himself except to raise his arms, offer them up to defensive wounds to deflect more deadly blows, and hope that his colleagues would overpower the man before he could do any worse damage. Even that might not work. He would have to bend down to take the knife, which made him mortally vulnerable to a sudden upward swing of the blade. If the woman's condition had been less serious, he might have waited for back-up, but with things as they were, that was out of the question. There was no choice. He was only a foot away now.

'I'll take that, sir, if you please,' he said, as calmly as he could.

There was no response at all. This was the moment. He was aware that Raymond was at the man's back, ready to pounce. He extended his right hand towards the man's right hand. Their hands touched briefly on the handle of the knife. To his amazement, the man did not resist at all. The officer simply lifted the knife from where it lay, on his palm and under his thumb. The man had almost no grip on the knife; it was a wonder he had not dropped it, and it took almost no effort for Webb to make it secure. He gave an audible sigh of relief, and for some moments he stood in the rain, holding the knife down and away to his right, his eyes shifting between the man and the woman, wondering what had brought them to this.

2

'You don't happen to have any evidence bags with you, I suppose?' Webb asked.

Williams was helping Raymond to lead the man, whose arms were now handcuffed behind his back, to a patrol car which had just screeched to a halt by the entrance to the mews, its blue lights still flashing.

'Sorry, guv,' Williams called over his shoulder. 'Didn't think I'd be needing one up in the canteen.'

Webb smiled. He had been holding the handle of the knife as delicately as he could under his raincoat. With any luck there would still be a print or two left on the handle, and the rain had not entirely removed the blood from the blade; there would be something left for Forensic to look at.

A few feet away from him the ambulance crew was still working feverishly on the woman, huge wads of gauze applied to her wounds in an attempt to stem the tide of blood, an impromptu intravenous drip inserted into an arm, the bag of fluids held high by one of the crew. All in vain: hopeless. Their leader had told him as much when they arrived, with a single shake of the head. It would not be long before they admitted defeat and removed her body to the ambulance.

Very gently, Webb slid his handkerchief from his trouser pocket, wrapped the knife in it, and walked over to the patrol car. The man was now sitting in the back seat, motionless, staring down at the floor. Webb opened the boot, removed a wheel jack from its cloth cover, and converted the cover into a makeshift evidence bag for the knife. He closed the boot and leaned against the side of the car with Raymond and Williams, watching the ambulance crew begin their disengagement.

The street was busy now. Two more patrol cars had arrived, the officers standing by uncertainly. There was nothing obvious for them to do. Scenes of crime officers would soon arrive to take control of the site. But they would not leave until Webb, the senior CID officer present, dismissed them. Next to one of the cars, the ambulance waited, its back doors open. On the other side of Dombey Street, a few people had opened doors and windows to see what was going on. One or two had ventured out into the street. A single officer stood in the middle of the street to make sure they did not encroach on the scene, though no one was showing even the slightest interest in coming any closer. The neighbours seemed calm and incredulous. It was a Wednesday afternoon, not long after lunch: not the time when you would expect something like this. But then again, when would you expect something like this?

'Did he say anything?' Webb asked.

'Not a word, sir.' Raymond replied. 'He didn't resist when we put the cuffs on him, either. He went completely limp. I thought we were going to have to drag him to the car, but he did manage to walk on his own.'

Webb shook his head.

'Well, I hope he has something to say for himself. It looks like he's made a real mess of her. Do we know who he is?'

Raymond made a tent of a fold in his raincoat and took two items from his jacket pocket, keeping them dry while allowing Webb a quick look.

'Driving licence and cheque book in the name of Henry Lang, with an address in Alwyne Road, N1. Where's that?'

Webb shrugged.

'It's off Canonbury Road, sir,' Williams offered. 'Bit of a posh residential area. You wouldn't expect to find people carrying knives up there.'

'I'm not surprised by anything very much any more,' Webb replied.

'There's a business card in the name of Mercury Mechanics,

with an address in King Henry's Walk, N1,' Raymond added.

'Not far from Alwyne Road,' Williams ventured, 'a few minutes' walk at most.'

'He didn't have any car keys with him,' Raymond said. 'Strange for a mechanic, wouldn't you think?'

'Perhaps he liked to walk, or take the bus now and then,' Williams suggested. 'Just a thought, sir,' he added in due course, having received no reply.

'Perhaps someone here knows him,' Webb continued, after a silence. He looked across the street. The neighbours were still looking on, but no one seemed to be in a rush to volunteer information. The houses on both sides of the street were four storeys tall and all had windows overlooking the narrow street. Surely to God, someone must have seen something? He pushed himself up from his leaning position against the car.

'Did she have anything with her?'

'A handbag, sir,' Williams replied. 'It's in the car.'

'All right. This patrol car can take Mr Lang to the nick and get him booked in. We will talk to him when we get back. Tell them to leave her handbag on the desk in my office. Start talking to those people over there and see if anyone saw or heard anything. If they did, make sure you get statements.'

'Yes, sir.'

'And when you've done that, knock on the other doors up and down the street, and see if there's anyone who's a bit shy about coming outside, but may have been peering through the lace curtains. If you need more help, call in and tell them I authorised it.'

'Yes, sir.'

The ambulance crew had lifted the woman on to a stretcher and removed the IV. They were carrying her slowly the short distance out of Harpur Mews towards the ambulance. Only the pool of blood, which seemed barely diminished despite the rain, remained to suggest that anything untoward had occurred to interrupt a peaceful Wednesday afternoon. Three scenes of crime officers had arrived. Webb knew them; he had worked with them before and they were thorough. If there was anything to find, they would find it. He saw them conferring with one of the uniformed officers. If they were lucky, the rain would have left them something to work with, some trace of evidence to seize and analyse. If not, they would have to gather evidence wherever they could.

Webb allowed his gaze to rest on the houses in front of him. As he watched, the front door of the house immediately across the street from the mews opened, and the figure of a woman appeared slowly and hesitantly. She stood for some time with the door slightly ajar before emerging fully into view. She was slightly built, with dark brown hair, dressed in a long, flowing white cotton skirt and a beige blouse, around her neck a thick silver-coloured necklace, rigid and unadorned, her feet in brown sandals with a slight wedge. Webb's first impression of her age was vague, somewhere between 30 and 40, but difficult to pin down more precisely. He could see little of her face, which was almost covered by the large white handkerchief she was holding up to her eyes. Her distress was obvious. He nudged Raymond, and they made their way across the street to her.

'Are you the police?' she asked quietly.

'Yes, madam. We are from Holborn Police Station. I am Detective Inspector Webb, and this is Detective Sergeant Raymond. And you are…?'

'Wendy Cameron.'

'Can you help me at all about what happened here?'

She nodded and pushed the door open.

'I saw it all,' she replied, 'through the window. You'd better come in.'

3

'Would you like some tea?'

They had closed the front door, leaving the horror of the mews behind them, and made their way through to the kitchen at the rear of the house. It was suddenly more peaceful, and for the first time Webb was able to release some of the tension he had felt building inside him since they had arrived on the scene.

'Yes. Thank you, Mrs Cameron. I'm sure a cup of tea would do us all some good. Just milk for me, please.'

'Two sugars, please,' Raymond said.

She struck a match and lit one of the burners on the gas stove. She filled the kettle and put it on to boil.

'It didn't take you long to get here,' she said, her tone still shocked, distant. 'Everyone says that when you call the police it takes them ages to come, but you were here in no time at all.'

'As I said, we are based at Holborn Police Station, at the top of Lamb's Conduit Street,' Webb replied, 'so we were almost on the doorstep. We were able to dash down here as soon as the call came in. Was it you who called it in?'

'Yes. Was the ambulance in time to save her?'

'No, I'm afraid not.'

She nodded, placed both hands on the kitchen table, and bent low over it, as if reminding herself to breathe.

'That's what I thought,' she said eventually. 'I didn't see her moving at all.'

'Did you go outside?' Raymond asked.

'No. I was too frightened. Shocked, too, I think.'

'Yes, of course,' Webb said. 'You did the right thing, staying inside. There was nothing you could have done out there, and it might have been dangerous for you.'

They waited in silence for the tea to be made and served, allowing her time to recover her composure. They sat around the table, Wendy on one side, the officers on the other. She opened a tin, a Delft blue with a windmill and tulips on the lid, and offered biscuits.

'So, do I take it you know these people?' Webb asked.

She nodded.

'Henry and Susan Lang. They were my clients.'

'Clients?' Raymond asked.

'I'm a welfare officer for the High Court – for divorce and child custody cases. The judges ask us to interview the parties and write a report if they need information or an evaluation for a case they're doing.'

'What kind of report would that be?' Webb asked.

'It varies. In most cases, I report on arrangements for children, to help the court to decide who should get custody, or how much access to allow the non-custodial parent. In some cases, it's just to assess the prospects for a reconciliation before the case goes ahead.'

Webb suddenly felt his stomach turn over. He glanced at Raymond.

'What kind of report were you doing in the Langs' case?'

'It's about the children. The divorce would probably have gone undefended – they couldn't wait to get rid of each other – but there was going to be a hell of a fight over custody and access. Mr Justice Wesley had given Susan interim custody, with liberal access to Henry. But that doesn't mean she would have got custody after a full hearing. There were two sides to that.'

'How old are the children?' Raymond asked.

'Marianne is seven, and Stephanie is five.'

'More importantly,' Webb asked, '*where* are the children?'

'Oh, they're safe,' Wendy replied. 'They will be with Susan's mother. That's where they spend most of their time, if the truth be known. Susan was always ready to fight for them and scream about how much she loved them when she was in court, or with me, but I'm not sure she thought about them very much the rest of the time.'

'But she was determined to get custody?'

'Yes. But so was he; even more so, if anything.'

'Were you ready to submit your report?'

'No. The judge asked for the report before he held the next hearing, but I told him I would need at least six weeks because of pressure of work and I still had some way to go. I would have had to do a detailed inspection of both homes – the matrimonial home, where Henry is still living, and Susan's flat. Then I would have met with both of them again, at least once individually and once together, before I prepared my final draft.'

'I see. And they were in a meeting with you today, between what times?'

'Between 12.30 and 1.30, or thereabouts.'

'Did you see either of them with a knife?'

She reacted sharply.

'Good God, no. I wouldn't tolerate anything like that. I would have called the meeting off immediately. Then I would have called the police, and reported it to the court.'

Webb nodded.

'So, what did you see through the window?'

She froze, cup in hand, and looked somewhere into the distance above Webb's head.

'As I say, they left at about 1.30,' she replied. 'I came back here to the kitchen to sort something out for lunch, but after a few minutes, I thought I could hear raised voices. I made my way back to the front room, and I saw Henry and Susan arguing. They were across the street, and they had stepped just inside the mews. I couldn't hear everything they were saying, but it was obviously about the children. We had been talking about the children during the meeting, of course. I was about to go outside and remind them that arguing in front of me wasn't the wisest thing for them to be doing, when I was going to report on them to the judge. And then...'

'It's all right, Mrs Cameron. Take your time.'

'And then it happened.' She put the cup down and held her head in her hands. 'I saw him strike blow after blow, six or seven in all, one after another, bang, bang, bang, just like that. I don't think she saw it coming. There was no struggle. I didn't see her do anything to defend herself. She just went down in a heap. I didn't even realise that he had a knife until I saw how much blood there was. And then he was just sitting there on the ground, doing nothing. I managed to lock my door, grab the phone and call the police. And then you came, and that was it.'

'Had you ever known Henry to be violent before?'

She shook her head firmly.

'Good God, no. He's a quiet, mild-mannered man. He's not some kind of…' She took a breath and visibly pulled herself together. 'The answer is no,' she continued. 'I would never have believed what I saw today.'

Webb drained his tea cup.

'All right, Mrs Cameron, you've had quite a shock. I'm not going to ask you any more questions now. I'll send a constable to take a full statement from you tomorrow. We will need to hear all about the Langs' divorce, in as much detail as possible. We will also need a copy of all the drafts of your report.'

She stood, as they did.

'I really want to help,' she replied. 'But you must understand, I am an officer of the High Court. Everything I do is confidential. I report to the judge. I will have to ask the judge first. I'm sure it won't be a problem, but…'

Webb nodded.

'I understand. But please ask the judge for permission as soon as you can. We will be questioning Mr Lang later this afternoon. It's going to be a lot easier getting to the truth if we know what's been going on.'

'I'm trying to make sense of this,' she said, as the officers were leaving. 'You know, if Susan had done something like this, I think I might be less shocked. She has a temper, and the meeting did get pretty heated. But Henry… something must have gone really wrong, and I can't believe I didn't see it coming.'

'You can't blame yourself, Mrs Cameron,' Webb commented. 'This is not your fault in any way.'

'No, I know. It's not that. It's just that I'm trying to explain it to myself, to make sense of it.'

'You did say that Henry wanted custody of the children even more than Susan did,' Raymond reminded her. 'What was it that made you think that?'

She considered for some time.

'Henry doesn't wear his heart on his sleeve,' she replied, 'and he never banged on and on about wanting the children in the way she did. But when he did say something, he seemed very intense. You could tell he meant it…' She stopped. 'I don't want to say any more now. I am sure it will become clear to you once you question him.'

'Are you going to be all right?' Webb asked. 'Do you have someone you can talk to?'

She smiled.

'I'll be fine,' she said. She had opened the door, and was staring fixedly across the street. 'Will they clean all that blood up this afternoon? It's so horrible. I can't bear having it there where I see it every time I open the door.'

Webb glanced at the three forensic officers who seemed intent on searching every last inch of the entrance to the mews for clues.

'I'm sure they will do it as soon as they can,' he replied.

4

On arriving back at the police station, Webb carefully repackaged the knife in a plastic evidence bag and assigned Raymond to make sure that it found its way to the forensic science laboratory without delay. He then made his way down to the cells. It was quiet. The previous night's consignment of drunks, working girls, and assorted nuisances had long since been dispatched to the Magistrates' Court to be dealt with, and the remands had not yet returned. He found the duty sergeant, PS Bert Miller, his feet up on his desk, with a cup of tea and a copy of the *Daily Mirror*. On seeing Webb, Miller threw the newspaper down on the desk beside him, and swung his feet down to the floor.

'I was wondering when we might see you, Johnny,' he smiled. 'You've got a right one here, and no mistake.'

Miller and Webb had joined the force at about the same time, more than 20 years before, but their career paths had been very different. While Webb had scrambled for a job in CID as soon as he decently could and worked his way up through the ranks, Miller's taste was for work in uniform, out of doors, away from the police station, dealing with the public.

His family had eventually persuaded him to apply for promotion to sergeant, which he had done reluctantly, and had regretted ever since they sewed the stripes on his uniform. As duty sergeant he spent far too much time on routine custody matters, which involved endless paperwork. He took every available opportunity to take part in any assignment away from the station, but sergeants were in short supply, and most of the outside jobs these days were entrusted to constables. In cases where a serious crime required a show of uniformed strength, a large drug bust for example, he always volunteered, but there was often some upstart graduate-entry inspector who wanted to prove to the world that he could handle the physical side of policing and pulled rank to take his place. Despite all this, Miller loved and respected the job. Even though he knew Webb well, he would have called him 'sir' or 'guv' if there had been another officer within earshot.

'Still not talking, is he?' Webb asked.

Miller snorted.

'Not a word. But that's the least of it.'

'Oh?'

'There's some kind of medical problem. I've got Dr Moynihan with him now.'

Webb looked at Miller in surprise.

'Medical problem? What medical problem? We didn't notice anything when we arrested him. He was quite capable of stabbing his wife violently just a few minutes before that, so I don't see what he would need a doctor for.'

Miller got to his feet and sipped his tea.

'All I can tell you,' he replied, 'is that I was checking on him every 15 minutes after I put him in the cell. Once the escorting officers told me the circumstances, I took it upon myself to put him on a suicide watch.'

Webb made a face.

'Come on, Johnny, don't look at me like that. You've known me long enough. I don't like taking chances, you know that – not when it's my responsibility. I don't want some poor sod offing himself on my watch, even if he has just killed his wife. Anyway, as I say, I'm checking on him regularly, and the third time I go in, he's sitting there on the floor of his cell, shaking. And I don't mean shivering. I mean shaking, uncontrollably. I go in and ask him if he is all right. No reply. So I approach him and take his arm, and...'

Miller stopped and shook his head.

'I've never felt anything like it. He was freezing, Johnny, absolutely bloody freezing. Talk about Scott of the Antarctic. You could have frozen water on his arms. That was why he couldn't control the shaking. He was just too bloody cold. And you know what it's like down here. It can be a bit on the warm side in the cells, even in winter. There would be no reason for him to be cold, much less shaking himself to death like that.'

Miller breathed out heavily and leaned back against his desk.

'So I grabbed all the blankets I could find and wrapped them around him, and then I made him some very hot sweet tea; lots of sugar. That seemed to help. He calmed down a bit, but he was still far too bloody cold. At which point I thought, I can't take chances with this. This bloke could be seriously ill. I need to know what I'm dealing with. You couldn't have interviewed him in that condition, anyway. So I called Dr Moynihan, and we will see what he has to say.'

Webb nodded.

'All right, fair enough, Bert. How long do you think Dr Moynihan will be with him?'

Miller shrugged.

'Your guess is as good as mine. He's been in there for a good half-hour already. Why don't you take yourself off to the canteen and have a cuppa? I'll let you know as soon as there is anything to report. The only thing is – I wouldn't be surprised if Dr Moynihan wants him taken in to Guy's or Barts for the night, for tests or observation. You know how careful he is.'

'All right, Bert, thanks,' Webb said.

He turned to leave, but then swung back abruptly.

'And he really hasn't said anything at all?'

'Not to me. Not a dicky bird. If it hadn't been for the documents he had with him, I would have had to book him in as "identity unknown". Don't we know anything else about him?'

'Not yet. I have a feeling we will get some more from our eye witness, the welfare officer, eventually. But she can't tell me any more without getting permission from the High Court. It's all confidential, isn't it?'

Miller smiled. 'Typical.'

'Yes, well, we'll get there,' Webb reflected. 'But I'm going to be a lot happier once he starts talking.'

5

Webb returned to his office. Susan Lang's handbag had been deposited in the centre of his desk. It was a large bag, filled to bursting with odds and ends – cosmetics, tissues, and packets of Polo mints. There were also two sets of keys, which looked like house keys and car keys. The car keys were on a Morris Minor key ring. There was a slim black address book. And, buried deep at the bottom of the bag, Webb found a packet of Durex condoms and a small plastic bag containing a white powder. He held the bag in his hands for some time, before opening it slightly, inserting a finger, and tasting with the slightest touch of his tongue. He nodded. Well, of course: what else could it have been? Picking up his phone, he summoned DC Simon Rice. When Rice arrived, Webb instructed him to prepare an inventory of the handbag's contents, placing each item in its own evidence bag with an identifying label attached.

'Then get this powder over to the lab as soon as you can,' Webb continued. 'I'm going to hold on to the address book and the keys for now. I will sign them in when I have finished with them.'

'Very good, sir,' Rice replied. He seated himself in front of Webb's desk, and began work on his list of exhibits.

DS Raymond came in just as Rice was finishing the last label. He inspected the items carefully.

'Is that what I think it is?' he asked. 'In the bag?'

'Yes,' Webb replied.

'Brilliant.'

'I know. What have you got?'

'The knife's on its way to the lab, sir. There was a green Morris

Minor parked just around the corner from the scene,' Raymond said, pointing at the car keys, 'in Orde Hall Street, I think it's called. It could be hers.'

Webb nodded. He turned to DC Rice.

'Simon, keep the car keys, and when you've dropped everything else off in the evidence room, take a walk and see if you can open a Morris Minor anywhere within a radius of a couple of hundred yards of Harpur Mews, using these keys. You might as well start with the green one in Orde Hall Street. If it's still there, I'd be very surprised if it's a coincidence.'

'Right you are, sir.'

'If there is a car you can open, don't interfere with it. Stay out. Call Forensic to look at it, and don't leave the car until they get there.'

Rice nodded, gathered up the evidence, and left.

'I've made inquiries about next of kin,' Raymond said. 'I've asked the High Court to release any names and addresses in the divorce court's files. We should know something soon. I phoned Mercury Mechanics and talked to a lad called Ernie, who confirmed that Henry Lang is the governor. Apparently they do very high-end repairs and maintenance, Bentleys, Jaguars, foreign sports cars, that kind of thing. I've arranged to go over there and take a look around later. We may have to wait to get entry to his house until we can contact the next of kin.'

'Any news about the children?'

'Yes, sir. Mrs Cameron was right – they're with her parents.'

'Good,' Webb said. 'Has anyone told you what's been going on here?'

'Yes, sir. I went down to the cells in case you were there. Bert told me all about it. What's going on?'

'I have no idea, but I'm sure someone will explain it all to us eventually.'

'Sounds to me like he's trying it on,' Raymond muttered sullenly.

'Yes,' Webb said, 'well, you may be right, but there's nothing we can do about it until we can speak to Dr Moynihan. Come on, let's go and get a cup of tea.'

6

Dr Moynihan found them in the canteen about 20 minutes later.

'Interesting case,' he observed, setting his mug of police station tea down on the table, and easing himself into a chair. 'Not the kind of thing a police physician has to deal with every day.'

Brian Moynihan was an amiable man in his mid-forties, transplanted years ago from his native Belfast when he went up to Cambridge to read medicine at Trinity Hall, and then moved on to a residency at the Royal Free in Hampstead. He had fallen in love with London instantly and had given up any thought of returning to Northern Ireland, though his accent remained intact. He had been the official police physician for the Islington and Bloomsbury area of North London for some seven years and, as such, was called in regularly to examine a wide range of people, from drunk drivers to drug addicts, whenever the duty sergeant thought that a medical opinion was needed. He wore a blue three-piece suit with a blue and white dotted bow tie, and well-shined light brown shoes.

'I've had to ask Sergeant Miller to have him escorted to Barts. He will be there for a night or two for observation. Don't worry. They will keep a close eye on him.'

Webb pretended annoyance.

'Is that really necessary, Doctor? You do know, I hope, that he was arrested for murdering his wife in very brutal circumstances? We are very anxious to question him.'

Moynihan laughed politely. He was used to pressure of that kind from police officers by now, and had become utterly impervious to it. Once he was called in, the welfare of a detained person was his responsibility and his alone, and no police officer, however senior, was going to influence his judgement on a medical question.

'Question him?' he replied. 'My dear Inspector, at this precise moment you would get more information out of my cat than you would out of Mr Lang. It would be a complete waste of your time, I assure you. In any case, I can't permit it, from a medical point of view.'

Webb drummed his fingers on the table in frustration for a few seconds, and then reluctantly relaxed. It was pointless to argue. He took a deep breath.

'What exactly is wrong with Mr Lang – from a medical point of view? Is it even a genuine medical problem?'

'Oh yes,' Moynihan replied at once. 'He's not malingering. There's definitely something wrong. I'm not exactly sure what, at this stage. They will perform a few basic tests at Barts to eliminate the more obvious physical causes – concussion, effect of drugs, and so forth. But my hunch is that it's not physical in that sense. My money is on shock of some kind, a very severe shock.'

Webb and Raymond considered this for some time.

'He was completely passive at the scene,' Raymond said. 'He didn't resist arrest, or try to run away – which he could have done, given that he had a knife. He didn't say anything in reply to the caution when he was arrested, and apparently he hasn't spoken to anyone since then.'

Moynihan nodded.

'All classic symptoms,' he replied. 'It is as though he's frozen, unable to function normally. The freezing expressed itself literally in his body when Sergeant Miller found him shaking uncontrollably in his cell. He had warmed up a bit physically by the time I saw him, thanks to the sergeant's quick thinking, but his mind is still frozen. He couldn't speak at all. I'm pretty sure he understood what I said to him, but he couldn't respond to me.'

'What could have brought this on?' Raymond asked. 'Could it be a reaction to what he did to his wife?'

'Certainly. The trauma of what he did – seeing the blood, perhaps, seeing that his wife was dying – could well have triggered it. Shock of that kind has been well documented. It was commonly observed in soldiers in both world wars.'

'What treatment will they give him at Barts?' Webb asked.

Moynihan shrugged.

'There's not a lot they can do, really. They just have to keep him warm and hydrated, and keep him under observation. If it is shock, sooner or later it will lift, and he should get back to normal. But they can't rush it. It may take a day, it may take two days or, if it is severe, it may take longer. In some of the wartime cases, it lasted for months, or even years. Of course, those were much more serious cases, but there's no way to tell. We will just have to wait and see.'

'Well, look on the bright side, sir,' Raymond said, turning to Webb. 'We have an eye witness, and we were on the scene ourselves a minute or two after it happened. Even if he never speaks another word again, the way I see it, we've got him bang to rights.'

7

Jess Farrar walked briskly into the ladies' robing room at the Royal Courts of Justice and gratefully dropped the heavy briefcase she had hauled from her chambers on to the floor with a loud thud.

'God, why do these cases have to have so much paper?' she asked.

Her opponent smiled, walked over, and gave her a hug and a kiss on the cheek.

'To drive us all mad, obviously. I always assume that at least 90 per cent of what solicitors give us is unnecessary in any given case. How are you, Jess?'

'I'm fine, Harriet, thanks. You?'

'I'm well. How is Ben? Did you have a good weekend?'

'Pretty good. Nice dinner in Islington on Saturday night. It was a bit fraught earlier in the day, though.'

'Oh?'

'West Ham lost again –'

'Oh, dear –'

'Yes, so Ben and Simon were pretty depressed for a while.'

'He still takes Simon to games, does he? He's been doing that ever since he and I joined chambers, just when Simon's mother, Anne Gaskell, was getting her divorce, before she and Kenneth were married.'

'Yes. He doesn't see him as often now. Simon's playing football himself most Saturdays, and when he is free to go to Upton Park he usually goes with his father. But he and Ben still go once in a while. He's grown into such a nice young man, Harriet, and he's already talking about which university he wants to go to. He's thinking of law. It's amazing how time flies.'

'Well, a lot of that is down to Ben. He took an interest in Simon when he must have been feeling very low.'

'It's been good for both of them. Simon really looks up to Ben and I think having someone who looks up to him has been good for him.'

Harriet smiled. 'Talking of Ben, has he had anything to say about our case today?'

Jess laughed. 'Not much. I have told him about it – well, we always talk about our cases – but with his wife on one side and his chambers room-mate on the other, he's been a bit coy about it. I get the impression he thinks that discretion is the better part of valour.'

'I can't say I blame him – especially with our former head of chambers trying it.'

'Yes, it all feels slightly incestuous, doesn't it?'

'Absolutely, and Bernard Wesley would be the first to applaud that. Keep it all in the club, as far as possible. That was always his motto as head of chambers.' She paused. 'And I know he will be scrupulously fair, but I have to admit, he's not the judge I would have chosen for my side of the case.'

'A bit too prim and proper for you?' Jess smiled.

Harriet nodded. 'I think my girl could have done with someone a tad more understanding of human foibles. Not that she has any, of course –'

'Of course not.'

'But I know your man is going to throw some mud at her –'

'The boyfriends, yes –'

'Whom she started seeing out of desperation only because he was working all the hours God sent –'

'In an effort to keep her in the lifestyle to which she had become accustomed –'

'Or because he didn't care about her any more –'

'Said lifestyle including a predilection for drink and drugs.'

Harriet did not reply immediately.

'I don't think you can prove that.'

'I think I can.'

Harriet nodded.

'Look, Jess, do we have to fight this all the way? Can we talk about it?'

'Maybe. What's she suggesting?'

'She's the mother. She wants custody. If he will give way on custody, she will allow him very liberal access, including nights and weekends to accommodate his hours of work. He can basically see them whenever he wants to. It will be a very good deal for him.'

'Harriet, she's running around with drug dealers. She's not a safe custodial parent for the children.'

'She denies that.'

'He is convinced of it.'

'I don't think you can prove it.'

'In front of Bernard Wesley? I think I can.'

They were silent for some time.

'I can't understand why she wants custody, anyway,' Jess added. 'Having to look after the children must be cramping her style a bit.'

'I don't think that's fair. She's entitled to a night out.'

'It's not just a night out though, is it? Our information is that the children spend more time with her parents than they do with her. She's out almost every night, getting back in the early hours. My man's not making this up, Harriet. This is coming from *her* friends. I'm going to ask Bernard to order a welfare officer's report.'

Harriet shrugged.

'Fine. I can hardly oppose that.'

'The welfare officer is bound to talk to the children. They're old enough to know what's going on, or at least to tell the welfare officer where they are spending all their time. The truth is going to come out.'

'She says she has nothing to fear from that.'

'I still don't understand why she wants to put herself through all this. I would have thought it would have suited her down to the ground to have access when it fits in with her social life, and not have to deal with the responsibility of full custody.'

Harriet nodded.

'I take your point, Jess. But at the end of the day, she is a full-time mother, even if she does venture out for some fun at night. And he's not exactly the perfect custodial parent, is he? He works all the hours God sends. He's never home, and that's not good for the children either.'

'It's not ideal,' Jess agreed. 'But if it comes to a choice between a father who's working too hard and a mother who is running round with drug traffickers, I think Bernard is going to go with the father. And frankly, if you fight this all the way in front of Bernard, and I can prove that she's taking hard drugs, he is quite likely to order that any access should take place under supervision – if he allows her any access at all.'

Harriet was silent for some time.

'Well, I'll speak to her again,' she said. 'But I can't hold out much hope, Jess. She's digging her heels in. She seems to feel that the whole world is against her.'

'Too much cocaine can do that to you, I'm told,' Jess replied.

8

'May it please your Lordship,' Jess began, 'I appear for the husband, Henry Lang, in this case. My learned friend Miss Harriet Fisk appears for the wife, Susan Lang.'

They were in one of the large, cavernous old courtrooms in the Royal Courts of Justice which looked as though it could accommodate a vast throng of spectators; but because the case involved children, the court was sitting in chambers, and the public were excluded. The small group of people present, seemingly huddled together in the small central space in front of the judge, looked almost comical set against the imposing dimensions of the room. The large empty spaces produced an eerie echo whenever anyone spoke. It was not a relaxing atmosphere, and even though she now had considerable experience of court appearances, Jess felt nervous. Behind her sat the reassuring figure of her instructing solicitor, Geoff Bourne of Bourne & Davis, and his presence was a comfort. Jess had worked for the firm before becoming a barrister, and so knew Geoff well. He could be relied upon to inject calm into tense situations, but she wondered whether today that skill might be pushed to its limits.

Henry Lang, looking uncomfortable in his best grey suit and a red tie, sat next to Geoff. He was visibly agitated, and was doing his best to ignore his wife, who sat only a few feet away with her solicitor, Val Turner, behind Harriet Fisk. It would not take much interaction between the two of them to set things off. Geoff was determined not to allow that to happen, and Jess had confidence that he would keep Henry in check. But Jess had met Henry Lang in two lengthy conferences, and his distress about the proceedings he was involved in was very obvious. It was not unusual for parties to divorce cases to have strong feelings, and any lawyer doing that kind of work had to get used to dealing with emotional outbursts. But there was something about Henry Lang, an intensity she could not quite define, but something that ran deep and which worried her. She could only hope that he would not reveal whatever it was to Mr Justice Wesley. Raw emotions, understandable as they might be, did not impress a judge who had to decide which parent was more likely to be a stable, cooperative force in the lives of the children.

'Yes, Miss Farrar,' the judge replied, with a broad smile in the direction of each of the barristers in turn.

The Bar was a small profession, and it was not unusual for a judge to know the barristers who appeared in front of him quite well. But the connection in this case was especially close. Mr Justice Wesley had only been on the High Court Bench for about a year, and as Bernard Wesley QC he had played an important role in recruiting Harriet Fisk to join his chambers – the first woman to do so – and in encouraging Jess Farrar to become a barrister. There was a strong personal connection, too. Bernard and Amélie Wesley were sociable people and gave regular dinner parties; both Jess and Harriet had been their guests more than once.

This familiarity was a challenge, of course. Wesley knew that it was more than usually important for him to be – and to be seen to be – objective and unbiased. He also knew that to be objective and unbiased was difficult, if not impossible, certainly once he had started to read the case papers. Written affidavits, even though sworn to under oath, were not the same as live evidence given in court by witnesses who could be cross-examined. But to someone with a lifetime of experience of reading case papers, even an affidavit could have the ring of truth or untruth to it, and Wesley's first impressions were rarely very wide of the mark. With the best will in the world, those impressions were already forming in his mind, which meant that he would have to take all the more care not to let them show.

'My Lord, this is the husband's application for custody of the two children of the family. Your Lordship should have affidavits from both the husband and the wife. May I ask whether your Lordship has had the opportunity to read them?'

'I have,' the judge replied.

'I am much obliged. My Lord, it will be my submission that this is a case in which your Lordship would be greatly assisted by a welfare officer's report. There is a huge conflict of evidence between the parties, which your Lordship will inevitably have to resolve, and I would submit that the full hearing of my application should await the report.'

She looked expectantly at the judge, who turned to Harriet Fisk. Jess resumed her seat.

'I don't disagree with my learned friend, my Lord,' Harriet said. 'Mrs Lang has no objection to a report being ordered, of course. The only application I am instructed to make today is for interim custody, pending the report. The children are with the wife, and it makes sense for them to remain with the wife until the matter is finally resolved.'

Jess sprang to her feet immediately.

'That might make sense if the court could be assured that the children were not being left alone.'

'Whenever my client has to go out, they are cared for by her parents, who live conveniently close,' Harriet countered.

'And if the court could be assured that the children were not being exposed to criminal influences,' Jess added.

'That is pure speculation,' Harriet replied. 'Your Lordship has heard no evidence about any criminal activity.'

'It's in the husband's affidavit.'

'On which I have not had the opportunity to cross-examine him. When I do, I am confident that your Lordship will reject those allegations as baseless.'

Bernard Wesley held up a hand.

'Yes, yes, all right, I've got the point.' He looked across to his right, where the welfare officer had been sitting, following the proceedings carefully. 'Mrs Cameron, how long do you think you will need for your report?'

Wendy Cameron consulted her notebook.

'My Lord, taking into account other work, and as we are about to run into Easter, can I ask for somewhere between six and eight weeks? I will speak to the parties today to make arrangements for an initial interview, which will save some time. But I can't really guarantee a report any sooner than that.'

Mr Justice Wesley nodded.

'Yes, very well. I'm going to ask the solicitors on both sides to keep in touch with the welfare officer and let the court know when it would be realistic to set a date for a final hearing.'

He paused.

'Assuming, that is, that the parties are not able to reach an agreement. Needless to say, it is always in the best interests of the children if the parties can reach an amicable agreement about custody and access. I hope both sides will bear that in mind.'

This was something Wesley always said to parties in custody cases, but in this case, even as he made the request, he had little confidence that it would have any effect.

'There remains the question of interim custody,' the judge added. 'Is there anything either of you would like to add before I give judgement on that matter? Bearing in mind that I have read the affidavits, but as yet have heard no evidence beyond the affidavits.'

'Nothing from me,' Harriet said.

'No, thank you, my Lord,' Jess added.

'Very well.'

Bernard Wesley donned his reading glasses and arranged his papers in front of him on the bench.

9

'This is the husband's application for custody of two children, aged seven and five. I stress that the judgment I give today is an interim judgment, and the parties should not assume that the ultimate result will be the same. I have read the detailed affidavits submitted by both parties, in which they set out their positions at some length. There is a considerable conflict of evidence between them, and I think it will be necessary for me to hear evidence from the parties, and perhaps from other witnesses. I have also decided to order a welfare officer's report, as both counsel agree this would be appropriate. The welfare officer, Mrs Wendy Cameron, is now present in court, and she will hear what I am about to say.

'The parties, Henry and Susan Lang, are now both 32 years of age. They were married on 9 June 1962. Their elder daughter, Marianne, was born on 8 October 1963, and their younger, Stephanie, on 4 February 1966. At first, all seems to have been well, and the marriage was reasonably happy. They had little money to begin with, but that does not seem to have caused any serious problems between them. They lived initially in a flat in the Dalston area. Mr Lang, I think both parties agree, is a hard-working and ambitious man, a mechanic by trade, and he quickly set about improving their fortunes. While many men in his position might have been content with a job as a mechanic, earning the standard wage, Mr Lang aimed higher.

'After gaining some experience with a well-known garage in Chelsea, he set up his own business, Mercury Mechanics, in King Henry's Walk in Islington, not far from the family home. The business is not the usual kind of garage that accepts almost any vehicle. Instead, it specialises in the repair and maintenance of high-end vehicles, expensive and unusual cars, including imported vehicles. Mr Lang quickly earned a reputation for providing a good, reliable service, and he began to be in demand by the owners of vehicles of that kind in London, and indeed, beyond. Not surprisingly, the business has done well. He now employs three mechanics, in addition to working in the business each day himself. I have been shown the accounts for the past five years, and it is clear that Mr Lang has become, if not rich, certainly quite prosperous. The family was able to move to a much larger and nicer flat in Alwyne Road, in Canonbury, again not too far from Mr Lang's business address.

'One might have thought that Mr Lang's success would have been good news for the whole family, but it appears that the long hours he was working to achieve it took their toll on the relationship between the parties. Because this is one of the main areas of contention, and I shall be hearing a good deal of evidence about it, I will say little about it today. But it is clear from the affidavits that the long hours of work caused a good deal of trouble between them. Mrs Lang says she felt ignored, being left at home all day with the children – at any rate until they were old enough to go to school – while her husband spent all day, and many evenings, at the garage. Mr Lang agrees that he was working long hours, but says that it was necessary to develop the business, and that the whole family, including his wife, benefitted from his success. They both agree that there were loud arguments between them, with both parties shouting. Mrs Lang says that the arguments turned violent, that he slapped her face on some occasions, and told her to shut up. Mr Lang strenuously denies that, and insists that he never hit her.

'In February of this year, Mrs Lang left the matrimonial home and moved into a flat of her own in Pimlico, taking the children with her. It was in response to this that Mr Lang brought his suit for divorce, and has made this application for custody of the children. Putting it simply, he says that Mrs Lang is no longer a parent who can be trusted with the custody of young children. He says that she started going out at night long before she left the matrimonial home, that she regularly came home drunk at 1 or 2 o'clock in the morning; and that she had friends, both male and female, whom Mr Lang thought unsuitable for a parent with young children. He says that she sometimes left the children unattended at home. Finally, he says, she started taking drugs and associating with drug users and dealers. Mrs Lang denies that. She admits that she started going out in the evenings with friends, but she insists that the children were always safe, with a reliable child-minder. After she left the matrimonial home, she always left the children with her parents if she was going out for the evening. She says that she never came home drunk, and she denies taking illegal drugs.

'These allegations are clearly of the greatest possible importance. They are bound to affect my decision about which of these parents should have custody of the children, and about the nature of the access which should be granted to the other parent. But they are not the only matters to consider. I need to know in far greater detail what living arrangements are proposed for the children by both parents, particularly what child-care arrangements they propose to make. I need to be satisfied that they will be safe, and I need to know what plans there are for their education. I shall, of course, also have to satisfy myself that the financial arrangements the parties propose to make are suitable.

'I cannot decide all this today. I shall, therefore, adjourn this application pending the welfare officer's report. The question is: what to do in the interim period? It is not an easy question. But I am persuaded, just, that the best course would be to keep disruption to a minimum. The children have already been uprooted once, when their mother moved them from Islington to Pimlico. It seems to me to be in their best interests not to uproot them again without good reason, when the court's ultimate decision cannot be foreseen. For that reason, I will award interim custody of both children to Mrs Lang, but Mr Lang is to have access to the children every other weekend. I hope the parties can make their own sensible arrangements about the times at which the children can be picked up and returned. I am sure their counsel and solicitors will give them appropriate advice about that. If they are unable to agree, a further application can be made, and I will decide for them, but I very much hope that they will be able to work it out for themselves. I stress again, the more they can reach agreement without the intervention of the court, the better it must be for the children.'

10

'I knew the judge would be against me,' Henry said quietly. They had settled down to a coffee in the crypt café in the Royal Courts of Justice.

'He's not against you, Henry,' Jess replied. 'All he decided today is where to place the children for a few weeks until we get the welfare officer's report. They were already with Susan. It does make sense to leave them where they are for now. But you heard what the judge said. That doesn't mean anything in terms of the ultimate decision. It's going to be very different when we come back for the full hearing.'

'Yeah, but now she's got six or eight weeks to clean up her act, hasn't she? She will be in every night, drinking lemonade and playing Monopoly with them, won't she? She will be putting on the full-time mother act, especially when the welfare officer comes to visit.'

'It's too late for that, Henry,' Geoff Bourne replied, shaking his head. 'We already have evidence of what she's been getting up to. Even her friends are concerned about her behaviour. I am very close to verifying that two of the men she has been seen with have previous convictions for supplying hard drugs. It's not going to work.'

'The children will tell the welfare officer the truth,' Jess added, 'and I think her parents will tell the welfare officer the truth. She will have to call them as witnesses, and I don't think they're going to lie for her to an officer of the court.'

'What you have to do between now and the final hearing,' Geoff said, 'is to make sure you can account for every moment in the children's lives when they are back with you. How are you going to get them to school? How are you going to get them home from school? How late at night are you going to work? And so on. You know the kind of thing. We've talked about it.'

Henry drained his coffee cup slowly.

'I can't help the fact that I have to work hard,' he said. 'Some people would even give me some credit for it.'

'Bernard Wesley will give you credit for it,' Jess reassured him. 'Believe me, I know the man. He is in favour of hard work, and he will want to reward it. All you have to do is show him how you're going to take care of the children.'

Henry shrugged. 'My parents live too far away to help regularly,' he said. 'My sister will help. She could collect them from school and stay with them until I get home.'

'The judge would prefer a professional arrangement,' Jess replied. 'Your sister has a life. She's not going to be on call the whole time. It's not as though you can't afford to pay someone. You work hard and you earn good money. Make your money work for you.'

He nodded. 'All right. I can do that.' He glanced at his watch. 'Talking of work,' he said, 'I have to be running along.'

'That's fine, Henry,' Geoff replied. 'Just keep in close touch.'

Henry shook hands with Geoff and Jess in turn, and seemed to be on the point of leaving, when he sat down again abruptly.

'You know what really hurts me about all this? It's not that she complains about my working all the time. I understand that, in a way. I'm sure there were times when she was lonely. I didn't do it deliberately to hurt her. It was just that I was trying to make a good life for us, and that's what it took. I could have dealt with it better. I know that now. But what hurts me is that she doesn't even *want* the children. They're just pawns in the game to her. She wants to get whatever she can out of our marriage, and if she has to use Marianne and Stephanie as bargaining counters to do that, she will.'

'That doesn't necessarily mean she doesn't want them,' Jess said.

'She's *told me* she doesn't want them,' Henry replied.

Jess and Geoff exchanged glances.

'When did she say that?' Jess asked.

'Lots of times, when she came home at God knows what time of the morning, half cut. She would say that she was much happier before she had children, and they just got in the way of her having a good time. She said she was too young to be a mother. She told me a lot of things, believe me: what a mistake it had been marrying me; what a sad little life I led being a mere mechanic; how much more interesting the people were that she was meeting on her nights out; even how much better than me the men were in bed –'

'Henry…' Jess began.

'But you know what? I don't care about that now. If she wants to screw around and throw her life away on drugs and all the rest of it, there's nothing I can do about it. If she wants to insult me, there's nothing I can do about that either. But she is not going to take my children down with her. I won't allow that. I won't allow it.'

He looked directly at Jess.

'Do you think the judge understands that?'

'Absolutely, yes, I think he is very capable of understanding it. He was a very successful Silk in family cases long before he became a judge. He has a lot of experience at seeing through people. So, yes, I do think he will understand it.'

'I can't take risks with my children,' Henry said.

'I'm not asking you to take risks,' Jess replied. 'I'm asking you to trust the process and the people involved.' She took his hand. 'Henry, listen, there are never any guarantees. But I have a good feeling about your case. I know Geoff does, too.'

'Absolutely,' Geoff said at once.

'We have a good case and we have the right judge. I really believe the judge is going to come down on our side. You just have to be patient. I know eight weeks seems like an eternity now, but in the context of your life with the children, it's a very short time.'

They shook hands again, and Henry made his way towards the exit. He stopped just before turning the corner and going out of their sight.

'Thank you. Thank you both, for all you've done for me,' he said. 'You're the best. I know that. You've helped me more than I can ever tell you.'

11

Harriet Fisk knocked on Aubrey Smith-Gurney's door and poked her head inside his room without waiting for an invitation. She had just returned from the Reading County Court after a gruelling day. Merlin, the senior clerk to chambers, had told her that Aubrey was in his room reading a morass of papers in preparation for a banking case in the High Court, and was not to be disturbed. Harriet had smiled to herself and made her way to Aubrey's room anyway.

'May I exercise my right to pick my former pupil-master's brains?'

Aubrey looked up from the huge stack of papers before him on his desk. He was a genial, portly man, and was second in seniority in the chambers headed by Gareth Morgan-Davies QC at Two Wessex Buildings in the Middle Temple. When Harriet had been his pupil, some nine years earlier, he had had a mixed range of work doing family and civil cases, often in the County Courts. But his career had since taken off in the wake of two major successes. He had recently taken Silk, and now enjoyed a high-powered High Court commercial practice which kept him frantically busy. But he always had time for Harriet.

As her pupil-master, he had mentored her and paved the way for her to be taken on as the first female member of chambers. At the time, it had been a contentious decision, which had divided chambers. Bernard Wesley had been head of chambers then. Harriet had good credentials. She was bright; she already had some of her own clients; and her father was the Master of the Cambridge

College both Aubrey and Bernard Wesley had attended. Even so, it had been a hard battle and, to this day, Aubrey was convinced he did not know the full extent of the political manoeuvres Bernard had resorted to in order to ensure that Harriet became a member of chambers. But whatever they were, they had succeeded, and he and Harriet had been close ever since. To her, his door would always be open.

'Of course, Harriet. Come in. You look as though you've had a hard day.'

She smiled and took a seat in one of the two armchairs in front of Aubrey's desk.

'Does it show? I'm not surprised. I've spent all day in Reading, trying to teach His Honour Judge Filby the basics of the law of nuisance, while pretending not to notice how rude he was being to me just for being a woman.'

Aubrey nodded.

'That man is a disgrace to the bench. I don't know how he gets away with it. Reading is not exactly the other end of the earth, is it? You would think it would be close enough for the Lord Chancellor to take some interest in what goes on there, wouldn't you? You could report him.'

She shook her head.

'I could, but my instructing solicitors are a local firm and they have to get on with him. I did tell him to bugger off in a very indirect way he probably didn't even understand.'

Aubrey laughed.

'Oh, he understood, I promise you. John Filby has many faults, but he's a bright man. He hides it well, but he will have understood, and in fairness, he will respect you for it. It's not personal. He's rude to everyone. He was rude to everyone when he was at the Bar, and that's something that doesn't change just because they make you a judge.'

There was a knock on the door. Alan, the junior clerk, entered bearing a tray with two cups of tea.

'Merlin thought you could both use a cup, sir,' he grinned, setting the tray down carefully on a rare empty space on Aubrey's desk.

'He was absolutely right, Alan. Thank you.'

Aubrey waited for Alan to leave.

Harriet sipped her tea gratefully.

'Are you sure you have time? That looks like quite a pile of paper on your desk.'

He shook his head. 'It can wait. Actually, I'm not staying late this evening. I'm going to a party.'

She laughed.

'That's pushing the boat out for you, Aubrey, isn't it? I have never thought of you as a party-goer.'

'It's true; I'm not usually. But this is not just *any* party. It's just been announced that a great chum of mine is going up to the High Court bench, and they are giving him a bit of a shindig in chambers this evening.'

'Really? Who's that?'

'Conrad Rainer, commercial Silk. Do you know him?'

'By reputation, of course. I've never met him personally. I'm impressed that he should be a chum of yours, Aubrey. The word is, he's something of a playboy when he's not working.'

He laughed. 'He does have that reputation, and it's fully merited. I've known Conrad all my life. We were at school together, and then at Cambridge; though he wasn't at your father's college: he's a St John's man. Anyway, how can I help? Is it about your case at Reading?'

12

'No. Actually, it's a custody case I have coming up in front of Bernard. I know you don't soil your hands with that kind of work now that you live in the exalted world of banking –'

He laughed.

'I still retain a distant memory of it. What's the problem?'

'Well, I've got the wife. There are two children, aged seven and five, who are with her at the moment. Bernard has given her interim custody, but only because they are with her, and he's made it clear that the final result may be different. He's ordered a welfare officer's report.'

'What's her complaint against the husband?'

'That's just it. She doesn't really have one, except that he works far too hard and gets annoyed with her if she goes out for a night on the town with her friends.'

Aubrey raised his eyebrows.

'That doesn't sound like a particularly serious complaint. Did she leave him?'

'Yes, and she took the children with her.'

'I'm afraid that sounds rather like desertion to me,' Aubrey said.

'Well, she does say they had violent arguments and that he hit her a few times. But he denies any violence, and he comes across as a decent, hard-working kind of man.'

'That doesn't mean he didn't hit her,' Aubrey pointed out. 'Domestic violence knows no social barriers.'

Harriet nodded. 'Agreed, but –'

'But you don't believe her?'

'I'm not sure I do. And it gets worse.'

'Oh?'

'The other side has been talking to her friends. Apparently, they're saying that she drinks too much, and that recently she's been taking hard drugs and associating with drug dealers.'

'Is that true, do you think?'

'Yes, I think it may well be.'

Aubrey looked up at the ceiling for some time.

'Who's on the other side?'

'Jess Farrar.'

He smiled. 'Mrs Ben Schroeder?'

'Don't be so sexist, Aubrey. You are as bad as Filby. She is Jess Farrar.'

'Sorry, no offence intended. She's very good, so I hear.'

'That doesn't get you off the hook. But yes, she is.'

He shook his head.

'Well, if she can persuade Bernard that anything like that is going on – drugs and the like – you can wave goodbye to custody. He may not even allow her access except under strict supervision. You know how conservative he is about things like that.'

'That's my problem, Aubrey. I'm not sure the other side can actually prove any of it. A lot of it sounds like hearsay. But with Jess against me –'

The phone on Aubrey's desk rang abruptly.

'Give me a moment,' he said, raising a hand. 'Yes? What? Oh, yes, she is, Merlin. Just one moment.'

He handed the receiver to Harriet.

'Merlin. There's a call for you.'

'You're busy,' she said. 'I can have it transferred to my room.'

He shook his head. 'That's all right.'

'Hello,' she said. 'Yes, all right, Merlin, put her through, please.' She put a hand over the mouth of the receiver. 'This is a coincidence. It's Val Turner, my instructing solicitor in the case I'm telling you about.'

'She must be psychic,' Aubrey smiled.

He turned his attention for a moment to the document he had

been reading when she came in. But the change in her face, as she listened silently, drew his attention back to her. Her complexion turned pale, then white, and then to a terrible grey.

'I'll call you back later,' she whispered, handing the receiver back to him.

He stood.

'Harriet, what's the matter? You look as if you've seen a ghost.'

For some time, he thought she had not heard him. She was staring vacantly at the wall above his head.

'Harriet?'

'He's killed her,' she said eventually.

'What? What are you talking about?'

'He's killed her. The husband. He's killed my client.'

She stood abruptly.

'I'm sorry, Aubrey. I have to go.'

13

Ben Schroeder threw the bag containing his robes on to the floor in the corner of the room behind his desk, and sat down wearily. He ran his hands through his hair, and looked through the large sash window out over the Middle Temple gardens. It was a calming sight after the exertions of the day. He had spent much of the afternoon trying to persuade a judge at the Old Bailey that there was some mitigation for his client, who had tried to solve his financial problems by driving the getaway car for two of his mates who had made an unsuccessful attempt to rob a bank using sawn-off shotguns. The judge had disagreed, and the client was now beginning a 12-year stretch, a sentence with which, despite his strenuous efforts to mitigate, Ben wholeheartedly agreed. That did not make the experience any easier when he had gone down to the cells to advise his client that there was no reasonable basis for appeal. It was fair to say that the client had not reacted well to that news.

Ben was a strikingly handsome man in his early thirties, with dark features. He had been a member of chambers for about eight years. As usual, he was immaculately turned out in a dark three-piece suit, a crisp white handkerchief fluted in the top pocket of his jacket and, despite the travails of the day, he somehow still managed to look as fresh as when he had started out first thing in the morning.

His copy of *The Times* lay on his desk. He picked it up, opened it, and began to search for the daily law report. Just as he found it, Merlin knocked and entered without waiting to be invited. The senior clerk's usually imperturbable demeanour seemed to have deserted him. He was breathing quickly, as if he had been running, and his cheeks were flushed.

'Sorry to disturb you, sir, but we have a bit of a crisis.'

'Oh?'

Before Merlin could reply, Jess entered the room with Barratt Davis and Geoff Bourne, the two partners in the firm of Bourne & Davis. Their office was nearby in Essex Street, just outside the Middle Temple, and they were frequent visitors to chambers. Both sent their work in the courts to Two Wessex Buildings. Barratt specialised in criminal law; Geoff dealt with the firm's civil and family work. Jess had first met Ben when she worked for Bourne & Davis after leaving university and was thinking about her career options. Since then, she and Ben had married, and she was starting her own practice as a barrister. She looked pale. She had been out of court for the day, working on an opinion, and was dressed informally in a brown blouse and grey slacks. Her luminous light brown hair was tied back, held in position by a bright green band. In her flat brown shoes she was shorter than Ben's six feet two, but not by much. He saw the lack of colour in her cheeks at once, and walked over to meet her.

'What on earth has happened?' he asked, hugging her.

Merlin closed the door and gestured all present to sit down.

'It's the Lang case, Mr Schroeder, which I have with Miss Farrar,' Geoff said. 'The police called this afternoon. It appears that our client, Mr Lang, killed his wife earlier today.'

'What?'

'They had been to see the court welfare officer. It seems he stabbed her in the street after the meeting. He's going to be charged with murder. I don't know anything more at this stage. I told Barratt, and we both thought we ought to come to chambers immediately. He will need criminal representation now.'

Ben nodded.

'Yes, I see.' He paused. 'Wait a minute. Am I getting mixed up or...? Jess, isn't the wife represented by...?'

'By Harriet. Yes.'

'Oh, my God,' Ben said. 'Where is she?'

'She's with Mr Smith-Gurney, Mr Schroeder,' Merlin replied. 'She's very distressed, but he has promised to look after her. She won't be in chambers long. I think he's arranging for her to spend the night with one of her close friends.'

'I should see her before she goes,' Jess said. 'I hope to God she doesn't blame me for this.'

'She could have no possible reason to,' Ben replied.

'Even so…'

'It might be better to leave it, Miss Farrar,' Merlin suggested. 'I'm sure she will be back in chambers in a day or two.'

Reluctantly, Jess sank back into her chair.

'We still represent Henry in the family proceedings,' Geoff said. 'Despite what's happened, we owe him a duty to safeguard his interests, such as they are. So I will still have a watching brief, as far as the children are concerned. But I've asked Barratt to deal with the criminal case. It's his cup of tea rather than mine.'

'Obviously,' Barratt said, 'we have a difficult situation here, and a very sad one. But we must arrange for Henry to be represented. He will be charged almost immediately, I assume, which means that he will be appearing before the magistrates, perhaps as early as tomorrow or Friday. Ben, I'd like you to represent him.'

'Yes,' Ben replied. 'Would you like Gareth to lead? I'm sure Merlin can give us his dates to avoid for the trial.'

'Yes, of course, sir,' Merlin said.

Barratt hesitated.

'Actually, I want you to do it,' he said.

Ben and Merlin exchanged glances.

'You mean, on my own?'

'With a junior.'

Ben looked again at Merlin, who was looking down, but smiling, his composure having apparently returned.

'Barratt, that's very flattering, but I'm a bit young to lead in a murder. I'm still fairly junior in chambers.'

'I know that. But I think you're ready, and I have a specific reason for wanting you in this case. I want you to lead Jess.'

Ben smiled. 'Barratt –'

'There's method in my madness. Let me explain. Geoff tells me that Henry trusts Jess implicitly.'

'Very much so,' Geoff confirmed.

'Jess also knows everything there is to know about the family proceedings, and that may be very useful in the criminal trial. So I want her to be involved in his defence.' He grinned. 'I take it the Bar doesn't have some arcane rule that a barrister can't lead his wife?'

'Not as far as I know,' Ben replied.

'Well, I have to ask. God knows, the Bar seems to have every arcane rule imaginable, and then a few. Are you all right with it, Merlin?'

'It's not really for me to say, sir,' Merlin replied. 'Choice of counsel is up to you. But since you ask, I would have every confidence in Mr Schroeder, and I am quite sure that Mr Morgan-Davies, as Head of Chambers, would agree.'

'Good,' Barratt said. 'Then it's settled. Geoff tells me that the officer in charge is a DI Webb. I'm going back to the office now to try to contact him, and see what I can find out. In the meanwhile, Jess and Geoff can fill you in about anything you need to know about the family proceedings. Merlin, could you book this in as a conference?'

'Certainly, sir.'

As Merlin and Barratt left the room, Jess caught a glimpse of Harriet, on her way out of chambers with Aubrey.

She stood and walked quickly out into the corridor.

'Harriet, I'm so sorry this has happened.'

Harriet did not reply. Jess approached, and put her arms around her. They held each other for some time.

'I'll be all right,' Harriet said.

'I know. But this is so horrible.'

'Let's talk in a few days.'

Jess kissed her cheek as she walked away.

14

Friday 30 April 1971

'Thank you for seeing us at such short notice, Mr Pilkington,' Webb said, offering his hand. 'I am DI Webb, and this is my colleague DS Raymond.'

'Good to meet you both.'

They shook hands.

'We weren't sure about the protocol,' Webb said. 'We wouldn't normally bother prosecuting counsel at this early stage of a case – particularly when it's Treasury Counsel at the Old Bailey. I was brought up properly to mind my Ps and Qs. But we've got a rather unusual situation on our hands; so I asked my Assistant Chief Constable to see if we could get some urgent advice, and they said you might be able to fit us in. I know you're busy, and I'm sorry to disturb you.'

'Don't worry. That's what we're here for,' Andrew Pilkington said. 'What seems to be the problem?'

'Well, sir, there was a murder two days ago, in Bloomsbury. The victim is a woman called Susan Lang. The suspect is her husband, Henry Lang. He had started divorce proceedings against her in the High Court. She had left him, walked out – in February, this was – and she'd taken the children with her, two girls aged seven and five. Henry asked the judge to award him custody of the children. They had a hearing at the law courts about three weeks ago. The judge said the children should stay with the wife for now, but he didn't make any long-term order and he said it could go either way at the final hearing. He also ordered a welfare officer's report. So they both went to see the welfare officer on Wednesday, around lunchtime, and apparently it didn't go entirely to Henry's satisfaction. They came outside after the meeting, and he stabbed her with a large knife, seven times, all up her front, pubis to breasts. The wounds were fatal, no chance of survival at all. The welfare officer saw it all through her window and called the police.'

Andrew raised his eyebrows and whistled quietly.

'Not a case for mediation, then?'

'Apparently not, sir. As it happens, Phil and I were in the vicinity. The murder took place in Dombey Street, and we are based at Holborn nick.'

'Right on the doorstep,' Andrew observed.

'Yes, sir. We were just starting a break, but when the call came in, obviously we rushed back out and we were on the scene within five minutes, tops.'

He paused, reliving the scene.

'When we get there, Henry's sitting there on the ground next to Susan, not moving a muscle, not saying a word, still holding the knife, and there's blood everywhere.'

'It sounds like a vicious attack.'

'It's the worst I've ever seen, sir. The pathologist, Dr Wren, thinks any one of the wounds would probably have been fatal in itself, without the others.'

'And the welfare officer didn't notice anything amiss during the meeting?'

'No, sir, and she is positive she didn't see a knife. She didn't actually see the knife until the attack was over.'

Webb paused.

'Susan was actually lying inside a mews entrance off the street, and Henry was sitting across the entrance, blocking access to her. So I had to disarm him immediately. For one thing, the ambulance was on its way from Great Ormond Street, but they couldn't get to her as things were; and there was a chance he might attack her again. So we approached him from two separate directions – and I had the jitters about it, I don't mind telling you. If he'd gone for me with the knife…'

'He won't say it, sir,' Raymond said, 'but it was the bravest thing

I've seen a police officer do in my time in the job. He should get a medal.'

'Yes,' Andrew said. 'A very brave thing to do.'

Webb shrugged modestly, but his face showed that what they had said had pleased him.

'All in a day's work, sir.'

'Hardly.'

'I had Phil and a uniformed officer, PC Williams, backing me up. They would have jumped on him if he'd started anything.'

'We wouldn't have been in time,' Raymond said, 'not if he'd swung at you with the knife.'

'It was certainly very brave,' Andrew repeated.

'Thank you, sir… anyway, now we come to the really interesting part…'

'Go on.'

'Well, when I approached him, it was the easiest thing in the world – like taking candy from a baby, as they say. No resistance at all. The knife was just lying in his hand, and I took it off him, just like that. Phil and PC Williams put the cuffs on him and he was nicked. Again, no resistance at all.'

Webb leaned forward in his chair.

'But the really strange thing is that he never said a word to anyone – not to us, not to the duty sergeant, not to anyone. And he still hasn't.'

'The Director's office said he was being treated for trauma-induced shock?' Andrew asked.

'Yes, sir. Our police physician, Dr Moynihan, diagnosed it, and Barts confirmed it.'

'Is he still in hospital?'

'No, sir. They kept him until this morning, to sort out the immediate physical symptoms, but they said there was no medical reason not to keep him in custody, subject to daily checks by Dr Moynihan. So he's back with us now.'

'And he still hasn't said anything?'

'Not a word. He hasn't asked to see his solicitor. He hasn't even asked us what he's doing in the nick.'

Andrew got up from his desk and stretched. He thought for some time.

'Do you have any idea at all what might have driven him to this kind of frenzied attack?'

'Not really, sir. We're assuming that it's tied to the children in some way, but it's not making sense yet. We're talking to Susan's solicitors, but they haven't been very informative. I think they're still in shock themselves, to be fair, though I do get the distinct impression that they were starting to worry about the divorce proceedings. Susan might not have come out of it too well in the long run.'

'Oh? Why do you say that?'

'Well, sir, Susan had parked her car, a green Morris Minor, a short distance from the welfare officer's house. When we searched it, we found a cigarette butt containing a mixture of tobacco and cannabis. And in her handbag we found a quantity of white powder containing cocaine, and an address book containing the names of three persons we believe to be involved in dealing hard drugs.'

Andrew raised his eyebrows.

'How much cocaine? Personal use, or supply?'

'Just under four grams,' Webb replied. 'Not a serious commercial quantity, but on the high side for personal use, at least for someone in her financial situation. I would say personal use plus supply to friends and associates. Decent purity too, around 40 per cent.'

'It would be interesting to know how much Henry knew about all that, wouldn't it?' Andrew observed. 'Does he have any form?'

'No, sir. Clean as a whistle.'

'In that case, I'm sure he wouldn't want his children getting mixed up with drug dealers.'

'That's one of the many things we would like to ask him, sir.'

Andrew nodded.

'Yes, of course. And the doctors haven't given you any idea of how long it might be before he can talk to you?' he asked.

'No, sir. They say it will happen in its own good time. But the problem is that we can't interview him until it does happen, and sooner or later we will either have to charge him or let him go. Obviously, it would be almost unheard of to agree to bail in a murder case, and he has more than enough means to do a runner if he's so inclined. His solicitors have asked when they can see him, and I'm running out of excuses for stalling them.'

'Who are his solicitors?'

Webb fumbled in his jacket pocket before pulling out a handwritten note.

'A firm called Bourne & Davis, with offices near the Temple.'

Andrew smiled.

'Do you know them, sir?'

'I do indeed. I've had several cases against them. They're very good, and absolutely honest. You won't have any problems with them.'

He paused for some time.

'So,' he said, almost to himself. 'What to do? '

He resumed his seat behind his desk.

'All right. First, you must at least try to interview Henry; go through the motions. It's very unlikely that he has total amnesia. Even if he can't remember what happened on Wednesday, find out who this man is, his life history, what he remembers about his marriage, his children, his wife leaving him, the divorce proceedings. I'd be amazed if he doesn't remember something, and with any luck that will jog his memory about the event itself.

'Worst case scenario, even if he says nothing, or he tells you that he can't remember anything, you are putting his reaction on the record, so he can't pretend otherwise when he comes to trial. I don't want the defence to complain that you made no effort to question him. Also, it will give you the chance to assess for yourself whether the amnesia seems to be genuine or not.'

Webb nodded. 'Right you are, sir.'

'Second, you can't stall his solicitors. You're not allowed to, and you don't want to. Let them see him as soon as possible. Again, it's about making a record. If he doesn't say anything to them either, they can't complain about you at trial. It may even be in his interests for his solicitors to cooperate with you.'

'How so, sir?'

'They may be thinking of some defence based on mental incapacity. We don't know enough about the case yet to know whether that might fly or not, but Davis might raise it with you. In any case, you need to get a second opinion from a specialist doctor or a psychologist familiar with the effects of shock and amnesia. Dr Moynihan is all very well and good, and he seems to have made the right calls so far, but he's a general practitioner, and eventually a judge is going to want to hear from an expert.'

Webb was rapidly making notes. Andrew waited for him to finish.

'Once you've interviewed him, go ahead and charge him, regardless of what he says or doesn't say.'

'Even if he doesn't say anything?'

'Yes. Why not? It's not exactly unknown for suspects to remain silent when interviewed, is it? That's why you caution them, to remind them that they have the right to remain silent. The reason for the silence may be a bit different in this case, but that doesn't alter the principle. It doesn't matter whether he says anything or not, as long as you give him the chance. You have more than enough evidence to charge him with murder. You may as well get on with it.'

15

The two officers stopped at the door of the interview room, opened the door gently and stepped inside. Henry Lang was waiting for them. He was sitting quietly at the table. His sister had brought him some of his own clothes and personal effects from home, and he was dressed in a clean grey shirt and jeans. He looked up as they entered. He looked tired, and there were dark lines around his eyes. The eyes themselves seemed empty, vacant. The officers looked at each other and sat down at the table opposite him.

'Mr Lang, I don't know whether you remember us?'

He stared at them blankly.

'No. Sorry. Should I?'

'All right, then. Let's start with introductions, shall we? I'm Detective Inspector Webb, and this is Detective Sergeant Raymond. Before I go any further, Mr Lang, I must tell you that we are investigating the suspicious death of your wife, Susan Lang, and that you are a suspect in her death. Therefore, I must caution you that you are not obliged to say anything unless you wish to do so, but what you say may be put into writing and given in evidence. Do you understand what I've just said?'

'Yeah.'

'Good. Sergeant Raymond is going to be taking notes.'

Henry nodded but said nothing. There was a silence. Webb laughed awkwardly.

'I must admit, Mr Lang, this is a new one for me. I'm not sure where to begin. Perhaps I should ask... do you even know where you are?'

Henry nodded again.

'I'm in custody at Holborn Police Station.'

'Very good,' Webb said. 'That's correct. How do you know that?'

'Sergeant Miller told me this morning.'

'This morning?'

'Yeah. I remember arriving here this morning in an ambulance, with a police officer, and when we arrived, Sergeant Miller said who he was, and told me that he was in charge of the people in custody at Holborn Police Station. That's how I know.'

'And you don't remember meeting Sergeant Miller before this morning?'

'No.'

'Do you know what day it is?'

Henry thought for some time.

'No. Not really.'

'Well, I can tell you: it's Friday 30 April,' Webb said. 'I'd be happy to find a newspaper with today's date on it, if you don't want to take my word for it.'

'No, I'll take your word for it.'

'Thank you, Mr Lang. Well... I'm not sure... can I just see if I understand this correctly? Is it your impression that you were brought here for the first time this morning, Friday 30 April?'

'As far as I know, yeah.'

'Do you know why you're here?'

'Sergeant Miller told me I'd been nicked.'

Webb nodded. 'That's right. Do you know why?'

Henry shook his head.

'Not really. He said my wife had been attacked, but I don't know anything about that.'

'I'm sorry to have to ask you this, Mr Lang, but did Sergeant Miller tell you that your wife had been killed? Do you understand that she's dead as a result of being attacked with a knife?'

'Yeah,' Henry replied quietly.

'Did he tell you when your wife was killed?'

'I'm not sure.'

'Or where?'

'I don't remember.'

Webb paused to allow Raymond to complete a note.

'So you don't remember being arrested by DS Raymond and myself on Wednesday, and brought to the station in a police car?'

'On Wednesday?'

'Yes.'

'No. I don't remember that.'

'You don't remember being put in a cell here just after lunch time, about 2.30 to 3 o'clock on Wednesday afternoon?'

'No.'

'Do you remember feeling very cold in your cell?'

'Cold?'

'Yes.'

'It doesn't feel cold in here.'

'No. I know. But I'm asking whether you remember feeling cold while you were in the cell on Wednesday afternoon?'

'No.'

'You don't remember Sergeant Miller bringing you a cup of tea, and then some blankets, and telling you to wrap yourself up in them to keep warm?'

'No.'

'You don't remember a doctor, Doctor Moynihan, coming to see you, and taking your temperature, your blood pressure, and so on?'

'No.'

'And you don't remember being taken to Barts hospital?'

'No. Is that where I came from this morning?'

'Yes. Do you remember staying the night there?'

'No.'

'Not last night, not Wednesday night?'

'No.'

'No? You don't remember being in a hospital ward, nurses putting an IV in your arm to keep you hydrated and medicated, doctors coming to examine you?'

'No.'

'Nothing about any of that?'

'Nothing at all.'

Webb sat back in his chair, and looked at Raymond in frustration.

'Well, what *do* you remember?'

Henry thought for a very long time.

'I remember being at home in the morning –'

'What, on Wednesday?'

'Yeah.'

'Home being your flat in Alwyne Road?'

'Yeah. I was at home until it was time to go out.'

'To go out where?'

'I had to… well, I'm involved in a divorce…'

'Yes. Go on.'

'And I'm trying to get custody of my two daughters.'

'Yes. I know.'

'The judge said my wife and I had to have some meetings with a court welfare officer.'

'And what's the welfare officer's name?'

He paused.

'Wendy Cameron. She lives in Dombey Street.'

'Yes,' Webb said. 'That's not far from here, is it?'

'From here?'

'Yes. Holborn Police Station, where we are now, is in Lamb's Conduit Street, right around the corner from Mrs Cameron's house. Why do you suppose I would know that?'

Henry shrugged. 'I don't know.'

Raymond was shaking his head. Don't push him too hard, he was suggesting.

Webb nodded.

'So you had a meeting scheduled with Mrs Cameron on Wednesday?'

'Yeah.'

'And that was to talk about your children?'

'To help her to decide what to recommend in her report. Yeah.'

'What time was the meeting supposed to take place?'

'We had to be there by 12.30.'

'And what time did you leave home?'

Henry shook his head.

'I don't know.'

'Well, how long would it take you to get from your flat to Mrs Cameron's house?'

'Not long.'

'Not if you drove, no. But you didn't drive, Mr Lang, did you? You walked.'

Henry looked up, apparently in surprise.

'Did I? Why would I do that?'

'I don't know, Mr Lang. I was going to ask you the same thing.'

'I don't know.' He looked closely at Webb. 'Did I really walk?'

'It seems so. We didn't find any car keys when we arrested you, and there was a red E-Type outside your flat when officers went there later in the day. Is that yours?'

Henry nodded.

'Yeah. I have a couple of cars I keep at my garage, but I do tend to run around in the Jag mostly.'

'We did wonder whether you might have gone by bus. Do you remember being on a bus?'

'No. I don't use the buses. I don't like buses, and anyway you can't rely on them.'

Webb reached into his briefcase, which he had placed beside his chair.

'While we're talking about your flat, Mr Lang, do you happen to recognise this?'

Webb put the knife, still in its evidence bag, on the table. Henry made a move as if to pick it up, but then withdrew his hand as if unsure whether he was allowed to touch. Webb picked it up and put it in Henry's hand.

'Don't be nervous about handling it, Mr Lang. It's in a bag, so you can't contaminate it. Do you recognise it? Take a careful look.'

Henry turned it over several times, peering at the knife through the plastic cover from different angles.

'I can take it out of the bag if you want…'

'No,' Henry replied suddenly, abruptly replacing the knife on the table. 'That could be mine. It's similar to a set I have in the kitchen. I think Susan bought them, in the West End somewhere, when we were first married.'

'If I were to go to your flat now, would I find the complete set of knives there, or would there be one missing?'

'I don't know.'

'This one, perhaps?'

'I don't know.'

'Don't you? Didn't you take this knife with you when you left your flat to go to Mrs Cameron's?'

'No. Why would I take a knife with me to see Mrs Cameron?'

'I don't know, Mr Lang. I'm asking you.'

'No. I can't see why I… I don't remember taking anything with me.'

He paused.

'Can I ask a question?'

'Of course you can.'

Henry picked up the knife again.

'What are all those brown stains on it?'

16

Webb took a deep breath.

'Mr Lang, before I answer your question, in fairness to you, I think it's time for us to put our cards on the table, and tell you what DS Raymond and I saw on Wednesday afternoon in Dombey Street.'

'All right.'

'There was a 999 call just after 1.30, asking for police and an ambulance to be sent to Dombey Street at the entrance to Harpur Mews. That's immediately opposite Mrs Cameron's house. DS Raymond and I responded, together with another officer, PC Williams.

'When we arrived, we saw you sitting on the ground, in the rain, holding this knife in your right hand. Your wife Susan Lang was lying on the ground, just inside the entrance to the mews. She was bleeding heavily from a number of wounds, and it was obvious to us that her condition was very serious. Are you with me so far?'

Henry nodded.

'The way you were sitting, there was no way for the ambulance to get to Susan, so it was necessary for us to take away the knife – which we did, and in fairness to you, you didn't try to stop us, or attack us, or attack Susan. You were totally compliant, and I want to thank you for that.'

'I don't remember any of this,' Henry said.

'You were arrested, and given the same caution I gave you today, and you made no reply. You were brought here to Holborn Police Station and checked in – in other words Sergeant Miller made sure he knew who you were and why you had been arrested – and you were then placed in a cell, just like the one you've been in this morning.'

Webb paused.

'But, I'm sorry to say, the ambulance crew weren't able to save Susan. They tried very hard, they did all they could, but our understanding is that she couldn't have been saved by the time they arrived. Her injuries were too severe. They were always going to be fatal.'

Henry was nodding.

'Meanwhile, you were apparently suffering from shock. You went very cold, and you weren't responding to anyone at all. Sergeant Miller was concerned about you, and called the police surgeon, Dr Moynihan, and he was the one who diagnosed shock and whisked you off to Barts for tests and observation.'

Henry was still nodding.

'So, they're blood stains?' he asked. 'That's Susan's blood?'

Webb nodded.

'It has been analysed,' he replied. 'It's her blood.'

Henry held his head in his hands for some time, and lowered his head towards the table. DS Raymond was rubbing his hands together, grateful for a break from his rapid note-taking. Webb said nothing for more than two minutes, allowing Raymond time to flex his writing hand a few times before picking up his pen again.

'We spoke to Mrs Cameron,' Webb said. 'She was the one who made the 999 call. She told us all about the meeting, and she told us she saw the whole thing from the window of her house. Do you want to know what she saw?'

'Yes,' Henry replied, his head still bowed.

'She saw you and Susan arguing by the entrance to Harpur Mews. She even heard you shouting at each other, though she couldn't hear what you were saying. And then she saw you strike Susan very hard, six or seven times, and she saw Susan fall to the ground. That's when she saw the knife in your hand. You sat down on the ground, exactly where you were when we found you. You hadn't moved at all.'

'So, I killed her?' Henry asked, raising his head and looking directly at Webb.

Webb was taken aback. Raymond had paused in his writing and Webb was aware of his questioning look.

'Yes… actually, Mr Lang, at this point, I think I ought to remind you that you are still under caution. That means that you are not obliged to say anything unless you wish to do so, but what you say may be put into writing and given in evidence. Do you understand what I've just said?'

'Yes.'

'Mr Lang, do you wish to say anything?'

'What do you want me to say?'

Webb stared at Henry for some time.

'Mr Lang, do you understand what we're talking about? Do you understand that you are going to be charged with the murder of your wife? I ask because, for a man who has stabbed his wife to death in such a violent manner, you seem remarkably composed. I think if I were in your position, I would be a basket case, and yet you seem completely calm.'

Henry remained silent.

'Well, would you like to tell us why you killed your wife?'

'I don't know,' Henry replied, after a long silence.

'Was it to make sure that she didn't get custody of the children?'

'No. Well, I don't think so. I can't remember.'

'You can't remember stabbing your wife six or seven times with this large kitchen knife? You can't remember sitting on the ground, watching her bleed out?'

'No.'

'Well, what *do* you remember?'

'I remember getting ready to leave home to go to Mrs Cameron's house. After that, I remember arriving here from the hospital this morning. That's it.'

Webb exchanged glances with Raymond.

'You don't remember anything between those two times?'

'Nothing at all.'

Webb banged both palms down on the table. He then stood,

and walked to the wall behind his chair and studied Henry's face. Henry looked steadily ahead of him and did not seem to react.

'You'll forgive me, Mr Lang,' Webb said, 'if I tell you that I don't accept that. It's very convenient, isn't it?'

'Is it?'

'Yes. If you can just answer "I don't remember" to any question I ask you, it means you don't have to give us an explanation, doesn't it? And I'm not sure what explanation you could possibly give us for what you did.'

'Neither am I,' Henry conceded.

'And to be perfectly candid, Mr Lang, I don't think a jury is likely to accept what you say about your loss of memory, any more than I do.'

'Well, it's not very convenient for me then, is it?' Henry replied.

17

Friday 1 October 1971

The prison officer unlocked the conference room and ushered
Ben, Barratt and Jess inside. It was a procedure that had become
wearily familiar: the trip from the Temple to Brixton prison,
where Henry Lang was on remand; the time-consuming process
of being checked in, having briefcases and handbags emptied and
examined; the delay while prison officials found an unoccupied
conference room, protesting surprise at the visit even though it
had been booked long in advance; the further delay while they
searched for an officer free to escort Henry; the discomfort of the
small claustrophobic windowless room with its hard metal table
and chairs. And, of course, the frustration of interviewing a man
who remembered everything except the events they needed him
to remember. But now, there was the added pressure of the trial.
This was Friday, and the trial was fixed for Monday. All they had
left was a weekend.

Time after time, Jess had used her knowledge of the family
proceedings to establish a full history of Henry's life – his home
background, education, business success; and the essential details
of his marriage, the birth of his children, the beginning of the
break-up, Susan's leaving home with the children, and his decision
to divorce her. Jess was patient in her questioning, and skilful in
drawing information out of him. The trust she had gained during
the family proceedings was intact, and he seemed at ease with
Ben, who deliberately stayed in the background, asking only an
occasional question to clarify something.

But each time, they had run into a brick wall which shut out any image of the occasion on which he had killed his wife. His last memory was leaving the house at about 11.30 in the morning on his way to see Wendy Cameron. After that, his mind was a complete blank until they returned him to Holborn Police Station from Barts hospital, two days later.

At first, Ben had found himself sceptical. They had confronted Henry time after time with the evidence of the police officers who had attended the scene. It was a compelling account of terrible violence wrought by a man with no history of violence, but with every reason to resent, and perhaps even to hate, his wife. As a trial lawyer, Ben struggled to believe that none of this vivid and dreadful evidence had released any fragment of memory at all, however small.

But as he got to know Henry better, he gradually came to share Jess's belief that the amnesia was not an act. If it was an act, he grudgingly conceded to himself, it was a performance worthy of an Oscar. Very few people, if any, could have acted so well over such a prolonged period. He and Jess were not Henry's only audience. Ben had seen the notes of two police interviews in which DI Webb and DS Raymond had gone over exactly the same ground as he and Jess, had tried just as hard, and had met with exactly the same result; and he had seen the report of a Dr Harvey, an expert in both neurology and psychiatry, whose opinion was that Henry's inability to remember was not inconsistent with the evidence of what had happened on the fateful Wednesday.

But while he was glad to think that Henry was genuine, Ben knew that it offered little hope for the trial that was about to start. If he couldn't offer the jury some explanation for what he had done to his wife, he would leave them with little choice. A conviction for murder and a sentence of life imprisonment were staring Henry Lang in the face.

Ben was arranging his papers on the table, Jess was whispering something to Barratt, when Henry entered the cell. The prison officer slammed the door shut and locked it from the outside, leaving the four of them alone together. Ben got up to shake hands, but Henry stood rigidly just inside the door, making no movement towards him.

'I've remembered,' he said quietly.

For some time, no one spoke.

'What?' Ben asked.

'I've remembered what happened,' Henry replied.

He suddenly sat down on the floor, and began to weep, more and more loudly until his weeping became a howl and finally a scream.

18

May 1970, almost eighteen months earlier

Deborah Rainer waited just long enough for her husband to lift himself off her and roll over on to his back before pulling her white lace nightdress down to cover her body. The gesture eased her anxiety a little. She was already fretting about how she was going to prepare for the Bible study she was supposed to be leading at church in two hours' time, and she was resenting him for asking for sex on a Wednesday afternoon, when he knew she always had Bible study on Wednesday evening. Their time for sex was Sunday afternoon, after lunch, when she had got through morning worship and Sunday school and could relax until it was time for evening worship. And he was still asking her to take off her nightdress, when he knew that she preferred to keep it on. She had pulled it up for him while they were under the covers, as she always did. What more did he expect?

He was still naked and breathing heavily, looking up at the ceiling as if he were unaware of her. Why hadn't he covered himself up? Why was he so remote, so inconsiderate? Did he still love her? Why didn't he hold her in his arms after sex any more? He used to when they were first married. Was it because she couldn't have children? What had she done to make God punish her like that?

He was aware of her. Out of the corner of his eye, he had watched her go through the routine of pulling down her nightdress, signalling the end of their intimacy for the day. And as he gazed up at the ceiling, he was wondering how he had allowed his life to come to this: to a childless house in Guildford; to sex once a week by appointment with a woman who fretted about Bible study and pulled her nightdress up and down to announce the beginning and end of play, like a referee with his whistle; to a sexual adequacy dependent on summoning up fantasies about old girlfriends, or women he met professionally, or socially, or saw at a distance on the train or in the street.

'I don't know why you have to stay up in town over the weekend, Conrad,' she was grumbling as she climbed out of bed and began to dress. 'You're going to miss church again on Sunday, and I know Pastor Brogan has started to notice; and I was hoping you might come to Bible study with me this evening. I feel more confident when you're with me.'

He got up and reached for his dressing gown.

'I'm sorry, Deborah. I can't. It's this fraud case I've told you about. It's coming on next month and I'm not ready. Besides, you lead Bible study perfectly well. You don't need me there every time.'

'Every time? I can't remember the last time you came with me.'

'It was last month.'

'It's been at least two months, closer to three.'

'Be that as it may, I can't do it tonight. I have work to do.'

'That's the excuse you make every time you stay up in town.'

'I'm a Silk now, Deborah, a QC. You know what that means. Professionally, I can only take more difficult cases, more complicated cases; and complicated cases take time. I explained all that to you when we took the flat in London. I told you there would be nights away. I don't know why you have to keep bringing it up.'

'It's not just nights away, though, is it, Conrad? You're sometimes gone for most of the week.'

'I'm gone when I have to be. I came home yesterday evening, didn't I? We've had a fuck on a weekday afternoon. I'm doing what I can, Deborah.'

'Don't use that word. You know I don't like it.'

She was dressed now, apart from her shoes. She looked at him in silence for some time as he opened the wardrobe to take out his suit.

'I need you for church committee next Tuesday evening. I

promised Pastor Brogan you would talk to him about planning permission for the new church hall.'

He nodded.

'Yes, all right; not that I know anything about planning permission – it's hardly my field.'

'You know a lot more than he does, and you know who to talk to about it.' She glanced at her watch. 'What train are you catching?'

'The first one I can get. I'm off to the station now.'

'Phone me before you go to sleep,' she said, leaving him alone in the bedroom.

It was after 7 o'clock by the time Conrad arrived at his flat in a fashionable block in the Barbican, the City of London's new upmarket residential area. He unpacked the few things he had brought with him. It didn't take long. There was not much he had to carry back and forth between Guildford and the flat any more. During the five years of his tenancy, he had made himself more or less self-sufficient there. Deborah still seemed to have a mental image of him camping out, sitting on packing cases and brewing tea over a paraffin burner, huddling over it to keep warm in winter. But Deborah, by choice, had hardly ever set foot in the place, and had no real idea of what it was like. She preferred to pretend that it was no more than a temporary expedient, or a fad of which he would eventually tire. But it had long since become a comfortable home from home. He had furnished it tastefully, with every imaginable comfort, and he lacked for nothing. It was an extravagance, but he could afford it. He was doing well in Silk, and if he ever had a quiet period there was always Deborah's trust fund, over which he now had as much control as she did. Just as well, too, given her propensity to be an easy touch every time Pastor Brogan came calling for a contribution to whatever new project he had in his sights.

Opening the sideboard in his living room, Conrad gratefully selected another reason for enjoying his London sanctuary – a bottle of good whisky. Deborah wouldn't have it in the house in Guildford. He could barely get away with a beer at the weekend, or wine with dinner once in a while. Pastor Brogan wouldn't approve even of that; there was always the feeling of dabbling in a forbidden pleasure, like some Prohibition-era American taking a solitary, nerve-racking drink of some nameless hooch in the darkness of his cellar. But not here. In the Barbican, he could enjoy a glass of beer, or wine, or whisky, or whatever else he wanted, whenever he wanted it; and now he sat relaxing on his sofa, nursing a large glassful, looking out over the quiet night-time City streets, and thinking again of Barbara, a free-spirited friend of his student days, the memory of whose generous hands had been the inspiration for his laboured passion with Deborah during the afternoon. Whatever had become of Barbara? He had heard that she had taken a job in Canada. Was that true? Had she stayed, or returned?

By 9 o'clock he was ready to eat something. The other benefit of the flat was that it had made him take an interest in cooking. Conrad would never be an adventurous or experimental cook, but he had taught himself to prepare a range of basic meals that didn't take too long and didn't leave a huge pile of washing up. He knew his limits as a domestic manager, and the rule was to keep it quick and simple. Tonight, a cheese omelette seemed right, with a glass or two of Beaujolais.

At 11 o'clock, he called Deborah to tell her that he was ready for bed, and listened patiently to her account of Bible study, and how much better it would have been with him there, and how Pastor Brogan sent his prayers and best wishes for his fraud case. When the conversation ended, he put on his jacket and adjusted his tie, switched off all the lights except the one by the front door, and made his way out of the building.

19

'Conrad, do come in.'

John Aspinall had walked down from his office on the top floor to welcome the Clermont Club's newest member personally. During the course of his progress from Oxford undergraduate with a passion – and talent – for gambling to the owner of London's leading gaming club, Aspinall had learned a few things about managing an exclusive clientele. It was the personal touch that mattered.

Opening his club in 1962 in the exquisite Georgian architectural masterpiece at number 44 Berkeley Square, he catered for the client with good taste in every department – and the money to pay for it. The building itself offered a peaceful, refined setting for high-stakes gaming in the heart of London. The food and drink, often free of charge to members who ventured large sums of money at the roulette wheel and the card tables, were superior to anything on offer in the Capital's more traditional gentlemen's clubs. A troublesome debt was dealt with by friendly advice in Aspinall's office, never by so much as the hint of a threat; after all, the whisper that a member was unable to pay his debts carried more weight in London than any threat, and it was said that because Aspinall knew how to whisper, he never had to. In any case, if you were rich and socially well-connected enough to be an asset to the Club, debts at the Clermont were sometimes negotiable.

But what summed it all up was the personal touch. Aspinall knew all his members, and their friends and spouses, by their first names, and he did his best to attend to their every whim. As a result, the right kind of people flocked to join. Conrad Rainer, successful Silk, whose wife had a trust fund, was one of them.

'Let me walk you through the Club,' Aspinall said, 'then we'll have a chat up in my office, and then I'll introduce you to whoever may be here and leave you to get on with it.'

They walked together from the front hall and, with the bar on their left, gazed up at the house's magnificent staircase.

'This isn't your first time in the building, of course?' Aspinall said.

'No. Ian Maxwell-Scott showed me around when he introduced me,' Conrad replied, 'though I didn't have time to take it all in properly. I've spent more time down in the basement, in Annabel's.'

Aspinall smiled.

'Ah, yes. Mark has done wonders with the place hasn't he? That's good for us, too, of course, having such a prestigious night club downstairs. It was the house's wine cellar originally, you know. There's a staircase just on your right there, that they would have used for access in the old days but I don't think it's seen any traffic for many years now. I'm not even sure it would be safe, so I've closed it off.

'Originally, the house was the residence of Lady Isabella Finch, a daughter of the Earl of Winchilsea. She was a spinster, quite a character by all accounts, well connected at Court – and she obviously wasn't short of money. She bought the land in 1740 and commissioned no less than William Kent to build this house on it. She lived here from about 1744.'

'I have to confess, I don't know much about architecture,' Conrad admitted, 'but the name William Kent rings a bell.'

'It should. He also built Devonshire House and Holkham Hall, though sadly this is the last surviving example of his London town houses. Just look at the staircase, and the way he's made the curves correspond to the curves of the dome.'

'It's marvellous,' Conrad said, as they looked up together.

'It's one of the glories of London,' Aspinall replied, 'and if I hadn't got my hands on it, someone like Charlie Clore would have bulldozed it to build more of his ghastly modern blocks of flats.'

They began to climb the staircase.

'But now, it's all ours. The staircase and landing are like

Holkham Hall in miniature. Kent reused a number of his best ideas, and you can see some of them in the rooms upstairs.'

They paused halfway up to admire the dome again.

'I took the name of the Club from a member of the Fortescue family, the Earl of Clermont. Lady Isabella died in 1771, and the house remained empty for five years or so, but eventually Clermont bought it and made it something of a social centre in London. Apparently, there were all kinds of notorious goings on involving the rich and famous of the day, but fortunately, he didn't do any damage to Kent's work. We'll come back down to the gaming rooms. Let's go all the way up to the top, to my office, for a minute or two.'

'So, it was Ian who introduced you?' Aspinall said, once they were seated. 'I've known him ever since we were up at Oxford. Have you known him for a long time?'

'Actually, I know Susie better than Ian,' Conrad replied. 'We're members of the same profession.'

'Oh, yes, of course,' Aspinall said. 'She was Susie Clark before her marriage, wasn't she? One of the youngest, if not the youngest, woman to become a barrister in England.'

'Yes, that's right. I met Ian through Susie.'

Aspinall laughed.

'They seem to do very well together. But to be honest – and I'm not telling tales out of school; they'll be the first to tell you themselves – it's something of a miracle they're not both bankrupt several times over.'

'Oh? Why?'

'They're both incorrigible – never satisfied unless they're betting huge amounts of money on something or other, and they don't have a lot of talent for it. But the gods of the tables seem to smile on them. They always seem to win big just when all seems lost, and they somehow keep their heads above water. I love them both dearly, but they do worry me.'

'Do you worry about all your members?' Conrad asked.

'Yes,' Aspinall replied. 'Well, they're all friends. That's the principle behind the Clermont: that you eat and drink with friends, and game with friends. Everyone knows the rules, and everyone knows their limits.

'Do you know, Conrad, when I started the Clermont, it was just a small group of us. There was Ian, Dai Llewellyn, Dominick Elwes, Jimmy Goldsmith, Mark Birley, Lucky Lucan, and me. All of us friends, all used to playing together. And everyone played a part. Ian was in charge of food and drink. He's quite an expert, by the way – that's why the food and drink are so good here compared to other clubs. Dai was our social secretary. Dominick was our one-man membership committee – still is, come to think of it: recommending new members, making sure they're suitable and all the rest of it. Then you've got Lucky and Jimmy, who know a lot of people, people with the right social background, with the right kind of resources to join a club like the Clermont. Of course, we have many more members now, but that's how it started, with an emphasis on quality rather than quantity.'

He looked up to the ceiling.

'Did you know I used to host games at the Ritz before I started here?'

'I had no idea,' Conrad replied. 'Was that legal?'

'Not at the time,' Aspinall laughed. 'But no one cared. And you know why? It was because it was all among friends, and they were the kind of friends no one was going to refuse, even at the Ritz – perhaps especially at the Ritz. And that's how it is today at the Clermont. So, Conrad, this is what I want to ask of you: be my friend. If you have a problem – with losses, with another member, whatever it is – you come to me. You don't go to anyone else, inside the Club or outside. You come to me. Agreed?'

'Agreed.'

They shook hands.

'Good. And you must know your limits. Members here tend to play high, but you don't have to try to match them. I'm sure you know what I mean. What interests you?'

'*Chemin de fer*,' Conrad replied immediately. 'I've played most of the card games, including classical baccarat, but never chemmy.'

Aspinall smiled. 'Ah, well, you've come to the right place. Chemmy is a house speciality, and there's a game on the go every night.' He looked at his watch. 'Getting on for 1 o'clock. Things should be warming up downstairs. Are you ready?'

'Ready,' Conrad replied. As they stood to leave, he said, 'I hope you don't mind my asking, John. What was it that made you offer me membership?'

Aspinall laughed.

'Dominick told Ian he thought you were all right,' he replied.

20

They walked down one floor to the heart of the Clermont Club, the first floor, which boasted the two gaming rooms, both exquisitely decorated with artwork and a rich, dark red velvet wall covering. A desk stood in front of them as they left the small staircase leading to Aspinall's office. There was not much space on the landing separating the desk from the magnificent main staircase, which with startling suddenness curved steeply away towards the ground floor. The view down from the landing was both exhilarating and vertiginous. Conrad felt a momentary wobble as he allowed his eyes to follow the sharp fall of the stairs.

'This is the cash desk,' Aspinall said, 'and this is Vicente, who will be in charge of giving you your chips and cashing you out.'

They shook hands.

'Good evening, Mr Rainer,' Vicente said. 'Welcome to the Clermont Club.'

'So this is your first port of call if you're playing. Then, you have a choice. To your right is the Holland Room, and to your left is the Blue Room. Take your pick. There was more action in the Blue than the Holland earlier. Is it still busier there, Vicente?'

'Yes, Mr Aspinall,' Vicente replied. 'There's been a good crowd in the Blue Room all night.'

'It changes from night to night,' Aspinall said. 'Let's go into the Blue Room, and I'll introduce you to whoever there is to meet, and then you're on your own. It would be a good idea for you to make a bit of a tour of the building tonight, even if you don't play very much, just so that people get to know you. Spend a bit of time in the Holland, and make an appearance in the Club Room downstairs.'

'I will,' Conrad promised.

To the right of the door of the Blue Room was a large green-covered table, shaped like an imperfect figure eight, with the eight's curves but without a coming together in the centre. Nine men were seated around the table, which was presided over by a dinner-jacketed croupier.

'Right, let's see who we have,' Aspinall said, leading Conrad into the room by his arm. He turned left, away from the card table.

'Can I have your attention for a moment, everyone? This is Conrad Rainer, a new member. He's a QC, so you'd all better be on your best behaviour, but Dominick has pronounced him to be a thoroughly decent fellow.'

There was some laughter.

'Perfectly true,' Dominick Elwes said, advancing and offering his hand. 'Welcome, Conrad.'

'This is Lord Lucan, "Lucky" to his friends.'

Conrad offered his hand to the Earl of Lucan, and noted his sharp features, his jet black hair combed back and parted so precisely, and his thick black moustache. Lucan took his hand briefly with a slight nod of the head, but said nothing.

'This is Lord Derby; and this objectionable fellow is the notorious Kerry Packer, who's doing his damnedest to ruin the sacred game of cricket. Typical bloody Australian. I can't imagine why we ever made him a member.'

'You like the money, mate,' Packer replied, laughing. 'You and everybody else.' He shook Conrad's hand. 'Welcome aboard, sport. I hope you've brought your wallet and your cheque book with you.'

'And you already know these two reprobates,' Aspinall smiled, as they approached Ian and Susie Maxwell-Scott.

'Conrad, darling,' Susie said, getting to her feet, cocktail glass in hand. 'How lovely to see you.'

She kissed him, and then John Aspinall, on both cheeks.

'You've arrived just in time. Ian is just off to join the table, and he's leaving me alone. You can keep me company for a while.' She took Conrad's arm and turned him away from Aspinall slightly.

'He's only just let me back in,' she added, in a stage whisper designed to allow Aspinall to hear. 'He had me banned for weeks. So unfair.'

'She was as pissed as a newt the last time she was here,' Aspinall said, 'and she got loud. The members were complaining – and if she doesn't behave herself tonight she'll find herself out on her ear again.'

She stuck her tongue out at him. 'Spoilsport.'

'Ian, thanks for the introduction,' Conrad said, offering his hand.

'My pleasure,' Ian replied. 'Make yourself at home, won't you. And you don't have to babysit Susie.'

'Yes, he does,' Susie insisted.

'It will be my pleasure,' Conrad grinned.

'Have you played chemmy before?' she asked, as Ian took his seat at the table. Kerry Packer had also joined.

'No,' Conrad replied. 'I've tried blackjack and I've played baccarat once or twice, but I'm interested in chemmy. I want to give it a try.'

'You'd better watch for a while,' she said, 'just to get the hang of it, and get a feel for how much money changes hands here. It moves at a pretty fast pace. Don't join till you've got a feel for it. You can lose a lot of money in a hurry.'

She took his arm.

'Come on, let's get you a drink and observe from a safe distance.'

She put her head around the door.

'Vicente, be a love and call down to the bar and get Mr Rainer a drink, will you? He must be dying of thirst. What will it be, Conrad, a G and T?'

'Whisky, with a splash.'

'The Famous Grouse, with a splash,' Susie said. 'Put it on my husband's account.'

'Coming right up, Mrs Maxwell-Scott,' Vicente grinned.

21

'If you've played baccarat,' Susie said, 'you'll know the basics. The main difference with *chemin de fer* is that the house doesn't act as banker. A player has the bank. The bank starts with the player on the croupier's right; so it would have started with whoever that is on Jean-Pascal's right – looks familiar but I can't quite place him – and as you see, it's already made its way down to Dai Llewellyn. A player keeps the bank as long as he's winning, but once he loses, the bank passes to the player to his right. That's where the name comes from. "*Chemin de Fer*" is French for "railway". The bank goes round like a train.'

'But if the house isn't the banker, how does the house get its cut?' Conrad asked.

'These days there's a standard table charge. In the old days, the house took 20 per cent of the amount wagered in each round, and Jean-Pascal would have raked if off into the *Cagnotte* before the cards were turned over. But that's not legal now. John still does all right out of the game, though, believe me.'

'I'm sure. Does the bank play against all the other players?'

'Yes.'

'That must mean that the bank stands to lose quite a bit on each hand? Can the banker give up and pass the bank to the next player?'

'Yes, but there's a certain etiquette involved. You can lose a lot as the banker, but you can also win a lot, and it's not the done thing to pass as soon as you're ahead.'

'You have to give the others a sporting chance to recover?'

'Yes. Two or three hands is usually enough to keep everyone

happy. But remember, the banker is either winning from, or losing to, every player who places a wager.'

'But not every player receives cards – otherwise the bank would be outnumbered.'

'That's right. One player represents all the others, however many there may be, and everyone lives and dies by the two cards the representative is dealt. So it's two cards against two.'

They were standing close enough to the table to see, but far enough away not to interfere.

'The bank wagers £300,' Dai Llewellyn was saying.

'Now the others have to decide whether to match the bank,' Susie was whispering. 'The player to his right – that's Henry Vyner, I think, I've only met him once – has first call. If he calls "*Banco prime*", the bank is covered and Jean-Pascal will announce no more bets. It's French again of course. What he says is, "*Rien ne va plus*".'

'What if Vyner doesn't cover the bank?'

'Then, any other player can cover the bank. If no one does, each player can wager at his discretion up to the amount wagered by the bank; and if the bank agrees, the amount can be increased, but the bank sets the limit. You see those two squares on the table? The first one, the *Banque*, is where the croupier places the amount covered, and the second one, the *Reliquat*, is for any uncovered amount.'

'*Banco*,' Ian called.

'There you go,' Susie smiled. 'Ian's in the game. It never takes him long.'

'So John was telling me.'

She smiled, but she seemed irritated.

'John can be such a killjoy. It's our money, for God's sake. There are times when he needs to… well, don't get me started on that. So now, Ian represents the players. If there had been a *banco prime*, he would represent; if not, it's the first player to call *banco*; and failing that, it's the player who lays the highest wager.'

Conrad's drink arrived. He thanked the waiter, who left quietly.

'*Rien ne va plus*,' Jean-Pascal called.

'Now we come to the cards,' Susie said. 'Always dealt from the shoe by the croupier, of course.'

'Using several packs?'

'Six to eight packs,' she replied. 'The house rule here is eight, or at least that's what Jean-Pascal always uses.'

'And the goal is nine points from two cards?'

'Exactly. A total of nine or eight is called a "natural". The nine is "*La Grande*" and the eight is "*La Petite*", and any natural means that no more cards are drawn. Nine wins, and eight wins unless there's a nine.'

'What happens if it's a tie?'

'The croupier calls, "*Égalité*", and rolls the wagers over to the next hand.'

They couldn't see the faces of the cards, but Jean-Pascal was announcing that the bank had won by *La Petite* to zero.

'Dai's in form tonight, apparently,' Susie said. 'You can score zero in any number of ways. All the picture cards are worth zero, so if you have a jack and a queen you have zero, and if you have a four and a king, you have four.'

'And there are several ways of making a natural.'

'Yes. Aces count as one, so to get to nine you can have ace plus eight, two plus seven, three plus six, and so on.'

'When can you draw an extra card?'

'That varies a bit from house to house. Here, the rule is that the players can draw on zero to four, they stand on six or seven, and they can either stand or draw on five. If the players stand, the bank is allowed to draw on zero to five but stands on six or seven. If your score goes above nine, you deduct ten, or twenty, so it always comes down to something between zero and nine.'

Jean-Pascal had raked the used cards into the *Panier*, and a short break had been declared to allow the players time for a drink; the Clermont did not permit drinking at the table itself.

'So, have you got the idea?' she asked, as the players dispersed.

'I think so. I'm going to watch tonight, and I'll take a hand next time I come in.'

'Very wise.' She took his arm and walked him away from the

table. 'I haven't even asked you how you're doing, Conrad. How's the practice going?'

'Busy. Commercial stuff, frauds, you know. How are the children?'

'Driving us mad as usual, but we can't complain. I'm sure we drive them even more mad with the lifestyle we lead. How are things at home?'

'Much the same, I'm afraid.'

'Bible studies and no booze?'

'That's about it.'

'How bloody for you, darling. I'm so sorry.'

She kissed him on the cheek. Ian was approaching.

'Don't forget to make the rounds, Conrad, will you?' She tapped him on the chest with her forefinger for emphasis. 'And don't forget the Club Room.'

'John told me to show my face everywhere.'

'Yes, but now *I'm* telling you. And *I'm* telling you not to forget the Club Room.'

'Why? Are there a lot of people down there?'

'Sir Jack Bristow – you know, the property magnate – was there earlier.'

'Is he someone I should meet?'

'Not particularly, but he was with someone you should definitely meet,' she smiled.

'Oh?'

'Yes. She struck me as someone who might be a bit of an antidote to the home situation, if you see what I mean.'

Conrad raised his eyebrows and returned her smile.

'I'll keep my eyes open.'

'Yes,' she said, 'do.'

22

The Club Room was almost empty. As Conrad entered, several members were making their way out, talking and laughing, one or two smoking cigars, en route to the Holland Room to start up a game. Only two or three tables were still occupied. Conrad approached a waiter and quietly asked where he might find Sir Jack Bristow. The waiter pointed discreetly to a corner table at the far end of the room. Conrad looked. He saw a short, fair-haired man in his fifties or sixties, wearing a suit – cheap-looking and a fraction too small for him, the fabric a far-too-light blue, the jacket already beginning to shine at the elbows. And then he saw her.

She was tall, with vivid red hair and green eyes, age hard to read – he put her in her early thirties but felt that he could well be off by several years either way – not slim exactly, but with no excess weight at all and perfectly proportioned. She was wearing a stunning low-cut cocktail dress, red, with matching high red heels and an elegant gold necklace, tight to her skin. She seemed to notice him too. Although she was speaking to Bristow, her green eyes strayed in his direction, and stayed on him as he approached.

'I'm sorry to interrupt, Sir Jack. Do forgive me. I'm a new member. John Aspinall has given me strict orders to introduce myself to everyone tonight before I'm allowed to leave, on pain of banishment, so here I am. My name is Conrad Rainer.'

Reluctantly, Bristow forced himself to stand, and offered his hand.

'I'm Jack Bristow. Allow me to present Greta Thiemann.'

She offered her hand, which he took and kissed lightly. Her

perfume was restrained but alluring, a fragrance he did not recognise but which recalled a scent of wild roses.

'Miss Thiemann.'

She sat back and lit a cigarette in an ivory-coloured holder.

'It would be Fräulein Thiemann, if you want to be formal,' she said, 'but I prefer just Greta.'

'Why don't you join us?' Bristow said, raising a hand to attract the waiter's attention. 'Greta gets bored listening to me talking about new buildings all night, and besides, I promised to go upstairs and lose some money in the Holland Room.'

'He'll be in trouble if he doesn't lose some money tonight,' she said.

Conrad walked around the table and took a chair between them. When the waiter came, he ordered a whisky. She ordered another glass of champagne. Bristow declined.

'What business are you in, then, Rainer?' Bristow asked, a little too directly.

'I'm a barrister, Queen's Counsel.'

'Oh? What kind of cases do you do?'

'Commercial.'

'Really? Well, you never know, I may need you one of these days. I don't tend to make many friends in my line of work. People are threatening to sue me all the time. My solicitors do very well out of me.'

'It's one of the hazards of doing business, of course,' Conrad replied politely. 'How about you, Greta?'

She drew on her cigarette, smiling. 'I don't approve of work. It gets in the way of pleasure.'

'So you're German?' he asked, after Bristow had left to lose his money in the Holland Room.

She smiled again.

'All I said was that my title should be Fräulein. I didn't say I was German. I could be Austrian, Swiss even.'

He shook his head.

'The accent's wrong,' he replied. 'You're German.'

She nodded, putting out her cigarette.

'I'm impressed. You have a good ear. Do you speak the language?'

'Not very well. But I took German in school and I've spent some time in the German-speaking parts of Europe. I think my family has German roots – though they prefer not to talk about it.'

'How boring of them.'

'Yes. They like to think of themselves as the quintessential English family. But they called me Conrad – with a C, not a K, which isn't very subtle – and I once saw some old family papers I wasn't supposed to see, in which our name was given as Reiner rather than Rainer.'

'How strange,' she said, 'to pretend to be something you're not. I think that must make life far more difficult than it's supposed to be. But I have noticed that the English have a tendency to want to be someone else – or at least, appear to be someone else. Why is that? Is it because you think it's glamorous?'

'It's probably because we like to look down on foreigners, and you can't do that if you suspect you may be a foreigner yourself.'

She laughed.

'Well, they must have a whale of a time looking down on me then. I'm from Leipzig, so I'm not only German, I'm a wicked communist German.'

He laughed with her.

'You don't come across to me as a communist,' he replied. 'Not that I've met many communists, but you don't quite have the hammer-and-sickle image.'

'No, thank God. I escaped from all that seven years ago, and I have no intention of going back.'

'Do you mean "escaped" in the literal sense?'

'I didn't climb over barbed wire fences with the Stasi shooting at me, if that's what you mean,' she replied. 'My father was a diplomat, and my family had many connections, so it was all done by diplomacy rather than cloak and dagger stuff. It's not hard if you know the right people. That's true the world over, isn't it? It doesn't matter where you are. East Germany is supposed to be the workers' paradise, but it's just like anywhere else. If you are connected to those in power, you can do whatever you want. If you are a worker, you stay put and do what they tell you to do.'

They sat silently for a minute or two.

'And you don't let work get in the way of pleasure? I'm sure that's easier here than in the DDR.'

'I told you,' she said, 'I have no intention of going back.'

She lit another cigarette and looked at him.

'I often take my pleasure downstairs,' she said.

'In the night club?'

'I'm a friend of Annabel and Mark. They were among the first people I met when I came to London. They were very kind to me, and introduced me to many of their friends. That's how I know people who are members of this Club.'

She drew on her cigarette.

'But I can't come here unaccompanied, of course. So when I'm on my own, I go to Annabel's. Perhaps you will come and meet me there one evening – when I'm not accompanied?'

'I would like that,' he said.

23

He found her in Annabel's, unaccompanied, two nights later. On this evening, the cocktail dress and heels were a dark green. As he kissed her cheek, the image of the wild rose returned. He had arrived back at his flat at 7 o'clock, having finished his work in chambers, and relaxed with a glass or two of whisky before making himself a light supper. At 10.30 he called Deborah to tell her he was going to bed and wish her good night, and at 11 o'clock, he made his way to Berkeley Square. It was Friday, and the club was packed with smart-set young people, the in-crowd, celebrating the start of the weekend. They had to cling to a corner of the bar just to make enough space to talk, and even then, it was hard for them to hear each other above the animated hubbub.

'I like to be taken to the Clermont Club,' she said. 'But as someone once said, I have always depended on the kindness of strangers. Who was that?'

'Blanche', he replied, 'in *Streetcar* – Tennessee Williams. But you're no Blanche DuBois, and hopefully they are friends now, rather than strangers.'

'Some of them are,' she said, stubbing out her cigarette and squeezing the butt out of the holder into the ashtray. 'But you never really know. Some of them just like to have me with them as an accessory, to show me off, as if they own me.'

'Even Jack Bristow?'

'Especially Jack Bristow.'

'Oh, come on, Greta, I'm sure –'

'You don't know the Clermont yet, Conrad. What do you think it's all about? Do you think John Aspinall makes men members of the Clermont because he likes them, because they're all friends? It's not true – whatever he may tell you. He makes them members because they're rich and powerful men, who can afford to lose a lot of money but can't afford to be seen as losers. Believe me, they don't care about me. They care about having a good-looking woman by their side when they gamble, because they think it makes them look even richer and more powerful than they are.'

She lit another cigarette.

'It's all about image. In any case, I know my place. I'm not welcome in the Clermont for who I am; I'm tolerated because of who I'm with. I don't fit in.'

'Of course you do. You're—'

'I'm a foreigner, Conrad. You said it yourself. The British love to look down on anyone who's different, and those aristocratic types who run the Clermont are the worst of all. Do you think men like Jimmy Goldsmith and Kerry Packer would be allowed in if they weren't made of money and didn't mind losing it? Not a chance.'

He signalled to the barman for more drinks. She smiled.

'I'm sorry,' she said. 'I didn't mean to get started on all that. Let's talk about something else. Let's talk about you. Who is Conrad Rainer – other than a barrister from a family that wishes it wasn't German?'

He laughed.

'That's a good question. I'm not sure I've ever thought much about it. Once you get started at the Bar and the work starts to flow in, you don't have time to breathe, much less think about questions like who you are.'

'Well, let's start with what you like to do in those rare moments when you're not working. You know about Tennessee Williams, so I assume you like the theatre?'

'Yes. But I can't remember when I last went.'

'Books?'

'Yes, but mostly stuff that's easy to read these days, a thriller when I'm on holiday – which I almost never am.'

'Music?'

'Yes, classical music, and some jazz, if it's well done.'

'Concerts?'

'Not these days; on the radio. I went to the Proms a few times, years ago, but not any more.'

'Eating well?'

'Ah, yes. That's one of the few cultural pursuits we do make time for as lawyers.'

'So you do go to restaurants? Well that's something. What sort of cuisine do you like? French?'

'Yes, but also Italian – and Portuguese, which is very underrated.'

'I agree,' she said. 'So, what have we established so far? I think we have established that you like good things but never make time for them: am I right?'

They laughed together.

'Spot on.'

'Doesn't your wife make sure you find some time to relax?'

'My wife? I didn't say I was married.'

She almost choked, inhaling from her cigarette.

'Oh, Conrad, please. The day I can't tell whether a man is married is the day I go back to Leipzig.'

They laughed together again.

'Do you have children?'

'No... she can't, you know...'

'I'm sorry.'

'It's all right. So... my wife. What can I say –?'

She put out the cigarette.

'I don't know. What *can* you say? I think, if you could say anything about her to me, you would have said it already, and I conclude from this that your wife does not support you in the things you enjoy. Am I right?'

He bowed his head. She did not rush him.

'Deborah is very different from me. She's very religious.'

'In what way, religious?'

'She's a Baptist. She takes the Bible literally, she believes in heaven and hell, and she doesn't hold with drinking, smoking, gambling, or anything else most people do to have a good time.'

'So I would guess you've never brought her to Annabel's?'

'You would guess correctly.'

'She's not just religious, then: she's a puritan?'

'I suppose you could say that. Yes.'

'But, of course. Look, I know lots of religious people. Some of them are against certain pleasures of the flesh, some are against others, but very few are against all pleasures. For example, the Catholics I know are usually against sex unless it's for making babies, but I know one or two Catholic bishops who could drink us both under the table before lunch and wouldn't think twice about it. The Protestants would be horrified by that, but they can be quite happy to jump into bed with each other if they get the chance. How does your wife – Deborah, is it? – how does she feel about sex?'

'Greta –'

'Oh, I'm sorry. I've crossed the line, haven't I? It's the one question you never ask anyone in England. Typical foreigner, you see. I told you, I don't fit in. Never mind. Let's talk about something else –'

'No,' he said. He paused for a few moments. 'No, since you've asked, let's talk about sex. Since you ask, she's not very keen on it. We have an appointment every Sunday, after lunch. Once in a while, I can make an appointment at some other time if I show good cause, and it doesn't get in the way of Bible study, or the church committee, or the youth group, or… whatever else may be going on. Once, in the missionary position, and she prefers to keep her nightdress on.'

He suddenly banged his fist down on the bar and bowed his head.

She finished her drink and looked at him carefully.

'How old are you, Conrad?'

He looked up. 'I'm 53. Why?'

She nodded.

'Come with me, please,' she said.

She led him quickly to a discreet door behind the bar marked 'Staff only', rummaged through her handbag for a key, and opened it. The door led to a narrow corridor. She took Conrad's hand and they began walking. A young man, wearing a chef's white hat and apron and carrying an empty metal tray, was coming the other way.

'Evening, Greta. All right?'

'Hello, Bobby. I'm fine. You?'

'Can't complain.'

She pushed open a door to her left, pulled him inside and bolted the door.

He looked around, startled.

'What is this?'

'Quite obviously,' she replied, 'it's a toilet. Don't worry, it's a ladies. It's for the staff.'

'But what if someone wants to come in?'

'They'll just have to wait, won't they?'

'But how can you…?'

'I told you on Wednesday. I'm a friend of Annabel's.'

'But…'

'Shut up, Conrad,' she said. 'Stand against the door.'

He obeyed. She expertly undid his flies, and he felt his trousers slip down around his ankles. His underwear followed. He felt suddenly faint, but he noticed that without any conscious input from him, his penis had risen naturally to meet her hand. She held it firmly and kissed its tip.

'What are you doing?' he breathed hoarsely.

'I'm doing what Deborah should have done, long before you reached the age of 53,' she replied.

Afterwards, she lit a cigarette.

'Do you mind if I have one of those?' he asked.

'Yes, I'm sorry.' She gave him a cigarette, and lit it for him. 'I didn't know you smoked. I haven't seen you with a cigarette.'

'I haven't smoked since university,' he replied. 'But I'm thinking of starting again.'

She smiled. 'Good for you.'

As they smoked silently, he ran his hand gently up inside her dress, feeling the top of her stocking.

'I'd be happy to…' he began.

But she put her hand over his and held it still.

'Yes, you will be happy to do that for me,' she said, 'but not now. We'll have plenty of time later. Now, I want you to take me to the Clermont Club. As my friend.'

24

They had a drink and a cigarette in the bar to settle his nerves. Conrad's life had changed in the space of ten minutes in a staff toilet at Annabel's. Nothing felt the same as it had before he left the Barbican some three hours earlier. He had an image of himself as a butterfly emerging from the chrysalis, testing its wings, learning to feel the caress of the wind and the touch of a flower. His body had transformed itself. His energy was running high; it made him feel light-headed, unfocused. He had the strangest desire to go outside into Berkeley Square and run into the night as fast as he could until his breath gave out. He was acutely conscious of his heartbeat, which seemed strong, but rather erratic. But he had the disquieting illusion that the Club staff, and even one or two of the members, were smiling at him in such a way as to suggest that they knew what had happened at Annabel's a few minutes earlier; and it was so strong that he had an impulse to tell them himself rather than submit to the scrutiny of their suspicious smiles.

All in all, he felt in no condition for a serious game of cards. Greta, on the other hand, was calm and composed, as if nothing out of the ordinary had occurred. She was her usual charming self, and wished everyone a good evening with her most winning smile. He sat back in his chair and allowed the warmth of the whisky to soothe him.

It was after 2 o'clock in the morning now, but in the gaming rooms of the Clermont Club time was an irrelevance. In the Blue Room, Jean-Pascal was presiding over a game of *chemin de fer* with nine players. As they entered the room, he recognised Dominick Elwes, Dai Llewellyn, Lord Derby and Ian Maxwell-Scott. Susie was sitting with a drink on the far side of the room. When she saw him enter with Greta, she gave a look of mock horror, with both hands over her mouth, before turning up both her thumbs with a gleeful private smile. He smiled back, quite sure that he must have looked like an adolescent confiding in a friend about an unexpected conquest, half triumphant, half embarrassed. Well, Susie knows now, Conrad thought, and if Susie knows, so will everyone else before the night is out. It was a thought that rocked him for a moment, but then, once the shock had subsided, rather pleased him.

Ian waved him into the chair on his right. Two chairs to Ian's left, Lord Derby had the bank, and to judge from his expression, and the quantity of chips in front of him, he was having a good night. To Lord Derby's left, Dominick Elwes, who must have surrendered the bank to Lord Derby, gave no indication of having a good night. Even in his short time as a member of the Clermont, Conrad had heard the rumours that Dominick was allowed to lose as much as he wanted within reason, on the house, because his charm and wit brought people into the Club and kept them happy while they played. If so, he was giving little indication of charm or wit at the moment. Vicente had supplied Conrad with £500 worth of chips against his cheque. Greta briefly stood behind his chair and squeezed his shoulders, allowing her hair to brush against his head, before moving away to talk to Susie, who had approached the table to see how her husband was faring.

'The bank wagers £500,' Lord Derby announced with an air of authority.

Dai Llewellyn, sitting to Lord Derby's right, had the right of *banco prime*, but he shook his head.

Conrad's light-headedness had subsided enough for him to be aware that serious money was at stake now, and John Aspinall's words returned to him: 'Members here tend to play high, but you don't have to try to match them. I'm sure you know what I mean'. Even with his lack of experience, Conrad knew that each table developed a life of its own as an evening wore on, and unless you joined early, you had to find a way of divining what that life was, and where it had led at the time you joined.

He saw at once that he had joined the table at a critical moment. Lord Derby had kept the bank for some time, and he had done some major damage. He wouldn't be starting out with a bet of £500; there was a history to it. The Clermont minimum was £100, and usually if the bank was winning, the banker would increase his bet in increments of £100, but there were some players who were far more aggressive. Lord Derby, Conrad felt sure, was throwing out a challenge to a fight to the death to opponents he had already beaten heavily. Every instinct Conrad had told him to stay out of it until he got the feel of the table. But he could still feel the blood racing through his veins, and there was a recklessness surging through him, which took him by surprise and yet, at the same time, felt entirely natural.

He and Ian shouted *banco* at the same moment. Looking to his right, he saw Greta flash her green eyes and smile. Susie was giving Ian a look that he could not quite identify. The table as a whole seemed to have lost whatever confidence it had started with. Only Ian, resistant to fear as ever, was still in the game. Whatever Lord Derby had been doing during the night, it had worked; he had the others thoroughly intimidated.

'Mr Maxwell-Scott has covered,' Jean-Pascal said. '*Rien ne va plus.*'

Conrad nodded. He had given way to his impulses, but he was not going to feature in this hand. The croupier was right. The player closer to the bank had priority.

Jean-Pascal quickly dealt two cards to Lord Derby and two to Ian.

Tentatively, Ian turned over his cards, and suddenly gave Conrad a smile, half relief, half delight. Two fours. The bank had a three and a king. Lord Derby's reign as banker had ended, but Conrad had not been part of it.

'The players win, *La Petite* to three,' Jean-Pascal announced. 'Mr Llewellyn has the bank.'

Dai Llewellyn started with the minimum £100. Ian covered at once, but lost the hand seven to zero, and Dai kept the bank.

Next, Dai ventured £250. Ian seemed momentarily subdued,

and kept quiet. No one covered. Conrad bet £100, and a taciturn man to Jean-Pascal's immediate right did the same. As the player closer to the bank, he had to represent the players. Conrad turned his cards over slowly. A five and a jack. He shook his head. He had to choose whether to stand or draw a third card. Impulsively, he called '*Carte*'. His third card was a queen, worth zero. His score remained at five. The bank had seven.

Dai was feeling bolder now, and jumped from £250 straight to £750. Conrad forced himself to think. Dai must have calculated that the lack of confidence that had gripped the table during Lord Derby's hold on the bank would continue, and that he would have only one or two small bets to contend with. Lord Derby himself seemed to have been affected. Even Ian seemed to have had the wind taken out of his sails and showed no inclination to react. Susie had gone quiet and had returned to her seat on the other side of the room. Greta had moved closer to the table. Conrad saw her looking at him with a look that said, 'Go for it'.

'*Banco*', he called.

He felt Dai's sharp glance from his left. Eyebrows were raised around the table. Finally, someone was trying to take the initiative.

Conrad was dealt a seven and a king. Unless the bank had a natural, he was going to win. The bank had zero. Conrad was ahead for the first time, and Ian Maxwell-Scott had the bank.

Conrad saw Ian smile to himself. Susie was still sitting quietly as if trying to distance herself from the action. He watched Ian closely, and suddenly understood what John Aspinall had said about him. He was an intelligent, thoughtful man, but once he was in the grip of the excitement of the game and had money in his sights, thinking took a back seat and the thrill took over; once that happened, there were no limits. Conrad pondered how to react. He could be patient, stick with systematic bids of £100 or £200, and wait out the hands when the bank was covered; or he could jump right in and try for a decisive advantage. He didn't need to look at Greta to know what she was willing him to do. He felt her presence from where he sat. He glanced at his watch. It was already nearly three. The recklessness had not left him.

'The bank wagers £1,000,' Ian declared. In the distance Susie had taken refuge in a fashion magazine.

'*Banco prime*,' Conrad responded, without hesitation. He saw Greta close her lips and nod her head slightly.

'*Rien ne vas plus*,' Jean-Pascal announced. He dealt the cards.

Conrad had a feeling about it the moment the cards were dealt. When he turned them over and saw the nine and the jack, he felt an immense rush. The bank had six. It didn't matter. He had won and the bank was his.

He was on a mission now. The lack of confidence around the table would not last indefinitely. Whenever the stakes rose at a table, the energy the high stakes generated began to spread; and the stakes were rising now. Besides, it was getting late. Time might be irrelevant to some, but he was all too aware that he would have to put in an appearance in chambers later in the morning, and he had made a promise to Greta, which he was sure she would require him to fulfil. Time was short. He would strike while he had the bank.

'The bank wagers £1,000.'

The repetition of Ian's bet was a deliberate provocation, one he knew would produce an immediate reaction. Ian responded with '*banco*' before anyone else could say a word. Ian did not have *banco prime*, but there was no challenge from his right. For the moment, it had become a personal duel, and the other players would be content to sit and watch for a while. Conrad had begun to feel the energy of the table now. It was a new experience for him, and he watched it carefully. It seemed to him that it had settled on him. He continued to watch it as the cards were dealt. He ended up with seven against Ian's three.

Susie threw down her magazine and stood very obviously behind Ian's chair. 'She sees it, too,' he told himself, 'the energy. She sees it's not with him.' She made very obvious comments about how late it was and the need to get up in the morning, and Ian reluctantly took the hint, bidding good night to those assembled. Conrad smiled to himself. It was a downhill run now. It took hardly any time at all. He kept up his £1,000 starting bid, sensing that no one would cover. No one did. He won four hands in succession. A number of players had recovered sufficiently to cover him partially, and adding it all together, he was substantially ahead. Not only that, but he had respected the convention. He had kept the bank long enough to give the table a fair chance to recoup their losses. He could not be criticised for calling it a night. He passed the bank on voluntarily and left the table. It was just before 4 o'clock as he lit one of Greta's cigarettes.

25

She hailed a taxi outside the Club, and without consulting him, gave the driver the address of her flat in Knightsbridge.

The flat was on the fifth floor of a block with a dated art deco feel; but a fine view looking out over Hyde Park from the front of the building more than made up for its appearance. The flat was furnished tastefully in a French style, with no references to her native Germany. Her bedroom was at the front, and she had left the curtains open to the view of the park.

They had said very little on the way back from the Clermont, but she had leant her head on his shoulder. They lingered in the living room only long enough for her to pour them both a whisky. She lit a cigarette and led him into the bedroom.

'Take your clothes off,' she said, as she disappeared into the bathroom.

He put his clothes on the armchair by the side of her dressing table, and walked naked over to the window. He looked down. The streets were deserted. People were sleeping. Certainly, people who had jobs to go to were sleeping. He himself had a job to go to. There was a fraud case waiting for him in chambers that wasn't going to prepare itself. Yet here he was, with the clock making its way towards five.

He shifted his gaze to the park, but in the darkness and the dim street lighting, he could not make out any of its features except for the tops of some trees. It was an interesting experience, he found – standing naked in front of a window open to the world. In most circumstances in his previous life he would have drawn the curtains, or beaten a retreat towards the bed, or at least looked around for a dressing gown. But now that his life had changed, he found himself enjoying what risk there might be of being seen. He was five floors up; it was barely conceivable, even if someone did happen to pass the building at that hour. But the thrill of the risk was undeniable. He stood right against the window, his hands deliberately clenched behind his back, offering the world maximum exposure, savouring the feeling. He wondered if Greta ever stood there naked, daring someone to look up from across the street. He felt sure that she did – and probably at times of day or night when the odds were better that someone would.

'Come here,' she said.

She was naked too, and she was sitting on the bed. He turned and walked towards her. He found her extraordinarily beautiful. She aroused him and he made no attempt to hide it. He knelt in front of her. The warmth of her body accentuated the wild rose perfume, made it more immediate. He found it intoxicating.

'Do you remember what you promised?' she asked.

'Yes, of course.'

'Well, then, let's see how well you do. You English men don't have a great reputation as lovers – but neither do German men, so who knows?'

She lifted herself on to the bed, lay on her back, her legs parted, and stretched out her arms above her head. She closed her eyes.

He lay on the bed on her left side, and kissed her full on the lips. She responded with her tongue. He moved down to her breasts, circling her nipples with his tongue. She allowed this for some time before she lifted his head.

'Feet first,' she said. 'For me, always feet first, then work your way up.'

He stood and repositioned himself at the bottom of the bed. He lifted each foot in turn, kissed her ankles, her soles, and her toes and then kissed his way along the inside of her right leg and thigh until he felt her hairs start to tickle his nose. He stopped. It wasn't a question of the reputation of English men, he thought. It was a question of his own lack of experience; that was all.

Years ago, once or twice, with Barbara, he had been on the brink of intimacy of this kind, but he had pulled back – his decision, not hers – and since then his sexual experiences had been strictly regimented. That was his own fault – he saw that clearly now – there was nothing to blame Barbara for; it was his own lack of… what: imagination, involvement, courage? After that, it was, from a practical point of view, simply too late. He would never have suggested such unconventional explorations with Deborah. But why? Was that her fault or his? He didn't know. Perhaps, if it had been early enough in their relationship, she would have been open to it. Before he got too busy and she got too religious. Perhaps she would even have reciprocated. Perhaps his life could have been reinvented without the need to visit the ladies staff toilets at Annabel's, with a woman from Leipzig who wanted him to be her friend.

There was no way to know now. It was too late. He had to do his best. He had read things in men's magazines from time to time – not in Guildford, obviously, but in the secrecy of his Barbican flat, when he had caught a glimpse of them in their discreet place on the news stand near his building and purchased one with an air of practised indifference, as if he were buying *The Times*. Five things every woman wants. Ten ways to drive your lover crazy. Twenty things every man should know. He pictured himself back at Annabel's and put his tongue and his fingers to work.

It seemed to have an effect. She began to move, and then she began to moan, and after some time, she dug her soles into the bed, arched her back, threw her head back, clutching the metal bars of her headboard, and gave a loud, deep sigh. Judging by what Conrad remembered from the magazines, she showed every sign of having come. He didn't know whether she really had or not. Even if she had, he had no way of knowing whether she was thinking of him, or of some equivalent of Barbara.

Eventually, she opened her eyes. She smiled.

'Not bad,' she said. 'Not bad for a first time. Next time, I will give you a few tips, but definitely not bad for a first time.'

Then abruptly, her manner changed.

She rolled quickly away from him across the bed, reached down, and picked something up. She was so fast that he didn't see what it was, or even exactly where it had come from. Turning back, she manhandled him with surprising strength, and turned him over on to his front. The next thing he felt was a hard, stinging blow across his buttocks. He was too surprised to react. But when it was followed by a second, and then a third blow, both hard and painful, he cried out and tried to push himself up. She pushed him down hard.

'Stop fighting,' she commanded.

Another blow followed.

'What the hell are you doing?' he demanded.

'Punishing you.'

Another blow.

'Punishing me? For what? What's going on, for God's sake?'

She paused.

'For giving up.'

'For giving up? What do you mean? Look, I did my best. You said it wasn't bad for a first time. What more do you want?'

She scoffed.

'You idiot. I'm not talking about that. I'm talking about the table, Conrad. You stopped. You gave up much too soon.'

'What? I stopped because I was ahead and it was almost 4 o'clock.'

'You never stop until you have risked as much as you can.'

Another blow.

'Greta, for God's sake! This is ridiculous. It's my money. I decide when to stop.'

'Not when you're with me.'

'What?'

'Haven't you wondered why I'm with you, why I asked you to take me to the Clermont?'

'I –'

'It's the excitement. That's what turns me on, Conrad, not your first attempts to please me in bed. I told you. I may not fit in, but I like powerful men who are not afraid to take risks, whatever the cost: men like Lucan and Elwes, and even poor little Ian Maxwell-Scott with his beloved Susie, God bless him. And I thought you were the same.'

'I am…' he protested.

'Tonight? You think what you did tonight was exciting?'

'I played the table. I came out ahead.'

'You played it safe,' she replied. 'God. You had them where you wanted them. You could have increased your bets.'

'Greta, I was already wagering a thousand.'

'A thousand? That's nothing. I want to see you taking risks – two thousand, five thousand, your damned house in Guildford, whatever. If you don't, you get punished. That's my house rule, Conrad, take it or leave it. And don't you dare try to wriggle or put your hands in the way. When I punish you, you take it. If I have to tie your hands to the bed I will, but I'll be disappointed if I have to.'

The blows continued. Part of him wanted to curse her and walk out. Although she had shown strength, she would be no match for him if he resisted; he could easily have thrown her off. But he was aroused again, aroused as he had been when she had taken down his trousers at Annabel's, and instead of throwing her off, he stretched his arms out and surrendered to her. She stopped after about twenty blows, by which time his skin was burning.

She threw whatever she had been using across the bed, and for the first time he saw that it was a pink ping-pong bat.

She turned him over on to his back, and once again, he could not hide his arousal. She smiled.

'I thought so,' she said.

She mounted him expertly and held his hands above his head with hers. She drove him steadily into the bed, not stopping, even when he came, until she was ready. When she did finally release him, she reached for a cigarette from her bedside table, and lit it.

'Now, get out,' she said. 'Go home. Please. I have to get some sleep.'

26

'The bank wagers £1,000,' Conrad said.

It was not a bet he particularly believed in. It was almost 3 o'clock, he had been playing for two hours, and he had not particularly believed in a single bet he had placed during that time. The table was trouble. He had seen that the moment he walked into the Blue Room. It was a ferocious table: angry and chaotic. He was used to seeing the energy now; it had become a physical phenomenon he could observe; he could watch it, predict it, track its progress. But it was different tonight. Tonight he saw the energy darting and bouncing this way and that around the table without any pattern, seemingly thrown into orbit around one player at random, then around another at random, by the sheer force of their wills. It was a table impossible to read or to predict: a very dangerous table.

It was a table Conrad would never have joined if Greta hadn't been with him, daring him, wordlessly cajoling, even threatening him, making it impossible for him to back away. James Goldsmith, Lucky Lucan, Lord Derby, Dominick Elwes, and the inevitable Ian Maxwell-Scott were among those at the table, and they were in a predatory mood. Lord Derby's last bid before losing control of the bank at a high cost had been £2,500. The bank had passed to Conrad. John Aspinall, advised of the mood in the Blue Room by some nameless member of his staff, had come to observe, sitting quietly but conspicuously across the room, facing the table. Susie Maxwell-Scott was sitting by herself in a corner, a nervous wreck.

His visits to the Clermont Club with Greta had become routine, at least once a week, sometimes twice or even three times, and they were taking a toll. Some of the toll was due simply to a lack of rest. He was waking up feeling exhausted, sometimes at Greta's flat – she allowed him to stay sometimes now, when it suited her – in which case he had to make his way home to change before going into chambers, or to court. His concentration was suffering. The fraud case had been tried over three weeks in October, and by the end the numbers had rearranged themselves in his mind into meaningless sequences, and he could no longer reconstruct all the complex financial history involved in the case. He was not sure his closing speech to the judge had even been coherent. The result was not a total catastrophe – fortunately the merits were largely on his client's side, and Mr Justice Overton had seen that long before the case came down to closing speeches – but it could have been much better. He was still worrying about it.

He worried about other things, too. Not, so much, about Greta: she still excited him, and she still seemed to enjoy him. Under her tutelage he had become a better lover, more precise and competent, and that increased his confidence. He no longer felt any need to feign resistance to the spankings, which he now accepted as part of his desire for her. On the surface, that was all going well. Still, he did worry about how important a part of his life she had become, and what would happen if one day she tired of him. He knew Greta well enough by now to know that the day she tired of him was the day she would throw him out of her life, like last season's cocktail dress, without remorse or ceremony. He was addicted to her now, and he worried about the coming of that day.

He worried about Deborah, too. Now that the fraud case was over, logically enough, she was expecting him to come home to Guildford at night. Every night away now required a plausible story. There were always chambers meetings, and parties, and other cases to work on; moreover, he had to justify the Barbican flat to the tax man and he couldn't do that without using it regularly. But he had to be careful about repeating the same story too often. He worried about making a mistake, and he worried about what would happen if she tried to call him during the night and he wasn't there. She suffered from bouts of insomnia, and there were times when, in her misery, she woke him to ask why

God had punished her by making her barren, or why the people she most looked up to at church never seemed to warm to her, despite everything she did for them. And what if there were an emergency at home, and she needed him, and he wasn't on the other end of the phone? Those were dangerous thoughts to have running through your head when you were at the table trying to read the energy.

And then he worried about money. When he first joined the Clermont Club, his luck had been good. There were nights when he won and nights when he lost, but once he had learned to see the energy, he learned to control his play well. He knew when to stop, and even if the punishment for stopping was sometimes severe later, in Knightsbridge, he knew how to walk away. But then – at some time he could never quite pinpoint – his luck started to change: imperceptibly at first, the sequence of losing nights becoming longer, the winning nights becoming fewer and farther between.

He had a successful practice in Silk and he was earning high fees. But as a barrister, he was self-employed, and being self-employed, he depended for his income on the cheques written by solicitors. The arrival of a cheque for a barrister's fee was a notoriously unpredictable event. The solicitors often kept barristers' fees for a year or more to boost the interest on their client trust accounts before sending a cheque to chambers. The practice was grossly unethical, but if chambers wanted the solicitor's work, nothing would be done except for the occasional gentle reminder by the senior clerk. Often, the clerk was fobbed off with the disclaimer that their client had not put them in funds, which was usually untrue. Conrad had heard that in Hong Kong the Bar had dealt with the problem by boycotting solicitors who treated them in that way, but in England, the prospect of the profession coming together with such a show of solidarity on a subject as *infra dig* as money was remote.

He had to budget for the many expenses in his life: the house in Guildford, the Barbican flat, his chambers rent, and his clerk's fees – which, alone, accounted for ten per cent of his gross income – not to mention putting something by for when the tax man came calling. His professional and personal survival depended on his ability to meet those expenses as and when they came due. And then, he needed enough money to go to the Clermont Club at least once a week, and keep Greta happy by being prepared to lose. He had tried once or twice to explain all this to Greta, but she seemed indifferent, and if she reacted at all, it was to punish him, for what she called his weakness, even more firmly than usual.

It was within his power, of course, to walk away; to resume the life he had led with some success before John Aspinall had made him a member of the Clermont Club; before he had met Greta. But he had to admit to himself that it was not only Greta he was addicted to. He had been a gambler before he met her. All she had done was raise the stakes. He was just as addicted to the thrill of the table as he was to Greta herself. He didn't want to walk away. He no longer saw a way back to his former life; and in any case, it had been a life to endure rather than to live. He was living now, and he was determined that nothing should get in his way.

The problem facing him tonight, as he sat amid the chaos and violence of that turbulent table, was that his adverse run of luck had taken him beyond the point where he could provide for his losses out of his income. He had a Post Office savings account in his sole name, which contained £10,000. It was an account he had opened as a student, and had paid into as and when he could, and which, as a prosperous QC, he had kept intact largely for nostalgic reasons. Tonight that money was with Vicente at the cash desk. Some £2,000 had already gone.

27

Lord Lucan was seated to his immediate right, and Lucan was harder to predict than anyone at the table. Conrad could read Ian Maxwell-Scott like a book now, and when he had won over the last few months, it had increasingly been at Ian's expense. Susie had been watching, and had deliberately distanced herself from him. It seemed to be as much as she could manage to say a polite hello when he came in now. Dominick, he could read, too: Dominick losing within reason for the house, taking one for the team. Conrad felt safe enough with him. Even James Goldsmith, with his relentless manic aggression, was usually predictable, up to a point. But tonight, Goldsmith seemed to have been caught up in the waves of the anger fuelled by Derby and Lucan. Their betting was more in the nature of terrifying emotional outbursts than rational calculation.

Having Lucan on his right at a chemmy table on a night like this was like sitting next to an unexploded shell. He knew it would be wiser to play respectably down until he lost something manageable, and passed the bank to Lucan, and could react to the explosion instead of being caught up in it. But she had been standing behind him, with her hands on his shoulders; her hair touching his head and her scent filling his nostrils; and now he had lit the fuse.

'*Banco prime*,' Lucan said, his tone harsh.

'*Rien ne va plus*,' Jean-Pascal announced.

As the cards were dealt, John Aspinall stood and came closer.

Lucan turned his two cards over: a six and a jack.

Conrad inhaled deeply before turning his cards over: an ace

and a king. In another card game it would have been a perfect hand, but it was of no value in *chemin de fer*. He closed his eyes and breathed out slowly.

'The players win, six to one,' Jean-Pascal announced. 'Lord Lucan has the bank.'

Aspinall called a break to allow time for the atmosphere to calm down, and a waiter took orders for drinks.

'All right, are we, Conrad?' he asked, while Greta was out of the room for a few minutes.

'Yes, John, of course. Why do you ask?'

Aspinall shrugged.

'Oh, I don't know. It just seems to be a bit competitive on this table tonight. I don't know what's got into everyone. Lucky seems wound up tight, and Jimmy looks as if he's ready to kill somebody. It does get like this sometimes for no apparent reason, but it's been a while since I've seen it this lively. It's a bit quieter in the Holland, if you fancy something rather more sedate?'

Conrad smiled, anticipating what Greta would have to say about a quieter table in the Holland and something more sedate.

'I'm fine, John, thank you. It's getting late in any case. I don't suppose I'll last much longer; work tomorrow, that kind of thing.'

'That might be very wise, Conrad, I think,' Aspinall replied, walking away as Greta returned.

The break did nothing to dissipate the violent atmosphere at the table, and try as he might, Conrad could not track the energy. Twice he suggested to Greta that it was time to call it a night, but her reaction was so strong that he was actually afraid she might cause a scene. Lucan seemed to have lost his grip on reality, and at one point Aspinall had to remind him discreetly of the house maximum of £10,000. With ill grace, Lucan reduced an absurd wager of £20,000 to the house maximum. Even for this out-of-control table, it was too rich. The highest response to his bet was £500, but he won and sulkily reduced his next wager to £5,000. Goldsmith pounced, covered the bank, and won for the players; and to general relief, the bank passed to Ian Maxwell-Scott.

By this time, Conrad was down more than £5,000. The sensible course was to leave now, while he still had some of his savings left. But she was there behind him, with her wild rose scent, and besides, he had the measure of Ian Maxwell-Scott. Susie was pacing up and down, desperate to take him home, but Ian was not about to give up now, not with the energetic anarchy around the table. Conrad decided to chase his losses.

'The bank wagers £1,000,' Ian said, with a strange calm.

Conrad looked around. The energy was still eluding him, but Ian sounded as though he had sight of it and believed it might be with him. Dominick Elwes had the right of *banco prime*, but Dominick was concerned that he had already lost more than John Aspinall was likely to write off to expenses, and he showed no inclination to intervene. Even Derby and Lucan seemed uncertain. These were important cautionary signs, and on a normal night he would have paid attention to them; but he chose to ignore them. He called *banco*, but Ian had a seven and a two. As lost as if he were in a fog, Conrad allowed himself to repeat the scenario twice, and in both hands, the result was the same except for the arithmetic of the bank's victory. After another hand or two, his savings were gone, and Susie was all over Ian, telling him how brilliant he was and cajoling him out of his chair to go home.

There was to be no punishment. On the contrary, Greta plied him with whisky, undressed him, and took him to bed, praising him to the skies for his courage. She laid him down on his back, and started to undress.

'You were magnificent,' she said. 'I want you to play like that every time.'

'I can't,' he replied. 'I don't have any more money.'

She laughed.

'There's always more money,' she said.

He was about to protest, but she was already naked and was beginning to kiss her way down his body from his chest. He swallowed his protests and, as she worked her magic on him, started to think about what she had said. Was there always more money? There were two assets left: the house and Deborah's trust fund. There would be certain – well, complications – involved in accessing funds from either source, but it could be done; as a temporary measure, obviously, just until his luck changed back again. Tonight he had been the victim of a freak table – even John Aspinall had said so. That shouldn't put him off. He would soon be back on track.

28

'Mr Rainer to see you, Mr Sawyer,' Annette said, smiling, and ushering him in.

'Ah, Conrad,' Jeremy Sawyer said, getting to his feet, 'I'm so glad you could come. Would you like some tea?'

'Yes, thank you.'

'How do you like it, Mr Rainer?' Annette asked.

'Just a little milk, please, no sugar.'

'Won't be a jiffy,' she said, breezing back out through the door.

'Come and sit down here so that we can enjoy the view,' Sawyer said, pointing to a sofa and two armchairs in front of the huge window at the front of his office. 'Much nicer than sitting around a desk, I always think.'

Conrad took one of the armchairs. The view over the river was magnificent. He was still in something of a daze after losing his savings the previous night. Greta had cheered him up considerably at Knightsbridge, but when he arrived back at his flat, desperately tired and in the usual rush to shower and change in time to take himself into chambers, the exhilaration was quickly replaced by the reality of a new day, for which he felt unprepared. To make matters worse, just as he was leaving, Deborah had called about some domestic matter. As far as he could tell, she had not tried to call the flat the previous evening; at least, she didn't say that she had. But then again, she didn't say that she hadn't, and the anxiety was still there. With such an unpromising start to the day, Conrad was taken completely by surprise when his clerk told him that Jeremy Sawyer wanted to see him at the House of Lords just after lunch.

He had heard about Jeremy Sawyer's office from others in chambers – others who had gone on to a judicial appointment. Jeremy Sawyer was known as the Lord Chancellor's right-hand man when it came to the appointment of judges, and his huge office with its commanding view of the Thames was something they all remembered. Conrad was astonished when he received the news. He had always considered himself judicial material, his practice in Silk more than justified an appointment, and he had hoped that one might eventually come his way; but with all the distractions in his life, in addition to his practice, it had been the last thing on his mind lately.

Annette served tea and retired discreetly.

'Conrad, I asked you to come this afternoon so that we can have a chat,' Sawyer said. 'I'll come straight to the point. The Lord Chancellor has taken soundings from the judges who know you well, and he is considering you for an appointment to the High Court bench – the Queen's Bench Division. Of course, the appointment is actually made by the Queen, not the Lord Chancellor. But once the Lord Chancellor decides to recommend someone, the Queen always agrees, so as a matter of protocol the Lord Chancellor never makes an offer of appointment without first making sure that it will be accepted.'

He paused and drank from his cup.

'So, I must ask you: if he were to make such an offer, would you be minded to accept?'

Conrad felt his whole body relax. He came alive again. The day had changed instantly from one of exhaustion to one of joy.

'Yes,' he replied. 'Yes, I certainly would.'

Sawyer smiled.

'Excellent. The Lord Chancellor will be very pleased. We'll be in touch about the paperwork in due course; no need to worry about that today. But there are a couple of other questions I need to ask you; all perfectly routine, nothing to be concerned about.'

'Yes, of course.'

'Firstly, as you know, all High Court judges are knighted on appointment, and the Lord Chancellor must make sure that the person appointed will accept the knighthood.'

Conrad's first thought was for Deborah. She would become Lady Rainer. Perhaps that would be some compensation for all the nights he had spent away, and for all the sacrifices they had made over the years, and perhaps even for the absence of children. He found himself happy for her.

'Why would someone refuse a knighthood?' he asked.

Sawyer laughed. 'It's very rare. You occasionally have a chap who's a bit left wing and fancies himself as a republican, or something like that, who turns his nose up at it; betrayal of his principles and so forth.'

'What do you say to people like that?'

'It's only happened once on my watch. I told him that he couldn't have the job without the K, and that I had any number of good chaps waiting in the queue who would be only too happy to step up if he really couldn't reconcile it with his conscience.'

'And what happened?'

'It did the trick. He's still on the bench, and doing a jolly good job, too.'

Conrad laughed.

'Well, you won't have any problem like that with me, I assure you.'

'I didn't think so. But I had to ask.'

He paused. 'There's another thing I need to ask, too.'

'Please,' Conrad said.

'The Lord Chancellor must know if there's any reason why it may be inappropriate for him to recommend you to the Queen.'

Conrad paused.

'Inappropriate? In what way?'

Sawyer shrugged. 'Well, I'm sure I don't need to tell you that the Lord Chancellor expects the highest standard of conduct from judges. It's particularly important at the High Court level. At the lower levels, the Lord Chancellor can dismiss a judicial office holder for misconduct. But High Court judges can only be removed by an address of both Houses of Parliament, which is something that has never happened to an English judge. That's a record we're rather proud of, and one the Lord Chancellor wouldn't want to lose.'

'Yes, I see that…'

'There was a case a few years ago,' Sawyer continued, 'which was on my watch, I regret to say. It's all in the public domain, and the man in question has retired, so it's quite proper for me to tell you about it – and indeed, the Lord Chancellor has asked me to tell everyone in your position.

'There was a man called Martin Hardcastle. I don't know whether the name rings a bell?'

'Yes, it does,' Conrad replied. The story had made the rounds at the Bar at the time; it was hard to imagine that anyone had not heard it. But Sawyer was going to tell him, regardless, and he would not interrupt him.

'Hardcastle was in Silk, and the Lord Chancellor offered him an appointment to the County Court bench, which he accepted. There had been rumours about the amount he was drinking, but neither I, nor the Lord Chancellor, had any reason to think that it would be a problem. I interviewed him in this very office, and the Lord Chancellor offered him an appointment.

'But when his chambers gave him a farewell dinner, he got very drunk – so much so, that on his way home he was arrested for being drunk and disorderly, and obstructing a police officer in the execution of his duty. A member of his chambers managed to get the obstruction charge dropped, but he was fined by the magistrates for being drunk and disorderly. Of course, yours truly then had to write to Hardcastle to tell him that the Lord Chancellor had withdrawn the offer. Not the kind of situation we like to be in.'

He paused to finish his tea.

'Conrad, I'm sure there are no skeletons in your closet, but the Lord Chancellor insists on my asking now, in all cases. I have to advise you that if there is anything that might embarrass the Lord Chancellor at some future time, you must let me know now. Speak now, or forever hold your peace, as the saying goes.'

Conrad felt Sawyer's eyes on him. For a moment he went hot and cold as images of Greta and the Clermont Club went through

his mind. There was nothing illegal in any of that, and if the Lord
Chancellor had taken soundings from judges who knew him, then
the Lord Chancellor already knew that he had a reputation for
liking a night out on the town. But he had never been arrested, or
even stopped by the police. Martin Hardcastle might have been
stupid enough to walk home after a dinner like that, but that
was his problem. Conrad took taxis, and always would. Then he
remembered his thoughts of the previous night about the house
and Deborah's – the future Lady Rainer's – trust fund. The Lord
Chancellor wouldn't like that, not one little bit. But the chances of
him finding out about that were negligible.

'No; no skeletons,' he replied.

'Splendid,' Jeremy Sawyer said. 'Then we'll put the wheels
in motion. The only other thing I have to tell you is that your
appointment has to be confidential until it's announced publicly,
which won't happen until the Queen has agreed to sign off on it. At
that stage, and not before, we'll let you know, and we'll announce
it in *The Times*. Until then, I'm afraid, the convention is that you
can tell your wife, your clerk, and your accountant; no one else;
and you have to swear them to secrecy.'

'Understood,' Conrad said. 'Thank you.'

29

It had always been an article of faith with Conrad that his luck would eventually change. It had not been consistently bad. There had been some ebb and flow, and there had been nights when he had come out ahead. But the one or two spectacular wins he had enjoyed in the early days had remained elusive, like lightning reluctant to strike in the same place again.

His luck was not the whole story; he knew that. The ability to watch and track the energy around the table had left him, too. He sensed that this was not random. In the beginning he had been focused on the game and the players, concentrating on the table, and nothing but the table. He could go for hours without being aware of anything else. But then, he had not been worrying about the money. He had been free to focus on the game. Now he was worrying about the money a great deal.

His visits to the Clermont Club were no longer a game; they had become a battle for survival. His losses were no longer simply the cost of a night's entertainment; they represented serious damage to family assets that should never have been at risk, that Deborah did not know to be at risk; and the circumstances in which they had been exposed to risk had his fingerprints all over them. He was smoking at the table now, too – another distraction he had never imposed on himself before. Things were critical. He was due to be appointed a High Court judge in a matter of weeks. The Queen's decision had been made, and was about to be made public. He couldn't afford skeletons in the closet, as Jeremy Sawyer had put it. If his luck didn't change soon, there was every chance that things would start to fall apart.

With so much to worry him, he was concentrating on the result instead of the game, the money instead of the energy; and when you focused on the money, the energy became invisible to you. If anyone was seeing the energy now, it was Ian Maxwell-Scott, who in recent weeks had played with such insight and precision that even Lucan and Goldsmith were nervous of him. He had asked Susie one night how such a transformation had come about. 'He has nothing left to lose,' she replied. 'He's way beyond worrying. He communes with death – in the gaming sense, you understand – every night, and he has no more fear of it.' Well, I'm very afraid of it, Conrad reflected, and I still have a lot to lose; which explained his state of mind, but offered no way out.

He had calculated as precisely as he could the amount of money he needed from his two sources of funding. He needed a prolonged winning streak to make good his losses, and a prolonged winning streak did not, could not, involve winning every hand. It involved having enough resources to allow his luck time to work; to let it materialise, hand by hand, night after night, with the wins outstripping the losses gradually and consistently over a period of time. For that purpose, in the high-stakes world of the Clermont Club, he estimated the minimum funding required at £30,000. If he could have put all the distractions out of his mind, kept his focus on the game; if he could have lost the fear of death, he might even have done it. When the table caught fire and the wagers escalated steadily up to half the house limit, a player who could see the energy clearly might walk away with most of what he needed to recoup his losses in a single night. Even if there was still some shortfall, he might be able to walk away happy.

But the fear had robbed him of the ability to see clearly; it had robbed him of his confidence; and he had begun to make mistakes. His worst mistake was to raid his two sources separately. He raised £20,000 from his first source, Deborah's trust fund, hoping – against his own calculations – that it might be enough; and putting himself under more pressure worrying that it might not be enough; leaving himself uncertain and vulnerable as his losses mounted. By the time he was forced to raise £10,000 from the second source, the house, by means of a mortgage, his fear had more or less wiped out his ability to play a table.

He had become easy prey. Even Dominick Elwes was able to keep pace with him. As banker, his betting was erratic. Instead of starting small and encouraging others to cover, upping the stakes gradually as they did so, he bid high and low without any pattern, and frightened the other players off until they saw the chance to pounce. As a player he offered the mirror image, alternating between recklessly covering the bank and offering only minimum stakes against a banker whose run was obviously coming to an end. He was rudderless in the midst of a chartless sea. He tried to look to Ian for inspiration, but Ian the Fearless was on another level now, on a planet of his own, with a manic Susie cheering him on, and Conrad could no longer read him. Periodically, he made a real effort to see the energy, and sometimes he thought he did, but he could not keep his mind from leaping in excitement at the thought of a win, and once his mind went there, the energy vanished as quickly as it had appeared. When the table was on fire, he was losing instead of winning; the amount of his resources merely postponing the inevitable, and making the inevitable worse when it came.

As the last remnants of his resources dwindled away, he tried to confide in Greta, but hers was a world in which there was always more money, and she seemed to have no understanding of his plight. He contemplated raiding his resources again, but if he did that, the amount he would have to chase would need luck of a different order, and his bankers would ask questions they had not asked so far. He started to float away into a melancholy fog in which the endless round of losses was all that remained visible to the human eye.

Then one day, by appointment, he went into his chambers for almost the last time, to make the necessary arrangements for his departure for the Bench. As chance would have it, he found himself alone in the clerk's room for some minutes, and looking serendipitously around, he suddenly saw a third source, an opportunity to fund one last despairing chase of his brutal losses.

Putting his judgement aside, he seized this final opportunity with both hands, and tonight, he had brought it to the Clermont Club. But now, he no longer had time to wait for a prolonged, gradual run of luck. The third source was one he could not conceal for long. He was holding a hand grenade, and the pin was halfway out. He needed to win now.

30

Lucan and Goldsmith were ready for him. By arrangement or chance – Conrad never knew – Lucan had been placed to his left, Goldsmith to his right. He had to deal with a Lucan bank and with a Goldsmith right of *banco prime*. John Aspinall, who had a nose for the big occasion, was on hand to watch.

Conrad had brought £14,000 with him, leaving the remaining £2,000 from the unexpected proceeds of the third source at home, as insurance. It was not enough. When he took over the bank, Lucan gradually increased his bids. Conrad bided his time, never covering the bank. In this way, he managed to break even after several hands, but as Lucan had calculated, breaking even was not on Conrad's agenda for the evening. His need, his transparent haste and anxiety, made him vulnerable. Abruptly, Lucan tempted him with a bid of £2,500. Conrad covered and lost. Without even thinking about it, Lucan upped his wager to £5,000. Conrad covered and lost again. On the following hand, he abstained. Lucan lost, and Conrad had the bank. It felt like a poisoned chalice.

Goldsmith called *banco prime* to cover Conrad's first wager. He had started modestly with a bid of £250, and had won two hands at that amount. But then, instead of proceeding incrementally, starting to ride his luck, he jumped nervously to £2,500, and lost. Greta was looking on impassively. Once Goldsmith had the bank, Ian Maxwell-Scott, who at times had seemed almost asleep at the table and had played no real part in the action, suddenly woke up and, with Susie standing behind him and willing him on, engaged Goldsmith in a short, fierce duel. Ian lost two hands, but then won on a £1,000 wager, and seized control of the bank.

Ian's recent run of form meant that most of those around the table were reluctant to match him. Apparently oblivious to his surroundings, Ian started high, at £1,000. Conrad watched for a hand or two, venturing only £200, and lost both times. The third time, he covered, and lost again.

After the fourth time, John Aspinall called for a break in the action, and took Conrad aside as the other players took advantage of the lull to go downstairs for a quick drink.

'I think that might be enough for this evening, Conrad, don't you agree?'

'He's fine,' Greta protested. She was standing a few feet away, behind them. 'Let him be.'

'I wasn't talking to you,' Aspinall replied tartly. 'Why don't you go and get yourself another drink? Tell them it's on the house.'

Furious, she turned and left the room.

'I'm concerned, Conrad. I think you're out of your depth at this table. Why don't you try the Holland Room? There's a lower-stakes game going on. You might feel more comfortable.'

Conrad bit his lip. He had not come to the Clermont to feel comfortable. But it would do no good to tell Aspinall what his goal for the night was, or what was riding on his achieving that goal. If he gave any hint of that, Aspinall would slam the door in his face and put the word out to every gaming club in London.

'I know what I'm doing, John,' he replied.

'Do you? I'm a very hands-on kind of man, Conrad, as you know. In this business, I have to be. Word gets back to me. I know how much you've been losing, and frankly with some people – Lucky or Jimmy, for example – I would turn a blind eye. I might have a quick word, a quick check that everything's all right, but I'd let it go. I know they're good for it, you see? Jimmy makes money just by waving his hands in the air, and Lucky has bankers who think it's a privilege to give his Lordship as much credit as he asks for. But with you… Conrad, I don't think I can. You're a successful QC, so I know you're not a poor man, but you've acquired an expensive habit. I've always thought you were a bit out of your depth in the Blue Room – financially, I mean. It's not good for you, and it's not good for the Club.'

Conrad did not reply immediately.

'As a successful QC, I think I might be trusted to know when I'm in over my head,' he said eventually.

Aspinall smiled.

'It's strange what the table can do to people,' he said. 'It creates all kinds of illusions, including a certain blindness to being in over one's head.'

'Perhaps the illusions affect club owners as well,' Conrad suggested.

'They do,' Aspinall agreed, 'more than anyone else, actually. But club owners end up carrying the can when things go wrong. I'll allow you £2,000, Conrad. If you lose any more than that tonight, I'll have to ask you to deposit at least £20,000 to continue in the Blue Room.'

He walked away before Conrad could say another word.

Later, in the Knightsbridge flat, while they were smoking, naked, on the bed, he told her what Aspinall had said.

'What does Aspinall know?' she demanded.

'It doesn't matter what he knows. It's his club. He makes the rules. If I don't come up with £20,000 I'm finished.'

'Then come up with £20,000.'

'It's not that easy, Greta.'

'You have assets, Conrad. Use them.'

'I can't – not without my wife finding out. I'm in enough trouble with what I've done already. If I try for more, I'd be putting my head in the lion's mouth.'

She allowed her hand to wander down between his legs.

'I like men who are willing to do that.'

He moved her hand away gently.

'I know you do. But this is reality now. I'm in a lot of trouble, Greta, and I don't see any way back except winning, and winning quickly. But to do that I need money, and I can't go back to the same assets.'

'Can't you ask your bank for credit?'

'To fund my gambling? In addition to my raids on my assets, which the bank knows all about?'

She reached over to put out her cigarette.

'What if I could arrange for you to have some money?' she asked.

'What? What do you mean?' He looked at her for some time. 'Greta, are you…? Look, if you mean that you want to give me money – no. I appreciate the offer but –'

She smiled.

'No, Conrad. I'm not offering to give you money. I like you, but not that much.'

'Well, what are you saying, then?'

'I know people: people who could make money available to you.'

He settled on to his back, and looked up at the ceiling.

'I'm not sure I like the sound of that.'

She shrugged.

'Well, it's true, these people are not bankers, but what is it you say in English? Any port in a storm? It all depends how much you want the money, doesn't it? You don't have to. You could walk away now, and perhaps your wife and your bankers would never know, and over time, you will replace the losses and you will live happily ever after.'

Perhaps, he reflected silently – if he got very lucky over a long period of time; if no one asked questions; if Deborah took no interest at all in their financial affairs. But even if that were possible, there was the third source. He hadn't told Greta about that, and there was no way back from the third source.

'What would I have to do?' he asked.

'I would call a man,' she replied, 'and you would meet him here, and talk terms.'

'When?'

'Give me a couple of days,' she said.

31

Conrad knew the man was trouble as soon as he walked into Greta's living room. They must have had some history together – she kissed him as he entered – but that did not reassure Conrad at all. She didn't look enthusiastic about it. In fact, she seemed nervous, and he had never seen Greta nervous, had never associated her with nervousness. The man's appearance was unpromising. He was wearing a suit, but it was a tasteless parody of a suit, dark blue, a little too short in the sleeve and in the leg, the three buttons of the jacket fastened and making it look too tight. He was wearing a parody of a tie, too, some kind of pattern of red and black, knotted too tightly and veering to the right, against a frayed blue shirt. Then, there was the cheap plastic briefcase. But it was the man's face that put the matter beyond doubt. It was a hard face, sporting a heavy black stubble, and scarred on the left side from just below the eye to the middle of the nose. The eyes were as hard as granite, dark and impenetrable.

'I'm Danny Cleary, Mr Rainer,' he said, offering his hand with an obviously false attempt at pleasantry. 'Greta's told me all about you. Very impressive. I understand you're interested in obtaining some cash?'

The accent was South London. Conrad's every instinct was to put a stop to it there and then. Nothing was looking right about this. He could still walk away. Whatever his problems, there was no point in making them worse. But then again, he had to find a solution somewhere. There could be no harm in learning more. Perhaps some ideas would come to him as a result.

'I'm interested in hearing what you have to say, Mr Cleary,' he replied.

Cleary smiled. 'Good. Well, no need to stand on ceremony, is there? Why don't we all have a seat, nice and friendly?'

'Do you want a drink, Danny?' Greta asked. She still sounded nervous.

'No thanks, darling. Not when I'm working. Got to keep a clear head, don't you, Mr Rainer? I'm sure you know that, in your line of work.'

Conrad lit a cigarette.

'So, you might want to borrow some cash?'

'I might.'

'Fair enough. I might be able to help. The thing is, Mr Rainer, I represent what you might call a syndicate.'

'A syndicate?'

'Yeah. Well, it's just a group of friends really, friends who have a few bob to lend, and don't mind lending it in a good cause.'

'A group of friends? So, it's not a company?'

Cleary laughed.

'A company? No, definitely not. More like a rabble, if you ask me, more like a mob. But they're good lads, you know. I can vouch for them. If they say they'll come up with the money, they will. I don't put up any cash myself. I only wish I could, but I'm not that fortunate. So I just represent them.'

'I see,' Conrad said. 'And what are your friends' terms for lending a few bob?'

'That depends on how much you want,' Cleary replied.

'So I assumed.'

'What did you have in mind?'

'What if I wanted £20,000?'

Cleary looked at him.

'Twenty grand? That's a fair chunk of cash, that is,' he said, his eyes never leaving Conrad's face. 'Usually, people want five hundred, or a thousand or two. It's not often we go very much more than that.'

'If it's not possible, I quite understand,' Conrad said.

Cleary did not reply at once.

'I didn't say it wasn't possible, did I? It might be. But I'd need to know a bit more.'

'Such as what?'

'Such as what you're going to do with it. I mean, that's enough for someone to disappear, innit? If you run off to Brazil or wherever, taking their twenty grand with you, and you're never seen again, my friends are going to be very unhappy with me, and I don't want them to be unhappy with me, if you know what I mean.'

'Conrad's not going to disappear anywhere,' Greta said.

'Darling, why don't you disappear somewhere?' Cleary replied, without turning to her. 'Why don't you go and powder your nose, or whatever?'

Greta shook her head in frustration, but retreated silently into the bedroom.

Cleary laughed.

'She's a very pretty girl, but pretty girls get in the way of business, don't they, Mr Rainer? I'm sure you've noticed yourself. Now, where were we?'

'You were suggesting that I might disappear,' Conrad replied.

'No offence, Mr Rainer, but it's my job to think of these things. My friends depend on me to think of these things. See, twenty grand buys you a lot. Look, truthfully, I don't care what you do with it, as long as my friends are going to see their money at the end of the day. That would be a lot of money to them. It might be their retirement money, or the money they were going to use for the villa in Spain, or the diamonds for the wife for their silver wedding, or whatever. So, they just need to make sure you're good for it. They don't want you doing a runner. As long as you're good for it, you can spend it all on the nags, or the latest fashions for your good lady wife, for all they care.'

'They'll get their money back,' Conrad said.

'I don't doubt it,' Cleary replied, 'you being a gentleman of the law, and everything. But what they're going to ask me is: what you're willing to do to show good faith.'

'Meaning what?'

Cleary shrugged.

'Well, they can't leave a loan of twenty grand out there for too long. We're not talking about a long time for repayment. They're going to insist on a substantial rate of return, and they're going to insist on regular cash payments on an agreed schedule.'

'How much?'

'I'd have to verify this with them, but I would think we're talking about half the amount in interest, so that's ten grand, and a monthly payment of two and a half, representing a payment of capital and interest, first payment in four weeks.'

Conrad almost choked on his cigarette.

'You're asking for £2,500 a month? You can't be serious.'

'I said I'd have to verify it. That's just my first impression. They have the last word, obviously.'

'That's outrageous.'

'Well, I could be a bit off, Mr Rainer, but honestly, I don't think so. I know these people, and I know how they think, and I'm usually pretty close. Look, on that schedule, the loan's outstanding for half a year, and that's much longer than they usually allow. They'd be doing you a big favour.'

'I don't believe it.'

'We're not a bank, Mr Rainer. I know you could go to the Midland and get a much better deal, but I'm thinking you have reasons for not wanting to go to the Midland. Am I right?'

Conrad did not reply.

'See, the thing is: this is what's known technically as an unsecured loan.'

'I'm aware of that,' Conrad said testily. 'I know what an unsecured loan is.'

'Yes, but I did say "technically",' Cleary said, 'meaning that we don't have any paperwork – we don't have a mortgage or a promissory note, or such like. But, just so there's no misunderstanding, that doesn't mean it's entirely unsecured.'

Conrad nodded.

'Meaning, if I don't pay, I will be in trouble, whether there's paperwork or not.'

'I didn't say that,' Cleary said. 'But let me put it this way: it wouldn't be advisable to default, which I believe is the correct legal term. So, what you have to decide is: how much you need the money, whether you really need twenty grand, and whether you are prepared to agree to the syndicate's terms now that you understand what would be involved if you were to default?'

He stood.

'Why don't you think it over? If you want to go ahead, Greta knows how to get in touch with me. Tell her to call me, and I'll have the cash for you in 48 hours.'

32

'Ben, come in. How are you?'

Andrew Pilkington lifted himself out of his chair and walked to the door to welcome his visitor. It was now almost 5 o'clock, and his case, a serious grievous bodily harm with intent – a Saturday night pub brawl that got out of hand – had ended with a satisfying verdict of guilty. He had returned to his chambers to find a message that Ben Schroeder wanted to see him urgently. That could only mean one thing. It was time to forget about the grievous bodily harm and turn his attention to the murder trial he was to start on Monday, the case of Henry Lang. He contemplated the message for some time, before asking his clerk to call Ben's chambers and invite him to come for a cup of tea.

On the face of it, the prosecution case he was about to present to a jury was rock solid. His police officers were competent and reliable, and he had an eye witness. But the defendant's claim of amnesia bothered him. In some ways, it would be the icing on the cake for the prosecution to have a defendant with such an obviously convenient gap in an otherwise excellent memory. But the medical evidence did not entirely support that sceptical view of the case; and Henry Lang was represented by solicitors and counsel he knew well and trusted implicitly – if there was anything suspicious about the defendant's claimed amnesia, it would not be at their instigation. In addition, he had a victim who, although she in no way deserved the violent death her husband had inflicted on her, was hardly the model wife and mother. DI Webb had unearthed enough evidence to implicate her in dealing hard drugs. Admittedly, it was at a low level, but she had clearly been associating with some unsavoury characters since walking out on her husband – characters who were dealing at a much higher level and using her as one of their street runners. That evidence had been disclosed to the defence, and it was inevitable that it would be dragged up repeatedly during the trial. There was nothing Andrew could do about that. In a perfect world, such considerations would not affect the outcome of a murder trial in which she was the victim, but Andrew had enough experience to know that juries were unpredictable, and in an imperfect world they sometimes seized on evidence of that kind to manufacture some undeserved sympathy for a defendant.

'Very well, Andrew, thank you. You?'

'Yes, well, thanks. Just finished a GBH, Saturday night glassing. Nasty little case; he ran self-defence, but they potted him in the end, thank goodness.'

They sat down next to each other in two armchairs, while Andrew's junior clerk served tea.

'I keep meaning to ask you,' Andrew said. 'Your Welsh lady, Mrs Finch, how is she doing? Has she got her son back?'

'I still haven't thanked you enough for what you did for her.'

Ben had represented Arianwen Finch the year before. She had been accused of being involved in a conspiracy to plant a bomb in Caernarfon Castle on the occasion of the Investiture of Prince Charles as Prince of Wales, a plot which had been foiled by her husband Trevor, who, unbeknownst to Arianwen, was an undercover police officer. Arianwen had been arrested with the bomb in the boot of her car, on her way, the prosecution said, to rendezvous with her brother Caradog, who was to carry it into the castle. But she had insisted throughout that she had not known about the bomb, and that she would never have agreed to carry it if she had known – especially with her four-year-old son Harri strapped in his seat in the back of the car. The case against her was strong. But the prosecution had misled the court and the jury by concealing the vital fact that Trevor was an undercover officer, and by painting him as a conspirator who had escaped arrest. When Andrew was brought into the case on appeal after

Arianwen's conviction, he saw at once that her right to present her defence had been hopelessly compromised by the deceitful way in which the case had been presented. He threw his hand in, invited the court to allow her appeal; and Arianwen Finch walked from the Royal Courts of Justice a free woman – a result that Ben had always believed to be the right and just one.

Andrew shook his head.

'There was nothing else I could have done. Her conviction was unsafe. I can't believe they let that man Evan Roberts prosecute her. He has no idea what goes on in a criminal court. And when it was all over, they bumped him up to the High Court, didn't they? Talk about the inmates running the asylum.'

Ben laughed.

'I couldn't believe it. At first I thought it was part of some massive cover-up, to protect him from any inquiry into what had happened, but Gareth said I was being too cynical about it.'

'Understandable, after what you had been through, I would say.'

'Anyway, Arianwen is doing well, so I hear. Barratt keeps in touch with her through her Welsh solicitor, Eifion Morris. She had to move away from Caernarfon because of all the publicity; but she's doing well, teaching music again, and Jess persuaded the local County Court judge to return Harri to her just before Christmas.'

'Good for her,' Andrew said. 'Well, let's talk about Henry Lang. I hear we've been assigned a new High Court judge called Conrad Rainer. He doesn't ring a bell with me. Do you know him?'

'Only by name. He was a commercial Silk, apparently.'

Andrew shook his head.

'Oh, that's perfect. Another one who won't know his way around a criminal courtroom. I suppose we will have to hold his hand while he learns how we do things at the Bailey. Why in God's name they can't appoint one or two High Court judges who have actually done some crime, I will never understand.'

'I don't think the Lord Chancellor entirely trusts those of us who do crime, Andrew,' Ben smiled. 'Too close to the sharp end, might have sullied our hands.'

Andrew laughed. 'What about those of us on the side of truth and justice?'

'Which side is that?' Ben asked.

'Good question. So, how does it all look for Monday?'

'His memory has come back,' Ben replied.

Andrew stared at him in silence for some time.

'His memory has come back? Just like that? On the eve of trial?'

'Yes. Well, yesterday evening, so he told us when we saw him today.'

'Unbelievable.'

'I wanted to see you as soon as I could. We're not trying to ambush you, Andrew. This has come as just as big a surprise to us as it has to you, believe me.'

Andrew nodded.

'I accept that, of course, Ben. But it's still a remarkable coincidence, don't you think?'

'I can't argue with that.'

Andrew was silent again for a minute or so.

'Well, can you give me a clue? What is the case going to be about? What's his defence? Does he *have* a defence?'

'I believe so,' Ben replied. 'I have instructions to offer you a plea of guilty to manslaughter on the basis of provocation. If the plea is not acceptable, that's the defence we will run at trial. If you need an adjournment to give you time to think about it, I can hardly object, but I'm hoping we can deal with it on Monday.'

Andrew shook his head.

'I can guess where you're coming from with the provocation. I'd half expected something like that. I don't need an adjournment. We might as well get on with it.'

He paused for some time.

'As to the plea, I will have to think about that over the weekend. I may have to consult with the Director's office before I can give you an answer.'

'That's fine.'

'But to be perfectly honest with you, Ben, I'm not sure I can recommend it to the Director.'

'Think about it a bit more. Sit with it over the weekend.'

'I will. But I see two problems. First, it's a bit too convenient that he suddenly remembers being provoked just before we start trial on Monday –'

'That's a point you can make to the jury,' Ben nodded, 'but I don't think they're going to hang a verdict on it.'

'Perhaps not,' Andrew agreed, 'but they will on my second point.'

'Which is…?

'A man doesn't take a large knife with him from home to a meeting with a court welfare officer, does he? Not unless he's already decided to kill his wife, before he even leaves his house.'

33

Monday 4 October 1971

It was a dark, raw Monday morning. Ben and Jess were glad to escape the biting wind and cold misty drizzle that had hounded them during the walk from Ben's chambers at Two Wessex Buildings to the Central Criminal Court: up Middle Temple Lane, along Fleet Street, crossing over briefly into Farringdon Road before darting into Seacole Lane, and finally turning into Old Bailey just a few yards from the court; time enough to get thoroughly chilled.

Having robed, they had a warming cup of coffee in the bar mess. It was 9 o'clock. Their case was listed in court two at 10.30.

'Why don't you find Barratt, and take him down to the cells to see if Henry's here?' Ben suggested. 'I'll look for Andrew and find out whether he will take a plea.'

Jess nodded and they separated just outside the mess. Ben made his way to the office occupied by Prosecuting Counsel to the Crown at the Central Criminal Court, generally referred to as Treasury Counsel. It was a hive of frenzied activity. In addition to the case of Henry Lang, the office had a substantial fraud and a second murder case starting that morning, and it seemed that no one had time to breathe. He found Andrew Pilkington tying his bands while giving instructions to a young, grey-suited assistant. His discarded tie and collar lay on the desk beside him, and his wig and gown were tangled up in an unceremonious heap nearby.

'Come on in, Ben,' he called out cheerfully, trying to extricate a thumb from the knot he had just tied in the bands. 'There's some coffee on the side. I can't say how warm it is. Take a seat.'

'Thanks, I've had some,' Ben replied, 'and I don't want to keep you. I know you're trying to get ready for court. I just wondered if you had any good news for me to pass on to Henry Lang.'

Andrew seated himself on the desk and released his grip on the bands.

'I'm sorry, Ben. I spoke to DI Webb, and I ran it by the Deputy Director. Webb was happy to leave it up to me. But the Deputy Director asked for my opinion, and I had to tell him I couldn't recommend taking the plea. We have no details of the evidence we can expect the defendant to give. We can't form any view about whether it's a genuine case of provocation, much less whether it satisfies the reasonableness test. And there's the knife he brought from home to the meeting with Wendy Cameron. At the moment this looks like a case of premeditated murder to me.'

Ben nodded.

'Understood. Is there anything else we need to talk about?'

'I don't think so.' Andrew reached behind him and plunged his hand into a morass of papers. 'Oh, I can give you this. It's the scale plan of the scene in Dombey Street. For some reason they only finished it late Friday afternoon. There's a copy of the maker's witness statement attached. Let me know if you have any problems with it.'

Ben scanned the plan quickly. 'It looks fine to me,' he replied.

'Good. I think I will call Wendy Cameron first, so that I can get her away today. You won't need to keep her until tomorrow, will you?'

'I'm sure I won't,' Ben replied. 'Any word from the judge?'

Andrew laughed.

'No cries for help yet. I have been half expecting an invitation into chambers for a quick consultation. Perhaps he's having a good read of *Archbold*. We shall see.'

'I hope he asks us if he's all at sea,' Ben said. 'Provocation is not the easiest thing to sum up to a jury.'

'We'll put him right if we have to,' Andrew grinned.

Henry Lang was dressed in his grey suit and red tie, the same suit and tie in which he had appeared in front of Mr Justice Wesley in the family court. He had shaved, and his hair was tidily combed back, but his face was grey and he looked ill-at-ease. Ben delivered the bad news as gently as he could.

'To be honest, Henry,' he said, 'it's what I'd expected. The prosecutor has no idea of what you're going to say. You had the knife. The prosecution are bound to think you planned it. We have to face that.'

'I don't know how I'm going to get through this,' Henry said.

'You will,' Barratt reassured him.

Jess reached out her hand and touched his arm.

'Keep thinking about Marianne and Stephanie,' she replied. 'If we can get manslaughter, there's every chance you will be back in their lives while they're still young enough for you to make a real difference. You need to be strong and think of them.'

Henry nodded. 'I'll try,' he said. 'It's just the thought of that day being brought up time and time again.'

'Keep thinking of the children,' Jess urged.

'What does our ideal jury look like?' Ben asked, as they made their way to court.

'Men who've been screwed over by their wives in divorce cases,' Barratt replied.

'Very helpful, Barratt,' Jess grinned. 'I would say older women and younger men, as long as they look old enough to have been around the circuit once or twice. No bank managers, military types, or women anywhere near Susan's age.'

'Keep a notebook between us and scribble an X for anyone you think I should challenge.'

'All right, but I have a feeling you'll be there before me.'

'Not necessarily', Ben replied. 'I need you to use your intuition, and don't hold back.'

'Good morning, Mr Schroeder. It's nice to see you back again.'

The speaker was a tall, elegant man wearing a dark suit, a starched white shirt and a red tie. His black gown bore the insignia of the Corporation of the City of London. He held the door of court two open for them as they approached.

'Geoffrey, sir. I was your usher in the Welsh case last year.'

'Of course, Geoffrey,' Ben smiled. 'This is Miss Jess Farrar.'

'Good morning, Miss Farrar.' He leaned in towards Ben confidentially. 'Mr Schroeder, I'm probably not supposed to, but I would like to say how pleased I was to read about what happened in the Court of Appeal. I thought that Mrs Hughes – well, Mrs Finch I should call her, shouldn't I? – was a very nice lady, and to be honest I'm surprised the jury ever convicted her. I think it was a very close call. How is she doing, sir?'

'Thank you, Geoffrey. She's doing very well, and she has her son back with her – thanks to Miss Farrar.'

'I'm delighted to hear it, sir.' He nodded respectfully. 'Miss Farrar.'

'Are you ushering for us today?' Ben smiled.

'Indeed I am, sir.'

An hour later the trial was ready to begin. After challenges, there were eight men, only two seemingly over forty, and four women, the youngest seemingly in her late thirties, the others into their fifties. Each juror in turn took an oath to faithfully try the defendant and give a true verdict according to the evidence.

'What do you think?' Jess whispered, as the judge was giving the jury an introduction to the criminal trial process with the air of one who had been doing it for years.

'It's your typical Old Bailey jury,' Barratt replied. 'Some good, some bad.'

'We couldn't have done much better,' Ben added.

'I'm not sure about juror ten,' Jess said. 'There's something about her I don't like.'

'Well, you'll just have to turn her around then, won't you?' Barratt said.

34

'May it please your Lordship, members of the jury, my name is Andrew Pilkington and I appear on behalf of the prosecution in this case. My learned friends Mr Ben Schroeder and Miss Jess Farrar appear for the defendant, Henry Lang.

'Members of the jury, you've heard the indictment read to you by the learned clerk, and so you already know that the charge in this case is one of murder. The prosecution say that this defendant, Henry Lang, stabbed his wife Susan Lang to death in a street in Bloomsbury on the afternoon of 28 April this year. He stabbed her seven times with a large kitchen knife, and the pathologist who examined Susan Lang's body and conducted a post-mortem examination will tell you they were savage blows, blows that destroyed internal organs and severed arteries. He will tell you that Susan Lang could not possibly have survived the defendant's attack on her. Any one of his blows, in itself, would have been fatal. She died there, in the street, before anyone could even try to save her. By the time the police and an ambulance arrived, it was already too late.

'Members of the jury, on any view, this is a tragic case. Henry and Susan Lang were married in June 1962, and they have two children, Marianne, born in October 1963 and Stephanie, born in February 1966. What, you may ask, led Henry Lang to kill his wife? What led him to make such a frenzied attack on her? Sadly, members of the jury, the reason will become all too clear from the evidence you will hear. Henry Lang killed his wife because he was afraid that a judge was going to award custody of Marianne and Stephanie to her.

'There had been difficulties in the marriage, and in February of this year, Susan Lang had left the home she shared with her husband in Canonbury, and made a new home for herself and the children in Pimlico. She had taken the children to live with her there. Henry Lang began divorce proceedings against her in the High Court, and had asked the judge to order that Marianne and Stephanie should return to live with him. There was nothing wrong with that, members of the jury. That's why we have family courts, so that people in Henry and Susan Lang's position can go before a judge and have their differences resolved by someone impartial, if they can't work things out between themselves. Such cases are never easy for anyone involved, of course, but in most cases the parties are able to cope with them, and can start rebuilding their lives. But in this case, Henry Lang was unwilling to let the proceedings take their course, and let the judge decide. Henry Lang decided that even if he couldn't have the children, he would at least make sure that his wife would never have them; and make sure of that, he certainly did.

'You will hear that there had been one hearing in front of the judge, Mr Justice Wesley, at the end of which the judge ordered that the children should remain with Susan until the case could be fully heard. You may think that was a sensible solution. It would have done no good to have the children moved to and fro unnecessarily, when the whole thing would have been over in one or two months. The children could then have looked forward to some stability, living with one parent while seeing the other as often as possible. The judge also ordered a court welfare officer's report. Members of the jury, court welfare officers are highly-trained men and women who interview the parties, and sometimes the children, look at the premises in which the children would be living with a custodial parent, and then report their findings to the judge. In this case, the court welfare officer was Mrs Wendy Cameron, who works from her home in Dombey Street in Bloomsbury.

'You will hear from Mrs Cameron, members of the jury, and she will tell you that she arranged to see Henry and Susan Lang together at about lunchtime on 28 April, a Wednesday. Mrs

Cameron will tell you about the meeting they had. She will tell you that Henry Lang appeared tense and anxious, and that he was very distressed whenever the possibility was mentioned that the judge might award custody to Susan. She will tell you that when the meeting ended, they left together, and she went to her kitchen to make herself some lunch. But within a short time, she heard the sound of a violent argument outside her house. When she returned to her front room and looked out of the window, to her horror, she saw Henry Lang stab Susan repeatedly with a large knife. She saw Susan fall to the ground, where she remained, motionless; and she saw Henry Lang sitting on the ground, next to his wife, making no effort to help her, or to seek help for her, just watching her die. Wisely, you may think, Mrs Cameron did not go outside, but she dialled 999 for the emergency services.

'Mrs Cameron will tell you, members of the jury, that she did not see a knife in Henry Lang's possession during their meeting, but clearly he had it with him when they left, and you may well conclude that he had concealed it in his coat until it was needed. You will hear from a police officer who searched Henry Lang's flat after he had been arrested, and found a set of seven kitchen knives, identical in appearance to the murder weapon. Each knife is different in size, and the murder weapon appears to form part of that set. You will be able to see that set of knives for yourselves and draw your own conclusions. You may well think that no other conclusion can be drawn but that Henry Lang took that knife with him when he left home to make his way to the meeting with Mrs Cameron and his wife. That is an important fact in this case, members of the jury, and I will return to it shortly.

'The first officers on the scene were Detective Inspector Webb, Detective Sergeant Raymond, and a uniformed officer, Police Constable Williams. You will hear, members of the jury, that Mrs Cameron's home in Dombey Street is a very short distance indeed from Holborn Police Station, where those officers are based, and so they were on the scene within a few minutes of her emergency call coming in. You will hear from those officers, and one thing you will hear, members of the jury, is that they each displayed remarkable courage, particularly DI Webb. Susan Lang was lying just off the street inside the entrance to a mews courtyard called Harpur Mews, and Henry Lang was sitting in the entrance itself, blocking access to her, and still holding the knife. DI Webb saw that it was necessary to disarm him, which he did by approaching him from in front, which inevitably meant exposing himself to the knife. If Henry Lang had attempted to use the knife against the Inspector, he would have had no real way of protecting himself from a very serious and potentially mortal wound.

'I make clear, members of the jury, and I do so gladly, that Henry Lang did not attempt any violence at all, with the knife or otherwise, against any of the officers. In fact, he surrendered the knife to DI Webb without any resistance, and he offered no resistance when he was arrested, handcuffed, and taken to Holborn Police Station. One of the curious features of this case is that, not only was Henry Lang totally compliant in that way, but he also remained silent throughout, during his arrest and when he arrived at the police station. When the officers interviewed him under caution two days later, he gave them no explanation of the events of 28 April. There are two things I must say about that.

'First, under our law, no suspect is obliged to answer any questions put to him by the police. That is a right we all have, and it is an important one. Members of the jury, his Lordship will direct you about the law later in the trial, and you must take the law from his Lordship, not from me. But I can safely tell you this: that you are not allowed to hold Henry Lang's silence against him in any way. It is not evidence of his guilt, because it was his right to remain silent, and it cannot be evidence of guilt if he chooses to exercise that right. The prosecution has the burden of proving the defendant's guilt if you are to convict. No defendant is called on to prove his innocence, and that is another reason why Mr Lang has no obligation to say anything, either before trial or during trial.

'I must also tell you that Mr Lang's silence was not entirely the result of a conscious choice on his part. You will hear that when he arrived at Holborn Police Station, he not only continued to say not a word, but he also became very cold, shaking uncontrollably. The custody sergeant, Sergeant Miller, who was responsible for

Mr Lang's welfare while he was in custody, became so concerned that he called in the police surgeon, Dr Moynihan, for advice. Dr Moynihan sent Mr Lang to Barts hospital, where he was found to be suffering from traumatic shock. They kept him for two nights and treated him as far as they could, and during that time Mr Lang recovered from the shock and was returned to the police station. The prosecution accept that Henry Lang had gone into shock after killing his wife. We say that it was simply an understandable reaction to the horror of what he had done.

'After his recovery from the shock, he did speak to the officers in interview on Friday 30 April, but he did not tell them anything about the events of 28 April. Again, as I say, that was his right, and you will not hold it against him. But there is another matter that you will have to consider. Henry Lang told the police that he had no memory of those events; that his memory ended with his leaving home on that morning, and resumed only with his return from Barts to the police station two days later. Everything in between, he claimed, including his stabbing of his wife, was a blank.

   'Members of the jury, the prosecution do not accept that Mr Lang was telling the truth when he claimed to be suffering from amnesia about that vital period of time. The reason we do not accept it is that last Friday afternoon, when this trial was set to begin today, Henry Lang suddenly claimed that his memory had now returned. He did not say that to the police, members of the jury. He said it to his solicitor and counsel, and I am grateful to my learned friend Mr Schroeder, who immediately reported it to me. It was a characteristically fair and proper thing for Mr Schroeder to do. But the fact remains that, in the prosecution's view, it is simply too convenient that Henry Lang's memory has returned just in time for trial, when it was too late for the officers to interview him and discover what he has to say about the events of 28 April, and to question him about them. We may find out during the trial what he has to say about it, or we may not. Mr Lang is entitled to give evidence if he wishes, but he has no obligation to give evidence. We will all just have to wait and see, won't we?

'There is one last matter to mention, members of the jury. My learned friend Mr Schroeder was good enough on Friday afternoon to tell me that the defence will be one of provocation. Again, members of the jury, the law is his Lordship's province, not mine, but I hope it will be helpful if I tell you briefly what that means. Provocation is a partial defence to murder. If you thought this might be a case of provocation, you would convict Mr Lang, not of murder, but of manslaughter. In other words, you will not be invited simply to find him not guilty of anything; that will not be an option in this case. If the prosecution proves beyond reasonable doubt that this is a case of premeditated murder – which we intend to prove, and are confident that we will prove – then you will convict him of murder. But if it may be that he killed only because he was provoked, then you would convict of manslaughter.

'Members of the jury, as you would expect, the test for provocation is not an easy one to meet. Provocation means, not only that the defendant was in fact provoked by his victim to do as he did, but also that what the victim said and did to provoke him not only caused the defendant to lose his self-control, but also was such that it would have caused a reasonable man in the defendant's position to do as he did. That is the question you will have to answer. Bear in mind throughout that the prosecution must prove its case, if you are to convict.

'But we say that, when you have heard the evidence, you will have no doubt whatsoever that this is not a case of provocation, but the clearest possible case of premeditated murder. There is one simple reason for that, which will become clear if you will ask yourselves this question: why did Henry Lang take a large kitchen knife with him from home to a meeting with his wife and a welfare officer? There can only be one sensible answer to that question, can't there? Henry Lang had decided to kill his wife before he ever left home.

'With your Lordship's leave, I will call the first witness.'

35

'Would you give the court your full name, please?'

'Wendy Cameron.'

Andrew Pilkington smiled. 'Mrs Cameron, please remember that this is a large courtroom and everyone has to hear what you say; and although I'm asking you the questions, try to direct your answers to the jury.'

'I'll do my best.'

'I'm sure you will. Mrs Cameron, what do you do for a living?'

'I am a welfare officer for the Family Division of the High Court.'

'How long have you worked in that capacity?'

'For about seven years. I started when it was still called the Probate, Divorce and Admiralty Division.'

'Can you explain briefly what a court welfare officer does?'

'Yes. In divorce cases the judges often have to decide where the children of the family will live, which parent they will live with, and how often the other parent will see the children. The judge can ask a welfare officer to prepare a report dealing with all these things, to assist him in reaching a conclusion.'

'Thank you. Just before I ask you about the report itself, what qualifications does a welfare officer need?'

She smiled. 'I'm not sure what the formal qualifications are, if there are any. The judges rely mainly on our experience. I had a number of years of experience as a child welfare officer in North London before I applied. It's mostly a question of knowing where to look and what questions to ask.'

'I'm sure there's no such thing as an average case, Mrs Cameron –'

'No, there's not –'

'No. But can you give the jury a general idea of what you would do in order to prepare a report for the judge?'

'There are certain things we always do. I'm not sure all officers necessarily do them in the same order, but they have to be done. I always begin by meeting with both parties, just to explain my role a bit more, and tell them what to expect, and hopefully to reassure them that I am neutral and I'm not starting out with any preconceived ideas.'

'Then, what?'

'Then I interview the parties in turn. I start with the party who has initiated the divorce or the proceedings for custody. There's no particular reason for that except that it's an objective reason to start with that party, so it doesn't give rise to any suspicion that I am starting out for or against either of them.'

'All right.'

'Then I interview the other party.'

'Let me ask you this. Do you tell each party what the other has said to you?'

'No. But I have to explain to them that the welfare of the children is the overriding consideration. So, while I will keep what they say confidential, as far as I can, and I certainly wouldn't repeat what they say for no good reason, at the end of the day there is no privilege involved. I must include in my report anything I think the judge should know in the children's best interests, which may mean telling the judge – and the other side – about things a party might prefer to keep quiet about.'

'What else do you do?'

'I also look at the accommodation and educational arrangements the parties are proposing. I take into account the parents' financial situation, of course, and I look at the living conditions before the break-up. A divorce always means that there is less money to go around than there was before, so you can't expect the same standard of living, and in any case that's not the only consideration.'

'Do you talk to the children?'

'If it's appropriate.'

'When is it appropriate or inappropriate?'

'It depends on a number of things. Age is always important. The older the children are, the more likely it is that I will talk to them. In fact, by the age of about twelve or thirteen, most judges will want to know whether the child has expressed any view about where he or she wants to live. But if the child is too traumatised, or I'm not sure he or she is mature enough to express a reliable opinion, I may decide not to speak to them.'

'Are the parents involved in your decision whether or not you talk to a child?'

'I listen to what the parents have to say, but it's my decision. If I decide I should talk to the child, I do it. If the parent resists, I simply tell them that I will ask the judge to make an order. That usually does the trick. Actually, the parents' reaction when I ask to speak to a child can be quite revealing, and I always pay attention to it.'

She paused to drink from the glass of water Geoffrey had placed in front of her on the witness box.

'Afterwards, I interview the parents again, separately and together, to give them the opportunity to add anything they wish to add, or to ask me any questions.'

'And based on everything you've done, do you then present a written report to the judge?'

'I make a written report, and I am available at the hearing to answer any questions from the judge or the parties.'

'Yes. Thank you, Mrs Cameron. Let me move on to ask you about Susan and Henry Lang. How did you become involved in their case?'

'I was assigned to attend the first hearing in front of Mr Justice Wesley. Both counsel agreed that a welfare officer's report would be useful. The judge accepted that view and asked me to prepare it.'

'And, it is not in dispute I think, the learned judge awarded interim custody to Susan Lang, but ordered that Henry, the defendant, should see the children every other weekend. Is that right?'

'Yes. The children were with Susan and the judge felt that it would be pointless to move them pending the final hearing. That's a common enough thing for a judge to do. He made it very clear that it was only an interim order and that the final hearing could go either way.'

'Can you please now tell the jury what you did in order to prepare your report?'

'I spoke to both parties and their solicitors that same morning, while they were at court, and I made appointments to interview Henry first, as it was his application for custody, and then Susan.'

'Typically, where do your interviews take place?'

'Whenever possible, I try to conduct the individual interviews at the party's home. They tend to be more relaxed there, and if home is the accommodation they are proposing for the children, it saves time because I can inspect the premises while I'm there. If a party prefers, he or she can come to my office instead, and I always use my office when I am interviewing the parties together.'

'What happened in this case?'

'Both Henry and Susan were happy for me to interview them at home, but they wanted me to come back for a formal assessment of the premises because there were changes they were planning to make for the children. That was fine. It's not unusual. It means that I can at least take a preliminary look around.'

'And did you in fact interview each of them in turn?'

'Yes, I did.'

'Did you meet the children?'

'No. They were not at home when I interviewed Susan.'

'And because of the way in which events unfolded, did you ever meet the children?'

'No.'

'What was the next step?'

'I arranged a joint meeting with Henry and Susan at my office.'

'When and where was that meeting to take place?'

'On a Wednesday, 28 April, at about lunchtime. Both of them said that was a convenient time.'

'And where is your office?'

'It's in my home, number 26 Dombey Street. It's a large house, and I use the first floor as my office space.'

Andrew turned to Mr Justice Rainer.

'My Lord, the jury are going to hear a great deal about the area surrounding Mrs Cameron's house. If there is no objection, we have a scale plan of the area. I ask that the plan become our Exhibit 1, and it may be convenient if the jury could see it now.'

Ben stood. 'I have no objection, my Lord.'

'Yes, very well,' the judge replied.

Andrew waited for Geoffrey to provide Wendy Cameron with a copy, and to distribute copies to the jury, one between two.

'Mrs Cameron, on the plan the usher has handed you, do you see your house, number 26, marked with an arrow?'

'Yes.'

'Do the front windows of your house overlook Dombey Street, and does your house face directly on to the entrance to Harpur Mews?'

'Yes, actually, the entrance leads into a courtyard, which goes all the way through past the mews itself, to Harpur Street, which runs parallel to Dombey Street.'

'Yes, I see. Now, I know this will be difficult for you, but I must ask you about the events of 28 April.'

36

'Do you remember at what time Susan and Henry arrived on that day?'

'They didn't come together, of course. She came first, about 12.20 to 12.25, and he arrived exactly on time, at 12.30.'

'What was Henry Lang wearing, if you recall?'

'He was wearing a jacket, brown I think, and grey trousers, and a light raincoat, which I thought was a bit odd because it was a pretty warm day.'

'Did he wear the coat during the meeting?'

'No, he hung it up. I keep a coat rack outside the office.'

'This may seem an odd thing to press you on, but did Henry hang the coat up himself, or did you take it from him?'

'He hung it up himself.'

'Thank you. How did the meeting begin?'

'The same way as usual. I made coffee and put out glasses of water and we started talking.'

'Could you give us a sense of how the conversation developed?'

'I began by inviting them both in turn to make any comments they wanted to about their individual interviews. Neither of them had much to say about that. So I began to explain where I wanted to go from there, a further inspection of both their homes, the possibility of interviewing the children, and so on.'

'All right. I want to ask you about your impression of both of them at that meeting. What, if anything, struck you about Susan?'

Wendy Cameron thought for some time.

'Susan was always very hard to read. She said all the right things. She knew how to sound like a devoted mother. She made all the right noises about how the children were the most important thing in the world to her. But if you challenged her, she would admit that they spent a lot of time with child minders, usually her parents – especially when she went out at night. Sometimes, I had the feeling that it was more important to her that Henry shouldn't have the children than that she should, if you know what I mean. She could be very controlling.'

'And on this occasion?'

'It was the same old story. She was a full-time mother, Henry was working too hard, he cared about nothing except his business, and he would never be there for the children. It was as much for Henry's benefit as mine. She knew how to wind him up.'

'What was your impression of Henry?'

Again, she did not reply immediately.

'Henry was far less talkative. At times, you had to push him pretty hard to get him to say anything at all. He didn't try to impress me with his credentials as a parent in the same way she did. But he loved the children. I never doubted that.'

'But how did he strike you on this occasion?'

'He was very quiet. It was an effort to get him to participate in the meeting at all. It was as if his mind was somewhere else.'

'Was there any discussion specifically about the possibility that Mr Justice Wesley might award custody to Susan?'

'Yes. I tried to make it clear to both of them that nothing had been decided, and that whichever way it went, they had to work together in the children's interests once it was all over. So we had to consider all the possibilities.'

'How did Henry react to that?'

She shook her head.

'The idea that the children might end up with Susan distressed him very much. He didn't seem able to get past that idea. I couldn't get him to move on and focus on what would be in the children's interests if that happened.'

'How did he show his distress? Visibly? Audibly?'

'Yes. I don't mean that he was shouting. Henry hardly ever raised his voice. But there was an intensity about him. I don't quite know how to put it, but whatever he was feeling ran very deep, and when he did say something, it came across very clearly.'

'Was it a productive meeting, would you say?'

'No. Not really. They were both too interested in making the same points over and over again. I tried to tell them that I understood what they were saying, but I wasn't the right person to say it to. They would have to say all that to Mr Justice Wesley, not me. But they weren't really listening. When I called time on the meeting at about 1.30, it was obvious that we weren't going to get anything done with the two of them together in the same room. I would have to rely on individual meetings if I was going to move them forward.'

'At which point, the meeting was adjourned, and they left?'

'Yes.'

'What did you do then?'

She closed her eyes and brushed away a tear.

'I went into the kitchen to make myself a sandwich for lunch.'

'Mrs Cameron, did you know that Henry Lang had brought a knife with him to the meeting?'

'No, I most certainly did not.'

'Would you have permitted it?'

'No, of course not. I would never tolerate anyone bringing a weapon to a meeting.'

'What would you have done if you had known that?'

'I would have cancelled the meeting, and reported it to the judge – and probably to the police.'

37

'As you were making your sandwich,' Andrew continued quietly, 'did you hear something?'

She nodded. She had taken a white handkerchief from her handbag, and was clutching it in both hands.

'I heard some loud noises, like shouting, coming from the street. At first I didn't pay much attention. I didn't associate it with Henry and Susan. I assumed they would have gone their separate ways by then. But when it didn't stop, I suddenly became alarmed, and I ran back to the front room to see what was going on.'

'Did you look through your front window?'

'Yes.'

'Please tell the jury what you saw and heard.'

'I saw them standing together across the street, by the entrance to Harpur Mews. They were both very angry, screaming at each other. I couldn't really hear what they were saying apart from the odd word here and there, but it was obviously about the children. I was about to go outside, and tell them both what a stupid idea it was for them to be arguing outside my front door, when they were supposed to be trying to impress me as responsible adults who could be trusted with the custody of children. But then…'

She stopped abruptly. She bowed her head and brought the handkerchief up to her face. She was crying softly.

'Mrs Cameron, do you need a break?' Andrew asked. 'I'm sure his Lordship and the jury won't mind.'

She shook her head.

'No, I'll carry on.'

'We will break for lunch when you have finished your examination-in-chief,' Mr Justice Rainer said. 'We will have cross-examination at 2 o'clock,' he added, with a glance at Ben. Ben nodded.

'Much obliged, my Lord. Mrs Cameron, you told us that you were about to go outside…'

'Yes. Just as I was about to go out, he struck her.'

'Where were they standing at that point?'

'In the entrance to Harpur Mews. He was to the right as I was looking at them, and she was on the left, but they were only inches apart.'

'And when you say he struck her, can you describe that action for us?'

She shook her head.

'It was a terrible thing to see. He had one hand on her shoulder, holding her. He raised his other arm – his right arm – very high and brought it down with full force on her body. It was sickening to watch. And then –'

'Let me stop you for a moment,' Andrew said. 'Were you able to see whether he hit her with his hand, or with something else?'

'I didn't see the knife until it was all over,' she replied. 'I don't know why. I think I was so horrified by the violence of it all, the huge arc he made with his arm, the force with which the blows landed. For some reason, the knife didn't register until it was all over and he was sitting on the ground.'

'When you say "until it was all over", do I take it from that that he hit her more than once?'

'Yes. It was six or seven times, at least. I can't be sure. I was so shocked, I felt paralysed. My mind seemed to have stopped working. It all seemed to be happening in slow motion. But I know he hit her six or seven times, and each time, with the same huge arc, the arm raised so high, the same violence…'

She wept quietly again. Andrew waited.

'I'm all right now. Thank you.'

'Thank you, Mrs Cameron. I know it's difficult. Can you tell us what happened to Susan after the first blow was struck. Did she do anything?'

'No. I heard her scream once, then she fell to the ground in a heap, and he kept hitting her when she was just lying there. She didn't move, and I didn't hear her call out again.'

'And what did Henry do when he stopped hitting her?'

'He just sat down in front of her, blocking my view of her. That's when I saw the knife. I saw him bring the knife down and sit holding it in his right hand.'

'Then what happened?'

'Nothing. That was the strange thing. He didn't move, and neither did I. I don't know how long I stood there before I reacted. When my mind finally started to work again, I dialled 999 to call the emergency services. I know this is going to sound odd, but it took a real physical effort just to pick up the phone and dial. It was as if my body had frozen along with my mind.'

'And we know that the police and the ambulance arrived soon afterwards?'

'Yes. They responded very quickly.'

'When the police arrived, had Henry moved?'

'No, he hadn't moved at all. He was still sitting on the ground, holding the knife, in exactly the same position.'

'I will call the police officers to deal with what happened next,' Andrew said. 'I needn't trouble you with that, except to ask you this: did the police in due course come to see you, and did you tell them what you had seen?'

'Yes.'

'Thank you very much, Mrs Cameron. That's all I have.'

Andrew turned to Ben and Mr Justice Rainer in turn.

'My Lord, may we now adjourn until 2 o'clock?'

Before the judge could reply, she spoke again.

'I didn't go outside,' she said quietly. 'I could have. I knew them both. Perhaps if I had…'

Andrew shook his head.

'Mrs Cameron, I assure you, and I think I speak for everyone in court when I say that no one blames you for that at all. There was nothing you could have done, except to put yourself in danger. No one would have expected you to do anything other than what you did.'

Ben stood.

'My Lord, I agree entirely with what my learned friend has said, and I will certainly not be suggesting otherwise.'

The judge nodded. 'Thank you, Mr Schroeder. We will adjourn for lunch. Be back for 2 o'clock, members of the jury.'

As the judge stood, there was a cry, a wail, from the dock. Ben turned round sharply. Henry Lang had risen to his feet. He had walked to the front of the dock, holding his head in his hands. He began to weep so violently that his whole body shook. The two prison officers who were with him also stood and approached, but without touching him.

'I'm sorry,' Henry said, just loudly enough for the court to hear. 'I'm so sorry.'

38

'Mrs Cameron, I won't keep you any longer than I have to,' Ben reassured her. 'But I'm sure you understand that there are certain things I have to ask you on Henry's behalf.'

'Yes, I understand. Thank you.'

'First of all, I would like to establish how much contact you actually had with Henry. Mr Justice Wesley assigned you to report on 5 April, during the first hearing. That's right isn't it?'

'Yes.'

'You may recall that my learned junior, Miss Farrar, represented Henry on that occasion?'

She looked over at Jess and smiled.

'Yes, I remember.'

'And we know that Susan was killed on 28 April, just over three weeks later.'

'Yes.'

'In the intervening period, on how many occasions did you speak to Henry?'

'I spoke to Henry twice before 28 April,' she replied. 'The first occasion was the first individual interview at his home in Alwyne Road. That was the following Tuesday, 13 April. I had arranged that meeting while we were at court.'

'Yes. And for how long did that interview last?'

'Between 45 minutes and an hour.'

'Was there any other meeting with Henry before 28 April?'

'Yes. At the first meeting, Henry had invited me to visit his garage in King Henry's Walk, to verify that he had a successful business. That was relevant to his financial situation.'

'Did you do that?'

'Yes, I did, a week later, on 20 April. But that was quite a short visit, probably no more than 20 to 25 minutes, and we didn't really talk about anything except the work he was doing. I also met one or two of his employees.'

'So, would it be fair to say that, as far as the question of the children was concerned, the only chance you had to speak to Henry before 28 April was the meeting on 13 April, which you told us lasted between 45 minutes and an hour?'

'Yes.'

'Mrs Cameron, would you agree that in those circumstances, you'd only had a very limited opportunity to assess Henry in terms of his behaviour, his personality, and so on?'

'I would agree with that. Yes.'

'You couldn't have based a report to Mr Justice Wesley on that alone, could you?'

'No. Certainly not. I needed at least one meeting with Henry and Susan together, and I would have had at least one further meeting with Henry on his own.'

'I want to ask you a bit more about the meeting on 13 April. When you held that meeting, you hadn't yet spoken with Susan, had you?'

'No. I hadn't.'

'Because, as you explained to us, you would first interview whichever party had started the proceedings, and in this case, that was Henry?'

'Yes.'

'But you had read the affidavits Henry and Susan had sworn and filed with the court?'

'Yes, I had read the court's entire file, including the affidavits.'

'And having read Susan's affidavit, you knew that she was accusing him of hitting her during some violent arguments in their flat in Alwyne Road before she moved out?'

'I was aware that she was claiming to have been hit, yes.'

'Did you ask Henry about that?'

'Yes, of course.'

'What did he say about it?'

'He said that there had been arguments between them that had got pretty loud, but he denied ever having hit her.'

'He denied it emphatically, didn't he?'

'Yes, that would be fair.'

'You had also read Henry's affidavit, and you knew that he was making certain allegations against Susan, didn't you?'

'Yes.'

'He was accusing her of neglecting the children?'

'Yes.'

'He was accusing her of staying out late and drinking too much on a regular basis?'

'Yes.'

'He was accusing her of taking drugs, and associating with men who dealt drugs. Isn't that right?'

She hesitated.

'I had no means of –'

'I understand that, Mrs Cameron. Of course, you had no way of verifying it. But that's what Henry said in his affidavit, and that's what he told you during the meeting on 13 April, isn't that right?'

'Yes.'

'And that kind of allegation would be very significant, wouldn't it? The judge would have to take that kind of allegation very seriously, wouldn't he?'

'Yes, of course.'

'When did you have your first interview with Susan?'

'Two days later, on 15 April.'

'Did you put those allegations to her?'

'Yes, I did.'

'What did she tell you about them?'

She hesitated.

'I'm very uncomfortable about getting into this when Susan isn't here to defend herself. Our conversation was confidential.'

'I understand,' Ben replied. 'My learned friend Mr Pilkington will object if I ask you anything I shouldn't, but as you told us earlier, there was no privilege involved, was there? Susan understood that you might have to repeat what she said in certain circumstances.'

'If it was relevant to the welfare of the children, yes. That's no longer the case now.'

Both the judge and the witness were looking at Andrew Pilkington, who remained in his seat. There was a silence.

'Are you going to object, Mr Pilkington?' the judge asked eventually.

Andrew stood.

'No, my Lord. Of course, I'm not aware of the nature of the defence in any detail, but it seems to me that my learned friend is entitled to ask about this if he thinks it may be relevant.'

'Even if the conversations were confidential?'

'Even then, my Lord. I'm not suggesting that the court should not respect confidentiality when it can, but if there's no legal privilege, the defence is entitled to present any relevant evidence. If your Lordship wishes, we can ask the jury to retire and I will refer your Lordship to *Archbold.*'

Mr Justice Rainer considered for some time.

'No, I'm sure you're right, Mr Pilkington.' He looked down towards Wendy Cameron. 'I'm afraid you will have to answer the question.'

She nodded.

'Susan admitted that she liked to go out with friends, and she admitted that she would sometimes drink a bit too much. But she insisted that the children were being looked after every moment she was away, usually by her parents.'

'What did she say about the suggestion that she was taking drugs?'

'She denied it.'

'What about the suggestion that some of the men she regarded as friends, and went out with at night, were drug dealers?'

'She denied any knowledge of that.'

'What about the suggestion that she was sleeping with some of these men?'

She reacted angrily.

'I can't see how that can possibly be relevant,' she replied.

'Neither can I, Mr Schroeder,' the judge added.

'Again, my Lord,' Ben said, 'my learned friend will object if he thinks I'm going too far. But the question the jury have to decide is one of provocation, and if I am allowed to continue, the relevance of the evidence will become clear in due course. If your Lordship wishes to hear argument in the absence of the jury...'

Again, Andrew Pilkington remained in his seat.

'Very well, Mr Schroeder, continue for the time being.'

'I am much obliged. Mrs Cameron?'

'She admitted that she had slept with one or two other men,' she replied reluctantly.

Ben glanced over at the jury. As he had anticipated, they were fully alert and taking notes.

'Was that something that might have been relevant to the question of custody that Mr Justice Wesley had to decide?'

'Yes.'

'Are you aware that Susan Lang had been smoking cannabis on 28 April, before she came to your house for the meeting?'

The witness looked genuinely shocked.

'No. I...'

'My Lord, I'm not sure the evidence quite justifies that conclusion,' Andrew said, rising slowly to his feet.

'I will rephrase the question,' Ben volunteered. 'Have you been told that when the police searched Susan's car on that day, they found a joint containing a mixture of tobacco and cannabis?'

'No. I have not been told that.'

'Have you been told that when the police looked inside her handbag – the handbag she had with her during the meeting – they found a bag containing a white powder, which was analysed and found to include almost four grams of cocaine of about 40 per cent purity?'

She turned pale.

'No. I...'

'So you had no reason to suspect that Susan Lang was taking drugs? She denied it?'

'Yes.'

'If you had known that she was smoking cannabis or taking

cocaine, was that something you would have brought to Mr Justice Wesley's attention?'

'Of course.'

'Did Susan mention a man called Daniel Cleary, otherwise known as "Danny Ice", as being one of her friends?'

Mr Justice Rainer looked up sharply.

'What? Who?'

Every eye in the courtroom turned to him.

'I… I'm sorry… I didn't quite get the name,' he said. 'I have to make a note. Daniel…?'

'I'm sorry, my Lord,' Ben replied. 'Daniel Cleary, C.L.E.A.R.Y. I am instructed that his nickname is "Danny Ice".'

The judge appeared to make a careful note.

'Thank you.'

'Mrs Cameron, does that name ring a bell?' Ben asked.

'No,' she replied, 'I'm not sure she gave me the name of any of her friends, except for one woman – who she said could verify that Susan had complained to her about being hit.'

'Did she ever tell you that this man Daniel Cleary had made threats against Henry Lang?'

'Threats?' the judge asked. 'What kind of threats?'

'Threats of violence, my Lord,' Ben replied.

'No,' Wendy Cameron said, 'I never heard about any threats being made against Henry by anyone.'

As Ben paused to look at his notes and consult in a whisper with Jess, Harriet Fisk quietly left her seat at the back of the public gallery to return to chambers.

39

'Let me turn to something else,' Ben said. 'My learned friend asked you what Henry was wearing when he came to your house on 28 April, do you remember?'

'Yes.'

'And you told my learned friend that Henry had been wearing a raincoat, which he took off and hung up himself?'

'Yes.'

'You were careful to emphasise that he hung it up himself, and that you had not taken it from him.'

'That's what Mr Pilkington asked me.'

Ben smiled. 'Fair point. You were just answering the questions put to you. I accept that, of course. But what you were trying to suggest was that Henry must have been wearing the raincoat only because it gave him a place to conceal the knife during the meeting. Would that be fair?'

'Well…'

'Let me help you. You didn't see the knife anywhere else on his person, did you?'

'No.'

'You told the jury you thought it was rather strange that he was wearing a raincoat because it was a warm day?'

'Yes.'

'And yet, when you were watching Henry sitting on the ground after he had stabbed Susan, it began to rain, did it not?'

She thought for some time, and then nodded.

'Yes,' she replied. 'Yes, you're right, there was a shower. I'd forgotten that.'

'By the time of the meeting on 28 April, had you come to any conclusions at all about the recommendations you were going to make to Mr Justice Wesley?'

'You mean, about custody of the children?'

'Yes.'

'No. I had much more work to do before I could think in terms of recommendations. Besides, judges vary in the kind of recommendations they like you to make. Some – the more senior judges usually – don't want you to say very much. They like you to give them a factual report and leave them to draw their own conclusions. But there are some who like you to spell it out for them a bit more. What Mr Justice Wesley may prefer, I can't say. He's a fairly new appointment, and I hadn't worked with him before, so I would probably have been quite conservative in the way I expressed myself. But I was nowhere near that stage.'

'But it would be fair, wouldn't it, to say that you had a few thoughts in your mind about Henry, as far as custody was concerned? You know, don't you, that the High Court has allowed us to see the notes you made as you went along, which you had in your file?'

She coloured slightly.

'Yes. I am aware of that.'

'Do you have a copy of your notes with you?'

'Yes.'

'Is it fair to say that you were satisfied about Henry from the point of view of what I might call his material circumstances – his home, the amount of money he was making, and so on?'

'Oh, yes, very much so. The children would never have wanted for anything if he had custody, and he had a sensible view about their education. He was very aware of the schools in the area, which were the best, and so on. In fact, they had been doing well in all those respects before Susan took them away.'

'And yet, you had a reservation about him, didn't you?'

'Well…'

'You were worried about how intense he was about the question of custody. You said so today in answer to my learned friend, and it is recorded in your notes, isn't it? You describe Henry as being "almost too quiet", "brooding", and having "feelings that run very deep". You were worried about a possible loss of self-control, weren't you?'

She hesitated.

'You must understand that I never expected anything like what happened...'

'I do understand that, Mrs Cameron. But Susan had complained that he had hit her; you sensed that he might have a short fuse when it came to the children. That must have caused you some concern?'

'Yes, it did. It was something that concerned me. But as I said before, she knew exactly how to wind him up. Away from her, and once the proceedings were over, he would have settled down. Most parents have strong views about the custody of their children. There's nothing unusual about that. It was just that, in Henry's case, while he was having to deal with her, there was always the potential for something to kick off. Even if the judge gave custody to him, he would still have to deal with her over access, so it was something I couldn't ignore.'

'All right. Let me ask you this. Reading your notes, it seems that when Henry talked about the children, he almost always referred to them as "my children" – not "our children" or even "the children". You've underlined the word "my" more than once, haven't you?'

'Yes. But again, that's not unusual in custody cases. Parents do tend to get a bit proprietary about their children when they're talking about where they should live, and it's not uncommon for them to downplay the other parent's involvement with the children.'

'I accept that, Mrs Cameron. But when you combine that with Henry's intensity, wouldn't you agree that this man, for whatever reason, thought of himself as their real parent, if I can put it in that way? Didn't he think that Susan had in a sense disqualified herself because of her lifestyle?'

'He certainly felt that way about Susan. Yes, I would agree with that.'

'You yourself would have brought her lifestyle to the judge's attention, to the extent you were aware of it?'

'Yes.'

'And knowing what you now know about Susan's lifestyle, Mrs Cameron, that was not an entirely unreasonable view for Henry to take, was it?'

'I wouldn't criticise him for thinking that.'

'No. And in consequence, he thought of himself as the only parent who deserved custody? Would that also be fair?'

'Yes, it would.'

'Custody of "his" children?'

'Yes. Always "his" children.'

40

'My Lord, I will call the next witness, Dr Joseph Wren,' Andrew said.

Dr Wren, a short dapper man in his mid-sixties, dressed in a brown tweed suit with a light blue shirt and a blue and brown striped bow tie, skipped energetically into the witness box. He was carrying a green file folder, which he deposited on the edge of the box. He took the Bible in his hand and took the oath without being asked.

'Joseph Wren, pathologist, my Lord,' he said, nodding in the direction of the bench.

'Thank you, Dr Wren. Would you please outline your qualifications for the jury?'

Ben had dealt with Dr Wren before, notably in the capital murder case of Billy Cottage some six years earlier. He stood at once.

'My Lord, there's no need for that as far as I am concerned. Dr Wren is a well-recognised and experienced expert witness, and his qualifications are not in doubt. Indeed, it may be helpful if I indicate that there is no dispute about the cause of death, and my learned friend may lead the witness if he wishes.'

'I'm much obliged, 'Andrew said. 'Then let me ask you this, just so that the jury will understand what it is that you do. Is a pathologist a doctor who specialises in the examination of bodies and determines the cause of death?'

'Among other things, yes.'

'Yes, of course, I'm simplifying –'

'For our purposes today, that is correct.'

'And have you practised as a pathologist and have you given

evidence in court about your findings on a regular basis for more than thirty years?'

'Yes, I have. I also speak at various seminars, write articles for respected journals, and participate in training for younger colleagues, which are all things we are expected to do, in addition to our usual professional work.'

'Thank you. Dr Wren, I see you have your file with you. Don't hesitate to refer to it as and when you need to. Did you conduct the post-mortem examination of Susan Lang in this case?'

Dr Wren took his reading glasses from his inside pocket and put them on. He opened his file.

'I did, my Lord. On Thursday 29 April of this year, at Guy's hospital, I examined the lifeless body of a female identified to me as Susan Lang. The body appeared to be that of a well-nourished young woman of about 30 years of age. I was unable to make any meaningful observations about her pre-mortem state of health because of the extent of the injuries she had sustained, but the cause of death was clear almost immediately.'

'Taking this quite shortly, did you find that she had sustained a number of wounds inflicted with a sharp object?'

'Yes. There were either six or seven wounds. The reason I put it that way is that there was what appeared to be one very large wound, the entry point being into the shoulder at the base of the left side of the neck. The blow had been struck in a downwards direction with a good deal of force, but the skin had been ripped sideways, and the width of the entry point was such that I could not determine with any certainty whether it was the result of one blow or two. If it was only one, the weapon was probably used also in a sideways direction, widening the area of impact.'

Ben glanced in the direction of the jury, and saw them grimace.

'I see. In addition to that wound, or those wounds, were there three blows to the chest or torso, also appearing to have been struck from above with a downwards motion?'

'Yes, two of those wounds were slightly left of centre, and one slightly to the right, all broadly speaking just below the breasts, though one of the blows on the left had penetrated the left breast and done considerable damage to it.'

'And finally, were there two wounds to the lower abdomen?'

'Yes. These wounds had a direct frontal entry point, as opposed to a downwards motion.'

'What conclusion, if any, did you draw from that?'

'I concluded that the blows higher on the body had probably been struck while she was still standing, and that these two blows lower on the body had probably been struck after she had fallen to the ground – which would have been almost instantaneous, given the severity of the injuries.'

'Dr Wren, my learned friend has indicated that there is no dispute about the cause of death, so perhaps you could state that to the jury in simple terms?'

'Certainly. Each of the injuries I have described would have been fatal in itself, either because it caused catastrophic injury to a major internal organ, or because it resulted in haemorrhaging which could not be stemmed. I can't say with certainty which blow caused Susan Lang's death, but the combination of all of them was certainly fatal. Her heart, lungs and liver were fatally compromised, and two major arteries were severed. The haemorrhaging from the arteries alone would have resulted in death within a short space of time, quite apart from the damage to the organs.'

'Did Susan Lang have any chance at all of surviving this attack on her?'

'None whatsoever. Death would have followed the attack very quickly.'

'With the usher's assistance, I would like you to look at a knife. My Lord, it will be formally identified later, but if there is no objection, may this be Exhibit 2?'

'No objection,' Ben said at once.

'Exhibit 2,' the judge confirmed.

It was the jury's first glimpse of the weapon used by Henry Lang to kill his wife. As Geoffrey passed by the jury box, they peered at it curiously, and some turned towards the dock to look at Henry. Since saying that he was sorry just before lunch, Henry had remained silent, sitting quietly and following the proceedings without comment like a disinterested observer. If the jurors were expecting him to react when the knife was produced, they were disappointed.

'Dr Wren,' Andrew was saying, 'have you had the opportunity to examine Exhibit 2 before coming to court today?'

'Yes, I have.'

'Can you say whether this was, or may have been, the weapon used to inflict the injuries you saw on the body of Susan Lang?'

Dr Wren took the knife from the usher and peered at it.

'I can say that the injuries I saw would be consistent with the use of this weapon, but –'

Ben stood.

'Again, my Lord, I can save my learned friend the trouble. There is no dispute that this knife was used to inflict the injuries.'

Andrew and the judge exchanged looks.

'Again,' Andrew said, 'I am obliged to my learned friend. In that case, Dr Wren, I don't think there is anything else I want to ask you at this stage. Please wait there in case there are any further questions.'

'Dr Wren,' Ben began, 'do I take it that you did all the usual tests for the presence of drug residues and other substances in the body?'

'I did, sir.'

'Your post-mortem examination was conducted on the day after her death, wasn't it?'

'Yes.'

'Did you find any evidence of recent sexual intercourse?'

'No. I did not.'

'Did you find any evidence of alcohol consumption?'

'No.'

'If she had consumed alcohol during the evening before, or the early morning of the day on which she died, would you have expected to find any evidence of it by the time of the post-mortem examination?'

'Not unless she had consumed a very large quantity, or there were very unusual physiological circumstances. The likelihood is that any alcohol in her body would have dissipated. And if she had been drinking enough the night before to leave alcohol in her blood for me to find the following day, Mrs Cameron would almost certainly have noticed its effects during the meeting. She would have been in a bad way.'

'She would have had a hangover?'

'She might still have been drunk.'

'I see. Did you find evidence of recent drug consumption?'

'Yes, I did.'

'Tell the jury about that, please, Doctor.'

Dr Wren turned over several pages of his notes, one at a time.

'I found evidence consistent with the recent consumption of both cannabis and cocaine.'

'"Recent" in this context meaning what?'

'Within 48 hours, and very probably within the 24 hours preceding death.'

'Thank you, Doctor. Is it within your knowledge that one of the effects of the consumption of cocaine may be a feeling of well-being and euphoria, which may cause the user to behave in a more excitable and perhaps even more reckless way than she otherwise might?'

Dr Wren nodded.

'I might not put it exactly like that myself, but I wouldn't disagree.'

'Is that effect capable of continuing for up to 48 hours after consumption?'

'Yes. Again, that depends on timing and quantity. But it would certainly be commonplace for it to continue for at least 24 hours.'

'Thank you, Dr Wren.' He glanced at Jess, who shook her head. 'I have nothing further.'

41

Andrew consulted his notes, and looked up at the judge.

'My Lord, I anticipate starting on the police evidence tomorrow morning. There is one short witness I can call now, and then I will ask your Lordship to adjourn for the day.'

Mr Justice Rainer looked up at the courtroom clock. It was approaching 4 o'clock.

'Yes, very well, Mr Pilkington.'

'I am much obliged. Jack Farmer, please.'

Jack Farmer, a tall, well-built man in his forties wearing a grey suit, made his way to the witness box and took the oath.

'Mr Farmer, what is your occupation?'

'I am a scenes of crime officer employed by the Metropolitan Police.'

'Tell the jury, please, what a scenes of crime officer does.'

'We are instructed to attend crime scenes and other relevant locations to secure the scene to the extent necessary; to identify items of evidence, to preserve and seize that evidence; and to work with the officer in charge of the case to ensure that evidence is then sent for forensic examination.'

'And does that mean that you may deal with evidence such as bloodstains and fingerprints?'

'Yes, sir.'

'In connection with this case, did you receive a call in the early afternoon of 28 April this year, to attend a scene?'

'Yes, sir. Together with other officers, I was instructed to attend Harpur Mews WC1. We were told that a stabbing had taken place, and we were asked to attend to make a search for any evidence, and to assist the officer in charge of the case in any way we could.'

'The officer in charge being DI Webb?'

'That is correct, sir.'

'On arrival at the scene, what did you notice?'

'We noticed two things. One was that the weather was unfavourable. It was raining. In some circumstances, that can lead to contamination of an outdoor scene and to the potential loss of evidence. That meant that we had to start work as soon as possible. But the second thing was that when we arrived, the ambulance crew was still working, trying to revive the victim, and we were unable to approach the scene until they had left.'

'Did that affect your work greatly in this case?'

'Fortunately not, sir. DI Webb and other officers had already seized items of evidence and got them out of the rain. These included the weapon allegedly used in the stabbing, and the victim's handbag. We recovered the clothing from the victim and the defendant later. There was a very large quantity of blood on all the clothing, and despite the rain, we were able to submit all of it for forensic testing.'

'Mr Farmer, I don't think there will be any dispute about this, and my learned friend will correct me if I'm wrong. Is it right to say that various items of bloodstained clothing from both Susan Lang and Henry Lang were sent for testing, and when compared to samples of blood collected by the ambulance crew from the body, the blood was found to be that of Susan Lang?'

'That is correct, sir.'

'And similarly with the knife, our Exhibit 2, which was recovered by DI Webb, did it prove to be the case that there was a sufficient quantity of blood remaining on the knife to permit a comparison to be made, and were the blood stains on the knife found to be the blood of Susan Lang?'

'Yes, sir.'

Andrew turned to the judge.

'My Lord, as there is no dispute about it, I now ask that the knife, Exhibit 2, be shown to the jury.'

Geoffrey once again brought the knife within close range of the jury, but this time he did not walk on past them to the witness box. This time, he stopped in front of the jury box and allowed the jury to see the dark stains for themselves. They nodded grimly.

'Mr Farmer, I'm going to ask you also to look at some other items. Usher, there are two cardboard boxes behind me. Can we begin with the one on the left, and my Lord, may this be Exhibit 3?'

The box was bulky, but not heavy, and Geoffrey carried it effortlessly over to the witness.

'Please tell my Lord and the jury what this is.'

'These are the items of clothing recovered from the victim, Susan Lang. Each item is in a separate plastic bag, including her shoes. Her handbag is also included, but not its contents. The individual items have been marked as Exhibits 3A to 3K.'

'Yes. And can the jury see for themselves the extent of the staining?'

'Yes, sir.'

'Actually,' Andrew said, 'if his Lordship will permit, would you please step down from the witness box and identify the individual items for the jury?'

Ben stood.

'My Lord, there is no need for the jury to have to see this. I have already made it clear that there is no dispute about the cause of death. My learned friend is indulging in a piece of pure theatre; he is simply trying to shock the jury while adding nothing of substance to the case.'

'I don't accept that, my Lord,' Andrew retorted immediately. 'The prosecution is entitled to show the jury how ferociously this defendant attacked Susan Lang. It is relevant to our contention that this was a very angry man who planned to kill his wife because he wanted to stop her getting custody of his children at all costs –'

'My learned friend has already established the ferocity of the attack through Dr Wren,' Ben countered. 'We do not dispute it. There is no need to expose the jury to graphic evidence of this kind, which has no value except to prejudice them against the defendant.'

Mr Justice Rainer nodded.

'I understand the objection, Mr Schroeder, but I think the

prosecution is entitled to ask the jury to look at the evidence and draw their own conclusions. You may leave the witness box, Mr Farmer.'

'As your Lordship pleases,' Ben said, resuming his seat.

'Mr Farmer, without removing any item from its plastic bag, would you take each in turn from the usher and show it to the jury, please?'

'Here we go,' Ben heard Barratt whisper behind him.

Piece by piece, Farmer held up for the jury's inspection each item of clothing Susan Lang had worn, and the handbag she had carried, when she met her death. Even to Ben, the extent of the bloodstains was horrific. To the jury, it went beyond anything they had expected to see in the courtroom. One or two looked as though they felt rather sick. Others had turned pale; others held hands up to their faces.

'It shouldn't hurt us,' Jess was whispering. 'It's just as consistent with a frenzy brought on by provocation.'

Ben nodded. In theory she was right, but the jurors were looking towards the dock again, as they had when the knife was produced, and their looks were not kind.

'I'm not going to repeat the exercise with the defendant's clothing,' Andrew said, once Farmer had regained the witness box. 'But can you identify the second cardboard box, Exhibit 4, please, my Lord, as containing the clothing worn by the defendant, again each item in a separate plastic bag and separately marked as Exhibits 4A to 4G, and is it all available if the defence wish to refer to it?'

'Yes, sir.'

'Thank you. Exhibit 5 is an album containing ten black and white photographs. There are copies for the jury. What do these photographs show?'

Geoffrey quickly distributed copies to the witness and the jury.

'They show the scene at Harpur Mews after the victim's body had been removed. There's actually nothing very much to see except for the dark stains on the ground, from which we took samples, which were found to be the blood of Susan Lang.'

'Thank you. Did you find any other evidence at the scene?'

'No, sir, I think we've covered it all.'

'All right. Let me come to the following day. Did DI Webb ask you to do something on that day?'

'Yes, sir. The next morning, at DI Webb's request, I went with DS Raymond to a flat at 36B Alwyne Road N1, which was identified to me as being the home address of Henry Lang. We were given a set of keys, and we were able to gain access without difficulty.'

'Did you and DS Raymond search the address?'

'We did, sir.'

'Again, I don't want to deal with matters that may have no importance, and my learned friend will be able to ask any questions he wishes. But did you find one item that struck you both as of potential value to the investigation?'

'We did, sir.'

'Exhibit 6, please, usher. Can you tell the jury what this is?'

'Yes, sir. This is a set of kitchen knives with blades of various lengths, each with the same brown handle stained to give the appearance of wood. These knives were found in the kitchen, and were contained in this stainless steel rack, as you can see.'

'The jury will see,' Andrew said, 'that one slot in the rack is empty.'

'Yes, sir.'

Ben stood. 'Again, my Lord, there is no dispute.'

'Be that as it may,' Andrew insisted, 'I would like the jury to see this. Would you please take Exhibit 2, the knife recovered by DI Webb from the scene, and tell the jury what you notice about it?'

'Exhibit 2 appears to be identical to the other knives, apart from its size and the length of the blade, and it appears that Exhibit 2 fits exactly into the empty slot in the rack. When you insert Exhibit 2 into the slot it completes the set.'

'And does Exhibit 2 appear to be the second largest knife in terms of the length of its blade?'

'Yes, sir.'

'What is the length of the blade of Exhibit 2?'

'It is approximately five inches in length, sir.'

'Did you feel the point to test its sharpness?'

'Yes, sir. It is very sharp indeed.'

'And does it have a serrated edge?'

'It does, also very sharp. I would ask, sir, if members of the jury plan to handle it, that they be very careful.'

'We will bear that in mind. Thank you, Mr Farmer. Wait there, please.'

'No questions, my Lord,' Ben said at once.

Mr Justice Rainer looked at the clock once more.

'Yes, well, we will leave it there. Be back for 10.30 tomorrow morning, members of the jury, please.'

Feeling drained, they started to gather up their papers.

'Let's go down to the cells and see Henry,' Ben said, 'then back to chambers to go over the police evidence before we go home.'

'I'm glad we've got the gruesome stuff over and done with,' Jess replied, with obvious relief.

Ben nodded. 'But it's not over for the jury. Some of them are going to have trouble enjoying their dinner tonight, and they're going to want to blame it on Henry.'

42

Harriet dropped off her coat in the room she shared with Ben, and made her way along the short corridor to see her former pupil-master. She had phoned in to chambers before leaving the Old Bailey, to make sure that Aubrey was available. Merlin had confirmed that he was in his room, working on an opinion for a banking client. Her tone of voice told the senior clerk that she needed to speak to Aubrey urgently, and Merlin had passed this on. He had made sure that she would have his undivided attention when she returned to chambers.

'Come on in, Harriet.' Aubrey said brightly. 'Would you like tea?'

'No, thanks. I'm fine.

'I saw in *The Times* today that your father is on the warpath again, saying we're not doing enough to make sure underprivileged children can get into higher education.'

'He's absolutely right,' Harriet said.

'I wouldn't have said this a few years ago, but I'm beginning to come round to his point of view.'

She smiled. 'Are you becoming a liberal in your old age, Aubrey?'

'Certainly not. But I've always liked your father. He's done a lot for the College as Master, and the government ought to listen to him. When are they going to send him up to the House of Lords? Surely he's done more than enough by now?'

'He certainly thinks so.'

They laughed.

He waved her into a chair. 'Merlin said you needed a spot of advice. What can I do for you?'

She leaned forward.

'It's a question of professional ethics, Aubrey, or at least I think it is.'

'Sounds intriguing.'

'You remember the client I had who was killed by her husband in April, Susan Lang?'

Aubrey sat up in his chair.

'How could I forget? You were with me here when they called to break the news to you. You were terribly upset – and understandably so. It was a dreadful business.'

'I was, and I'm grateful for you taking care of me that afternoon. I was a mess.'

'You had every right to be.'

She paused.

'Aubrey, the husband's trial for murder began at the Old Bailey this morning. Ben and Jess are representing him. I decided to go and listen for a while.'

Aubrey raised his eyebrows.

'Incognito, I assume, given the way you're dressed.'

She laughed, looking down at herself. She had deliberately worn light-coloured clothes to avoid looking like a lawyer.

'Why did you feel the need to be there?'

'I didn't want to distract Ben and Jess, or get in their way. That's why I dressed down. I sat at the back of the court and generally tried to keep a low profile. I don't think they knew I was there.'

'I repeat my question,' Aubrey said.

She did not reply immediately.

'I'm not sure, to tell you the truth. I had no reason for being there, except, I suppose, some kind of morbid curiosity. It made such an impact on me emotionally when I heard about Susan. For some reason I felt I had to hear for myself what had happened.'

'Was your morbid curiosity satisfied?'

'As much as it could be. I listened to the evidence of the welfare officer they had visited just before he killed her. She saw the whole thing through her front window. It was ghastly just listening to her evidence. He stabbed her over and over again with a large kitchen knife. It was a really vicious, relentless attack. She never stood a chance.'

Aubrey nodded.

'It all sounds very nasty. But how does all this involve your professional ethics?'

'Ben told the court that the defence was going to be provocation, which would reduce the charge from murder to manslaughter. The jury hasn't been told yet what the provocation was, and they probably won't know until the defendant gives evidence, but the pattern seems clear from Ben's cross-examination.'

'She was being cruel to him, was she, getting him worked up?'

'That's one way of putting it. The welfare officer painted him as a bit obsessive when it came to the children. She thought he might be liable to lash out if the wife gave him too much of a hard time over custody, and by all accounts, she was pretty good at giving him a hard time.'

'So presumably Ben was cheering the welfare officer on. That's good for him, yes?'

'Yes. He wants the jury to think of Henry Lang as the textbook example of a man who might lose his self-control if provoked far enough. He even got the welfare officer to agree that she had picked up on his obsessive streak and made a specific note about it after just one meeting with him.'

'Do I recall correctly? I seem to remember that he was accusing her of running around, staying out late, and generally hanging around with the wrong sort of people?'

'Yes, and there's a lot more than just the accusation now. She admitted to the welfare officer that she was sleeping with other men and drinking too much. But that wasn't all. After her death, the police found that she was using cannabis and cocaine.'

Aubrey sat back in his chair and nodded.

'So, in addition to everything else, the husband was fully justified in worrying about the children while they were with her?'

'Aubrey, my instructing solicitor, Val Turner, and I had both warned her that she was skating on thin ice, and that we might reach the point where we couldn't in all conscience support her claim for custody unless she made some changes to her lifestyle.'

'Was she listening?'

'I don't think so. She would go through the motions of agreeing with us, but I don't think she meant it.'

Harriet stood, walked around her chair, and leaned against it, her arms over the top.

'But here's what I want to ask you about. Ben asked the welfare officer whether Susan had ever mentioned a man called Daniel Cleary as one of the men she was running around with.'

'Who is Daniel Cleary when he's at home?'

'He's reputed to be a drug dealer and a fixer for certain criminal elements. He has form for violence and blackmail, among other things. If I tell you that he rejoices in the street name of "Danny Ice" that should give you a pretty good idea of what you're dealing with.'

Aubrey laughed. 'He does sound like a charming fellow.'

'Ben also asked the welfare officer whether she knew anything about Cleary making threats of violence against Henry Lang. She said she knew nothing about that.'

'And this is important because...?'

'Aubrey, the prosecution's case is that this was premeditated murder, not provocation. Their trump card is that on the morning he killed his wife, Henry carefully selected a large kitchen knife from a set he had in his kitchen, concealed it in his raincoat, and took it to the meeting.'

'Thereby demonstrating that he intended to kill Susan all along?'

'Exactly.'

Aubrey nodded.

'Well, I'm no criminal lawyer, Harriet, as you know, but even I can see why that might make it difficult to run provocation with a straight face.'

'If that were the whole story, it would make it almost impossible,' she said. 'But it's not the whole story.'

She hesitated.

'Go on,' he said encouragingly.

'It would be different if Ben knew about a conversation Val and

I had with Susan a week or so before the killing.'

She took her seat again. He did not rush her.

'Aubrey, when we warned Susan about her lifestyle, she didn't just ignore us. She told us we didn't have to worry about it. She said that Henry wouldn't go through with his custody application; she said he would withdraw it and allow the court to award custody to her.'

'Oh? And why would he do that?'

'That's what we wanted to know. She said it was because her friend Danny Ice was going to make it clear to Henry what would happen to him if he didn't.'

Aubrey brought his hands up to his face.

'God Almighty,' he said quietly. 'I assume you –'

'Yes, of course. We read her the Riot Act. We made it clear that we could have nothing to do with it, and that if the court ever got wind of it, not only would she lose custody, but she might well be in danger of prosecution. We couldn't have been much more forceful, and by the end she was backing right down, blaming Danny Ice for it all, insisting that it was all his idea, and had nothing to do with her.'

'Just an act of pure, unsolicited friendship on Danny's part, out of the goodness of his heart?'

'Something like that.'

Aubrey smiled.

'And you would like to tell Ben all about it, but you're worried because what she told you is privileged?'

She nodded. 'Aubrey, I don't even know for a fact that Ben is going to offer Danny Ice as an explanation for Henry carrying the knife. I can't ethically plant ideas in his head.'

'I don't think there's any risk of that,' Aubrey replied. 'Ben can't invent defences for his client, can he? He can only go on what Henry tells him, so Henry must have told Ben that he was so scared of Danny Ice that he thought he needed the knife for protection. It was a bloody silly thing to do, obviously, but that may just go to show how scared he was. Anyway, what other reason could he have had for taking the knife with him – unless, of course, he did intend to kill her?'

'I can't think of any. But what should I do? When we spoke

to Susan, we were acting as her legal advisers. Anything she said to us was privileged, and we can't ethically reveal it without her permission – and it's too late for that now.'

Aubrey stood and walked over to his bookcase.

'The first thing you should do is talk to Val and see if you can agree on exactly what was said. Make a note of it as accurately as you can, and list any points that you can't remember, or remember differently.'

She nodded.

'Yes, all right. I'll call her now.'

'In the meanwhile, I will consult *Cross on Evidence* and see what I can find about the law of legal professional privilege.'

'What's your instinct?' she asked.

He thought for a moment.

'Well, on the one hand, the law takes legal privilege seriously – as it should. Clients must be able to trust their lawyers to keep their confidences; if they can't, no client will trust a lawyer enough to tell the truth, and the whole system will break down. Not only that, but the privilege belongs to the client, not to you or Val. You can't waive it for her.

'On the other hand, the client is dead; there's no obvious reason to keep what she said confidential after her death; and the defence of a man charged with murder may depend on the jury hearing about it. My instinct is that there will be a way to do it. We just need to come up with the right legal argument.'

She smiled.

'I may ask you to represent me. After all, we will be in front of a good friend of yours, and there's no harm in having a friendly tribunal.'

'Oh?'

'Mr Justice Rainer is trying it.'

He laughed. 'Conrad? Trying a criminal case? God help us all. What is the world coming to?'

'Don't sound so smug, Aubrey. The same may happen to you one of these days, when you take your rightful place among the great and the good.'

'If I ever end up trying a case at the Old Bailey,' he replied, returning the smile, 'that may be the end of the criminal trial as we know it. I'm not sure they would ever recover from the experience.'

'Oh, stop it. You are both more than competent to try any case you turn your minds to,' she said.

'Well, I'm sure that Conrad will cope perfectly well with the law of privilege. Our job is to find the right way to put it to him. Not a word to Ben yet, obviously. When will he be ready to present the defence case?'

'Not for a couple of days at least, I would say.'

'More than enough time,' Aubrey said.

'Thank you,' she said.

As Aubrey began to explore *Cross on Evidence,* his phone rang. He picked it up absent-mindedly, his attention focused on a passage in which Professor Cross appeared to offer some hope for the argument he had been asked to make.

'Aubrey, is that you? It's Conrad.'

It took Aubrey a moment or two to adjust.

'Conrad? Well, this is a coincidence; we were just talking about you.'

There was a silence.

'Talking about me? Why? Who with? What do you mean?'

The voice had become shrill, as if alarmed. Aubrey's attention quickly shifted from *Cross* to the voice.

'It was nothing, Conrad. I was talking with my former pupil, Harriet Fisk, and your name came up, that's all.'

'Are you sure that's all it was?'

'Yes, of course... Conrad, what's the matter? You sound distressed.'

Another silence.

'Aubrey, I need to see you. I need to talk to you. Can you meet me at the Club?'

Aubrey closed his eyes. His family home was in Sussex. He kept a flat in London, in the Temple, and it was not unusual for him to stay in town if he was working late. But this evening he had promised his wife and daughters that he would be home for a family dinner. He was on the brink of making his apologies to Conrad.

'Aubrey, it's a matter of life and death. Literally. Please.'

Aubrey looked at his watch. There was something about Conrad's voice. He couldn't quite place it, but there was no doubt about the urgency.

'All right, Conrad. I'll see you at the Club at 6 o'clock,' he promised.

'Thank you, Aubrey. Thank you.'

After Conrad had hung up, Aubrey sat quietly for several minutes, contemplating what he had casually called a coincidence, and suddenly feeling by no means sure that coincidence was the right word for it. Eventually, he took one or two deep breaths and called home.

'I'm sorry, Sandra,' he said, 'I really am…'

43

When Aubrey arrived at his Club in Pall Mall at 6 o'clock, Conrad Rainer had already taken possession of a confidential corner table in the larger of the two lounges on the ground floor. He had a large glass of whisky in front of him, and the bottle from which it had been poured stood alongside the glass. He was lighting a cigarette, and the ashtray already held four butts. As he took his seat, Aubrey caught the eye of Luke, the waiter on duty in the lounge, and ordered his usual pre-dinner Campari and soda with no more than a wave of his hand, a gesture he had refined at the Club over many years and with which the staff were by now thoroughly familiar. He looked closely at Conrad. He seemed pale and preoccupied. Aubrey decided to do what he could to keep the atmosphere light.

'I didn't know you smoked,' he said. 'Is the stress of the new job getting to you already?'

Conrad shook his head quickly.

'No, not at all. I used to smoke a bit at university, if you remember. For some reason, I seem to have picked the habit up again; can't think why.'

There was a silence.

'You sounded rather upset earlier, on the phone,' Aubrey smiled. 'I do hope no one in my chambers is to blame.'

There was no smile in return.

'Why would anyone in your chambers be to blame?'

Aubrey looked away briefly, and then back.

'You have Ben Schroeder in front of you, don't you?'

'Yes. But Schroeder seems very good. He's done nothing to

upset me.' He paused. 'Why were you talking about me with your former pupil?'

Aubrey sat back in his chair. Out of the corner of his eye, he saw Luke putting the finishing touches to his Campari and soda. He turned away to watch him approach, buying time, sparing himself the necessity of an immediate reply. He calculated quickly as he watched Luke expertly serve his drink from a silver tray, a pristine white tea towel lying neatly over his shoulder. Having served the drink, he removed the ashtray and instantly replaced it with a clean one.

'Will that be all, Mr Smith-Gurney? Sir Conrad?'

'Yes, thank you, Luke,' Aubrey said.

He waited for Luke to retreat out of earshot.

'I wasn't talking to Harriet *about* you in that sense, Conrad. Your name came up because she mentioned your trial. Harriet represented Susan Lang in the family proceedings in front of Bernard Wesley. She was very distressed when her client was stabbed to death, needless to say, and she's not quite over it yet. She noted that the husband's trial had started today.' He hesitated. 'That was all there was to it.'

He raised his glass in a silent toast and took a drink.

'Now, since you're keeping me from Sandra and the girls on what was supposed to be a family evening, why don't you tell me what's really bothering you?'

Conrad nodded. Aubrey watched the man crumble before his eyes. His hand shook as he raised his cigarette to his mouth, and his voice was hoarse when he eventually spoke.

'I don't think I can go on, Aubrey. I've been dreading saying what I'm about to say for a long time, because I know that once I tell someone, my life is over. While it's just in my head, it's not real, but once I say the words it takes form, and once it takes form, my life as I know it is gone. I've been thinking that I may need to find a way out.'

For a brief moment, Aubrey felt an urge to take one of Conrad's cigarettes; but he had given up the habit on his doctor's advice three years earlier, and if Sandra knew he had started smoking again, even the occasional one, she would have a few words to say on the subject. It wasn't worth it. Instead, he took another drink from his glass.

'Conrad, I'm here to listen, and whatever you say to me in the Club is said in confidence. But in all honesty, I have no idea what you're talking about. It seems like only yesterday I was at your party, celebrating your appointment to the bench. You had capped a successful practice with a High Court judgeship. You seemed to be on top of the world. And now you're talking about finding a way out? For Heaven's sake, what's happened to make you talk like this?'

'It's not anything that happened overnight, Aubrey,' Conrad said, refilling his glass generously from the bottle. 'It's been going on for a long time now. But it's finally come to a head. It was bound to, sooner or later, and now it has.'

He put out the cigarette and immediately lit another.

'I gamble,' he said. 'I'm a gambler. I'm sure that's not news to you. I'm sure everyone knows that by now.'

Aubrey nodded. 'I know you like a flutter when you go out for the evening, Conrad. Of course I do. Everyone knows you enjoy the good life. You've never made any secret about it. And why shouldn't you? You've always worked harder than anyone I've ever known, and I've known you a long time now. I'm sure you've toned it down a bit since you went on the bench, but –.'

'It's not a question of a flutter,' Conrad interrupted. 'It's not a question of putting a fiver on a horse, or a tenner on the Boat Race, for God's sake. I'm talking about *gambling*, Aubrey. I'm talking about losing five thousand or more in a night. *Gambling*.'

Aubrey finished his drink quickly and waved in Luke's direction. Luke had already anticipated the request, and another Campari and soda was in front of Aubrey in a matter of seconds, together with yet another clean ashtray.

'All right,' he said.

Conrad seemed absent for some time, smoking his cigarette and gazing up at the ceiling. Eventually, his eyes returned to the table.

'It all started about 18 months ago,' he began. 'I was at Annabel's one night. It's always been a favourite haunt.'

'I've passed the odd evening there myself, with Sandra, I seem to recall,' Aubrey smiled.

'Yes. I don't know what it is about the place. It's just an old wine cellar, isn't it? But there's something about what Mark Birley has done with it. It's easy to forget the cares of the day.'

'Indeed.'

Conrad hesitated.

'And in my case, I was doing a bit more than forgetting the cares of the day,' he said quietly. 'I was on the lookout, and there was someone I'd been introduced to a day or two before. I went there to meet her. I don't mind admitting it. I'm sorry if I shock you.'

'Not at all.'

'You've met Deborah. She's the perfect wife, in many respects, into all manner of good works and all the rest of it, and perfectly happy to spend her life in Guildford. But that wasn't enough for me.'

He paused for a long sip of his drink.

'Specifically, Aubrey, once a month in the missionary position after Sunday lunch wasn't enough for me.'

Another cigarette replaced the one just extinguished.

'Her name is Greta Thiemann. She's German, from the East, Leipzig. I'm not entirely sure how she got over here, what her citizenship is, and all the rest of it. But she seemed well established, with a flat in Knightsbridge. She didn't mention a job. It crossed my mind that she might be a hooker. With her looks she certainly could be if she wanted to. But she's not. So I assumed she must be a woman of independent means. Well, at least, that's what I thought then; now, I'm not so sure.'

'Why not?'

'I'll come to that.'

Aubrey nodded. 'All right.'

'You should see her, Aubrey. My God, she was a sight for sore eyes.'

Aubrey raised his eyebrows and allowed himself a drink.

'I'm sure.'

'She didn't waste any time, either. We have a few drinks, and then I'm telling her all about the deprivations of marital life in Guildford; and the next thing I know after that, I'm in the staff toilet with her, with my trousers down around my ankles, she's on her knees in front of me, and she's—.'

'Yes, I get the picture, Conrad.' Aubrey waved again at Luke. 'And actually, contrary to what I said before, you are shocking me.'

Conrad smiled briefly. The thought occurred to Aubrey that it might have been the first smile he had given anyone that day.

'I'm sorry. In any case, we did a bit of gambling, and then she whisked me away to Knightsbridge.'

'You didn't go home to Guildford?'

'No. I'd told Deborah I was staying up in town for a few days, working on a fraud case – which was true, although obviously I wasn't working on it that night. As you know, I have my flat in the Barbican. It wasn't unusual for me to spend weeknights in town.'

He paused.

'We spent the whole night having sex – and not just in the missionary position, I don't mind telling you. It was unbelievable. I'd never experienced anything remotely like it before. I can't even describe it to you…'

'That's perfectly all right, Conrad,' Aubrey said. 'No need.'

'Anyway… then I had to rush home and get ready for court. But I was hooked. And, as Humphrey Bogart said in *Casablanca*, it was the beginning of a beautiful friendship.'

He took a long sip of his whisky.

'The only problem was, Aubrey, I didn't know what Greta expected of her friends.'

44

'I take it she made it clear eventually, whatever it was?' Aubrey asked.

Conrad nodded.

'Excitement,' he replied, refilling his glass and lighting a cigarette. 'As long as there was excitement, she was happy. If there was no excitement, she got bored rather quickly, and you didn't want to be with Greta when she was bored, believe you me.'

'Excitement in what sense?'

Luke had arrived with yet another Campari and soda. He served it and withdrew.

'In every sense. The episode in the toilet was a good example, if I'd only realised it, but that was only the start. She seemed to enjoy sex anywhere, whether it was in the ladies or a taxi, or anywhere else – as long as there was a risk of being caught.'

He paused.

'Go on,' Aubrey said encouragingly.

'That was what it was all about. It wasn't so much the sex that did it for her. It was the element of risk. She liked men to take risks for her. That's what turned her on.'

'I see. And one of those risks was…'

'Gambling, yes. And I was a sitting duck because I've always had a weakness for the cards and the roulette wheel. I'm sure she knew that. I probably told her. I told her all kinds of things. We gambled that very first night. We went upstairs from Annabel's to the Clermont Club.'

Aubrey raised his eyebrows.

'John Aspinall's place? You're a member there?'

'Yes. I'd just joined when I met Greta. That's where I met her. She was with that man Bristow, you know, the property magnate as he likes to call himself – stuffy, self-important little man. She'd been there with other men, too, she told me; she loved every minute of it. After the first time, we were there at least once a week, and before too long we were up to two or three times.'

'What did you play?'

'I play *chemin de fer*. I don't know whether you've ever...?'

'No. I've never seen the attraction, I'm afraid.'

'I envy you,' Conrad said. 'It's a seductive game. You can lose a lot in a night, and you can win a lot in a night. The point is, you never know. It's non-stop risk, non-stop adrenalin, and that's what Greta loved – as long as she wasn't the one taking the risk. She enjoyed the action, and I paid for it.'

Aubrey finished his drink and sat back in his chair.

'Conrad, forgive me for putting it this way. I know you were doing well at the Bar, making a fair bit of money, but you hear things about the kind of people who play at the Clermont. You couldn't have been in the same league as people like Lucan and Derby. How on earth –?'

'Did they let me in?' He laughed. 'They're not vulgar enough to inquire about your means, Aubrey. They assume that you wouldn't join unless you had enough money to throw around. Ian Maxwell-Scott introduced me to Aspinall – Ian is Susie Clark's husband. You know Susie from the Bar, don't you?'

Aubrey nodded.

'Once Ian had introduced me, the only question was whether the other members thought I was a good chap, and that meant getting on well with Dominick Elwes, the resident wit and raconteur. The rule was, if Dominick thought you were all right, you were in. Apparently, he did. And once I started showing up with Greta, people noticed me. Greta knew Annabel, you see, and if Annabel liked you... well, it all went from there.'

Aubrey held up a hand.

'I'm sorry, Conrad. I've had three Camparis on an empty stomach, and if I don't eat something soon, I'm going to start seeing double. Do you fancy going in to dinner?'

'Not really, Aubrey. I can't eat at the moment. I'm being a pain, I know, but…'

'No, that's all right.'

Aubrey turned round and summoned Luke.

'Yes, Mr Smith-Gurney?'

'We're not going to dine tonight, Luke. Do you think you could find us some sandwiches and crisps, something like that?'

'I'm sure I can, sir.'

'Excellent, and why don't you bring us a bottle of the Club white Burgundy to wash it down, if you've got one chilled?'

'Certainly, sir. It will be just a few minutes.' He changed the ashtray and walked discreetly away.

'For a while it wasn't a problem,' Conrad said. 'I got away with wagering small sums, a hundred or two on a hand, that kind of thing. I was even winning quite a bit at first – beginner's luck, I suppose. Greta would laugh and say she was my lucky charm. But…'

'I'm sure that didn't last long.'

'No. If you get up from the table too soon, people take exception, especially if you're winning and you don't give them the chance to win some of it back. The other members start whispering, and it all gets a bit unpleasant. I wasn't going to let that happen to me. And Greta wasn't happy if I gave up too early.'

'What do you mean, she wasn't happy? Did she make a scene?'

'In public, in the Clermont? God, no. No, she was more sophisticated than to embarrass herself in public. No, she would wait. But then, when we got back to Knightsbridge and we were undressed, she would lay into me with a ping-pong bat, and I just had to lie there and take it.'

Aubrey snorted.

'You *had* to? What do you mean you had to? Why didn't you just tell her to get lost and walk out?'

Conrad refilled his glass.

'Easy for you to say, Aubrey. You don't know what this woman could do with a man's body.'

'Whatever she could do, surely to God it wasn't worth giving her that kind of hold over you?'

'Yes, you're right, Aubrey, you're right, of course you are. But at the time, it wasn't that simple. She never stayed angry for long. It was as if spanking me got it out of her system, and instantly she went back to being her usual charming self. And every time I got ready to say enough was enough, she would give me a special treat. I'm sure I don't have to spell it out for you. She knew exactly how to make me stay with her.'

Aubrey shook his head.

'All right. Go on.'

Conrad lit another cigarette.

'So I started playing for longer and raising the stakes. But I seemed to be winning less than I had when I first joined. In fact, I was beginning to lose a few hundred on a regular basis. At first, I could cover it out of my income, but eventually I had to dig into some savings I had stashed away in a Post Office account – a few thousand. I always thought I could win it back, of course. That's the great illusion – that you can chase your losses and win them back in one great coup. And they say there are cases where that has happened. But they are pretty rare, and it's even rarer still to do the sensible thing and walk away once you've recouped your losses, because then, you think you're on a roll and you want to go on and come out ahead. It's madness, obviously – but you can't see that when you're in the midst of it.'

'So, the savings…?'

'Went the same way, of course. And that's when I started to get a bit desperate.'

45

Luke brought smoked salmon, and ham and cheese sandwiches, with a huge bowl of crisps and some salted peanuts. He set out the white Burgundy in a cooler. He changed the glasses and ashtray. Aubrey poured himself some wine and tasted it appreciatively.

'This is very nice. Can I pour you a glass?'

Conrad shook his head, raising his whisky glass.

'No, I'll stay with this.'

Aubrey started on the sandwiches with a vengeance. He had not realised how hungry he was.

'I was in the hole for a few thousand by then. But it seemed manageable. John Aspinall had torn up a few of my IOUs to the House. He's that kind of man, you know. It's something he does for some of the members. I know he's done it for Lucky Lucan several times.'

Aubrey shrugged. 'That would just be good business sense, wouldn't it, apart from anything else? You don't want your punters going under, do you?'

'I suppose not. But that only goes so far. You can't rely on it. In any case, I had every confidence that I would recover. The only problem was, I needed some seed money.'

'To fund the effort to chase your losses?'

'Yes. There's something of a science to that in a sick kind of way. Once funds become available you have to make sure that you don't run out of money for necessities – paying the mortgage, your clerk's fees, your chambers rent and so on. You have to be aware of how much is coming in for your fees, and calculate how much you can risk to start with. The hope is always that you can start out with a thousand, say, and win a few hands, and get there, or almost there. Then you can relax, even if you haven't got it all back.'

'But if that doesn't work…?'

'Then you have to decide whether to chase an even bigger sum. In my case, I could never quite give up on the idea that one day it was all going to work out well.'

Aubrey drained his glass and allowed the wine to linger on his palate before pouring himself another.

'But it didn't work out well, I take it?'

Conrad drank from his glass, shaking his head.

'I came damn close once or twice, Aubrey. And perhaps if I'd stopped then… but who knows? I didn't stop, and I still needed more money.'

'Where did you get it?'

Conrad did not reply for some time.

'Deborah has a trust fund,' he replied eventually.

'She's the one with the real money,' he continued. 'I didn't have much when I started – well, you remember those days, when we were starting out. We'd only just come down from Cambridge and taken our Bar finals. Neither of us had two pennies to rub together.'

Aubrey smiled. 'I remember very well.'

'I was lucky, I suppose. I married a woman who could support me while my practice got off the ground. Deborah had money from her parents – a lot of money – but she has never been all that interested in it.'

'She's very involved in her church, isn't she, if I remember rightly?' Aubrey asked.

'That would be putting it mildly. The local Baptist church is her second home. She gives the church a lot of money and takes part in most of their activities. That's been her life for many years now. She likes to show me off to the people there, but she takes very little interest in me, or my professional life, any more. Even when I became a judge, she wasn't very impressed. She smiled and said "well done" and she came with me to see the Queen when I got my K. But that was about it.'

Aubrey paused in the middle of eating a sandwich. An uneasy feeling was coming over him.

'I can't see Deborah as the kind of woman who would give you money from her trust fund for gambling. How did you persuade her to – ?'

'I didn't.'

Aubrey replaced the half-eaten sandwich on his plate.

'I see.'

'She got sole control over the fund when she turned twenty-five. That's the way her father set it up. Both her parents are dead now, and she's always been too busy with the church to take much day-to-day interest in money, so she gave me power over the fund as a joint signatory. That made sense, actually. If either of us ever becomes too ill to cope, the other can access the fund without any problem. But I never touched it until I got into trouble, I swear. I mean, we raided it together for certain purposes over the years – to get our deposit when we bought our house, to make improvements here and there, that kind of thing. But I never touched it for any other reason until…'

'How much?' Aubrey asked.

'Twenty thousand.'

'Any of it left?'

'Not a penny.'

'And when the twenty thousand went the same way as your savings?'

'I took out a second mortgage on the house for ten.'

'What? How…? Is the house in your sole name?'

'No, joint names.'

'But you couldn't… didn't the bank need a signature from Deborah?'

'Of course; and I gave them one.'

46

There had been a long silence. Aubrey had lost interest in the sandwiches, and was pouring himself more wine. Conrad was well into his bottle of whisky and had eaten nothing. A new sprinkling of cigarette ends was accumulating, despite Luke's attentive replacements of the ashtray.

'All right, Conrad,' Aubrey said, 'let's see where we stand. You are in the hole for a lot of money – let's say somewhere in the region of £30,000 to £40,000. Yes?'

'Something like that.'

'But it's something you could sort out with Deborah, isn't it? That's the good news. There's no need for any of this to become public knowledge. At least you're in debt to her, not to John Aspinall, and I imagine there's still something worthwhile left in the trust fund?'

Conrad smiled. 'I can just imagine having *that* conversation with her.'

'It's better than talking about reaching the end and finding a way out, for God's sake,' Aubrey said. He had raised his voice without intending to, and he looked anxiously around him, but most of the members were at dinner, and the few left in the lounge seemed to be absorbed in their newspapers or books.

'Conrad, the answer is staring you in the face. Break it off with Greta now, stay away from the Clermont, and make a clean breast of it to Deborah. You've got your judicial salary. You have fees still coming in from your practice. You will get back on an even keel. It may take a while, but time is one thing you have on your side. And it will all remain a private matter.'

'Will it? I don't think so, Aubrey. You don't know Deborah. She would divorce me in the blink of an eye, and take me for what little I have left. She might even tell the police I forged her signature on the mortgage deed. And that would be a very public matter.'

Aubrey smiled thinly. 'I thought Baptists were supposed to believe in forgiveness.'

'They believe that God will forgive you,' Conrad replied. 'That doesn't mean *they* have to.'

He smiled grimly for a second or two.

'Besides,' Conrad said, 'I'm afraid the mortgage wasn't quite the end of the story.'

Aubrey felt his stomach begin to twist.

'I was sick with worry about the mortgage,' Conrad said. 'I had all the correspondence sent to chambers, of course, not to the house; but even so, it would have been easy for Deborah to find out about it if she suddenly began to take even the slightest interest in our bank accounts. It was about the time the Lord Chancellor was making overtures to me about going on the bench, and obviously anything like that coming out would have scuppered my chances completely. I needed to find a way to pay off the mortgage. I couldn't try winning at the Clermont again – I had nothing left to play with. Even I could see that. But Greta was on my case all the time. So eventually, I told her the truth.'

Aubrey gasped.

'About everything?'

'About everything – the trust fund, the mortgage, the whole nine yards. I knew it was unwise –'

'Unwise?' Aubrey had raised his voice again. He lowered it anxiously. 'That wasn't unwise, Conrad, it was insane. What were you thinking?'

'I wasn't thinking – well, certainly not clearly. I was desperate, Aubrey. I was clutching at straws. I thought, if I told Greta the truth, she could hardly blame me for not wanting to chase the money I'd lost. I hoped she might even have some sympathy for me.'

'And did she?'

He smiled. 'Yes, in a manner of speaking, I suppose she did. But she didn't show it in quite the way I'd hoped. She laughed. She was almost offhand about it. It was as if I'd told her I wanted to borrow a tenner. She asked me how much I needed to chase my losses. I told her £20,000. She said she could arrange it for me.'

'Arrange it for you? What did she mean by that?'

'Well, she wasn't talking about going to the bank, Aubrey. And she wasn't talking about lending it to me herself. What do you think she meant?'

Aubrey sat back in his chair.

'Oh, my God. You didn't…'

'Two days later she introduced me to a gentleman who said he represented what he called a syndicate. In view of my well-known success at the Bar, and their confidence in my ability to repay them, the syndicate was prepared to lend me up to £20,000, unsecured, to be repaid in monthly instalments, the money to be provided in cash, and the payments to be made in cash, no questions asked on either side.'

'You idiot,' Aubrey breathed.

'His name was Cleary,' Conrad said. 'Pleasant enough fellow if you like that charming South London brogue. He didn't say it in so many words, but let's just say he left me in no doubt that it wouldn't be a good idea to be late with the payments.'

Aubrey felt his blood run cold.

'Did you say "Cleary"?'

'Yes.'

'Not… not Daniel Cleary, by any chance, also known as "Danny Ice"?'

Conrad paused in the act of lighting a cigarette, and looked up sharply.

'That's the fellow. How on earth do *you* know him? Aubrey, don't tell me…'

'Don't play games with me, Conrad, please. Daniel Cleary's name came up in your trial today, as you well know.'

Conrad inhaled deeply from his cigarette and watched the smoke thin out as it rose towards the room's high, ornate ceiling.

'How would you know that?'

'Because Harriet Fisk was in court this morning, and she told me. Besides, criminal proceedings are a matter of public record. Why shouldn't I know?'

Conrad laughed.

'And I suppose now you're going to tell me that I should withdraw from the case because of a conflict of interest, and let it start all over again in front of another judge? I can just picture that scene, can't you? "I regret to inform counsel that I am unable to continue as your judge because I'm on the hook to the same villain who was threatening Henry Lang, over a small matter of £20,000 I borrowed from him to cover my gambling debts." What would the Lord Chancellor think of that, I wonder? I might as well throw myself straight under a train and have done with it.'

Aubrey was silent for some time.

'I shouldn't be telling you this,' he said, 'and you didn't hear it from me, but you might as well know. You haven't heard the last of Cleary. You will probably have to rule on an application to admit some evidence involving him.'

Conrad nodded.

'I'm sure I can manage that – just as long as they don't want to call him as a witness.'

'I don't think there's any danger of that. But what happened? Did you borrow the whole £20,000?'

'Yes.'

'The rate of interest?'

'You don't want to know. It would make your eyes water. Usury's not a strong enough word.'

Aubrey refilled his wine glass.

'Why didn't you use it to repay the mortgage, or put a few thousand back into the trust fund?'

'I told you. I needed it to chase my losses.'

'Conrad –'

'I had to, Aubrey. I needed some seed money to get back in at the Clermont. In any case, Greta would have beaten me within an inch of my life if I'd got all that money and not taken her to the Clermont again. That's why she set me up with Cleary. She didn't give a damn about my mortgage. She wanted to make sure I could still play – and besides, I still believed that my luck was bound to change. I'd had a bad run. I was due for a break.'

'Of course you were. Did you get one?'

'No.'

Aubrey drank deeply from his glass.

'How long ago was this?'

'February, not long before I was appointed to the bench.'

'So, by February you still had something owing on the mortgage, and you had to start making payments to Cleary?'

'Yes.'

'How much?'

'Two and a half a month.'

'How did you plan to do that?'

Conrad was lighting another cigarette.

'The original plan was to pay from my winnings once my luck changed. When it didn't change, I used my salary, and I dipped into the trust fund again.'

'Have you kept up with the payments?'

'More or less. I missed once. Cleary sent me a message suggesting that I should make every effort not to miss again.'

Aubrey nodded.

'Well, I understand why you're feeling desperate,' he said.

'That's not quite all,' Conrad said.

Aubrey swallowed hard.

'After I lost the £30,000 from the trust fund and the mortgage, Cleary wasn't my only source of money,' Conrad said. 'Some other money became available, unexpectedly. But I'm afraid it meant crossing the line.'

'What line?' Aubrey asked.

47

'Just before I left chambers to take up my appointment, I stole some money from three members of chambers.'

'Stole? How? What in God's name are you talking about?'

'I needed money.' Conrad said. 'I was still in a deep hole, but I still had this idea that all I needed was one good night at the table. If I could just keep myself going until my luck changed, I could win enough to turn things around. Obviously, that didn't make any rational sense, but when you're in that kind of spiral you don't think rationally.'

'You seemed quite normal at the time,' Aubrey said. 'I would never have guessed there was anything wrong, much less something like this.'

'My professional life was my only refuge,' Conrad replied. 'It was the only thing I had left to cling on to. At least that part of my life was still working. As long as I could pretend to myself that all was well, I could keep up a façade in front of other people. All wasn't well, obviously. I was living in fear that I would run out of money and the whole house of cards would collapse – sorry, bad choice of imagery in the circumstances.'

Aubrey smiled thinly.

'One day I found myself alone in the clerk's room; it must have been a week or so before I left chambers. Jeffrey was away from his desk somewhere, and I was looking at the pigeon-holes where he put our briefs and letters – and, of course, the cheques for our fees. You could tell when it was a cheque because Jeffrey always put them in the same small brown envelopes. There was nothing in my pigeon-hole. I was still owed quite a lot, but it was still the same old story – bloody solicitors taking forever to pay, no way of making them. But there were three small brown envelopes in other pigeon-holes: one for Frank Reilly, one for Jonathan Weatherall, and one for Martin Cohn. I took the envelopes and got out of chambers before anyone saw me. I endorsed the cheques to myself and paid them into my account.'

'You forged their signatures?'

'Yes. I didn't think of it as stealing at the time. It was just a loan. I was going to take the money, and –'

'Repay them when your luck changed,' Aubrey said. 'Except that it didn't.'

'Exactly. So at the end of it all, I've compromised every aspect of my life and I haven't solved any of my problems. In addition to owing a lot of money to Daniel Cleary, and still having a second mortgage Deborah knows nothing about, I'm not even sure how I can stay afloat, let alone pay my clerk's fees and put something aside for the tax man. And any day now, it's all going to come crashing down on my head in a very public way.'

'How much?' Aubrey asked.

Conrad seemed flustered.

'What?'

'How much did you steal from chambers?'

'I don't know: £8,000, £10,000, something like that.'

He paused.

'So I hope you see now why there's nothing left for me, except to find the way out. It's over, Aubrey.'

The lounge was almost deserted now. Voices could be heard in the corridors, as members finished dinner and made their way to the main bar for port and coffee. Luke was leaning against a wall, wondering whether it was the right moment to clean up their table again.

'And yet, you came to me,' Aubrey said. 'You asked to talk to me. Why?'

Conrad shrugged.

'I'm not sure. Perhaps I hoped that if I just talked it over with you, some ray of light might emerge. But it hasn't.'

'Or perhaps you were going to ask for my help in some other way?'

'I don't think there's any way for you to help.'

'I can't begin to bail you out financially, Conrad. I'm sure you understand that; and even if I could... frankly...'

'Why would you? I don't have a great track record, do I?'

'I couldn't trust you. Not at the moment.'

'I understand. I wouldn't trust myself.'

Aubrey shook his head. They were silent for some time.

'Have you at least told me the whole story?'

'Yes.'

'Are you sure?'

'Yes, I'm sure.'

'Then at least we know where we stand, don't we? Now, I want you to promise me that you won't do anything drastic. I want you to give me a day or two to think things over, to see if I can come up with something – anything – to start things moving in the right direction.'

'It's good of you Aubrey, but...'

Aubrey leaned forward in his chair.

'Conrad, listen to me. We go back a long way. We've known each other since prep school. You are my oldest friend – well, you and Gerry Pole – the Gang of Three as we used to call ourselves.'

Conrad laughed quietly.

'The Gang of Three. Yes. My God, we got up to a few tricks when we were younger, didn't we?'

'Yes, we did, and we will again. I'm not giving up on you, Conrad. I'm in no state to come up with anything tonight. My head's spinning. I need to sleep on it and kick my brain into gear tomorrow morning, and you have a trial to finish. So let's call it a night. But I'm not leaving until you promise me you won't do anything drastic.'

Conrad took a deep breath and released it slowly.

'I won't do anything until we've spoken again,' he replied.

'Thank you,' Aubrey said.

It was after 11 o'clock by the time the taxi dropped Aubrey off at his flat. He called Sandra to say goodnight and asked her to kiss their two girls for him. She said she would, but she was already in bed, and her voice was sleepy. A minute or two later, and he would have woken her up. He suddenly wished he could be there with her. He wished he had gone home that evening as they had planned; he wished that he had never set foot in the Club; that he had not had to hear and come to terms with the story he had listened to for what seemed like an eternity. The experience had drained him. He had drunk far more than he was used to. When he had left the Club, he had expected the fresh air to hit him; he had expected to feel the full effects of the Campari and the wine. Indeed, he had longed to feel it. He had hoped to be drunk; if the alcohol would anaesthetise him, if it would numb his distress, if only long enough for him to fall asleep. But there was to be no such relief; he felt as coldly and relentlessly sober as he ever had in his life.

Slowly, he removed his jacket and his collar and tie, and threw them on the bed. Rummaging through his briefcase, he found his address book and flipped through the pages until he found the number he wanted. Checking the time by his watch, he dialled the number apologetically.

'Hello?' It was a woman's voice. Aubrey cursed silently to himself.

'Rosemary, I'm sorry to call so late. Is Gerry still awake? Could I speak to him?'

'Aubrey, is that you? How are you? It seems ages since we spoke. How are Sandra and the girls?'

'They're fine, Rosie, thanks. They send their love.'

'Is Sandy asleep? Can I have a quick word?'

'I'm not down in Sussex, Rosie. I'm at the flat in town. Work, you know. But I'll tell her we've spoken, and I'm sure she'll call.'

'Please do, Aubrey. Here's Gerry. He's coming to see what all the fuss is about. Take care, darling, see you soon.'

'You take care too, Rosie.'

There was a moment and whispers as the phone changed hands.

'Aubrey, good to hear from you, old boy. What brings you to the phone at this hour?'

Aubrey hesitated.

'I may need your help,' he said, 'or rather, Conrad may need your help. I had rather a long session with him this evening.'

Gerry laughed. 'How is his Lordship? Is he becoming insufferable on the bench? It wouldn't surprise me at all. It was bad enough when he got Silk.'

'Actually, Gerry,' Aubrey said, 'he's not doing well.'

'I'm sorry to hear that. What seems to be the problem?'

'I'd prefer not to go into it on the phone,' Aubrey replied. 'Are you in town tomorrow? Is there any chance we could get together for lunch?'

'Yes, I don't see why not. I've got a meeting at 11 o'clock, but it shouldn't last more than an hour or so. Shall I come to chambers, or do you want to venture into the City?'

'I'll come to your office. Would 12.30 be all right?'

'Perfect. I'll book us somewhere decent.'

'Somewhere discreet, please, Gerry,' Aubrey said.

'Yes, all right. 12.30, then. Are you sure you don't want to give me some clue…?'

'No. Not tonight.' Aubrey paused. 'Gerry, you still have your holiday home on the Isle of Wight, don't you?'

'Our place on the Island? Yes, of course. Why?'

'Thanks, Gerry; again, sorry for the late call. See you tomorrow.' He hung up.

Albert saw him coming from a distance. Berkeley Square was quiet at that hour on a weekday evening. The figure approaching from the direction of Piccadilly was a familiar one. Albert prided himself on his talent for recognising members, and putting names to faces, welcoming each one by name. It was one of the personal touches Mr Aspinall liked and expected from his staff. A small group of young men and women, laughing and jostling each other, emerged from Annabel's and made their haphazard way towards the man. He ignored them, passing straight through the middle of the group, and continued his fast-paced, determined walk towards number 44. Albert opened the door of the Clermont Club with perfect timing, so that the man could enter almost without breaking stride.

'Good evening, Sir Conrad,' he said. 'Not a bad night for the time of year, is it?'

48

'I swear by Almighty God that the evidence I shall give shall be the truth, the whole truth, and nothing but the truth. John Alan Webb, Detective Inspector, attached to Holborn Police Station, my Lord.'

Webb returned the New Testament to Geoffrey, and clasped his hands behind his back.

'Thank you, Detective Inspector,' Andrew Pilkington said. 'Did you make any notes in connection with your inquiries in this case?'

'Yes, sir.'

'Are you asking the court to allow you to refresh your memory from those notes?'

'Yes, sir.'

'When were your notes made?'

'As soon as practicable, sir. I made the notes as and when I had the chance. It was a very hectic day, but I would say that my notes were made within two or three hours of the events in question.'

'And were the events still fresh in your memory when you made your notes?'

'They were, sir.'

'Did you make your notes alone, or with anyone else?'

'Most of them I made with DS Raymond, and if he wasn't there, I checked my recollection with him before completing the note.'

'And was that to ensure that you had the most accurate and complete recollection of the events?'

'Exactly, sir, yes.'

Ben stood. 'No objection, my Lord.'

Mr Justice Rainer did not seem to react.

Andrew glanced at Ben quickly. 'My Lord…?'

A second or two passed.

'I'm sorry, Mr Pilkington. What was that?'

'My learned friend has said he has no objection to the Inspector refreshing his memory using his notes.'

'Oh. Yes, of course. Please refer to your notes whenever you wish, Inspector.'

'Thank you, my Lord.'

Webb produced a small police notebook from the right inside pocket of his jacket, opened it, and placed it carefully on the edge of the witness box.

'Detective Inspector, on 28 April of this year, at about 1.45 in the afternoon, were you on duty?'

'Yes, sir. I was on duty in plain clothes with DS Raymond. We had just returned to Holborn Police Station after interviewing a number of witnesses in connection with some commercial burglaries in the Clerkenwell area.'

'What were you doing when you got back to the police station? Were you dealing with evidence from the burglaries?'

The Inspector smiled.

'No, sir. It had been a long morning, and DS Raymond and I had just settled ourselves in the canteen with a nice cup of tea.'

There was some sympathetic laughter from the jury box. Andrew returned the smile.

'I'm sure it was a well-earned break. But did something happen to interrupt it?'

'Yes, sir. We received a message that an emergency call had come in. There was information that a serious attack had taken place, and that the assailant might be armed. We were asked to attend the scene immediately.'

'Yes. Now, the jury have a plan of the area around Holborn Police Station. My Lord, that is our Exhibit 1…'

The judge seemed engrossed in his notebook.

'My Lord…?'

He looked up.

'Yes, Exhibit 1. I have it. Thank you, Mr Pilkington.'

'Inspector, the usher will provide you with a copy.' He paused to allow Geoffrey time. 'Is Holborn Police Station marked at the top right of the plan?'

'Yes, sir.'

'And can you show the jury where the assault was alleged to have taken place?'

Webb spread the plan out in front of him and studied it.

'We didn't have far to go, sir. If you turn right out of the police station, and continue a few yards – down the plan and to the left – along Lamb's Conduit Street, you come to Dombey Street. If you turn left into Dombey Street, about 50 yards along, you come to the entrance to a mews called Harpur Mews. The information was that the attack was taking place in that area.'

'Yes. Did you and DS Raymond make your way to the scene immediately?'

'We did, sir. We took a uniformed officer with us, PC Williams. There was no point in taking a car. We ran as quickly as we could. We were there in two or three minutes.'

'As you approached the entrance to Harpur Mews, what did you hear or see?'

Webb looked down and nodded for several seconds.

'It was very quiet. I couldn't hear anything at all. When we got to the entrance to the mews, I saw a man sitting on the ground with his legs drawn up towards his chest. I looked more closely and saw that the man had something in his right hand.'

'Could you see what it was?'

'Yes, sir. It was a large kitchen knife. There were dark red stains on the blade, which appeared to be blood stains.'

'What else did you see?'

'Beyond the man, inside the mews entrance, I saw a woman lying on the ground. She was lying on her back, with both arms out to her sides. Her legs were bent at the knee towards her right, and her head was bent the other way to her left.'

'What else did you notice about the woman?'

'She was bleeding heavily from the neck and torso. It appeared that she must have been bleeding for some time, because there was a large pool of blood around her body, and I could see some blood still seeping from her wounds.'

'Detective Inspector, do you now know that the woman you saw was Susan Lang?'

'Yes, sir.'

'What did you decide to do?'

'I realised immediately that it was necessary to disarm the man.'

'Inspector, let me ask you this: at that time, did you know what had happened?'

'No, sir.'

'Were you concerned for the man's welfare as well as the woman's?'

'Yes, sir. At that point, I had no idea whether he was the perpetrator or whether he was also a victim of the attack.'

'Did he say or do anything?'

'No. He said nothing. He remained sitting as he was, not moving at all.'

'What did you do?'

'I moved a bit closer. I knew he must have realised I was there. I was only a foot or two away. But still, there was no reaction at all. He didn't move, and he didn't say anything.'

'What was your main concern at that point?'

Webb shook his head.

'I had to find a way to get to the woman. She was obviously very seriously injured, and I needed to have access to her.'

'Did you have to call the ambulance, or was one already on its way? Did you know?'

'I knew that an ambulance was on its way from Great Ormond Street. It had been requested during the emergency call.'

'Was there a problem for you in gaining access to the woman?'

'Yes, sir. The man. When he didn't say anything, I had to assume that he was involved in the assault on the woman. He was still holding the knife and he showed no sign of putting it down. That meant that he was free to attack the woman again, or that he was free to attack me or my colleagues if we tried to assist her.'

'Did the man appear to be injured?'

'Not that I could see, sir, no.'

'What did you do?'

'I didn't want to give him any warning, so I didn't speak. Instead, I gestured to DS Raymond and PC Williams and hoped they would understand. My plan was that I would pass the man on his left side, try to get directly in front of him, and try to disarm him. At the same time, DS Raymond would approach from behind, and stand directly behind him so that he could try to restrain him if he tried to move. PC Williams would pass him on the left immediately after me, and try to get to the woman and stand in front of her, to protect her from further attack.'

Andrew paused for some moments.

'Detective Inspector, were you or your colleagues armed in any way?'

'No, sir.'

'Did you have any special clothing that might have protected you against stab wounds?'

'No, sir.'

'Did you appreciate the danger you were putting yourselves in?'

Webb exhaled audibly.

'Yes, sir. I think that was obvious to all of us. But it was also obvious that the woman needed help immediately if there was going to be any hope for her, so I had to clear a path for the ambulance crew. As it happened, sadly, it was already too late. But we had to try.'

'Did you approach the man, passing him on his left, as you planned?'

'Yes, sir. I was able to pass and position myself in front of him. I was standing about a foot away from him. I saw PC Williams run past me and kneel in front of Susan Lang, and I saw DS Raymond standing directly behind the man.'

'Then what did you do?'

'I asked the man to hand over the knife, and I reached out my right hand towards the knife.' He paused for a moment or two, closed his eyes, and shook his head.

'Are you – ?'

'I'm fine, sir. Thank you. To my surprise – and relief, obviously – he didn't try to stop me. In fact, he still didn't move at all. The knife was more resting in his hand than he was holding it, and I was able to disarm him without any difficulty.'

'What happened then?'

'By that time, the ambulance had arrived, and the crew set about doing what they could for Mrs Lang. Some additional uniformed officers had also responded, and they were ensuring that the ambulance crew had full access and that the scene was secure pending the arrival of scenes of crime officers. DS Raymond informed the man that he was under arrest on suspicion of causing grievous bodily harm and cautioned him. He made no reply. He was handcuffed and escorted to a police vehicle by DS Raymond and PC Williams.'

'Detective Inspector, please tell the jury the words of the caution.'

'Yes, sir. The words of the caution are: "You are not obliged to say anything unless you wish to do so, but what you say may be put into writing and given in evidence."'

'The man had still not identified himself to you?'

'No, sir.'

'But from documents he had in his possession, were you able to establish that he was, in fact, the defendant in this case, Henry Lang?'

'That is correct, sir.'

'Did you take possession of the knife?'

'I did, sir.'

'The jury has already seen it; it's our Exhibit 2. But just to confirm, with the usher's assistance, would you please confirm that this is the knife you seized at the scene?'

Webb looked at the knife carefully as Geoffrey held it up for him.

'Yes, sir, that is the knife.'

'Did you take possession of any other items at the scene?'

'Yes, Mr Lang's driving licence and one or two other documents we used to identify him, and Mrs Lang's handbag.'

'After Mr Lang had been taken to the police station, did you speak with Mrs Wendy Cameron? The jury will recall that she was the court welfare officer who made the emergency call and who gave evidence yesterday.'

'Yes, sir, I did. Mrs Cameron opened the door to her house on the other side of Dombey Street, and invited us in to speak to her.'

'Just answer yes or no, please, Inspector: did Mrs Cameron indicate to you that she had witnessed what had happened, and did she give you an account of what she had seen?'

'Yes, sir.'

49

'Finally, Detective Inspector, when you returned to the police station, would the usual practice have been to interview Mr Lang under caution, to ask him about what had happened, and to give him the opportunity to explain himself if he wished to do so?'

'That would have been the usual practice, sir, yes.'

'Were you able to follow the usual practice in this case?'

'No, sir – at least not immediately.'

'Why was that?'

Webb shook his head.

'When I returned to the police station, I was informed by the custody sergeant, Sergeant Miller, that Mr Lang had still not spoken a word to anyone; that he was not well, and that the police surgeon believed that he required medical attention in hospital. He was not fit to be interviewed at that time.'

'Yes. I will be calling medical evidence later, so I needn't trouble you with that, but did it appear that Mr Lang was suffering from shock?'

'So I was told, sir, yes.'

'Were you able to interview him at a later time?'

'Yes, sir. Mr Lang spent two nights in Barts hospital. He was discharged and returned to the police station on Friday morning, 30 April. By that time, there was no medical objection to DS Raymond and myself interviewing him, which we did.' Webb glanced at his notebook. 'That was at 11 o'clock that morning.'

'Was Mr Lang cautioned at the start of the interview?'

'Yes, sir.'

'And was that the same caution he had been given when he was arrested, the same wording you gave to the jury a few moments ago?'

'Yes, sir.'

'And did he answer any questions?'

'He did, sir.'

'But, taking it briefly, did he tell you that he had no recollection of anything that had happened between the time he left home to go to Mrs Cameron's house on the Wednesday morning, and returning from Barts hospital shortly before you interviewed him on Friday morning?'

'Yes, sir.'

'Inspector, do you have a note of the interview in your notebook?'

'Yes, sir. This is a note originally made by DS Raymond while the interview was taking place. After the interview had finished, DS Raymond and I read over his note together to ensure that it was complete and accurate. I then copied it into my notebook.'

'Taking it slowly, Inspector, would you please read the interview to the jury?

DI Webb took a drink of water, and read each question and answer to the jury. When he had finished, Andrew continued.

'Thank you, Inspector. Did you make any further efforts to interview him?'

'Yes, sir. He was later able to give some information about his marriage to Susan Lang, the divorce proceedings, and he told us about his garage business, but still nothing about the event itself.'

'Unless my learned friend asks me to, I'm not going to ask you to read any of that to the jury.'

'No need, thank you,' Ben said.

'I'm obliged. What did you do next, Inspector?'

'At that stage, sir, having consulted my senior officer and spoken to Treasury Counsel –'

'Myself,' Andrew smiled.

'Indeed, sir, yes; having received advice from yourself, I decided to charge Mr Lang with murder. He was in due course charged with the murder of Susan Lang by Superintendent Naismith and cautioned, and he made no reply to the caution.'

'Detective Inspector, did Henry Lang ever mention to you the name of a man called Daniel Cleary, otherwise known as "Danny Ice"?'

Ben stood.

'My Lord, I object to that question. The jury are not allowed to draw any conclusion against Mr Lang because he may not have mentioned something to the police. He was entitled not to answer any questions from the police, and he was cautioned to remind him of that right.'

'That doesn't make my question improper,' Andrew replied. 'It's obvious from my learned friend's cross-examination of Mrs Cameron that the defence considers Daniel Cleary to be important to this case in some way; and given Mr Lang's claim of amnesia, it's not unreasonable for the prosecution to explore what he claimed to remember, and not remember, at the time following his arrest.'

Mr Justice Rainer was staring blankly.

'Daniel Cleary?'

'Yes,' Andrew replied. 'Your Lordship will recall –'

Suddenly, the judge seemed irritated.

'Yes, of course I recall, Mr Pilkington. But why are we hearing about this man Cleary? What has he got to do with anything?'

Ben stood.

'My Lord, if I may assist, Mr Cleary will play a significant role in this case.'

'Then why are you objecting to Mr Pilkington's question?'

'I'm not objecting to any mention of Mr Cleary, my Lord. I'm objecting to my learned friend's suggestion that Mr Lang had some obligation to mention him to the police when he was interviewed. He did not. He had been cautioned that he was not obliged to say anything.'

'What role is this man Cleary going to play in this trial?'

Ben turned to Andrew, who raised his eyebrows and shook his head.

'My Lord, I don't want to appear to give evidence myself with the jury present. If your Lordship prefers, we can ask the jury to retire for a few minutes so that I can explain. But Mr Cleary will have a role of some importance in the defendant's case.'

'I expect counsel to keep to matters that are strictly relevant,' the judge said. 'I'm not going to have the trial diverted into all kinds of highways and byways.'

'We're doing our best to stick to what is relevant, my Lord. If the jury may retire for a few minutes, I will explain why Mr Cleary is relevant.'

The judge sat shaking his head for some seconds.

'No. I'm not going to waste time on this. The… the witness will… answer the question.'

'Answer the question, please, Detective Inspector,' Andrew said. 'Do you remember the question?'

'Yes, sir. The answer is no: Mr Lang did not mention Mr Cleary to us at any time.'

'Did Henry Lang ever offer you any explanation for having taken the kitchen knife, Exhibit 2, with him to the meeting with his wife and Wendy Cameron on 28 April?'

'No, sir. He did not.'

'Thank you. Wait there, please.'

50

Ben stood slowly.

'Detective Inspector, first, may I make it clear that like everyone else in this courtroom, I'm sure, Mr Lang and I have nothing but admiration for the way in which you and your fellow officers dealt with the situation at Harpur Mews on the afternoon of 28 April. It was extraordinarily courageous.'

Webb bowed his head.

'Thank you, sir.'

'You had no way of knowing what might happen, did you?'

'No, sir.'

'But in fact, Henry Lang was entirely passive, wasn't he – saying nothing, doing nothing, offering no resistance when you disarmed him?'

'That's correct, sir.'

'In the course of your long experience as a police officer, had you ever, before this, known someone in his position – apparently caught red-handed having committed a serious offence – not to react at all when confronted or arrested?'

'No, sir. It was a first for me.'

'Are you now aware from the medical evidence that he was in a state of clinical shock when you found him?'

'So I am given to understand.'

'Shock which required medical treatment and a short stay in hospital?'

'Yes.'

'Henry Lang is a man of previous good character, isn't he?'

'Yes.'

'So that the jury will understand, when we say that someone is of previous good character, we mean that he has never been convicted of any criminal offence?'

'That is correct, sir.'

'And as a result of your inquiries, you were able to establish that Mr Lang is the owner of a very successful garage business in Islington, specialising in the repair and maintenance of high-end cars, including foreign imports?'

'Yes, sir.'

'Do you know, or do you know of, the man Daniel Cleary, otherwise known as "Danny Ice"?'

'I know *of* him, sir, yes.'

'Is there police intelligence about Daniel Cleary?'

Andrew began to push himself to his feet.

'My Lord –'

'I'm not authorised to make public details of police intelligence,' Webb replied. 'It would be for more senior officers to decide whether that would be appropriate.'

'The police are entitled to keep intelligence confidential,' Andrew added.

'All right,' Ben said. 'Let me try it this way. Is Daniel Cleary reputed on the street to be high up in the chain of command of an organised crime ring, people who supply hard drugs – heroin and cocaine – who lend money to people who wish to buy drugs at extortionate rates of interest, and who have violent methods of making sure the debts are repaid?'

Andrew hovered for a second or two before resuming his seat. Webb looked at him, offering him a chance to object, before he replied. Andrew remained in his seat and shook his head.

'Yes, sir, I am aware of that reputation. I'm not sure quite how high-ranking he is; I don't think we are talking about the very top, but he is certainly reputed to be an influential player.'

'Thank you. Daniel Cleary also has a number of previous convictions, doesn't he?'

This time, Andrew did spring to his feet.

'My Lord, that is not a proper question. Daniel Cleary is not here to defend himself, and whether or not he has previous convictions has no relevance to this case.'

'On the contrary, my Lord,' Ben replied. 'It is of considerable relevance. Mr Lang will say that Daniel Cleary had threatened him –'

'I would prefer that my learned friend not give evidence –'

'I'm not giving evidence. I'm simply trying to show the court why this line of inquiry is relevant. I offered to do so in the absence of the jury, but your Lordship appeared to think that it was unnecessary...'

Ben stopped abruptly. Mr Justice Rainer did not seem to be listening. He was staring vacantly up at the ceiling. Ben noticed that the jury were also glancing in the judge's direction.

'My Lord, again, if your Lordship would like me to explain in detail...'

The judge stood.

'I do apologise,' he said. 'I'm not feeling very well today. We will take a break, members of the jury.'

He rose without another word, left the bench, and made his way to his chambers.

Andrew looked at Ben.

'Detective Inspector, don't discuss your evidence with anyone during the break,' he said, loudly enough for the jury to hear as they were leaving court.

'No, sir.'

Andrew made his way over to Ben's side of counsel's row.

'The judge seems to be a bit off his game today, Ben, doesn't he?'

'That's putting it mildly.' Ben replied. 'Why didn't he just send the jury out for a few minutes, instead of going on and on about Cleary? I tried to tell him.'

'He's been acting strangely ever since we started,' Jess added. 'I've been watching him. There's something the matter with him. It's almost as if he's somewhere else, not here with us at all.'

'He's been a spectator so far,' Barratt added.

'Well, we'll have to pay attention to the summing-up,' Andrew said. 'God knows what he might come out with. It's bad enough that it's his first criminal trial, without having him not paying attention.'

'It's not his fault that he's not feeling well, Andrew,' Jess protested, 'and at least he's told us about it.'

'Perhaps so, but I don't think any of us wants to do this case all over again,' Andrew replied. 'If there's a chance he can't continue, it would be better if he told us now.'

Barratt shook his head.

'He doesn't look ill to me. He just can't concentrate for some reason. Perhaps he ate something that didn't agree with him, or perhaps he had a late night at some bigwig's party in the City. It's an occupational hazard for Old Bailey judges, isn't it?'

'If so, he will have recovered by the time he has to sum up,' Ben said.

'Well, let's hope you're right,' Andrew said. He dropped a document on top of Ben's notebook.

'What's this?'

'Daniel Cleary's antecedents. You might as well have them. I don't think I'm going to talk Rainer into keeping them from the jury. The last three convictions are probably the ones you want.'

Ben picked up the antecedents and flipped through them quickly. He smiled.

'Yes. I see what you mean. Thank you.'

'Do you mind if I talk to Webb, just to tell him I've given them to you?'

'No, of course not.'

Geoffrey was approaching.

'Sorry to disturb you, Mr Pilkington, Mr Schroeder, but the judge said to let you know that he will not resume until after lunch. He's released the jury until 2 o'clock, and you're also released.'

Andrew exhaled loudly.

'Thank you, Geoffrey. Please tell the judge we hope he feels better by then.'

'I will, sir,' Geoffrey replied.

51

'Detective Inspector, before lunch I was asking you about Daniel Cleary's criminal record,' Ben began. 'Do you now have a copy of his antecedents in front of you?'

'I do, sir.'

Mr Justice Rainer seemed to have regained some of his colour and poise during the lunch break. He had apologised again to the whole court, and hinted at a stomach upset. Andrew had assured him of the entire court's best wishes for a quick recovery, and had recalled DI Webb to the witness box.

'Is he now a man of 39 years of age, and does he have a total of 12 convictions recorded against him?'

'That would seem to be correct, sir.'

'I'm not going to go through them all. In 1964, at this court, was he convicted after a trial of causing grievous bodily harm with intent, and was he sentenced to imprisonment for four years?'

'Yes, sir.'

'Being released after serving two-thirds of that sentence in 1967?'

'Yes, sir.'

'In 1968, at Middlesex Quarter Sessions at the Guildhall, did he plead guilty to two offences of demanding money with menaces, and was he sentenced to 18 months imprisonment, being released in 1969?'

'Yes, sir.'

'And last year, at the Inner London Sessions House, having pleaded guilty to one count of assault occasioning actual bodily harm and one count of being concerned in the supply of a controlled drug, namely heroin, was he sentenced to a total of nine months imprisonment?'

'Yes, sir.'

'Thank you, Inspector. Lastly, I want to ask you a few questions about Susan Lang. You gave evidence earlier that you recovered her handbag from the scene at Harpur Mews.'

'That's correct.'

'Did you examine the contents of the handbag?'

'Yes, sir.'

'And among other items, did you find an address book?'

'I did, sir.'

'In that address book, was there a telephone number known to police to be associated with a man called Tommy McMahon?'

'Yes, there was.'

'And is Tommy McMahon a known associate of Daniel Cleary?'

'Mr McMahon was convicted together with Mr Cleary of the two offences of demanding money with menaces at Middlesex Sessions in 1968, and I understand that they continue to associate together.'

'Did you also find in Mrs Lang's handbag a small plastic bag containing a white powder?'

'Yes, I did.'

'Was that powder sent for analysis?'

'Yes, sir.'

'Please tell my Lord and the jury what the analysis showed.'

'The analysis showed that the powder contained approximately 3.88 grams of cocaine, having a purity of just under 40 per cent.'

'I see. Detective Inspector, during your many years as a police officer, have you had some experience of dealing with drugs, including cocaine?'

'Considerable experience, sir.'

'When we refer to the purity of a quantity of cocaine, what do we mean by that?'

'By purity, we mean the extent to which the powder is actually composed of cocaine itself. When the drug is supplied from a source close to the top of the chain of command, it will be of a very high purity. But it won't find its way on to the street in that condition. As it moves down the chain of command, each wholesaler and retailer will adulterate the powder, so as to reduce the purity. This is known as cutting the drug, and it is done by adding so-called cutting agents, which are hopefully otherwise harmless substances, such as baking soda.'

'Presumably, that has to do with each wholesaler or retailer in turn trying to maximise his profits?'

'Exactly. They then have a greater quantity of powder to offer for sale, but of course, it is less pure in terms of the percentage of cocaine.'

'By the time the cocaine hits the street, what would the average purity be?'

'I can't answer that. It depends very much on the history of that particular batch, how many times it has been sold on, and so on.'

'Would a purity of almost 40 per cent be usual or unusual at street level?'

'It would not be unknown, but I would say it would be relatively unusual.'

'Unusual because it is on the high side, or the low side?'

'The high side.'

'Thank you. Now, let me ask you about the quantity. When police seize a quantity of a drug such as cocaine, do they always consider whether it could be for the personal use of the person in possession of it, or whether it is more likely to be a commercial quantity, indicating that the person in possession might have intended to supply it to others?'

'Yes, of course. That's a basic consideration, before we can decide what to charge him with. It's an offence to possess the drug in itself, but obviously if he is part of a chain of supply, it is a lot more serious, and the higher up the chain of supply he is, the more serious it becomes.'

'In the case of the cocaine found in Mrs Lang's handbag, you had a quantity of 3.88 grams with a purity of almost 40 per cent. What conclusions did you draw from that?'

Webb paused.

'Well, it could possibly have been for personal use. When

cocaine is sold on the street, it's generally sold in quantities of about 0.2 of a gram, so she's carrying a quantity with a fair street value, and your first thought is lower-level commercial supply. On the other hand, many dealers give a purchaser a discount for buying in bulk, as you commonly find in any business, legal or otherwise. So you can't rule out the possibility of this quantity being for her personal use. But when you consider the purity, and when you consider her financial situation, being unemployed and separated from her husband, it becomes more likely that some element of supply was involved.'

'In fairness,' Ben said, 'she wouldn't have been anywhere near the top of the chain of supply, would she?'

Webb shook his head firmly.

'No. Certainly not. I would say we are looking at two possibilities. One, she bought in bulk on behalf of some friends, or to share with friends, and intended to pass some of it on; not to make a profit necessarily, but to be reimbursed and perhaps make a few quid to fund her own habit. Two, she was running a low-level street business as a runner for someone higher in the chain, and was paid a commission for her services by that person.'

'Someone like Daniel Cleary?'

'Perhaps. But we haven't investigated her activities in any detail, so anything beyond identifying those two possibilities would be no more than speculation.'

'Thank you, Inspector. Lastly, when officers searched Mrs Lang's car, did they find a cigarette butt which contained a mixture of cannabis and tobacco?'

'Yes, sir.'

'And when they searched her flat, did they find a small quantity of herbal cannabis consistent with personal use?'

'Yes, sir.'

'In the flat where she presumably would have lived with her two children if she had been granted custody by the High Court?'

'Presumably, sir.'

52

'My Lord, I now call Dr Cedric Harvey,' Andrew said.

Andrew had offered to call DS Raymond and PC Williams, but Ben was satisfied with his cross-examination of DI Webb, and saw no need to expose the jury to more evidence about the gruesome scene at Harpur Mews. They were released, to remain on call in case they might be required later.

Dr Harvey was tall and thin, dressed in a light grey pin-striped suit, a white shirt, and a red tie. He carried a thick file folder. He put on reading glasses to take the oath.

'Dr Harvey, would you give the court your full name?'

'Cedric James Harvey.'

'Are you a medical doctor by profession?'

'That is correct.'

Ben stood.

'My Lord, there's no dispute about Dr Harvey's credentials. My learned friend can take it quite briefly.'

'I am much obliged. Taking it briefly then, Dr Harvey, did you read medicine at Cambridge University, did you do your residencies at Guy's Hospital here in London, and have you been practising as a doctor, and teaching younger doctors and medical students, for more than twenty-five years?'

'I have.'

'And have you, during that time, acted as a consultant at a number of teaching hospitals, not only in this country, but also in Canada?'

'That is correct.'

'Do you have a particular speciality or specialities within the field of medicine?'

'I have a dual speciality in neurology and psychiatry.'

'Could you tell us what those terms mean?'

'The formal definitions are: that neurology is the study of the anatomy, functions, and organic disorders of the nerves and the nervous system; whereas psychiatry is the study and treatment of mental illness, emotional disturbances, and abnormal behaviour.'

'Doctor, please explain to my Lord and the jury in what way those two disciplines are related.'

'Well, they're not related as such, but they are often of interest to doctors at the same time in a particular case. It often happens that patients present with symptoms which could either have a neurological cause or a psychiatric cause. It's essential to diagnose correctly before the proper treatment can be identified, so you can't make assumptions; you can't jump to a psychiatric cause without first eliminating the possibility of neurological injury.'

'I see. I want to ask you in particular about clinical shock. Is shock a matter of interest to a doctor in your fields?'

Dr Harvey laughed politely.

'Clinical shock is a condition of interest to any doctor. It's a potentially life-threatening condition, which must be identified and treated promptly and correctly.'

Andrew smiled.

'Perhaps I should ask you first, then, what shock is.'

'Shock itself is simply a condition the body finds itself in when the flow of blood is suddenly reduced or interrupted, resulting in a lack of blood flow to the body's cells and its vital organs. It can be a serious condition, which may result in extensive damage to the internal organs, or even death, if not diagnosed and treated promptly.'

'What are the possible causes of shock?'

'There are any number of possible causes. If I could just name some of the most common: shock may occur as a result of cardiac arrest or heart failure; as a result of an infection of some kind; as a result of an allergic reaction to some substance, including medications; or as a result of some damage to the nervous system.'

'What symptoms may the patient experience?'

'Depending on the degree of shock, it may be simply a visible agitation; or sensations of faintness, dizziness, confusion, disorientation and so on. There may be chest pains, difficulty in breathing, a weak pulse, and of course the patient will almost certainly present with low blood pressure. In a serious case, there may be a loss of consciousness.'

'Thank you, Doctor. Is it possible for shock to be caused by a trauma of some kind?'

'Certainly. It's not uncommon, for example, for shock to be observed in a patient who's been involved in a car accident, or who has simply witnessed some shocking event.'

'What would be the physical cause of shock in such a case?'

'It depends. If the patient has been injured in the accident, for example, it could be due to the injury itself, or some neurological damage. But it's not necessary for there to be any injury. Sometimes shock can occur simply by the body reacting to something the patient has witnessed.'

'So the cause could be psychological?'

'Partly psychological. There would still be some physical reaction that reduces the flow of blood.'

'Dr Harvey, have you been asked by the prosecution to evaluate and give an opinion about some evidence relating to Henry Lang in this case?'

'I have.'

'Let me ask you this first. Have you ever examined or spoken to Henry Lang?'

'No. I have not.'

'What have you relied on in forming your opinions?'

'I have read the witness statements: particularly those of the police officers, DI Webb and his colleagues, who attended the scene; and the welfare officer Mrs Cameron. I have read the statement of Sergeant Miller, who was in charge of Mr Lang while he was in custody at the police station. I have read the report of the police physician, Dr Moynihan, and I have a copy of Mr Lang's file from his stay at Barts.'

'Based on those materials, and of course on your many years of professional experience, have you reached any opinion as to whether Henry Lang may have been suffering from shock at any time on the 28 April, the day on which he killed his wife, or on the following day?'

'I have.'

'Please tell my Lord and the jury what you have concluded.'

Dr Harvey turned over a number of pages in his file.

'Well, the first thing I should say is that I worked backwards in this case to some extent. The only medical evidence I had to rely on was Dr Moynihan's examination, and the examination at Barts, all of which took place after the event. Dr Moynihan noted that Mr Lang, though conscious and alert, and apparently responsive to touch and vocal stimuli, was not engaging with those around him; also, his blood pressure was low. Dr Moynihan also noted a severe reduction in body temperature. All of those symptoms are consistent with a diagnosis of trauma-induced shock. I should add that Sergeant Miller had also observed the low body temperature, and his reaction in dealing with it using blankets and then calling for medical help was highly commendable.'

'Did Sergeant Miller contribute to the successful treatment of Mr Lang's condition?'

'Undoubtedly. If he had simply assumed that Mr Lang would warm up again, and done nothing, the consequences could have been very serious. The Barts file notes the same symptoms, and records that Mr Lang was warmed with thermal blankets, and that they succeeded in getting him to drink some hot tea, and later hot soup. He was also somewhat dehydrated, and an IV line was used to rehydrate him. With that treatment, the symptoms subsided, and he was fit to return to police custody by the Friday morning. Barts also gave him a thorough physical examination, of course, and did the usual tests, and they note that no neurological injury was observed.'

'How does that medical evidence relate to the police evidence about his behaviour at the scene?'

'The police evidence is quite consistent with the medical evidence. Mr Lang suffered no neurological injury. He was conscious and alert, and was able to respond to physical stimuli, for example: releasing whatever grip he had on the knife; standing up, and placing his arms in a position to be handcuffed; and walking to the police car when he was arrested. At the same time, he was probably already suffering from the symptoms observed by Sergeant Miller and Dr Moynihan; we can safely assume that they didn't start spontaneously when he got to the police station. His apparent immobility, his lack of reaction to what was going on around him, and his failure to say anything, are all consistent.'

'And your conclusion from all that evidence…?'

'My conclusion is that Mr Lang was suffering from trauma-induced shock on the 28 and 29 April, and there is obviously a very high probability that the trauma that caused this condition was his act of stabbing his wife, launching a violent and prolonged attack on her, and then witnessing the consequences of what he had done.'

'So, it was a genuine case of shock?'

'Oh, yes. I don't think there can be any doubt about that at all.'

53

'Now, Dr Harvey,' Andrew continued. 'I want to ask you about something rather different. Have you been made aware, through your reading of the documents, and through your conversations with me, that Mr Lang did not give the police any account of what happened on 28 April, and that he claimed to have no memory of any events after leaving home some two hours before he stabbed his wife?'

'I am aware of his claim of amnesia, yes.'

'And once again – because all of us in court probably think we know what amnesia is, but it may be that we really don't – would you please give us the clinical definition of amnesia?'

Dr Harvey smiled. 'Actually, the popular concept of amnesia is quite close to the clinical view of it. For our purposes today, amnesia is simply the loss of memory of certain events or certain periods of time preceding the onset of the amnesia. That's the kind of amnesia most people are familiar with. Technically, it's called retrograde amnesia. There is a different kind of amnesia called anterograde amnesia, which refers to an inability to create new memories because of brain damage, but we're not concerned with that.'

'Doctor, what can cause a person to suffer from the condition of retrograde amnesia?'

'Again, just as in the case of shock, it can be caused by neurological damage, a head trauma, a brain injury of some kind, damage to the tissue of the brain; or by a very serious pathological event such as a stroke or cardiac arrest which results in loss of consciousness; we would call that kind of amnesia, "traumatic amnesia". But amnesia can also have a psychological origin, as a result of a person being involved in or witnessing some traumatic event, while not actually suffering any physical trauma oneself. That often takes the form of dissociative trauma, meaning that the mind will not allow the patient to access certain memories, to protect the patient from the pain those memories may cause.'

'Assuming that Mr Lang's claim of amnesia is genuine – and you understand, I'm sure, that the prosecution do not accept that it is genuine: on the basis of the evidence you have studied, what kind of amnesia are we dealing with in Mr Lang's case?'

'On the basis of the evidence, including the lack of any evidence of head trauma or neurological injury, I would assume that the claim would be one of dissociative retrograde amnesia. He witnessed the consequences of his attack on his wife, and the trauma of what he saw – and possibly heard, or even smelled – were such as to cause some limited retrograde amnesia.'

'Dr Harvey, are there any methods or procedures for determining whether a patient's claim of dissociative retrograde amnesia is genuine or otherwise?'

Dr Harvey thought for some time.

'There are a number of matters to consider there. First, unlike shock, which has obvious physical symptoms, a claim of amnesia is essentially subjective.'

'Meaning that we only have the patient's word for it?'

'Yes, and in a forensic setting such as a criminal prosecution, the patient may think it's in his own best interests to claim that he can't remember a particular event. For example, someone driving a car at the time of a fatal accident may choose to say that he doesn't remember what happened because he thinks it would look bad for him if he told the truth. But, of course, it's important to stress that the amnesia can be perfectly genuine, even under those circumstances; the accident may be just as traumatic for someone who is at fault, perhaps even more so than for an innocent victim.'

'Are there any possible indicators? For example, what kind of memory is generally lost? Would it be the memory of a particular event, or could it extend to the memory of your own circumstances

– your identity, your family, your job, and so on – or the general knowledge you have accumulated during your lifetime?'

Dr Harvey considered for some time.

'There are documented examples of all of those things. Total retrograde amnesia, including loss of memory of one's identity and personal circumstances, is extremely rare. But there are such cases, and there are cases of so-called dissociative fugues, which are recurring episodes of loss of memory, during which the patient may set out on apparently illogical journeys, appearing not to know who he is, or where he is going, or why he is going anywhere. It's also very rare for a patient to experience loss of his ability to write, or do arithmetic, or get dressed in the morning, because those long-term learned skills are stored in a different part of the brain which seems to be less affected by transient events. So those kinds of memory loss are not usually involved in dissociative amnesia.

'On the other hand, the loss of memory of a specific event, for example an accident in which the patient has been involved, is quite common, and it's usually no more than the body protecting us from the pain of reliving an event of that kind. That's the kind of memory loss one would expect to find in a case of dissociative amnesia, and it's the kind that Mr Lang claims to have suffered.'

'Are there any features of Mr Lang's claim that you find in any way suspicious?'

Dr Harvey smiled. 'I hesitate to use the word "suspicious" because, as a doctor, I am naturally inclined to take the patient's symptoms at face value, especially in an area such as this, where the nature and extent of memory loss can legitimately vary considerably from case to case.'

Andrew returned the smile. 'I keep forgetting to suppress my natural instinct to question everything –'

'No, I'm sure that's a quality you need in your line of work, just as I need a certain degree of mutual trust in mine. You must bear in mind that my concern is to treat the patient's condition, and I am asking myself how I might be able to restore his memory – assuming that it is desirable to restore it.'

'Of course. Let me ask it this way. Are there any features of Mr

Lang's account of his amnesia that would lead you, as a doctor concerned about his treatment, to ask further questions?'

'Yes. One thing that struck me as odd was the fact that his claim of amnesia goes back some two hours before he stabbed his wife, to the time when he left his house. This means that he doesn't remember how he got from home to Mrs Cameron's house, what they talked about during the meeting –'

'Why he took a large kitchen knife with him from home?' Andrew interjected.

Ben stood at once.

'My Lord, I think the jury already have that point, since my learned friend has gone back over it time and time again, but if not, he will have plenty of opportunity to return to it yet again at the proper time.'

Mr Justice Rainer looked up abruptly.

'Yes… let's keep to… shall we?'

Andrew glanced at Ben.

'Yes, my Lord. Dr Harvey, why did that strike you as odd?'

'Because dissociative amnesia generally operates from a moment immediately before the traumatic event itself. For example, a driver may well remember setting out from home, driving along the road, seeing the oncoming headlights, but have no memory of the collision that occurred seconds after that last memory. The loss of memory may then extend forward to subsequent events; for example, the patient may have no memory of being thrown clear of the car, of being attended to by passers-by, of the ambulance arriving, and so on. His next memory may be of something happening in hospital. But in Mr Lang's case, there is something odd about the amnesia beginning such a long time before the event. In fact, I have never known another case where that has been claimed.'

'Is there anything else that struck you as odd?'

'Well, of course, I was intrigued by the fact that his memory returned last Thursday afternoon, just as his trial was about to begin. But I must stress that I haven't really had much chance to consider that question.'

'No. In fact, were you unaware that Mr Lang's memory was said to have returned until I informed you of it this morning?'

'Indeed so.'

'In general terms, Doctor, for how long does a loss of memory of a particular event last in cases of dissociative retrograde amnesia?'

'There is no general rule at all. Each case is different. In the vast majority of cases, memory returns spontaneously, but the timing varies considerably. Sometimes the memory returns within a matter of an hour or two; sometimes it doesn't return for weeks, or months, or even years in a very severe case. In the absence of physical injury, a lot depends on how traumatic the event was, and how firmly the brain has repressed the memory to spare the patient the pain of remembering it.'

'What kinds of things can help in restoring memory?'

'Well, the most obvious treatment is to confront the patient with the facts of whatever it is he can't remember, and see if that jogs his memory. Often, it does. You can show him a photograph, or let him talk to other people involved in the accident, and so on, and very often that does the trick almost immediately. In this case, Mr Lang was confronted with the facts by the police, and no doubt by his own legal advisers, so on the face of it there is nothing inconsistent with his memory returning at any particular time. The only comment I would make is that, given that degree of confrontation and the stress of the circumstances in which he found himself – in custody, charged with the murder of his wife – it is surprising that his memory loss continued for some five months.'

'And that his memory returned on the eve of trial?'

'Quite so.'

'Thank you, Dr Harvey. Wait there, please. There may be further questions.'

'Dr Harvey,' Ben began, 'in psychiatric work, where you are dealing with mental illness or an emotional imbalance, it's important to speak with the patient, isn't it?'

Dr Harvey hesitated.

'Yes, in general, I would agree with that.'

'It's an important tool in making a psychiatric diagnosis, isn't it, to listen to what the patient says?'

'Yes, it certainly can be.'

'*Can* be?' Ben picked up a blue hardback book from the bench top. 'I was quoting from your introduction to the fifth edition of the *Handbook of Psychiatric Diagnosis*, published in 1969, in which you say, "Listening to the patient is *always* an important tool in psychiatric diagnosis". Have you changed your mind about that since 1969?'

Dr Harvey smiled and nodded in acknowledgement.

'No. I would agree with that.'

'You haven't spoken to Henry Lang, have you?'

'No. I was told by the prosecuting solicitor that, as he had already been charged, it would not be possible for me to see him.'

'Were you? Did you know that Mr Lang is represented by a solicitor, Mr Barratt Davis, the gentleman sitting behind me?'

'I assumed he had a solicitor, of course.'

'Would it have been possible for you, or the prosecuting solicitor, to contact Mr Davis and ask if you could see Mr Lang? He was in custody, wasn't he? He wasn't going anywhere.'

'As I say, I was told that it would not be appropriate after he had been charged.'

'It wouldn't have been appropriate to give Mr Lang and his solicitor the chance to arrange a consultation if they thought it might help? Did you question the prosecuting solicitor about it, ask him to take Treasury Counsel's opinion?'

'No. But I would like to add that the only psychiatric diagnosis of Mr Lang I made was one of trauma-induced shock, which I understand is not disputed.'

It was said defensively, almost petulantly. Ben paused.

'But your diagnosis of shock is not the only observation you've made about Henry Lang, is it, Dr Harvey? When my learned friend gave you the chance, you jumped in enthusiastically to support the prosecution's theory that Mr Lang's amnesia is not genuine, didn't you?'

'No. I said that there are some parts of his account that I find odd.'

'"Find odd" meaning that you don't believe it?'

'Not necessarily.'

'Well, do you believe it, or don't you?'

'I have insufficient data to say whether I believe it or not. I find some of it odd, that's all.'

'Is the fact that you haven't spoken to Mr Lang one reason why you have insufficient data?'

'It might have assisted to some extent to speak to him. I can't say. This isn't a diagnosis.'

'Without speaking to Mr Lang, your finding that something about the account he gave is odd is essentially speculation, isn't it?'

'I wouldn't go that far.'

'Well, let's look at it, shall we? One thing you find odd is that his loss of memory goes back to the time when he left home, some two hours before he killed his wife? You find that odd?'

'Yes.'

'Did it occur to you that if the use of the kitchen knife to stab his wife was part of the trauma he experienced on 28 April, then picking up the knife at home in the first place might have been part of the trauma?'

Dr Harvey looked startled.

'No, that did not occur to me.'

'Can you rule that possibility out?'

'I suppose not, altogether. But –'

'Dr Harvey, isn't it true that doctors still don't entirely understand how dissociative amnesia works?'

'There are some aspects of it which cause difficulty, yes.'

'And there can always be cases which don't correspond with the usual models, can't there?'

'Yes.'

'And for all you know, this could be one?'

'As I say, I can't rule it out.'

'Meaning, that there is at least some doubt about it?'

'Yes.'

'You also find it odd that his memory returned spontaneously last Thursday afternoon?'

'Yes, I do find that odd.'

'Even though you have already told the jury that it could have returned at any time in response to being reminded of the facts by the police and his own legal advisers?'

'Yes, that's true. Nonetheless, the timing seems odd.'

'Doctor, is it possible in a case of dissociative retrograde amnesia for memory to return as a result of a further traumatic experience related to the original event?'

'Yes, that does happen. For example, if someone dies as a result of an accident, some time after the original event, that sometimes brings back memories in others who were involved.'

'Yes. Dr Harvey, would you agree that going on trial for murder is a stressful experience for a defendant?'

'Certainly.'

'Could being brought to trial for murder properly be described as a traumatic experience occurring some time after the original event?'

Dr Harvey smiled.

'Yes,' he replied. 'I suppose it could.'

54

Aubrey knocked on the door, opened it and stuck his head inside. As he had hoped, Harriet had returned from court. She was sitting at her desk reading the day's law report in *The Times*.

'Ah, I was hoping I might catch you,' he said. 'Merlin said you were on your way back to chambers. Is Ben around?'

'I haven't seen him.' She looked at her watch. 'But he should be back from the Bailey any time now.'

'In that case,' Aubrey said, 'let's talk in my room. Alan will bring us some tea. I want to revisit our conversation about legal privilege and our mutual friend Danny Ice.'

They walked together along the corridor. She thought he looked tired and rather pale.

'Are you all right, Aubrey?'

'What? Oh, yes, fine. Bit of a late night, that's all. Come in. Have a seat.'

Alan had already left a pot of tea and a plate of digestive biscuits for them on an occasional table behind Aubrey's desk. Harriet tested the tea for strength and poured.

'I pored over *Cross* for quite some time,' Aubrey began, 'and as far as I can see, there is no rule that the privilege ends automatically just because the information would be useful to the defence in a criminal prosecution. Technically, the privilege relating to communications between lawyer and client lasts indefinitely, even after the client's death.'

'That doesn't seem right to me,' Harriet replied. 'The whole purpose of the privilege is to encourage the client to speak freely to her lawyer; once the client is dead, it's hard to see what purpose it could still have.'

'I agree, and that's why I think you should raise it with Conrad Rainer.'

Harriet looked at him quizzically.

'Raise it with him, how? Val and I are not parties to the case. We have no right to a hearing, and we can't tell Ben to raise it without violating the privilege.'

'Write Conrad a note and ask him to see you privately in chambers tomorrow morning before court sits,' Aubrey suggested. 'Explain what you want to see him about, without going into detail, obviously. Tell him you have some evidence which might be important in the case he is trying, but you would need a ruling from him before you can disclose it to the parties. Then he'll have to make up his mind. Either he will decide to make some new law, which we both agree ought to be made, or he will say he can't interfere with the privilege – in which case you have done all you can.'

'If he says no, there's nothing more we can do?'

Aubrey shook his head.

'Harriet, disobeying an order of a High Court judge is called contempt of court. You don't need me to tell you that. It's too much of a risk. Both you and Val could get into serious disciplinary trouble.'

'But if it would make a difference to the defence of a man charged with murder –'

'Harriet, you don't know whether it would make a difference or not, but even if it would, if a High Court judge rules that the privilege survives, you can't go against that.'

'In that case, maybe it would be better not to ask the judge to make an order. Maybe I should just tell Ben and let him handle it with the judge.'

'How would that help? You would still have violated the privilege.'

'But I would have done it for the right reason, wouldn't I? It just seems wrong to let it go without doing everything I can.'

'That wouldn't help you with the Bar Council, and it wouldn't help Val with the Law Society. You would both be in hot water.'

'Unless they agreed with us. There are times when you have to stand up for what you believe to be right.'

Aubrey shook his head, but smiled. 'That's the pupil I know talking.'

She returned the smile. 'Don't give me that, Aubrey. You've tilted at a few windmills yourself in your time.'

'Yes, but I tilted as counsel on behalf of others, Harriet, not as a potential witness.'

'You sailed close to the wind once or twice when you thought you were right – and you *were* right.'

'Talk to Conrad first,' Aubrey advised. 'If he says no, let's think about whether there's a way to go to the Court of Appeal. I will represent the two of you there and perhaps we can have a second bite of the cherry.'

'Thank you, Aubrey. That means a lot to me –'

'But if we lose in the Court of Appeal, you have to promise me that it will end there. I can't live with watching my star pupil get disbarred after all the efforts I made to get her taken on in chambers.'

'I have no intention of letting myself get disbarred – if I can help it,' Harriet replied. 'I need to think this through, and I need to talk to Val.'

'You need to talk to Conrad,' Aubrey said. 'And take *Cross* with you. There's no rule at present that the privilege must yield if it may affect the question of guilt or innocence in a criminal trial, but unless I'm misreading him, Cross thinks there should be. Perhaps it will persuade Conrad to go out on a limb.'

Aubrey's phone rang as Harriet was leaving.

'I have Mr Phillips QC on the line from Crown Office Row, sir,' Merlin said.

'Thank you, Merlin. Put him through.'

'Aubrey, how are you?'

'I'm very well, Stephen. I hope you are too.'

'Yes. Thank you. Aubrey, look, I don't want to stick my nose in where I shouldn't, but my clerk tells me you've asked for a confidential meeting with three members of my chambers, and

I must admit I'm a bit curious as to why. You and Gareth are not trying to lure anyone away to Two Wessex Buildings, are you?'

Aubrey laughed.

'No, Stephen, certainly not. You're quite right. I've asked to see Frank Reilly, Jonathan Weatherall, and Martin Cohn, and your clerk suggested Thursday afternoon, after court. But I can assure you that neither Gareth nor I have any improper designs on them.'

There was a silence on the line.

'As I say, Aubrey, I don't want to pry, but you must admit, it is a bit irregular to see members of another set of chambers in this way without asking first. I *am* their head of chambers after all, and if only as a matter of courtesy –'

'I apologise, Stephen. All I can tell you over the phone is that it's a very sensitive matter.'

'Have they done something wrong that I ought to know about?'

'No, not at all.'

Aubrey thought for some moments.

'Look, Stephen, if you're concerned, why don't you join us on Thursday? You'd have to be involved eventually, whatever happens, so there's no reason why not. Please, just keep it confidential for now. I think you'll understand why once you know what it's about.'

Another silence.

'All right,' Stephen replied. 'We can meet in my room. We won't be disturbed there. But I must say, Aubrey, I still find it all rather extraordinary.'

'Extraordinary doesn't begin to cover it,' Aubrey replied.

55

'Is the plan still for Jess to take Mrs Pettifer on cross?' Barratt asked.

'Yes,' Jess replied.

They had gone over every line of Mrs Pettifer's long, rambling witness statement in detail. It had taken well over two hours, and they had almost exhausted the subject of the cross-examination that would be required the next morning.

Ben nodded. 'We want to avoid getting into a pitched battle with her if we possibly can. She's on Susan Lang's side, she makes no secret of it, and she's fairly hostile about it. If I go after her, I will just come across as aggressive, and it will all become very confrontational. Jess's style of cross will be more effective with her.'

Barratt nodded, and suddenly seemed to relax a little, leaning back in his chair.

'What style is that?' he grinned.

Jess leaned forward in her chair and punched him playfully on the arm.

'I'm a Siren, Barratt. I lure them on to the rocks with my sweet singing, and they never know what hit them.'

Barratt nodded.

'Of course. I remember that ability from the days when you used to work for me. Is she like that at home as well, Ben?'

'No comment,' Ben smiled. 'But I think there's every chance Mrs Pettifer will end up on the rocks tomorrow, and in any case, Jess will give the jury a welcome break from having to listen to me all the time.'

Barratt nodded in agreement. 'I have every confidence in you, Jess,' he said more seriously. 'You know that. It's just that I'm nervous about Mrs Pettifer. She's the only witness who paints Henry Lang as the kind of man who might actually decide to kill his wife.'

'Yes,' Jess agreed, 'but if she goes after Henry too much, the jury will see right through her. If I can give her enough rope, she'll hang herself, and if we can make the jury see her as someone who's taken sides and isn't interested in being fair-minded, they won't be very impressed with her.'

'I hope you're right.'

'In the end, Barratt,' Ben said, 'this case is going to come down to Henry, not Mrs Pettifer. If he makes a good impression in the witness box, and we can show he has a serious case of provocation, I don't think the jury will be too concerned about what Mrs Pettifer may or may not have heard going on upstairs. All that is going to fade into the background once they hear what happened at Harpur Mews.'

'Sorry to interrupt,' Harriet said.

She had knocked softly at the door and waited until Ben had responded before she entered. Val Turner, formally dressed in a black two-piece suit, followed closely behind her.

Ben looked at his watch.

'Oh, I'm sorry, Harriet. How long have you been waiting? You should have banged on the door earlier. We can move on if you need the room.'

'No, no, we don't need the room. We'd agreed that you would have it tonight. No, Val and I have been over to the Devereux for a drink.'

'Lucky you,' Barratt said. 'You've been having more fun than we have.'

'Not necessarily,' Harriet replied. 'Barratt, Ben, this is Val Turner, who was Susan Lang's solicitor. Val, this is Geoff Bourne's partner, Barratt Davis, and Ben Schroeder, who's leading Jess in Henry's trial.'

They shook hands.

'If it's a bad moment, we can come back later.'

'No need,' Ben replied. 'We're just about finished.'

'Perhaps it's our turn to pop into the Dev?' Barratt suggested, turning towards Ben and Jess. 'Are you up for a quick one?'

'No, actually, Barratt,' Harriet said, 'we are here to see you. Val and I have something we feel we should tell you.'

She walked to her desk, opened a drawer, and took out a number of sheets of paper.

She looked at Val.

'Last chance. Are you still OK with this?'

Val nodded. 'I'm OK.'

'These are draft witness statements Val and I have made,' Harriet said. 'We haven't signed them yet. There's also a transcript of a conversation which we refer to in the witness statements. Why don't you read these first, and then we can talk about them?'

Harriet placed the documents on Ben's desk, and returned to her own desk to sit down. Jess and Barratt stood behind Ben and read over his shoulder. When they had finished reading, Jess and Barratt quietly resumed their seats. No one spoke for a considerable time.

'What you're saying,' Ben began, 'is that Susan Lang told you she had asked Daniel Cleary to threaten Henry, to persuade him to drop his custody application?'

'In effect, yes,' Harriet replied. 'She tried to back off when we challenged her, but that's what she told us.'

'Cleary was going to strong-arm Henry into giving up the children?' Barratt asked.

'Who better?' Harriet replied. 'You've seen his record, Barratt. He's already done four years for GBH with intent.'

'Not to mention demanding money with menaces,' Val added.

'He's the kind of man who wouldn't think twice about doing a little favour like that for one of his street drug runners, to keep her sweet,' Harriet said, 'especially if she was giving him a bit on the side.'

Ben ran his hands through his hair, and stared at them.

'Harriet, when Susan told you all this –'

'She was our client, yes. We are very aware of the privilege, Ben. That's what we've been talking about all evening.'

'But if she was speaking to you as her legal advisers –'

'Hear me out, Ben, please. Look, this has been preying on my mind for a long time now. I know privilege is important; I understand that. But Susan Lang is dead, and Henry Lang is on trial for her murder. I suspected his defence might be provocation and, if so, I knew immediately how important this was. Just to make sure, I was at the Bailey for the start of the trial. I skulked at the back of the court just long enough to confirm my suspicion.'

'Really? We didn't see you,' Jess said.

'I was fiendishly disguised as a member of the public,' Harriet smiled. 'Once I knew for sure, I went to see Aubrey to get some advice. He's my pupil-master, after all. Who else would I go to?'

'No one better,' Ben agreed. 'But surely Aubrey, of all people, would have told you that you couldn't tell anyone – least of all Henry's counsel and solicitor?'

'Ben, I don't feel right about defending the privilege in this situation, and I asked Aubrey to find me a way around it. We looked at *Cross* and we talked about it, and we agreed that the law ought to be that the privilege ceases to apply if the privileged information would tend to establish the innocence of a person accused of a serious criminal offence.'

'*Ought* to be?' Ben smiled.

'Yes. We can't actually find any such rule, but we think that *should* be the rule, and so does Cross. Ben, I'm right aren't I? This could make a difference to Henry's case, couldn't it?'

'It would make a massive difference,' Ben replied quietly.

'Well, then…?'

Ben thought for some time.

'You do both understand that, even if there were such a rule, the only way to get the information in front of the jury –?'

'Would be for one or both of us to give evidence? Yes, we understand that. But before we can give evidence, you'll have to convince Conrad Rainer to create a new rule of law.'

Ben took a deep breath.

'I can give it a try. It's not a bad argument: you have a client who has no further use for the privilege, and allowing the jury access to the information might help to prevent a miscarriage of justice. I can argue that with a straight face.'

'I think we're making this more difficult than it has to be,' Jess said. 'There's another argument we can make, surely, based on existing law?'

Every eye in the room turned to her.

'Pray, tell,' Barratt said.

'There's no privilege between a lawyer and her client if what is said between them is in furtherance of a crime by the client. Making threats of violence to get someone to drop a case has to be a criminal offence, doesn't it? I don't see how there can be any privilege for that. That's old law. We don't have to ask Rainer to create a new rule.'

Ben nodded slowly, and smiled.

'That sounds right to me, Harriet. Didn't Aubrey come up with that one?'

Harriet laughed.

'Neither of us came up with that one; it never occurred to us – or to you, apparently, until Jess thought of it. Well done, Jess.'

'Amen to that,' Barratt agreed, 'But you still have a problem, don't you? The moment Ben gets up to make the argument, it's obvious to everybody that you two have already violated the privilege.'

'That's what we were talking about at the Dev,' Harriet agreed. 'Aubrey suggested that we should ask to see Rainer in chambers without telling you, and make the case to him ourselves. Then, if he turned us down, we would go to the Court of Appeal, to see if they would listen. But we didn't like that idea. If Rainer turned us down and we said anything to you, we would automatically be in contempt of court. Aubrey knows Rainer well, and he thinks there's every chance he will go for it, but –'

'That's the other problem,' Barratt said. 'I'm not sure you could get Rainer to go for having a cup of tea at the moment.'

'What do you mean?'

'There's something going on with him, Harriet,' Jess explained. 'He's told us he's not feeling well, but there's something not right.

Whatever it is, he's not concentrating on the case; his mind is wandering the whole time. Ben and Andrew Pilkington are having to repeat themselves twice or three times, just to get his attention.'

'Aubrey didn't mention that he wasn't well,' Harriet said. 'I could ask him if he knows anything.'

'Forget about that for a moment,' Ben said. 'The real question is whether you want to do this. It seems to me that we're on solid enough legal ground, but if for any reason Conrad Rainer doesn't agree with us, you're both hung out to dry, and there's nothing I can do about it, and there's nothing the judge can do about it. He's bound to report you to the Bar Council and the Law Society.'

'Then we'll make the same argument to them,' Harriet said. She looked at Val, who nodded.

'You could be committing professional suicide,' Ben added.

Harriet shrugged. 'I think we're right, and I think Rainer, or a higher court, or someone will agree that we're right.'

'Harriet, do you really want to stake your entire future on that?' Jess asked. 'Do you, Val?'

'Yes, I do,' Val replied. 'Susan Lang is not our client any more, and we have a duty as lawyers to do the right thing.'

'I'm just hopelessly stubborn, I'm afraid,' Harriet said. 'I get it from my father. I grew up while he was a diplomat in some very dodgy places, and he taught me that when you are surrounded by villainy, you have to stand up for what you know to be right. So for me, it's a case of "here we go again".'

'Well, I admire your courage,' Ben said, after a silence, 'both of you. But let me suggest that you sleep on it tonight. I don't have to say anything to Rainer tomorrow; in fact, I can easily put it off until Thursday, perhaps even Friday morning at a pinch. Think about it. Make absolutely sure before you jump.'

56

When Aubrey arrived at the Club, Conrad Rainer was waiting for him at the same table as the previous evening. The sight unsettled him. The man was one of his two oldest friends, but he was stretching their friendship more than was comfortable, and Aubrey was feeling very conflicted. Not only had he admitted to committing more than one serious criminal offence, but he had also suggested that his life had spiralled out of control, threatening disaster not only to himself but also to anyone who got too close. Aubrey felt he was already too close, and he was being pulled even closer tonight, just by meeting Conrad again. Not to mention that he had already arranged a meeting with three barristers from whom Conrad had stolen a lot of money; and not to mention that he had already approached Gerry Pole, their mutual friend who had a house on the Isle of Wight – and a 60-foot ocean-going yacht, with all the latest technology, conveniently moored in a marina not a quarter of a mile from his house. Aubrey was a conventional man, who liked to feel he was standing on solid ground, but tonight he was beginning to feel the ground shifting beneath his feet.

'I can't do a repeat of last night, Conrad,' he said, as he took his seat. 'I had far too much to drink, and I didn't eat enough. I haven't felt well today. It's 6.30 now, and I'm going in to dinner at 7.30. You're welcome to join me if you like, but that's what I am going to do, with or without you.'

The trace of a smile crossed Conrad's face. Luke had approached. Conrad already had a glass of whisky in front of him, but Aubrey was relieved to see no trace of the bottle. Conrad raised his glass by way of request. Luke nodded.

'Just a tonic water for me at the moment, Luke,' Aubrey said. 'Ice and lemon.'

'Yes, Mr Smith-Gurney.'

'I'm sorry I kept you so late last night,' Conrad said. 'I needed to talk; I needed to tell someone all about it. Thank you for being there for me, for listening. It made a difference. I went home feeling some hope I hadn't felt for some time.'

'I'm always happy to be there to support you, Conrad, but I'm doing a bit more than just listening, aren't I?'

'Are you? I can't ask any more of you, Aubrey. It's up to you.'

Aubrey shook his head.

'We've been friends all our lives. Of course I'm going to do whatever I can to help. I have no choice. But you must understand, Conrad, I'm Queen's Counsel. There are some things I can't do, some things I can't know...'

He paused as Luke brought their drinks and exchanged the ashtray.

'There are lines I can't cross.'

'I'm asking nothing of you, Aubrey, except to listen and give me any advice you can,' Conrad replied. 'I won't be surprised if you have no more to give. If I don't know what to do, I have no right to expect you to know.'

He lit a cigarette.

'When all's said and done, I'm in this on my own. I know that. I stand to lose everything – my judgeship, my wife, my home, everything I have. I stand to end my career in public disgrace. Don't think I don't know that, and don't think I don't know it's entirely my own fault.'

Aubrey took a sip from his glass.

'Well, let's not assume the worst yet. I've been chewing it over since we talked last night, and I think it may be possible to salvage the situation. I can't guarantee it, but there may be a way. We're going to need a certain amount of luck, and you're going to have to play by certain rules from now on.'

'Discipline isn't my strong point, Aubrey, as you know only too well; never was.'

'Well, that's going to have to change if you want to survive this.'

Conrad drank, then inhaled deeply from his cigarette.

'It sounds as if you have a plan of some kind in mind.'

'It's not a plan exactly,' Aubrey said. 'It's just a matter of being realistic about where you stand. You're heavily in debt, and some of that debt is linked to serious criminal behaviour. I'm sorry to be blunt about it –'

'Be as blunt as you like. You're absolutely right.'

'You have to deal with Daniel Cleary first. You owe him a lot of money at an exorbitant rate of interest, and if you don't pay, you're very likely to come to serious harm. All right, you could go to the police, but that would have certain consequences –'

'Out of the question.'

'That's what I thought. So make sure you pay him in full every week, or month, whatever it is, and don't worry about anything else for now.'

'What if he keeps coming back for more after I've paid?'

'Then you may have to go to the police, to save your life, but let's look on the bright side for now.'

'All right.'

'Assuming you've got Cleary out of the way, then you have to deal with Reilly, Weatherall and Cohn.'

Conrad closed his eyes.

'In some ways, I'd rather deal with Cleary. I feel sick to my stomach every time I think about those little brown envelopes. If I could wind back the clock, that's the one thing –'

'You can't wind the clock back, Conrad. What's done is done. But we can talk to them about what was done.'

'Talk to them?'

'Yes. Actually, I want you to let me do the talking, at least to begin with.'

Conrad took a long drink.

'How are you going to do that?'

'I've arranged a meeting with all three of them in chambers on Thursday afternoon, after court. Stephen Phillips will be there as well, as head of chambers. He would have to know eventually, anyway.'

Conrad did not reply immediately. He extinguished the cigarette and lit another.

'What are you going to say to them?'

'I'm going to say that you got in over your head through gambling, and that you owe people a lot of money. I'm not going to mention the mortgage or Deborah's trust fund, but I'm going to have to tell them exactly what you did with their cheques, and I'm going to have to tell them about Daniel Cleary.'

Conrad sat up abruptly.

'No, for God's sake. Why do you have to tell them about Cleary?'

'Because I have to give them a reason not to go straight to the police, and I have to give them a reason to wait their turn in the queue to be repaid – to let you pay Cleary off first – and I can't think of anything else I could say that would have any chance of persuading them to agree to that. If you're feeling embarrassed about any of this, Conrad, don't. We're a long way past embarrassment now.'

'But what if they say no? What if they go straight to the police?'

'I told you we would need some luck.'

'Aubrey…'

'Conrad, how long do you think it will be before they find out? All it takes is for one of them to ask the clerk about a cheque that's gone missing. The clerk will tell the solicitor, the solicitor will check his bank records and discover that the cheque has been paid, and your chambers will have a major scandal on its hands. The solicitor will be going back over every cheque he's sent to chambers for the past ten years. How much sympathy do you think you're going to get then? I'm amazed your luck has held until now. Trust me, it's not going to last.'

He took a drink.

'We must talk to them now. And, of course, it goes without saying that you will repay them in full as quickly as you can, as soon as you've got rid of Cleary. I have to be able to tell them that, Conrad, and I have to be sure you mean it. Otherwise, I'm at risk of being an accessory after the fact to a large-scale theft, and I'm not prepared to put myself in that position. Do I make myself clear?'

Conrad nodded.

'Perfectly.'

'Do you agree?'

'Yes.'

'Good.' He paused. 'If all of that goes well – and it's a big "if" – you're left with the mortgage and the trust fund; but at least those are private matters, and even if you have to tell Deborah, at least there's a chance that they will remain private. Does that make sense?'

'Yes,' Conrad replied. 'But as you say, we're going to need a large slice of luck, and that's something I haven't had much of recently.'

Aubrey shrugged. 'That's something we can't control. We need to take charge now of the things we *can* control. That means: making the repayments; ending it with Greta once and for all; and staying away from the Clermont Club. Those are the rules from now on, Conrad, and unless you agree to play by those rules, luck won't enter into it. You will go down without a trace.'

'I had lunch with Gerry today in the City,' Aubrey went on.

'Yes?'

'I told him in general terms what has happened. I left out as much detail as I could.'

'Thank you.'

'Gerry said you are welcome to contact him whenever you need him. He asked me to tell you that he understands the situation you are in.'

'And he still has his place on the Island?'

'Yes.'

'And his yacht?'

Aubrey brought both hands down forcibly on the table top.

'That's all I have to say on that subject.'

'I was only asking –'

'That's something you will have to ask Gerry. I told you, Conrad, I'm Queen's Counsel. There are certain things I can't know.'

'Are you going to join me for dinner?' Aubrey asked, after a prolonged silence.

'No. I still have no real appetite. I'll grab a bite later.'

'You didn't eat yesterday evening either,' Aubrey said, concerned. 'You can't go on like this, Conrad. If your health suffers, you're not going to be able to push yourself through this.'

'I know. I will eat something later, I promise.'

'All right. I'll need to know all about the cheques you took from the clerk's room: cheque numbers, the amounts, whose cheque it was, and so on. Can you send the details to chambers by tomorrow evening?'

'Yes, of course.'

'Thank you. There's one more thing, if I may.'

'What's that?'

Aubrey took a deep breath.

'In the next day or so, you're going to have to make a decision about some evidence involving Daniel Cleary.'

Conrad looked up sharply.

'So you told me yesterday. What of it?'

'It's my turn to ask something of you. Please understand, it's something I would only ask in the Club.'

'Go on.'

'My former pupil, Harriet Fisk, and her instructing solicitor, a woman called Val Turner, have some evidence in Henry Lang's case which may be very important, perhaps even decisive.'

'Then, why don't they come forward with it?'

'The evidence consists of a conversation they had with Susan Lang at a time when they were her legal advisers. On the face of it, it's privileged.'

Conrad took a drink.

'I'm not sure what you mean by "on the face of it", Aubrey. Surely, it's either privileged or it isn't?'

'I've advised Harriet that the privilege should be overridden in this case.'

'Overridden? By what?'

'By the fact that Susan Lang is dead and has no further need for it, and the fact that the evidence is relevant to the defence of a man charged with a criminal offence. I can't find a rule to that effect, but *Cross* suggests that it should be the law, and...'

'And you're asking me to allow the evidence in?'

'I'm asking you not to allow Harriet and her solicitor to get into trouble for coming forward with it,' Aubrey replied. 'How you do that, I don't really care. Actually, I do think it ought to be the law, and I think you'd be doing the right thing if you gave a judgment to that effect. But whether you let the evidence in or not, Harriet and her solicitor are acting out of conscience, and they don't deserve to suffer for it.'

He paused.

'Harriet means a great deal to me, Conrad.'

Conrad nodded.

'In the circumstances, I can hardly say no, can I?'

'Yes, you can, if you wish, and it will make no difference to my efforts to help you. I can't dictate to a judge in a case I'm not involved in. I know that. I can only ask.'

57

After Aubrey had gone in to dinner, Conrad ordered another whisky and sat quietly in the lounge, drinking and smoking, for almost an hour. Finally, he pushed his glass away decisively, said goodnight to Luke, and left the Club. He stood for a moment, allowing the brisk October breeze to chill his face, before turning to his left along Pall Mall, then right on to St James's, and then left on to Piccadilly. Just before Green Park he crossed the street and made his way along Berkeley Street the short distance to Berkeley Square. Albert was in place outside number 44, ready to open the door for him, with his usual cheery words of welcome.

Conrad felt some remorse about breaking his word to Aubrey. Aubrey was a good friend, and he was doing his charming, naïve best to help. But he couldn't allow the remorse to get in the way of what he had to do. It wasn't as though Aubrey's plan was exactly foolproof; on the contrary, the path he had suggested was a minefield and even one false step would prove fatal. Aubrey was asking him to take a colossal risk, and Aubrey wasn't the one facing the exposure. The headlines in the press weren't hard to imagine. They had been dancing before his eyes for weeks now. *High Court Judge to be charged with Forgery. Top Judge stole to satisfy Mistress. Judge borrowed from Loan Shark to finance Gambling Addiction.* They would have a field day, but not just for a day, for months on end. 'Skeleton in the cupboard' didn't begin to describe it. He would be removed as a judge, prosecuted, and imprisoned – and that was before Deborah decided what to do with him. Well, at least he would have earned his place in history, but somehow that wasn't of much comfort.

Of course there was one obvious way out. But what if he still had a chance to turn things around? What if he could still beat the odds?

After so long, the odds of winning at *chemin de fer* were no mystery to him. The probability of accumulating nine points with two cards, given a full pack of cards, was a simple question of arithmetic. In all the time he had been winning and losing, that probability had not changed; it had remained a constant. The only thing that had changed was his luck. It had been bad for a long time now, but that must mean that it was due to change. That was how luck worked. It was good or bad for a while, then it changed. You had to ride it like an unruly horse, until it bent to your will. You just had to hold your nerve long enough.

And with his experience, of course, Conrad would not make the mistake of pushing it too far. He would not press on recklessly in search of sudden wealth. All he needed was enough to pay everything off. He owed a lot, but it was nothing a good night couldn't take care of. He had seen it happen. He had seen men walk away from the Clermont with twice that much after a single night's play. Once he had what he needed, he would stop. He would walk away from the Clermont, and from Greta. He would once again become what the world believed him to be. If he started with £2,000 and there were some high stakes men at the table, a few hands would see him safe.

What was the worst that could happen? He would have to raid the trust fund one last time, to make sure he could pay Daniel Cleary. The next payment was due now, and from tomorrow it couldn't be avoided. But Aubrey didn't have to know that, and it couldn't make the situation much worse. And he might walk away from his problems that very night. He might be buying Aubrey dinner the following evening to celebrate the end of the nightmare. Might? He would; of course he would. No one's luck could be that bad. He just had to believe.

He left his hat and coat in the cloakroom, and walked briskly into the Clermont. He paused at the bar for a whisky and soda. It was still early, not even 10 o'clock. He had planned it that way. It meant that the gaming rooms might still be quiet, that there might be fewer players than he would have liked, but it gave him a sporting chance of avoiding Greta. The last thing he needed tonight was Greta standing behind him, bending over him, the warmth of her body and the scent of her perfume taking his mind off the cards as she goaded him on to ever greater risks. With any luck she would not come much before midnight, if she came at all. With any luck, by the time she arrived... there was that word again: luck. He chatted to Mario, the barman, for a few minutes as he drank, and bought another drink to take with him.

He made his way upstairs just after 10.15 and, feeling suddenly exposed, looked around him awkwardly before approaching Vicente at the cash desk to exchange his £2,000 for the chips that represented his path to freedom. The Blue Room was quiet, as he had expected. Play was not yet under way, but Jean-Pascal was preparing the table; unwrapping eight new packs of cards, positioning the shoe and his rake. He exchanged greetings with the croupier, and watched him work for a few moments before standing back to survey the room.

'Lucky' Lucan was sitting by himself in a corner, reading *The Times*. Dominick Elwes was chatting to Ian and Susie Maxwell-Scott in a corner. Susie waved and blew him a kiss. In another corner, John Aspinall was listening – probably involuntarily, Conrad thought to himself with a smile – to Kerry Packer. Conrad's lips tightened. How that man had ever become a member... well, money talking, obviously. The cricket magnate's brash Australian speech was jarring, and it was non-stop – the man couldn't keep his mouth shut for a minute, not even during a game. He was a disconcerting presence at the table. Conrad was aware enough to know that it was a deliberate tactic, designed to keep his opponents off balance; but knowing that didn't make him any less difficult to deal with. It would be a better table without him, but that choice wasn't Conrad's to make. He would just have to tune Packer out. At least there was no Goldsmith tonight.

With a visible effort, Aspinall detached himself from Packer and approached Conrad, putting a hand on his shoulder.

'Evening, Conrad,' he said affably. 'How are things?'

'Oh, can't grumble, John, how about you?'

'Oh, very fair, very fair. Overworked as usual, but there we go… are you sitting in for a hand or two this evening?'

Conrad displayed his chips. 'All set.'

Aspinall had left his hand on Conrad's shoulder. He squeezed gently, and steered Conrad to the door and out on to the landing by the cash desk. Vicente immediately became intensely absorbed in some papers on the far side of the desk.

'Conrad, I hope you don't mind my mentioning this,' Aspinall began confidentially, 'but are you sure you're all right to play this evening?'

Conrad stared at him. 'What do you mean?'

'Well, it's just that… I can't help noticing – just part of being in charge of things, you know, it's the kind of thing I have to notice – but I can't help noticing that you haven't had much of a run of the cards recently. I don't want to be presumptuous, but I just want to make sure everything is all right. Greta came in last night, you know, after you'd gone, and she seemed to think – well, she seemed to think that perhaps things might be a bit difficult at the moment.'

He paused.

'We love having you here, Conrad, goes without saying. I'm just asking because I'm concerned – as a friend, you know.'

Conrad repressed a flash of anger.

'You don't want to pay too much attention to Greta, John. She doesn't know everything about me.'

'No, no, of course. I don't take her at face value. Certainly not. To be perfectly honest, Conrad, if Annabel wasn't so keen on her, she wouldn't necessarily be the kind of person we would expect to see at the Clermont –'

'No, I'm sure –'

'But she's welcome whenever she's with you, of course, goes without saying. It's just that, from what one hears, she has some rather dubious connections…'

Conrad forced himself to smile.

'Yes, I'm well aware of that, John. I keep her at arm's length, believe me. I have to, given my job and everything.'

'Yes, of course. I just wanted to make sure, you know…'

'Yes. Thank you John.'

There was an awkward silence.

'It's just that I couldn't bail you out again, Conrad, you see? You understand that, I'm sure. I have to think of the other members, and…'

From inside the Blue Room, they heard Jean-Pascal's voice.

'Gentlemen, please take your seats for *chemin de fer*.'

'Of course, I understand,' Conrad replied brusquely.

'Good,' Aspinall said, finally releasing his shoulder. 'Just wanted to make sure. Well, *bonne chance*, Conrad.'

58

Kerry Packer had taken the seat to Jean-Pascal's right, whether by virtue of a cut of the cards, or simply by choosing it, Conrad didn't know; it had happened before he came back into the room. Lucan had taken the seat to Packer's right, and to his right sat Ian Maxwell-Scott, with Susie hovering, drink in hand, behind him. Conrad took the seat to Ian's right and placed his chips in front of him. Dominick Elwes finished a confidential conversation with John Aspinall at the door of the Blue Room, and sat down on Conrad's right. Two men Conrad didn't know, who had apparently hurried upstairs from the bar when the start of play had been announced, joined to complete the table.

'The game is *chemin de fer*,' Jean-Pascal announced. 'The minimum stake is £100. Mr Packer has the bank.'

The ritual of shuffling and cutting the pack was carried out quickly.

'The bank wagers £500,' Packer called, his Australian accent a strange foil to Jean-Pascal's Parisian French. The croupier reached out with his rake and pushed Packer's chips on to the *Banque*.

Conrad took a deep breath. He was not ready to cover Packer's bet in its entirety. He ventured £100. Lucan and Elwes quickly bet £200 each, and the bank was covered.

'*Rien ne vas plus*,' Jean-Pascal said briskly.

The cards were dealt, Lucan representing the players. Packer turned over his cards, a four and a three. Lucan turned over the players' cards: a ten and a six.

'The bank wins, seven to six', Jean-Pascal announced.

Packer gave the table a huge smile.

'It's with me tonight, I can feel it. The bank wagers £1,000.'

Conrad felt the familiar churning in his stomach. This was the moment to test his luck. Packer was playing aggressively, setting out to intimidate the table. He felt instinctively that a response was called for. This had nothing to do with probability, he knew, but it might have a lot to do with the way the players bet as the game wore on. He glanced at Lucan and Maxwell-Scott. Neither seemed in a hurry to intervene.

'*Banco*,' he called out, as casually as he could. He felt, rather than saw, other players looking at him.

'Easy there, big spender,' a female voice behind him whispered softly. He turned. Susie was giving him a broad grin. 'The night is young.'

He saw her glance at her husband, who grinned back at her mischievously.

The bank's cards were a queen and a king. Packer cursed silently. The players had a three and an ace.

'The players win, four to zero,' Jean-Pascal confirmed. Suddenly Conrad was up £900. 'Lord Lucan has the bank.'

'The bank wagers £500,' Lucan said quietly.

Ian Maxwell-Scott looked as if he would intervene, but Susie was standing with a hand on his shoulder behind him, as if saying 'not yet'. He remained silent.

'*Banco*,' Conrad called.

'*Rien ne va plus*,' Jean-Pascal said.

Lucan flipped his cards over quickly: a two and a five.

With a smile, Conrad turned his over: an eight and a king.

'The players win, *La Petite* to seven. Mr Maxwell-Scott has the bank.'

'Up £1,400,' Conrad said to himself.

Susie bent her head over and kissed Ian on the forehead.

'The bank wagers £1,500.'

Jean-Pascal, sensing a shift in the mood of the table, glanced to his right. There was something troubling him, something in the atmosphere, but he couldn't quite place what it was. John Aspinall was watching from across the room. He showed no sign of concern, so the croupier relaxed. He had seen the scale of wagers escalate quickly before. He had imagined it. There was nothing to worry about. He dismissed the thought from his mind.

'*Banco prime*,' Conrad pounced.

'*Rien ne va plus*.'

The cards were turned over. The bank had seven. Conrad turned over a nine and a Queen. He was up £2,900. His luck had returned to him. It was working.

'The players win, *La Grande* to seven,' Jean-Pascal said. 'Sir Conrad Rainer has the bank.'

59

The energy had become visible to Conrad again, and he watched it ebb and flow around the table. He watched it settle on the table in front of him. It was a long time since he had felt this good about a table. He had achieved the first part of his goal: he had the bank and he was already ahead. The rest was management. Packer and Lucan had been subdued since losing control of the bank, though Packer was showing signs of coming back to life. Ian Maxwell-Scott's smile had vanished. Susie was massaging his shoulders. Now was the time to strike.

'The bank wagers £2,500,' he declared boldly.

Ian made a token wager of £100.

Dominick Elwes exchanged a look across the room with John Aspinall.

'*Banco prime*,' he said.

'I accept Mr Maxwell-Scott's bet in addition,' Conrad said.

'*Rien ne va plus*,' Jean-Pascal intoned. He dealt.

With a steady hand, Conrad turned his cards over: an ace and a four. He closed his eyes. It was a critical moment. He could either take a third card or stand at five. The probabilities were beyond his estimation now. This was sheer intuition, watching the ebb and flow. He had seen the luck settle.

'I stand,' he called after some seconds.

Conrad watched Elwes carefully as he turned over his cards: a two and a jack. Two points. Elwes smiled. He was about to gamble with £2,500 of John Aspinall's money. He relished the thought.

'*Carte.*'

A third card was dealt to him, which he flipped over: a three. A total of five. The points were equal.

There were gasps and some laughter around the table as the tension broke.

'*Égalité*,' Jean-Pascal announced. 'The wagers will stand for the next round.'

'Win one more hand and I'm up about £8,000,' Conrad calculated silently.

'Unbelievable,' Lucan said quietly.

'The bank will wager the same amount,' Conrad said.

The room was quiet for some time. John Aspinall had left his seat and was leaning against the wall to the left of the table, just beyond the door. Conrad sensed a mood of defiance around the table – just what he wanted. If his luck held, he had them. If not, it was over; but it had been over when he started, and there was no backing down now.

'*Banco prime*,' Elwes responded. He said it fiercely, as a challenge. If he'd had access to a gauntlet, he would have thrown it down.

'*Rien ne va plus*,' Jean-Pascal said. He dealt the cards.

Conrad turned over a nine and a King.

Dominick Elwes turned over a jack and a ten.

'Up, give or take £8,000,' Conrad said to himself.

'The bank wins, *La Grande* to zero,' Jean-Pascal said.

Aspinall smiled from his position leaning against the wall.

'Nicely done, Conrad,' he said.

Conrad ran away with the next eight hands. The fever, the intoxicating sensation of being in control, was upon him, and he had to struggle to keep a clear sight of his goal: enough money to get him out of the hole he was in. He was the best part of £20,000 up now. Well, he would have to contribute to the table charge, but even so, with that he would be able to pay back almost all of what he owed Cleary tomorrow. There was still the matter of the cheques he had stolen from the members of his chambers, but Aubrey seemed to think he could buy him some time there. There was still the matter of the trust fund; and there was the remainder of the mortgage. But as Aubrey had pointed out, those were not matters to attract public attention – at least, not unless Deborah was determined to unleash the full force of her anger against him. There was nothing he could do about it, if that was what she chose to do.

Rationally, he knew, it was time to quit: walk away from the table, collect his winnings from Vicente, walk down the staircase, out into Berkeley Square, wish Albert goodnight, go home. Go home. It was the only thing that made sense. He must have allowed his intention to show somehow, made some unconscious movement, gathering in his chips, moving his chair back – something – because he heard Dominick Elwes, in his irritating Mayfair drawl, comment about it being a bit impolite to pass now, without giving the table a chance to win back some of its money – isn't it, old boy? He prepared a glib answer, but before he could deliver it, he felt familiar hands on his shoulders.

He hadn't seen her come in. How could he have missed her? She must have come through the door and walked around the table right in front of him; there was no other way in. But he hadn't seen her. He had been absorbed in the table, the ebb and flow. She kissed the back of his neck.

'You're not bailing out on me, are you, darling? Not when your luck is in?'

She squeezed hard, digging her nails painfully into the hollows of his shoulders.

'You're not going to disappoint me, are you?'

He felt every eye in the room on him. She was standing directly behind his chair, taking away the option of pushing it back, unless he wanted to risk a scene. Her face was brushing against his cheek; her perfume was filling his nostrils, overwhelming his senses. Looking across the table, he saw Aspinall looking at him inscrutably. To his right, Dominick Elwes was giving him that supercilious grin of his, the grin he had always wanted to wipe off his face. The mist descended. This was his chance. He could shut Elwes up; shut Aspinall up; shut Greta up; shut them all up, and walk away. He could solve the whole problem tonight, get it over with. Let's get this done.

'The bank wagers £5,000,' he announced.

She bit him playfully on the neck and traced a line with her tongue up and under his right ear.

'That's my boy.'

The table did not respond immediately. Jean-Pascal looked up at Aspinall, who was hovering nervously. It wasn't the done thing to ask a member of the Clermont Club whether he could cover his bets, but in this instance he was thinking about it. He took too long. Before he could react, Elwes had covered the bank and the cards were being dealt. With a total of four against the players' four, he drew a third card, a jack. The players drew a five.

'The players win, *La Grande* to four,' Jean-Pascal said dispassionately. 'Mr Elwes has the bank.'

Of course, now, he had to chase his losses; no real choice about it, not with Greta standing behind him; perhaps there was no choice, with or without Greta. He had come too far along the path to let it go now. The Clermont Club would never allow a member to leave without some money for a taxi home and a cup of coffee. So he had that much to count on. But apart from that, six hands later, Conrad's money was gone. All of it.

60

It wasn't until the taxi got within striking distance of the Barbican that he realised they weren't going to Knightsbridge. That was where they always went when they left the Clermont, although at that precise moment, for all he knew then, they might have been heading for Paris or Milan. The mist was still in his eyes, making him oblivious to his surroundings. But as they approached the City, the mist was lifting, and the familiar cold touch of reality was beginning to take its place.

'Have you got anything to drink?' she asked. She had folded her arms in front of her, and was walking slowly into the living room on her high heels, gingerly, as if she did not entirely trust the carpet to support her weight.

He pointed to the bottle of scotch on the small mahogany table by the fireplace. She poured a glass for each of them, neat.

'Did they clean you out?' she asked.

He stared at her for some time. Incredibly, even now, a desire for her was stirring in him.

'Yes.'

She looked away from him.

'Do you have anything left to pay Danny?'

'Not tomorrow – or today, I should say. I will have to make some arrangements.'

She frowned, agitated.

'Arrangements again? Arrangements are not going to cut it, Conrad.'

He felt himself getting angry.

'What else can I do? I'm not a millionaire with an endless supply of money to throw around all over the place, Greta. I never have been. I'm sorry if that disappoints you.'

It was the kind of reply that, at Knightsbridge, in the past, when they had undressed, would have led to a vigorous spanking. But not tonight. She barely reacted.

'I'm not talking about me,' she replied quietly. 'I'm saying that won't cut it with Danny. Danny isn't interested in arrangements; he's interested in money, and £20,000 is a lot of money.'

'Well, he will just have to be patient won't he?' he said.

He had sat down on the sofa. She came to sit by his side.

'Conrad, do you know who Danny Cleary is? Do you know anything about him?'

He looked at her.

'Yes, I know about Cleary. His name has come up in the trial I'm doing. He's a small-time drug dealer who thinks he's big enough to be a loan shark, a big bad man who will shake people down if they don't pay.'

'He is a loan shark,' she replied. 'He's not at the top of the syndicate, but believe me, he has some very unpleasant associates, and he has some even more unpleasant people he has to report to. He can get very nasty if his clients don't pay.'

'He'd better not try to mess with me,' he said, with a burst of bravado which surprised both of them. 'I'm a High Court judge. There are security arrangements in place for people like me. Cleary doesn't know who he's dealing with. He's out of his depth.'

'Don't underestimate him, Conrad,' she replied. 'He knows some serious people.'

'*I* know some serious people,' he said.

She was on the verge of replying, but she checked herself.

'I will deal with it,' he said. 'I will deal with Cleary.'

'Oh? How will you do that? He's not the kind of man who waits for people to make arrangements, Conrad. He's going to come calling for his money today or tomorrow, or if not tomorrow, very soon, and believe me, there are no security arrangements that can protect you from him.'

'We'll see about that. It's going to be difficult for him to break my door down if he doesn't know where I live, and I'm very careful not to give out that information. He will have to find me first.'

She took a deep breath.

'I'm afraid that won't take him long,' she replied.

'What…?'

'Look, I'm sorry, but he came round to my flat last night, late, after I got home from the Clermont. He said there were rumours that you weren't going to have the money. I said I didn't know, I hadn't seen you; but he didn't believe me. And he was right, wasn't he? Aspinall told me he thought you weren't good for your debts any more, and if he told me, he's told everybody; the word is out on the street. Danny wanted to know your address. I tried to convince him that I didn't know, but he didn't believe me about that either, and he had a hunting knife with him… I'm really sorry, Conrad.'

'You gave him this address?'

'Not the number of the flat. I didn't know the number before tonight. I told him what I knew – which was that you lived in the Barbican. That was all. But that's more than enough information for Cleary, with the contacts he has.'

Conrad paced around the living room for some time. She never took her eyes off him.

'You told him where I lived?'

'Yes. It was that or get my face carved up. I'm sorry, Conrad, but that's the way it was.'

'How do you come to know someone like Cleary anyway?' he asked, after a silence. 'When you introduced him to me, you told me nothing about him, except that he was a friend.'

'You didn't ask any questions,' she pointed out. 'The man was telling you he represented a syndicate that made loans, and you didn't ask him a single question. What did you think was going on?'

'I needed the money,' he replied weakly, 'to stop you beating me up all the time.'

She shook her head.

'For a judge, Conrad, you are a very naïve man. Were you really just thinking about sex games like some frustrated 16-year-old?

Didn't you even ask yourself why I would know a man like Cleary? How do you *think* I know him?'

He shrugged.

'You seem to move in some exotic circles. I know there are people with criminal connections who like to spend their money in Mayfair. I assumed –'

'I buy from him,' she interrupted. 'He's my dealer, for God's sake.'

His jaw dropped.

'Your dealer? But I've never seen you –'

'Snort a line? In front of you?' She laughed. 'Conrad, give me some credit, please.'

'But…'

'Look, you want to know the truth? OK. I'll tell you the truth. I do cocaine, and Danny supplies me. I know who he is and what he does. I've always known. Shall I tell you how I know? Because I've been there. I've been where you are. I've been desperate for cocaine when I had no money to pay for what I'd already had. I know what it is to have Danny Ice threaten me, to lie in bed at night with the door locked, wondering whether he and his friends are outside waiting to break it down.'

She closed her eyes briefly and shook her head.

'So one night, I made a deal with him – because I had to; I had no choice.'

'A deal?'

'Yes. One night – after I'd let him into my flat before he could break the door down, as he was holding his hunting knife to my face, and explaining to me in great detail what was going to happen if I didn't have his money in 24 hours – I made a deal with him.'

'What kind of deal?'

'The only kind I could make. I offered him the only thing I had to offer to a man like Cleary.'

'Which would be what, exactly?'

'I know men, Conrad – rich men, men with money to spend and expensive habits to spend it on. Some spend it on cocaine, and some spend it on *chemin de fer*, but they all have one thing in common. They all want to take me to bed, because I give them something they don't get from their wives – excitement, adventure, real no-holds-barred sex. They all like their special treat, Conrad, and they all like to be punished severely if they let me down in my quest for excitement. So they spend their money with me, and at some point, they need a bridging loan; and as it happens, I know exactly where they can go to get it.'

He put his glass down on the side table by the sofa.

'You set Cleary up with clients?'

'I make introductions; and in return, my supply is secure, and I don't get my face carved up.'

He stood slowly.

'So I wasn't the only man you were seeing?'

She did not reply.

'And that was all I was to you? Another client for Daniel Cleary?'

She smiled.

'No. Actually, that's not all you were. I like you.'

'Oh, really?'

'Yes, really. Unlike most of the men I know, I can have an intelligent conversation with you. You are an interesting man to have dinner with. That's more than I can say for most of them. Most gamblers are very boring people, Conrad. Haven't you noticed? You're different.'

'That didn't stop you setting me up.'

'I didn't set you up, Conrad. You did that all on your own. You're not a child. You knew exactly what you were getting yourself into, you chose to get into it, and now you have to deal with it.'

He nodded vigorously. His anger was rising.

'You set me up. I'm just another of the men you sent Cleary's way. Well, you had me fooled, Greta. I have to hand it to you. I thought there was something real between us.'

His tone alarmed her. It was intense, menacing, and his face had turned a bright red. But how was any of this her fault? He was the one who had borrowed £20,000 from a loan shark.

'There was… there is…'

'Instead of which, you set me up with Cleary, and when it came time for me to pay up, you told him where to find me.'

She felt her anger rising to meet his.

'Don't put this on me, Conrad,' she replied defiantly. 'You're the one who screwed up. How much did you win tonight? Twenty? You had enough to pay Cleary off, didn't you? You had it in the palm of your hand. Why didn't you walk away?'

'Why didn't I...?'

Why hadn't he...? The mist began to descend again.

'You could have had everything you needed. All you had to do was get up like a man, pass the bank to Dominick Elwes, and you were home free.'

'With you sitting there?'

She laughed scornfully.

'Oh, so that's my fault too? It's my fault that you couldn't walk away? What did you think I was going to do? Take a ping-pong bat to you right there in front of everyone in the Blue Room? Grow up, Conrad. You're pathetic.'

Even with the mist in his eyes, Conrad had some insight, some awareness of what he was doing. This is what it must have been like for Henry Lang, he thought: knowing that he was about to do something terrible, something beyond recall; knowing also that there was in a sense a choice about it, that in a different universe it would have been possible to step back, to take time to reflect; but knowing also that the choice was not humanly possible in the face of the tide of anger rushing to the surface and engulfing him. It was certain that he would act; just as it was certain, as soon as he had struck the blow and she had instantly crashed to the floor, that she was dead. The bust of Mozart he used to kill her had stood on the coffee table, within easy reach. It was an unusual piece, made of cast iron, which he and Deborah had found in some back-street antique shop during a visit to Vienna, years ago. It was heavy, and the single blow was always going to be enough. He could tell that from the sound it made when it struck her skull, and from the expression on her face when she fell.

61

He sat on the sofa for some time, staring blankly at her body, and found himself wondering to what extent the man who had just killed Greta Thiemann – could it be Henry Lang? – had had control of his actions, and to what extent his actions had been the result of the irresistible, engulfing power of the mist. He was watching the scene and the man, as a neutral, uninvolved observer: an outsider trying to penetrate the secrets of someone else's free will; trying to analyse the problem presented; trying to follow a chain of reasoning – but losing track before he could arrive at a solution.

Then he became aware, dimly, that he was losing each line of thought as soon as it came to him; he wondered whether there was something wrong with him. He tried to go back over it. Something was wrong, felt wrong. Was he tired? Did he need to sleep? Yes, he felt as though he could sleep forever, and for a moment that thought pleased him and he tried to give way to it. But there was another physical sensation, one that seemed familiar, not from recent experience, but from something he had heard at some time. But when, and where? He couldn't quite place it, but forcing himself to concentrate with a massive effort as the shivers began to wrack his body, he remembered some words.

Dr Moynihan also noted a severe reduction in body temperature. All of those symptoms are consistent with a diagnosis of trauma-induced shock. I should add that Sergeant Miller had also observed the low body temperature, and his reaction in dealing with it using blankets and then calling for medical help was highly commendable.

That case he was trying. Henry Lang. The medical expert. What was his name? He couldn't remember, but that wasn't important.

Blankets. Highly commendable. Just as his body began to shut down, he dragged himself desperately towards the bedroom, his legs feeling as though they were made of lead, every step like wading through mud. There were two thick blankets, one on the bed, one on a chair. He seized both and, struggling to make his hands cooperate with him, he wrapped them as tightly as he could around him. The warmth of the wool comforted him, and the walk back to the living room was slightly easier. His glass of whisky was still on the side table where he had left it. He picked up the bottle as he passed the fireplace on the way back to the sofa, and once he was seated, with shaking hands, he methodically poured and drank three glasses one after the other without pausing. The shock to his body felt massive. For several moments, his breathing almost gave way and he felt that his heart was about to explode. He sat still and waited, and gradually the feeling subsided, and some warmth began to return to his body.

By the time his body and mind had recovered sufficiently to work together, and he had realised that he was not a neutral, uninvolved observer, and that he – not Henry Lang – had killed his lover, Greta Thiemann, it was almost 5 o'clock in the morning. At about the same time, he remembered that he was a judge, and that within a few hours, he was expected at the Old Bailey to continue the murder trial over which he was presiding; and he realised that he had recovered his capacity for abstract thought sufficiently to appreciate the irony of his situation. His body was exhausted. He wasn't sure he could even stand, but when he tried, it worked, and though his movements were slow and painful, he was able to walk the few steps to where her body lay. She was definitely dead, and her expression remained just as it had been when she had crashed to the floor. The bust of Mozart was lying beside her. He picked him up and replaced him on the coffee table.

Finally, approaching 6 o'clock, he felt strong enough to review his situation. Thoughts were coming to him thick and fast now: thoughts of having had almost £20,000 in his hands; thoughts of Greta being still alive. He fought to repress them. He had to concentrate on the matter in hand. He sat down and tried to force his brain to work.

Who knew that Greta was here? No one. He didn't remember bumping into any other residents when they entered the building and made their way up to his flat in the lift. Any number of people had seen them together at the Clermont Club, of course. Albert would have seen them leave together by taxi. But Albert wouldn't know where the taxi had taken them: probably wouldn't know, unless Greta (or he?) had told the driver the address as Albert was holding the taxi door open for them. He didn't know whether that had happened or not; he had no recollection of anything after losing the final hand until they were almost at the flat. What time had it been when they left the Club? At least 12.30 to 1 o'clock: had to be; so they must have arrived somewhere between 1 and 1.30. The taxi driver could identify the building, but he didn't know the flat number, and he couldn't possibly know where Greta might have gone later, after he had dropped them off. So no one really knew anything, not for certain, which was good. He could easily come up with a scenario that had her leaving his flat in the early hours after they'd had a drink. So, the main problem was that her body was still there, lying on his floor, and there was a lot of blood. By the time he had forced these thoughts into an orderly sequence, it was after 7 o'clock. He stood to look at the body again.

Looking more closely, he suddenly realised that she had collapsed on to a large rug, and that, although there was a lot of blood, it seemed to be confined to the rug, apart from a few splatters on a chair and the coffee table, and on Mozart, of course. He had no way of removing her body from the flat, and in any case, this wasn't the time to try something like that, with the residents up and about, leaving for work, with cleaners and handymen arriving to service the building. But if he could keep her on the rug, he could put the body somewhere out of the way for now, until he could think of what to do with her; and if he wiped away the blood spatters, there would be nothing to show that anything had happened. In any case, he had no intention of letting anyone into the flat, and as long as he let no one come in, he should be able to control the situation long enough to find a way out. Because now, of course, that was the only realistic goal. He had to find a way out. Not even Aubrey could argue with that now.

Just to the left of the front door there was a storage space where he kept his vacuum cleaner, his brooms, brushes and cleaning materials, two suitcases, and other odds and ends. He carefully lifted the coffee table and a chair off the rug to free it, and pulled it tentatively to see whether the body would remain in place when it was moved. To his relief, it did, although its weight was almost more than his exhausted frame could cope with. He opened the door of the storage space, pushed the cleaning materials and suitcases tightly against the walls, out of the way, and made sure there were no obstacles in his path. With luck, there should be just enough room if he could arrange the body diagonally. Bending his knees slightly to ease the pain in his back, he began to pull the rug, inch by inch, towards the door. When he was about halfway there, the phone rang.

He dropped the rug as his stomach tied itself in knots. It was 7.30. Surely no one had missed Greta yet? It wasn't possible. But if somehow…? What could he say? What was his story? They had come back to the flat together from the Clermont Club; no point in trying to deny that. They had had a drink, then she had left. Why had she left? Why wouldn't she stay? They had quarrelled; no, not that. She had said she had something to do early in the morning; but if so, why had she come all the way to the Barbican for a drink? The phone continued to ring. He had to answer. It would look suspicious if he didn't. If he wasn't at home at this time of the morning, someone might draw all kinds of conclusions. He dropped the end of the rug and walked to the telephone. He picked up the receiver.

'Conrad?' she asked.

He had to test his voice to see if it still worked.

'Yes… good morning, Deborah.'

There was a short silence.

'It took you long enough to answer the phone. Are you all right? You sound a bit strange. Are you getting a cold?'

'No, no. I'm fine. I was in the bathroom. I had to rush out when the phone rang. I'm a bit out of breath, that's all.'

'I don't want to keep you. I know you have to get ready for work,' she said. 'But I've got the builder coming round this morning to show me the plans for the new conservatory.'

'Oh, yes... is that today? I'd...'

'You don't remember, do you? Of course you don't. You never do. At times, it's as though we're living in different worlds.'

'I'm sorry, Deborah, I've got this case, this trial...'

'You've always got a case, Conrad. Anyway, look, I didn't call just to argue with you. The point is, if I like the plans and we agree to go ahead, I'm going to have to give the man a deposit. I don't know whether I can do that out of the bank account, or whether you want me to withdraw a couple of thousand from the trust fund.'

His brain froze.

'Conrad?'

'Yes, yes... no, don't bother with the trust fund. Give him a cheque. Yes, that's the best thing. There's no need to go to the fund. Give him a cheque and I'll make sure we can cover it.'

'All right, if you're sure.'

'Yes, that's fine. Call me later, after court, and tell me if you like the plans.'

'I'll call this evening. I have a meeting with Pastor Brogan this afternoon to talk about the outreach programme.'

'Call me when you can,' he said. 'I'll be back from court by 6 o'clock at the latest.'

He replaced the receiver and walked back to the rug.

62

They had brought Henry Lang up to court from the cells, and Barratt was standing by the dock talking to him. Ben and Jess were going over their notes. Andrew Pilkington walked hurriedly into court. He seemed rather out of breath.

'Morning Ben, Jess. I've had a message saying that the Pettifers are going to be late, something to do with the buses. I've asked DI Webb to send a police car to pick them up, so hopefully they won't delay us too long.'

'I wouldn't worry, Andrew,' Ben replied. 'The clerk just came in to tell us that the judge isn't here yet. He called in to say he wouldn't get to court until 11 or 11.30 at the earliest.'

Andrew looked concerned.

'Is he still feeling unwell?'

'No one knows. Apparently he didn't explain.'

Andrew nodded. 'Both the Pettifers are coming,' he said, 'to give each other moral support, but she's the one you really need, isn't she?'

'Yes,' Jess replied. 'He didn't hear anything, did he?'

'No. He's stone deaf, apparently. She says he wouldn't wake up at night if they dropped a bomb on the building; and he didn't really get to know either Henry or Susan.'

'In that case, no, I don't need him.'

'Thanks,' Andrew said. 'I'll tell him when he arrives, and he can either sit in court and not hear a word of what's going on, or he can take himself off to the cafeteria.'

'And you'll be closing your case when we've finished with her?' Ben asked.

'Yes, subject to one or two odds and ends, formal stuff, proving one or two exhibits. I take it you'll be calling Henry to give evidence? Are you going to raise this mysterious point of law of yours before or after?'

'After. The judge needs to hear his evidence before we argue it; and there's nothing mysterious about it. I have evidence that Susan Lang arranged for Daniel Cleary to threaten Henry with violence if he didn't drop his claim for custody.'

'What evidence?'

'Susan told her counsel, Harriet Fisk, and her solicitor, Val Turner, what she had done.'

Andrew thought for some time.

'I see,' he said. 'Well, it sounds like hearsay, but I'm sure you will say it goes to Henry's state of mind, so I probably won't waste the judge's time with that. But I'm not sure that Harriet or her solicitor can give evidence about it. Whatever Susan told them must be privileged, mustn't it?'

'We say not, in the circumstances,' Ben replied. 'If you look at *Cross*, you'll see where we're coming from.'

'I'll take a look at it later,' Andrew said. He glanced at his watch. 'I'm going to grab a cup of coffee. I'll let you know when the Pettifers arrive.'

'Mrs Pettifer,' Andrew began, 'would you please give the court your full name?'

'Violet Pettifer, sir.'

She was a short, plump woman with grey hair, wearing a brown coat with a grey scarf around her neck, and heavy-looking brown shoes. She was holding a pair of gloves in her hand, together with her handbag.

'Thank you. And if you don't kind my being a bit impertinent, what age are you?'

She smiled. 'I don't mind at all, sir. I'm not embarrassed about my age. I'm 67. My husband, Fred, is 69, and I'm 67. We're retired now, of course.'

'Do you live with your husband Fred in a flat at 36A Alwyne Road, London N1?'

'Yes, sir.'

'How long have you lived there?'

'Oh, a long time, sir, more than 20 years. We used to live over in Hackney years ago. Fred and I are both from Hackney originally, but we've lived in Alwyne Road, at number 36, for years now.'

'I see. Tell us a little bit about the house, Mrs Pettifer. For example, your address is 36A, isn't it, rather than just 36? How did that come about?'

'Ah, well, when we moved from Hackney, we bought the whole house, didn't we? £350 it cost us.' She laughed. 'We thought it was a fortune at the time, but it's worth a lot more than that now. Prices just seem to go up and up. It never stops, does it?'

She was looking at the jury, who were smiling and nodding sympathetically.

'I don't know where young people find the money to buy a house these days.'

'No, quite,' Andrew said. 'But did there come a time when you changed the house?'

'Yes, sir. After the children had left home, it was more space than we needed, really. So Fred converted the house into two flats, one upstairs and one downstairs. He's ever so good with his hands. Well, he was in the building trade all his life, wasn't he? He did it all himself – except for the electricity, of course. You can't take a chance with that, can you? It's too dangerous. So he got one of his mates from work, who was an electrician, to help him with that. But everything else he did himself. We thought if we lived in one flat ourselves and let the other one out, it would be a bit of extra money on top of our pensions.'

'Yes, I see. And you called one flat 36A and the other 36B. Is that right?'

'Yes, sir. The downstairs is 36A. That's where we live. We thought it was more sensible to live on the ground floor, so we didn't have to worry about the stairs as we got older. The upstairs is 36B.'

'Is it quite a large house?' Andrew asked.

'Oh, yes, sir. Even when we divided it, it made two big flats. There was plenty of room.'

'Dealing with upstairs, 36B, how many rooms does it have?'

'There's a living room and dining room combined, three bedrooms, bathroom and toilet, and a loft where you can store things. There's a nice garden at the back, too. We left part of it for whoever was upstairs, in case they wanted to grow vegetables, or flowers, or something.'

'And did there come a time,' Andrew asked, 'when you let the upstairs flat, 36B, to Henry and Susan Lang?'

Mrs Pettifer's smile disappeared and she stared down for a moment or two into the dock. Henry, as he had throughout the trial, was also looking down at the floor, and he gave no sign of recognition.

'Yes, sir.'

'When was that, do you remember?'

'I can't remember the exact date,' she replied. 'It was about a year ago, between a year and 18 months.'

'So, the girls, Marianne and Stephanie, would have been what, about seven and four when they moved in: would that be right?'

'Yes, sir.' Tears formed in her eyes, and she rummaged in her handbag for a handkerchief. 'Those poor little girls. I don't know what the world's coming to.'

'Yes. Mrs Pettifer, after the Langs moved in, did you get to know them well? I assume you must have had dealings with them as your tenants, but were you able to get to know them, or did they keep themselves to themselves?'

Mrs Pettifer considered for some time.

'I hardly ever saw Henry, to be honest. I saw him if he came down to pay the rent, or take the milk in, or leave the bins out. But even then he didn't talk very much, and most of the time he was at work. A mechanic he was, and he was gone from early in the morning until the evening. So I never saw him enough to get to know him.'

'And what about Susan?'

'I saw a lot more of her. The older girl was at school, and the younger one was either in a nursery or just starting primary school, so Susan was at home for a lot of the day. We used to talk if she came down to hang washing out to dry in the garden, and she would come into my kitchen for a cup of coffee as often as not. So I did see her quite a bit.'

'How did you get on with her?'

'Very well. She struck me as a nice young woman, friendly, and the children were lovely, poor dears.'

'Did she ever talk to you about her life?'

Jess stood.

'My Lord, I would ask my learned friend to be careful. As he well knows, whatever Mrs Lang may have told this witness about her marriage is not evidence.'

'I am aware of that, my Lord,' Andrew replied, 'and I wasn't proposing to ask the witness about the marriage…'

He paused because Mr Justice Rainer seemed to be staring down at the top of his bench. He had not reacted at all to what had been said.

Aware of the jury's questioning eyes on him, Andrew quietly moved to within whispering range of Jess.

'I'm not sure he heard any of that,' he said.

'There's something wrong, Andrew,' she replied. 'He's been like that ever since we started today, and he hasn't taken a single note of the evidence.'

Andrew nodded. He deliberately raised his voice.

'My Lord.'

This time it worked. The judge looked up.

'Yes, Mr Pilkington?'

Andrew took a deep breath.

'My Lord, my learned friend had expressed a concern that I was venturing into hearsay territory, and I was reassuring your Lordship that I had no intention of going there.'

The judge seemed to stare at him for some time.

'So, nothing you need my ruling on?'

'Not at this stage, my Lord.'

'Anything you want to add, Mr Schroeder?' the judge asked.

'Miss Farrar, my Lord,' Jess said.

'What? Oh, yes. Yes, of course, Miss Farrar.'

'I have nothing to add, my Lord.'

'Mrs Pettifer,' Andrew continued reassuringly, for the jury's benefit as well as that of the witness, 'just so that you will know what's going on, we have a rule in these courts that witnesses can tell the jury what they saw or heard themselves, but they can't tell the jury what someone else told them they saw or heard. Miss Farrar was just making sure that we keep to the rule. Do you understand?'

'I suppose so, sir. Yes,' she replied, in a tone of voice which suggested the opposite.

'Well, don't worry about it. It's up to me to ask you the right questions. Just answer the questions I ask, and we will be fine.'

'All right, sir.'

'Did Susan tell you how she occupied her time from day to day, the kind of things she liked to do?'

'Well, yes. She didn't go out much during the day. She couldn't, could she, not with the children? She'd go up to the shops, of course, and she always asked if there was anything I needed, and if there was, she would get it for me. She was very good that way. She would go up to the library to get books for the children, things like that. But she was at home most of the time.'

'And what about during the evenings?'

'Well, like I say, Henry was never home until the evening. It was often 7 o'clock or later before he got home from work, and I got the impression she wasn't too happy about that, but I think he was making good money, so she wasn't complaining too much.'

'Did you ever see Susan going out in the evenings?'

'Do you mean at weekends? They used to go out together sometimes on Friday night, the pair of them. They'd get a babysitter and go out for a drink and a curry. I looked after the children for them once or twice myself when she couldn't find anyone else.'

'I was thinking more about weeknights, after Henry got home from work. Did she ever go out then, on her own?'

Mrs Pettifer took some time before answering, and frowned.

'Well, yes, she did. But why shouldn't she? The poor girl was stuck there all day in the flat, wasn't she? And –'

'I'm not being critical of her, Mrs Pettifer,' Andrew said, aware that Jess was grinning at him. 'I'm just asking whether she went out.'

'Yes, sir. She did.'

'At what time would she go out, and at what time would she get back?'

'She would leave around 8 o'clock usually, and get back…well…'

'Was it late?'

'It would be after midnight.'

'How many times would that happen in the average week?'

'Twice, three times at most. There were weeks where she didn't go out at all, or perhaps she only went once.'

Andrew smiled. 'Forgive my asking this, Mrs Pettifer,' he said, 'but so that the jury will understand, how did you know that she was going out?'

'Well, I saw her, didn't I? You could hear when someone came downstairs, and when she went out she would wear high heels. You could tell by the noise they made on the stairs. So I would look out of the window and I would see her.'

Jess glanced in the direction of the jury, and saw that they were smiling. The judge had not reacted at all. He was still staring down.

'I wasn't spying on her, if that's what you're implying,' the witness said. 'I'm not a nosy parker. I just happened to see her.'

'Of course,' Andrew said soothingly. 'I wasn't suggesting otherwise, Mrs Pettifer. It's just that it's important for the jury to understand how you knew about her going out. Same question about her coming home.'

'I would hear her high heels going upstairs when she came home,' Mrs Pettifer replied. 'I don't sleep very well, you see; well, I haven't for years. The doctor keeps prescribing pills for me, but they never do any good. I still don't sleep, or if I do, I wake up at the slightest sound. I would wake up whenever I heard footsteps on the stairs, and I would look at the alarm clock, and it was always after midnight, usually 1 or 2 o'clock.'

'And did you ever hear any noises from upstairs after Susan had got home?'

'Yes, sir.'

'Tell the jury about that, please.'

Mrs Pettifer paused for some time. 'I heard them having words, arguing, you might say.'

'Could you ever hear exactly what they were saying?'

'Not really. You could catch the odd word. He would start on her when she came in.'

'When you say "start on her", what do mean? Why do you say that?'

'Well, I would hear her high heels on the stairs, I would hear her close the door when she went inside, and then I would hear his voice. He would be shouting at her, asking, "What time do you call this?" or "Where the hell have you been?". That kind of thing. Once or twice I heard him say she was drunk.'

'And you were able to hear that?'

'Some of the words, yes; enough to know what was going on.'

'How loudly was he speaking? Can you give us some idea? Was he talking normally, raising his voice, shouting? How would you describe it?'

'He was shouting.'

'Let me ask you this, Mrs Pettifer. Would your husband Fred be with you in bed on these occasions?'

'Yes, of course he was; he was always there, in bed with me.'

'Did Fred ever hear any of this, to your knowledge?'

She smiled.

'Oh, no, dear. Fred's as deaf as a post, isn't he? Once he's asleep, he wouldn't hear an air raid siren if it went off in the next room.'

'On these occasions, when Henry was shouting, did Susan respond?'

'Well, yes, sir, I could hear her too. But she wasn't anywhere near as loud as he was, so you could never hear what she was saying. Defending herself, I'm sure. But what she said, I couldn't say.'

'What else did you hear?'

'I heard him hit her.'

Jess saw the jury sit up in their seats.

'How do you know he hit her, Mrs Pettifer?'

'I heard him. It was like a slapping sound, two or three times usually, and she would cry out. And he was shouting when he did it, too.'

'So, you're describing the sound of a slap, is that it?'

'Yes, sir.'

'If you can tell us, Mrs Pettifer, how often did you hear him hit her?'

'I can't say how many times exactly, but it was at least once every two or three weeks. It wasn't every time they argued, but it was fairly often.'

'Is there anything else you heard that you haven't told us about?'

'No, sir. I don't think so.'

'All right. Do you remember the time when Susan Lang moved out of the flat, taking the girls with her?'

'Yes, sir, I do.'

'Did she move during the day, or over a weekend?'

'She moved on a weekday, a Monday, I think it was. A van came one morning, just after Henry had gone to work, a removal van with "Highbury Removals" or some such thing on the side; and she piled in a few suitcases and bags, took the girls, and that was it. I never saw her again.'

'Had she told you in advance that she was going to move out?'

'No, sir. But I wasn't really surprised. If you ask me –'

'I can't ask you about that, Mrs Pettifer. As I said before, we have rules of evidence.'

'Yes, sir. I'm sorry.'

'I think that's all I have. Wait there, please.'

63

'Mrs Pettifer,' Jess began, 'My name is Jess Farrar. I have a few questions for you on behalf of Henry. I won't keep you very long.'

'I'm not in a rush, dear,' Mrs Pettifer replied. 'I don't have anywhere else to go, except home.'

The members of the jury were smiling; Jess returned the smile.

'Thank you. You told the jury that you would see Susan when she came downstairs to hang washing up in the garden, and when she'd been to the shops and brought you something: is that right?'

'Yes, it is.'

'So, you would see her, what, two or three times a week to talk to?'

'I suppose so, yes.'

'On the other hand, you never really had the chance to talk to Henry, because he was always at work?'

'Yes, he was.'

'I'm not going to ask you what Susan told you; but would it be fair to say that anything you heard about their marriage came from her, rather than Henry?'

Mrs Pettifer hesitated.

'I never asked her about her marriage, Miss, it wouldn't have been polite, would it? I'm not one to pry into other people's affairs.'

'No, no, of course. But you know how it is when women get together over a cup of coffee. I'm sure you shared a few confidences now and then.'

She smiled. 'A truer word was never spoken, dear. We do like to gossip, don't we?'

'Yes, of course we do. And I'm not asking what you may have

heard about their marriage. My suggestion was that whatever you heard, you heard from Susan, not from Henry?'

'Well, yes… that's true.'

'Thank you. Mrs Pettifer, you saw Susan go out in the evenings twice or three times a week, is that right?'

'More or less, yes.'

'Leaving aside Friday nights, when she and Henry might go out together, she would go out on her own twice or three times a week?'

'Yes.'

'Leaving somewhere around 8 o'clock, and getting back as late as 1 or 2 in the morning?'

'Yes, Miss, that's true.'

'And when she went out, would it be fair to say – tell me if you don't understand this phrase – she would be "dressed up to the nines"?'

Mrs Pettifer frowned. 'I understand what you're saying, but…'

'She would wear high heels, yes?'

'Yes.'

'And a cocktail dress?'

'Yes.'

'Her hair nicely done, nice makeup?'

'Yes, quite true.'

'Mrs Pettifer, I don't mean to be rude, but people don't usually dress up like that to go out for the evening in Islington, do they?'

Mrs Pettifer thought for a moment or two.

'We did have a French restaurant once, and people dressed up a bit for that, but it only lasted a year or so. I suppose there wasn't the call for it.'

'They wouldn't dress up like that to go to the pubs near you, would they?'

She laughed. 'Oh, no, dear; not unless you wanted people staring at you.'

'It was more the kind of thing you would wear for a night out in the West End, wasn't it?'

'I wouldn't know, dear. I don't get up to the West End much these days.'

The jury laughed, and Jess joined in.

'Fair enough. But would you agree with this? She was dressing up to look sexy, wasn't she?'

Mrs Pettifer looked uncomfortable.

'Well, she was a good-looking woman. But why do you have to call it sexy just because she dressed up nicely to go out?'

Jess smiled. 'I won't press it, Mrs Pettifer. But the pattern was that two or three times a week, Henry would come home from work, and a short time later, Susan would go out, dressed up to the nines, and she wouldn't come back until the early hours. Is that what you saw?'

'I suppose so, dear, yes.'

'Mrs Pettifer, was Susan sometimes drunk when she came home in the early hours?'

The witness seemed taken aback.

'How would I know that?'

'You said that Henry would sometimes accuse her of being drunk. I wondered whether you ever saw or heard anything yourself to suggest that she had been drinking?'

'What kinds of things? I don't understand.'

'Well, you heard her footsteps on the stairs. Did she ever seem unsteady? Did she have trouble getting up the stairs? Could you hear her saying anything? Did anything ever happen that made you look out of your window?'

'No. Not that I remember.'

'When you heard her voice, was her speech ever slurred?'

'I couldn't hear her clearly enough to tell. I could hear him, but not her so much.'

'When you would see her for coffee, did she ever seem hungover, a bit under the weather?'

'She did look a bit pale some mornings, but I assumed that was just because she was tired.'

'Did she ever tell you that she was seeing another man?'

Mrs Pettifer gasped.

'What? What do you mean "seeing"? What are you suggesting?'

'I'm asking whether she ever told you she was going out with a man other than Henry?'

'No, Miss, she certainly did not.'

Jess paused.

'I'm sorry to have to ask you this, Mrs Pettifer, but do you know what cannabis is?'

She chuckled.

'Well, of course I know what it is, dear. It's what those hippies and such smoke instead of proper cigarettes, isn't it?'

Jess smiled. 'Yes, exactly. Mrs Pettifer, do you know what cannabis smells like when it is smoked?'

'No. Well, at least I don't think so. I've never known anyone who smoked it, as far as I know.'

'No, I'm sure you haven't, but did you ever smell anything from upstairs that seemed strange, something very pungent that didn't smell like food?'

The witness pointed a finger.

'Now you mention it, Miss, there was something. I thought it was just some different kind of coffee, you know, Turkish coffee or the like – not that I've ever had Turkish coffee, so I don't know really, but they say it's quite strong, don't they? I did smell something during the week sometimes, but I couldn't tell you what it was. She never smoked it in front of me. She smoked regular cigarettes sometimes, but not that cannabis, or whatever you call it.'

'Did she talk about the children very much?'

'No, not very much, come to think of it,' Mrs Pettifer replied. 'If I asked her about them, she would tell me how they were doing, but I don't remember her just talking about them for the sake of it, or showing me photographs, or anything like that.'

'And lastly, Mrs Pettifer, I want to ask you about the evidence you gave when you said you heard Henry hit Susan. You said this happened when they were arguing, after she got home late from her evenings out: is that right?'

'Yes. Not every time, but...'

'What you heard was the sound of a slap, is that right?'

'More than one.'

'All right, two or three slaps, or however many; but you were describing something you heard going on upstairs?'

'Yes.'

'Just so that the jury are clear about this, you never saw Henry hit Susan, did you?'

'I never said I did.'

'No, that's quite right, you didn't. It's just so we are clear. It's what you heard, not what you saw?'

'Yes.'

'You think you heard one person slapping another?'

'Think I heard...?'

'You couldn't see what was going on. You heard what you thought were a number of slaps.'

'Yes.'

'Let's assume for a moment that you are right about that –'

'I know what I heard, Miss –'

'You couldn't see upstairs, could you? But let's assume for a moment that you are right, that you did hear some slaps. You can't say who slapped whom, can you?'

'What...?'

'You hear a couple arguing, they're both angry, shouting at each other, and then you hear what you think are slaps. Assuming they were slaps, what I'm suggesting is that you can't say whether he slapped her, or she slapped him, can you? You weren't there.'

There was a silence.

'I heard her cry out,' she replied, after some seconds.

'Cry out, or shout?'

'Well...'

'Mrs Pettifer, did you ever see any marks or bruises on Susan?'

She shook her head. 'No.'

'Thank you, Mrs Pettifer. I have nothing further, my Lord.'

Andrew stood.

'My Lord, I have one or two short, formal matters, and I will then be in a position to close my case. After that, may I suggest that we adjourn and begin the defence case after lunch?'

'Yes, very well,' the judge replied. 'Isn't there going to be an application of some kind, a matter of law?'

'My Lord?'

'I thought someone said there was going to be a matter of law for me to decide, a matter of whether certain evidence is admissible?'

Ben got to his feet.

'My Lord, there will be a question of law, but not today. It's a matter I will raise after Mr Lang has given evidence.'

The judge nodded.

'Yes, very well. Then we will rise for lunch before you call Mr Lang.'

'I'm much obliged, my Lord,' Ben replied.

Andrew approached Ben to whisper.

'How did he know about the point of law? Did you tell him?'

Ben shook his head. 'I have no idea. He didn't hear it from me. Perhaps he's imagining things.'

Andrew grimaced. 'Great. That's all we need.'

64

Henry Lang made his way slowly from the dock to the witness box, accompanied by a uniformed prison officer. He wore the same suit he had worn in early April – it felt like a lifetime ago now – for his appearance before Mr Justice Wesley in the High Court. His hands were shaking.

He took the New Testament from Geoffrey.

'I swear by Almighty God that the evidence I shall give shall be the truth, the whole truth, and nothing but the truth.'

'Mr Lang, please give the court your full name.'

'Henry James Lang.'

'How old are you?'

'I'm 32, going on 33.'

'Mr Lang, have you ever been convicted of any criminal offence?'

'No.'

'Before your arrest, were you living at 36B Alwyne Road, in Islington?'

'Yeah.'

'Is that the flat you rented from Mrs Pettifer, the witness who gave evidence this morning?'

'Yeah.'

'Has it been your address since January of last year, 1970?'

'Yeah.'

Ben paused.

'Mr Lang, it's important that his Lordship and the jury hear what you say. Can you keep your voice up, please?'

'Yeah, I'm sorry. I'm nervous.'

'I understand, but it's important that we hear you.'

'I'll do my best.'

'Are you a mechanic by trade?'

'Yeah.'

'For how long have you been a mechanic?'

'I started an apprenticeship with Mick's Motors in Dalston when I was 16, as soon as I left school.'

'Did you work for Mick's Motors after completing your apprenticeship?'

'Yeah, they took me on, gave me a regular job, and I was with them for almost eight years, until I started my own business.'

'Your own business being Mercury Mechanics, based in King Henry's Walk in Islington?'

'That's it, yeah.'

'What sort of work do you do at Mercury Mechanics?'

'We are more of a specialised firm. We handle cars that most firms won't touch.'

'Such as…?'

'It's mostly foreign imports: your basic European models – your Renaults and such, and the higher-end European models, your Ferraris and Lamborghinis. We also get a certain number of American cars that find their way over here. We even get some of the more exotic British models, Rolls Royce or Bentley, and the odd Jag or MG, the older models.'

'That must be a bit different from the cars you worked on at Mick's Motors –'

Henry grinned. 'I should say so, yeah.'

'How did you get into that kind of work?'

'One of my mates worked for a high-end garage in Mayfair, and he was doing a bit on the side on his own account. I used to help him out at weekends. I made a few quid, and I learned a lot from him. After a while, I thought I could do just as good a job as they were doing in Mayfair and, being based in Islington, my overheads are lower, so I could be competitive on price. I got started by putting a few ads in the right kind of magazines, and once you get started, it's all word of mouth after that.'

'I understand you've been quite successful.'

'Yeah, touch wood, it's gone very well. I've got three mechanics working with me now. My foreman, Ernie, has been looking after the business while I've been in prison.'

Ben paused again.

'Mr Lang, on 28 April this year, did you stab your wife Susan Lang to death in Dombey Street, or Harpur Mews, as the prosecution allege?'

Henry looked down, and Ben saw tears in his eyes. He did not rush him.

'Yeah,' Henry replied, after some time. 'I did.'

'Thank you. What I want you to do this afternoon is to tell the jury, as far as you can, what happened before 28 April of this year, that led to what happened on that day. Let's start with how you and Susan first got together. How did you meet?'

'We met at a New Year party at my mate's parents' house in Dalston.'

'What year would that have been?'

'That would have been the end of 1960, beginning of 1961.'

'What happened at that party?'

'Nothing much happened. We were having a couple of drinks, and they had a record player, so we were dancing. It was your typical New Year's Eve party. We waited till midnight, and we drank a toast to the New Year, and did the *Auld Lang Syne* and the *Hokey-Cokey* and all the rest of it. Oh, and yeah, my mate's mother was Scottish, so his elder brother as the first-born son had to come through the door carrying coal into the house just after midnight. It's a Scottish custom, apparently.'

'What about Susan?'

'Susan was there. She was with a couple of her friends. I can't say it was love at first sight or anything like that, but we noticed each other – let's put it that way. We danced a few times, and it was obvious that we were attracted to each other. I asked how I could get in touch with her, and she gave me her phone number, and that was it, really.'

'Did you have a girlfriend at that time?'

'Not a regular girlfriend, no. There were two or three girls I took out, but no one steady.'

'Did you contact her in the New Year?'

'Yeah.'

'And did you start going out?'

'We did, yeah.'

'And soon you were going steady?'

'By about May, April or May, we were, yeah.'

'And in due course, did you agree to get married?'

'Yeah. I think I asked her in September, October, but we didn't get married straight away. We tried to save a bit of money first. We got married in the June of the following year, 1962.'

'You then had two daughters, didn't you? Marianne, who was born on 8 October 1963, so she's – well she's going to be eight on Friday as a matter of fact, isn't she?'

There was no reply. Looking up, Ben saw that Henry was weeping quietly.

'I'm sorry, Mr Lang. I know this is hard for you.'

'Too hard,' Henry breathed, after some time.

'And then you had Stephanie, who was born on 4 February 1966, so she's now five.'

'Yeah.'

'And we will come back to this, but since Susan's death, have both children been living with her parents?'

'They have, yeah.'

He was weeping again.

'I'm sorry, my Lord,' Ben said, 'but could we take a break, just for five or ten minutes, to allow Mr Lang to compose himself?'

At the second time of asking, Mr Justice Rainer agreed.

After Henry had returned to the dock and the judge had risen, Ben turned to Jess and Barratt.

'Is he taking any interest in the proceedings at all?'

'Not noticeably,' Jess replied.

'He's still not taking any notes of the evidence,' Barratt said. 'God knows how he's going to sum the case up to the jury.'

'We need to take our own notes then,' Ben said, 'as detailed as possible.'

Barratt grinned. 'I've been gripping my pen so hard I can hardly feel my right hand any more. I may have my arm in a sling by tomorrow. But don't worry. Between us, Jess and I will have it word for word.'

65

'Are you all right to continue, Mr Lang?' Ben asked.

'Yeah. I'm sorry. It's just when I think about the girls…'

'I understand –'

'But I'm all right.'

'Good. Then, let's move on. Thinking back to that party on New Year's Eve 1960, can you tell the jury what it was about Susan that attracted you?'

He shook his head. 'She seemed different, you know. She'd taken a lot of trouble over her appearance. She'd put her hair up at the back, and she was wearing a nice dress, and makeup. Her friends hadn't bothered very much at all. I remember one of them was even wearing a cardigan, but Susan looked really pretty. She was interesting to talk to, and there was something – I don't know – something a bit exotic about her: the way she talked about herself; the way she wasn't shy about talking about sex; and there was a smile she would give you when she really wanted to get your attention. I can't really describe it, but…'

'I'm sure the jury will understand,' Ben said. 'And when you were seeing each other after the New Year, did she still seem exotic?'

'Yeah. She talked to me non-stop. She used to say that she wasn't going to spend all her life in Dalston, that she wanted to move up in the world; and I could sympathise with that because I wanted to move up as well. She said she had smart friends in Chelsea who were members of the Conservative Party. She even said she might support the Conservative Party herself, which wasn't the kind of thing people said in Dalston, if you know what I mean.'

One or two members of the jury laughed, and several were smiling.

'What else did you find attractive about her?'

He hesitated.

'Don't be uncomfortable about it, Mr Lang,' Ben encouraged him. 'I want the jury to understand everything that led up to 28 April.'

'She was very open about sex,' Henry replied, after several seconds.

'Open in what way?'

'Well, the girls I'd dated before were always very shy about it...'

'Go on.'

'They might let you touch under their bra, and even lower down, if you were really lucky; and they might touch you through your trousers, you know. But that was about it. They were all so terrified that they might get pregnant somehow; everyone knew of someone that had happened to, and it was like this giant black cloud hovering over us and holding us back. We were all terrified the whole time, to be honest, and none of us really knew what we were doing. But not Susan. Susan was different.'

'In what way?'

'It wasn't that she was reckless, or that she didn't care. She was very careful indeed. But she wasn't scared, and she always seemed to know what she was doing; she was confident about it, and very matter-of-fact. She had no patience with fumbling around through layers of clothes. Susan's approach was that we would both undress and do it properly.'

'So she gave you your first real sexual experience?'

'Yeah.'

'Did she give you the impression that she had already had sexual experience?'

'She told me she had experience. She didn't make any secret of it. But it didn't matter to me because she was so exciting, and it made me feel like a grown man instead of a timid boy.'

'How was your marriage in the first years?'

'At first, it was great. I was still working at Mick's and she had a job with an insurance company somewhere near Moorgate, the same job she had before we were married. So we were all right for money, and we had a flat in Dalston. Yeah, it was going well.'

'When did you first notice a change?'

'It was after Marianne was born. We agreed that she would give up her job once we had the baby. But I noticed that she would get a bit restless at times. There was nothing wrong, as such. It was just that some of the glamour had worn off, and she was adjusting to having a baby and being in the flat all day. And I was working hard at Mick's and spending time working with my mate at the weekends, and then when Marianne wasn't much more than a year old, I was starting up Mercury Mechanics.'

'This may be an obvious question, Mr Lang, but how did that affect life at home?'

'I was working long hours. I know she got bored, being on her own so much, and then Stephanie came along, and she had two kids to cope with. And at some point – I can't tell you exactly when – she began to change. It was as if she was losing interest, and there wasn't anything I could do about it.'

'Losing interest in what way?'

'We weren't having sex much any more, and when I got home I couldn't get her to talk. It was as if the spark she had when I first met her had gone out, and I couldn't find any way to bring it back.'

'Did things change at all when Mercury Mechanics started to become successful?'

'To some extent, yeah. I was making good money, and I went out of my way to make sure she had more than enough. I encouraged her to spend some money on herself. It was ages since she had bought any new clothes, and she used to love her clothes, so I encouraged her to go up the West End and treat herself, and for a while she did, and things picked up a bit.'

'But not entirely?'

'No. It was still difficult.'

'When did she start going out on her own in the evenings?'

He shook his head and looked down for a moment.

'It was about a year before we moved to Alwyne Road. Stephanie would have been about three. She'd been helping out part-time again at the insurance company, just a few hours a week, to get her out of the house. I didn't mind that, to be honest, as long as she was happy, and it was a few quid more in her purse. But I noticed that she was changing again. It was as if she had a new life outside the home that I wasn't involved in. She started talking about having friends again, and eventually it led to the nights out.'

'How did you feel about that?'

'It's hard to say. In one way, I was pleased that she had friends she could go out with, and she was finally interested in something again. But it was her attitude. It was almost as if she was going to go out whenever she wanted, with whoever she wanted, and what I thought didn't count. She would just go upstairs, get changed, and come back down and tell me she was going out. That was it; never where she was going, or who with, or what time she would be back.'

'And what time would she be back?'

'At first it was before midnight, but before long it was 1 o'clock in the morning, or later.'

'Did that make things difficult for you?'

'Yeah. I was getting up early, 6 o'clock or sometimes even earlier, to get to work. She should have been dealing with the children, getting them up and ready to go, but she didn't want to get up herself. She was tired, and as often as not she was hung-over, and half the time I had to get the children up myself.'

'How often was this happening?'

'To be fair, before we moved to Alwyne Road, it was usually once a week, and that was it.'

'How would she dress when she went out?'

'She looked the same as when I first met her at the party back in 1960; not the same clothes, obviously, but the same look. She was taking a lot of care with her appearance, and she always wore a nice smart dress and high heels.'

'How did you feel about that, Mr Lang?'

'I wasn't happy about it, obviously. I was stuck at home after a hard day's work, and she was getting all dolled up for other people – and I didn't even know where she was or who she was with. If I asked her where she'd been when she got home, she would just say "out".'

66

'Let's talk about the move to Alwyne Road at the beginning of last year, 1970,' Ben said. 'How did that come about?'

'We both wanted to move,' Henry replied. 'With the children getting older, the place we had wasn't big enough. We needed more space. The business was doing well, and we could afford it, so we were looking around. We both liked the flat as soon as we saw it, it was close to work and school, and the Pettifers seemed like a nice couple, so we took the plunge and signed the lease.'

He paused.

'And, I don't know how Susan felt, but I hoped it might give us a fresh start, you know, new place, moving on, moving up a bit.'

'Did anything change?'

'Again, for a short time, it did seem to, but it wasn't long before she started going out on her own again, and it started happening more often. Now she might be out twice or three times a week, and I was exhausted. And there were other things I was noticing.'

'Tell the jury about that, Mr Lang.'

He breathed out sharply and shook his head.

'I knew she was drinking. I could smell it on her breath when she got home, and she would slur her words, and she was obviously hung-over in the mornings. But after a while, I started smelling cannabis on her, and there were times when I got home from work when I could smell it in the flat.'

'Did you ask her about it?'

'Yeah. She said some of the people she went out with smoked cannabis, but she didn't do it herself.'

'Did you believe her?'

'No. The smell was too strong, and as I say, I was pretty sure she was having a smoke in the flat.'

'What did you say to her?'

'I told her it had to stop. We had some pretty loud arguments about it. She always denied that she smoked, but at the same time she was saying that there was no harm in it, and everybody did it. I said I didn't want drugs in the flat, I didn't want all that going on around the children, and I was worried that we might lose our lease if the Pettifers knew she was doing drugs.'

'Did she respond at all? Did she make any changes?'

'No, she didn't.'

'Mrs Pettifer told us that she heard arguments between you when Susan came home at 1 or 2 o'clock in the morning; she said you would ask her where she had been and accuse her of being drunk. What do you say about that?'

'That's true. I'd had about enough of it, to be honest, and yeah, I did shout at her, and she would shout back, and we would have a right old go at each other.'

'Did you ever hit her?'

'No.'

'Mrs Pettifer says she heard the sound of slaps.'

'She would try to hit me sometimes. She could get herself wound up when she was drunk, and when we argued she would try to hit me. She never managed to do it, but there were times when I would put my hands up to defend myself, and she hit my hands, so it's possible that Mrs Pettifer heard that.' He grinned. 'But she must have pretty good hearing if she did. I think, more likely, Susan was feeding her a line when they were drinking coffee downstairs.'

'Did you ever strike Susan under any circumstances before 28 April?'

'No. Never.'

'Mr Lang, did there come a time when you decided that you needed to find out what was going on when Susan went out at night?'

'I did, yeah.'

'Why was that?'

'Well, as I said, I didn't like the situation, and I wanted to know who she was with. To be honest, I was worried that she was doing some other stuff, apart from the cannabis. Her eyes would look, what's the word – dilated?'

'Yes.'

'Yeah, dilated. And she was acting all hyper when she got home. It was getting out of hand.'

'What did you do?'

'I was pretty sure that one of the people she used to go out with was a friend of hers called Louise Farley. I knew Louise and her boyfriend used to drink at the Canonbury Tavern, so I went down there one night and found them, and asked Louise to tell me what was going on.'

'When was this?'

'Just after New Year, this year.'

'What did Louise tell you?'

'She didn't want to tell me anything at first, but I insisted, and her boyfriend backed me up; he said I was entitled to know, and eventually she opened up. She said it started innocently enough, with her and Susan and one or two other friends going out for a few drinks, here and there, sometimes even up to the West End, Soho. But she'd decided not to go with Susan any more because she didn't like the crowd she was hanging out with.'

'Did she tell you what she meant by that?'

'Yeah. She said they would go to bars and clubs where people would do drugs. She told me that Susan was doing drugs – not just cannabis, but cocaine as well – and that she'd been introduced to some men who were involved in dealing drugs, and other criminal stuff. She also said…'

Henry bowed his head, and the tears came again. Ben was about to offer another break, but he recovered.

'She also said that she was carrying on with at least one of these men, you know, they would disappear somewhere in the club for a while, and it was pretty obvious what was going on.'

'Did Louise mention any names?' Ben asked.

'Yeah, she gave me the names of one or two places they went, but I don't remember now. She also told me the names of some of the men she had met. One of them was known as "Danny Ice".'

'That's Daniel Cleary.' The interruption from the bench took the whole court by surprise. 'Is that who you mean, Mr Lang, Daniel Cleary?'

Henry looked questioningly at Ben, who nodded.

'Yes, my Lord.'

'A man with a serious criminal record,' the judge added, looking at the jury.

'I know that now, my Lord,' Henry replied. 'All I knew then was that he was involved with drugs.'

'Involved with drugs,' the judge said, looking at the jury again. 'Yes.'

Ben waited for some seconds in case the judge had a question, but he gave no sign of asking one. He glanced at Andrew, who shrugged and raised his eyebrows.

'Mr Lang, we know that in February this year, Susan left the flat at Alwyne Road and moved into a flat of her own in Pimlico, taking the children with her. Did she give you any advance warning of her intention to move, or take the children?'

'Not a word. I left for work one Monday morning, and when I came home she was gone, and so were the children. I don't even know where she got the money for a place of her own. It certainly wasn't from me. I had to phone her parents to find out where my children were. She wasn't going to tell me, was she?'

Ben nodded.

'Mr Lang, with everything that had gone on, everything that you've told the jury about, did it ever once occur to you to kill your wife?'

He shook his head. 'No, of course not.'

'What did you decide to do?'

'A couple of days after she left,' Henry replied, 'I went to see Geoff Bourne, my solicitor, and began divorce proceedings.'

'And did you, at the same time, make an application for custody of the children?'

'Yeah. Well, that was the main point, really. It wasn't whether we got divorced or not. I didn't care about her any more. I just wanted to make sure my children were safe – that was my first concern. I wanted them away from drugs, and away from people like this Danny Ice. I wanted them safe at home with me.'

'We will leave it there until tomorrow morning,' Mr Justice Rainer announced abruptly. 'Mr Lang, we will conclude your evidence tomorrow. You won't be able to speak to your counsel or solicitors until you have finished giving evidence.'

67

When the courtroom was almost empty, Andrew Pilkington approached.

'Ben, I'm not happy about the way this trial's going. We've got a judge who barely seems to be paying attention most of the time, and then, when he does say something, it doesn't seem to have any purpose. I don't know how he is ever going to sum up to the jury. I think we have a problem.'

'I agree,' Ben replied, as Jess and Barratt gathered round. 'But what can we do?'

'I've been giving that some thought. What if you and I ask to see him in chambers with the clerk, and tell him frankly what our concerns are? If he really is ill, he may not even be aware of how he's behaving in court. Of course, it may mean an adjournment.'

'It would mean more than an adjournment,' Barratt said. 'If it's anything serious, we would have to discharge the jury and start again in front of another judge.'

'We may have to do that in any case,' Andrew pointed out. 'If he's not capable of summing up, as the prosecutor I would have to make the application to discharge the jury myself; and frankly, I think it would be in Lang's interests just as much as the prosecution's to be tried by a judge who's in command of his faculties.'

'That's something we need to discuss among ourselves,' Ben said.

Andrew nodded. 'All right, fair enough. I'm just putting you on notice that I can't stand by and watch the trial fall apart. I'm having a conference with someone from the Director's office at

5 o'clock. I have to let them know what's going on and give the Director the chance to tell me what he thinks.'

'I'm sure the Director will leave it up to you,' Ben said. 'He doesn't dictate to Treasury Counsel.'

'It's not a question of him dictating to us,' Andrew replied. 'But there's a protocol that we have to report to him if we think there's a serious problem with a judge, particularly if it may attract the attention of the press – which it will if Rainer has some kind of public breakdown. I just wanted to let you know what I'm thinking. If you don't want to see him with me, then I'm going to have to think about whether I can allow this trial to go on. I would rather have that conversation with the judge in private, but if necessary, I will do it in open court.'

Ben nodded.

'Let us think about it overnight, Andrew, and we can talk again tomorrow.'

'All right,' Andrew said. He turned to go, but stopped, smiling. 'Jess – nice job with Mrs Pettifer.'

She smiled back. 'Thank you.'

They met in Ben's room in chambers.

'Andrew has a point,' he said. 'Provocation is not an easy thing to sum up. It's Rainer's first criminal trial, and he hasn't even been taking notes of the evidence. It could turn into a real disaster.'

'But if we have to start again,' Barratt protested, 'we lose the benefit of our cross-examinations of Cameron and Pettifer. We won't have the element of surprise the second time around. The prosecution and the witnesses will know exactly what's coming.'

Ben nodded. 'I know, but I'm not sure we have any choice. We have no idea what the jury are thinking, but in a case like this it's entirely possible that they are depending on the judge to explain the law to them, and tell them how to apply it to the evidence. If he gets it wrong and Henry is convicted, we may not get much sympathy in the Court of Appeal if we do nothing when it seems clear that the judge has lost control.'

'If we do support Andrew,' Jess said, 'perhaps we ought to do it straight away, before Henry tells everyone what happened at Harpur Mews on 28 April.'

They were silent for some time.

'That would mean seeing the judge first thing tomorrow morning,' Barratt said.

'Or just making an application to discharge the jury in court,' Ben said. 'I'm not sure I want to approach the judge in chambers. I'm thinking of the Court of Appeal again. Rainer doesn't have to discharge the jury just because we ask him to.'

'No,' Jess replied, 'but Ben, if you see him in chambers, you'll have a better chance of finding out what's going on. Whatever it is, he won't be comfortable talking about it in open court. It might be the only way. Maybe it will turn out that a visit to the doctor and a day or two off will take care of it.'

Ben turned to Barratt.

'What do you think?'

'Jess may be right,' he agreed. 'He might talk to us, and then at least we can make an informed decision about whether to call a halt or take our chances and forge ahead.'

'All right,' Ben said. 'Let's do it.'

The door opened suddenly, and Harriet Fisk entered, followed by Aubrey Smith-Gurney.

'Ah, just the people I was hoping to see,' Harriet smiled. 'Do you still need me tomorrow morning?'

'Yes,' Ben replied. 'With any luck Henry's evidence will be finished before lunch.'

'I'll call Val, then,' she said.

'Ben,' Aubrey asked, 'It's got nothing to do with me, of course, but if the judge lets you do this, have you decided whether you would call Harriet or Val, or both of them?'

'We hadn't decided that finally,' Ben replied. 'We were going to talk about it at court tomorrow, but I would have thought it would be best to call them both.'

Aubrey shook his head.

'It's not usual to call counsel as a witness about a case in which she has been engaged professionally. It's not seemly, is it? The better practice is to call the solicitor, surely?'

'I'm not concerned about it, Aubrey,' Harriet said. 'I'm not representing Susan Lang any more. As long as the court gives me cover by dealing with the privilege question, I don't have any problem with giving evidence.'

'Their evidence won't be challenged,' Jess offered. 'I'm pretty sure of that. The only point the prosecution is taking is the privilege. They're not even concerned about it being hearsay. They understand that we're only calling the evidence to explain why Henry may have been scared enough to take a knife with him on the day. I don't think the prosecution will want to cross-examine.'

'Even so…' Aubrey said.

'Let's talk about that tomorrow,' Ben suggested. 'We are unlikely to get a clean start tomorrow, Harriet, so 12 o'clock at court should be fine.'

'Why aren't you getting a clean start?'

'We may have to see the judge in chambers.'

He paused.

'Aubrey, you know Conrad Rainer, don't you?'

Aubrey seemed momentarily taken aback.

'Yes. Yes, I know him very well. Why do you ask?'

Ben hesitated.

'I'm not sure how to put it really, but there seems to be something wrong with him. He's not participating in the trial at all, and we're not sure he's even listening. You have to repeat yourself to get his attention. It's as if his mind is somewhere else, and he's not taking notes of the evidence. We think it may be a medical problem of some kind.'

Aubrey sat down in a chair in front of Ben's desk.

'Really? How odd. That doesn't sound like Conrad. But I wouldn't worry about him, Ben –'

'We have to worry, Aubrey,' Ben replied. 'We're not sure he's in a fit state to carry on with the trial. How is he going to sum up without a note of the evidence?'

Aubrey laughed.

'You obviously don't know Conrad,' he replied. 'He has a remarkable memory. He could probably reel off the evidence of every witness you've had, more or less word for word. He's one of those irritating fellows who never had to open his brief in court. He always had it all in his head.'

'I don't think he's got this case in his head, Aubrey,' Barratt replied. 'The prosecution are thinking of applying to discharge the jury, and we may have to support them.'

'Did you say you were thinking of seeing him in chambers?' Aubrey asked.

'Yes. We need to know what's going on.'

'That may be a private matter,' Aubrey said. 'I don't think it can be right to turn up in chambers and question a judge about things that are private to him.'

'We shouldn't have to,' Barratt insisted. 'If there's something wrong that makes it impossible for him to conduct the trial, he should be telling us about it without being asked. I have a client charged with murder, who's entitled to a fair trial.'

'Aubrey, do you have any idea what the problem might be?' Ben asked.

Aubrey hesitated.

'Conrad has always had his ups and downs, but it's never stopped him from performing in court. Why don't you wait for the summing-up and see what happens?'

'Because by that time, it may be too late.'

There was a silence.

'Another strange thing,' Ben said, 'is that Rainer appeared to know, or said he knew, that we were going to make an application to him to admit some evidence. We didn't tell him that.'

Harriet was taken aback.

'Did he know what the evidence is?'

'Not that he said.'

'But how could he have known about that?' she asked.

Ben shrugged, looking straight at Aubrey.

'One of the many mysteries in this case.'

68

'Do you have a moment, Aubrey?'

Aubrey looked up to see Ben leaning against the door frame, one leg crossed in front of the other.

'Come in, Ben,' he replied. 'I thought you were all going to the Dev for a pint?'

'I told the others I'd follow them.'

Ben closed the door and walked across to Aubrey's desk. Aubrey waved him into a chair.

'What can I do for you?'

'I'd like some assurance that I still have some control over my case,' Ben said.

Aubrey smiled.

'Ben, you've been around too long to believe that any of us has any control over our cases,' he replied. 'We do our best, but at the end of the day the result usually depends on forces outside our control.'

'Perhaps so. But I prefer to know what those forces are. I don't like them working behind the scenes, behind my back, where I can't see them.'

'Whatever I may have done can only benefit your client,' Aubrey said.

'I think I should be the judge of that,' Ben insisted, 'but I can't because I'm in the dark. I don't know what's been going on. I know something's going on, because Conrad Rainer knows that I'm about to apply to admit some evidence, and he didn't hear that from me. I'd like to know how that happened. I'd like to know exactly what you've told him.'

'I told him nothing that could do Henry Lang any harm.'

'I'm representing Henry Lang on a charge of murder, Aubrey. If he's convicted, he's facing a mandatory life sentence. You don't know the details of the case I'm presenting, so you don't know what might do him harm. This case is my responsibility. I want to know what's going on behind my back.'

Aubrey nodded.

'Fine. All that happened was that Harriet came to see me to explain the dilemma she was in. She was privy to a privileged conversation which might support Henry Lang's defence. She could have hidden behind the privilege and said nothing, but her conscience wouldn't let her do that. I looked into the question, and I concluded that there was a good legal argument for overriding the privilege and letting the evidence in. I told Harriet that, but I also warned her that she was playing a dangerous game. If Conrad didn't agree with her, she and her solicitor could get into a lot of trouble. She decided to go ahead anyway. I did what I could behind the scenes to protect her.'

'You mean you asked Rainer to let the evidence in?'

'No. I didn't ask him that, as a matter of fact. I asked him to make sure that Harriet didn't get into trouble. I said I didn't care how he did it.'

Ben shook his head.

'That's the same thing, isn't it? The only way to be sure of keeping Harriet out of trouble is to override the privilege and let the evidence in.'

Aubrey smiled.

'Yes, you're probably right, and I did take the opportunity of telling him what I thought the law should be. For what it's worth, I think he agrees with me, but that's not because of what I think. Conrad is more than capable of deciding the law for himself, and now that Jess has come up with an even better argument than mine, I would say you're on pretty safe ground.'

'What else have you said to him?'

'About the case? Nothing.'

Ben nodded slowly and got to his feet to leave.

'And you don't want to tell me why Rainer is acting so strangely in court – especially when someone mentions the name of Daniel Cleary?'

Aubrey closed his eyes.

'Sit down for a minute, Ben, would you?'

Ben resumed his seat.

'Have you ever thought about what privileges are?' Aubrey asked.

'What they are?'

'Yes. I mean, forget about this case for a moment, and think about privileges as a concept. Have you ever asked yourself what purpose they serve?'

'There's nothing complicated about that, is there?' Ben replied. 'A privilege is just a legal device for protecting information from disclosure.'

'Yes,' Aubrey agreed. 'Exactly. It's a legal device, and that's all it is. The privilege isn't what's important; it's the information it protects that matters. But what kind of information does it protect, Ben? Privileges protect information given by one person to another in confidence – secrets, if you will.'

'The law doesn't like secrets,' Ben said. 'They make the work of the court more difficult. They make it harder to get to the truth.'

'Quite so. That's why the law takes the view that the court should have access to all relevant information unless there's a good reason why someone should be allowed to withhold it. Privileges are the exceptions to the general rule.'

'Yes, and surely that's how it should be?'

'I don't know, Ben. Yes, we have to make sure the court has the information it needs to deal with a case. But I sometimes wonder why we have to take such a narrow view of privileges.'

'What do you mean?'

'The only privileged conversations you can have in English law are with your lawyer or your spouse. That's pretty narrow, don't you think?'

'As opposed to what?'

'Well, in America, for example, they protect communications with other professionals – clergymen, doctors, therapists. But what I'm saying, Ben, is that in this country, we don't show much respect for confidentiality. We don't encourage people to confide in others – in a friend for example – even though the need to confide is something we all feel from time to time.'

Ben nodded.

'Speaking for myself,' Aubrey continued, 'my friends have always been a very important part of my life, and I don't know what the point of friendship is unless you can tell your friends things you wouldn't want repeated elsewhere.'

'Where are you going with this?' Ben asked.

Aubrey stood and leaned on the chair behind his desk.

'You asked me whether I knew what might be ailing Conrad – why he doesn't seem to be concentrating on the case as much as he should.'

'I think I have every right to be concerned about that,' Ben said.

'I agree. All I'm saying is that there may be things Conrad has told me in confidence, things I'm not at liberty to share with you. I've known Conrad almost all my life. He's one of a small circle of my very closest friends. And while I agree that not all information can be privileged, I think we lose a good deal of the quality of our lives if we can't show some basic loyalty to our friends. That's something we all need from our friends at some point in our lives.'

Ben stood.

'Aubrey, the only question I have is whether Conrad Rainer can hold himself together long enough to finish my case. Selfish as it may seem, that's my only concern. I don't want to impose upon your friendship with him, and I don't want to interfere with his confiding in you. I don't need to know, and I'm not sure I want to know all the details. I just want to know whether Henry Lang is in safe hands.'

'As far as I can judge,' Aubrey replied, 'he's in perfectly safe hands.'

69

Conrad Rainer unlocked the door of his flat, looking warily up and down the corridor, and went inside with a sigh of relief. He had considered asking for a police escort home. There would have been no difficulty about it; the City of London police would arrange protection for any Old Bailey judge who had reason to believe that he might be in danger as a result of a case he was trying. But why he might be in danger from Daniel Cleary because of the case of Henry Lang would have been difficult to explain and might have led to some awkward questions. Instead, he made his way home on foot as quickly as he could, scanning the rush-hour crowds for any sign of Cleary, or anyone seeming to take an undue interest in him, anyone who looked like the kind of person who might work for Cleary. On arriving at his block, he waited until he was sure he was not being observed, before entering the building and running to the lifts which would take him to the sanctuary of the flat.

Having closed and locked the door behind him, he stood, leaning his back against the door for some time, getting his breath back. Everything was as he had left it: the blood spatters on the furniture and on the bust of Mozart; the empty path he had cleared to drag the rug across the floor; and the body of Greta Thiemann, propped up in the storage space.

First things first. With a massive effort, he lifted his sofa and pulled it by the end until it was in line with his front door, then pushed it, corner by corner, across the stubbornly resistant carpet until it came to rest against the door. He turned it sideways on to give the maximum area of contact. That ought to do it. Even if

Cleary gained access to the building, even if he had a key to unlock the door, or a crowbar to prise it open – in which case he would have to make some noise and draw attention to himself, and give Conrad the chance to dial 999 – the sofa would at least slow him down, make it difficult for him to open the door. Still, for good measure, he wedged the coffee table hard against the back of the sofa.

Deborah called just after 6.30.

'I'm not sure about the plans,' she said. 'I want you to look at them and tell me what you think.'

'Yes, all right.'

'I've asked the builder to come back on Saturday morning at 11 o'clock so that we can both talk to him. I take it you will be coming home at the weekend?'

He hesitated.

'Yes.'

'You don't seem too sure about it.'

'I'll come at the weekend.'

'The courts haven't started sitting on Saturdays, have they?'

'No, Deborah, we don't sit on Saturdays.'

'Thank goodness for that.' She paused. 'How is your trial going?' It was asked as a matter of formal politeness.

'Oh, fine,' he replied. 'We should get a verdict on Friday.'

'What is it he did, again?'

'He killed his wife, stabbed her a number of times with a kitchen knife.'

He heard her sniff contemptuously.

'Why would anybody need a verdict, then? Why can't you just sentence him to life in prison?'

'Because we don't know whether it was murder or manslaughter. He's saying she provoked him.'

'Provoked him? How can you provoke somebody to kill you?'

'It's not as difficult as you might think,' he replied.

He opened a new bottle of whisky, drank two glasses quickly, and foraged in the cupboards for odds and ends to eat.

Just before midnight, leaving the lights on throughout the flat, he changed out of his suit into a sweater and slacks, and lay down on top of the bed with a glass in his hand. He felt utterly exhausted, but very wide awake.

70

Lewis, a retired barrister who was the Old Bailey's most experienced court clerk, came out into the judicial corridor where he had asked Andrew and Ben to wait.

'The judge will see you now, gentlemen,' he said.

They followed him inside.

Conrad Rainer was sitting at his desk. He had put on his wing collar and bands in preparation for court. His tie and street collar lay on the desk next to a cup of coffee which was already cold. There was no sign of any of the case papers and his copy of *Archbold* was closed. He looked pale, and there were dark rings under his eyes.

'Counsel in the Lang case to see you, Judge,' Lewis said, before taking an inconspicuous seat in a chair by the door.

'Come and have a seat,' Conrad said. 'We're making quite good progress, I think, aren't we? We'll finish your client this morning, will we, Schroeder?'

'I would think so, Judge. I don't have much more for him – just the event itself on 28 April, which won't take long. I don't know how long Pilkington will need with him.'

'I won't have all that much, Judge,' Andrew said. 'It's a straightforward issue. I don't see why we can't finish with him by lunch.'

Conrad nodded.

'Good. Then we have your point of evidence, and if I agree to let it in, that will take how long?'

'It will be very short,' Ben replied. 'Half an hour at most, I would have thought.'

'I'm anxious to conclude this trial tomorrow,' the judge said. He paused. 'I have other matters to attend to next week. Pilkington, I would like to get your closing speech in this afternoon, then defence speech and summing-up tomorrow. Any problem with that?'

Andrew looked at Ben. Even with his considerable experience, he was nervous. In the past, while he had sometimes found it necessary to speak directly to a judge in court about the way in which he was conducting a trial, he had never confronted a judge in chambers about whether he was in a fit state to conduct a trial. But there was no turning back now. The Director of Public Prosecutions had given him his support, but Andrew would have to take it from there. The moment had come.

'I don't see any problem with the timetable,' he replied. 'But, Judge, the reason we're here is because Schroeder and I are concerned about the way the trial is going.'

Conrad raised his eyebrows.

'Oh? It seems to be going smoothly enough to me. Of course, I don't have your experience in criminal cases, so I may be missing something.'

'Judge, both Schroeder and I have had problems getting your attention in court, when something arises that we need your guidance on. We've both had to repeat ourselves. You give the impression of being far away, and not concentrating on the case, and we have noticed that you haven't been taking notes of the evidence. Frankly, we're worried. We don't want to pry, but it has occurred to us that you may still not be feeling well. You did mention before that you weren't feeling 100 per cent, and from the Bar it does seem that it may be affecting you. If you would like us to apply for a short adjournment, or if we should apply to discharge the jury, we would be grateful if you let us know.'

Andrew glanced quickly at Ben.

'I agree, Judge,' he added. 'Obviously, my man is charged with a very serious offence, and I am anxious that the summing-up should be as complete as possible. Provocation is not the easiest of things to sum up.'

Conrad nodded thoughtfully.

'I'm not feeling particularly well,' he replied. 'I'm not sleeping as well as I should. I've... I've suffered a... well, a bereavement, you see, and...'

'Oh God,' Andrew said at once. 'Judge, we had no idea. Our condolences, of course.'

'Of course,' Ben added. 'I'm very sorry to hear that, Judge.'

'There was no way you could have known,' Conrad said, 'and I wasn't going to mention it in open court, for obvious reasons. But you're quite right to raise it with me. I know I've been somewhat preoccupied. But I'm going to finish the trial, and I don't want to adjourn it.'

There was a silence. Eventually, Conrad smiled.

'You're worried that I may not be taking in the evidence?'

'It is the practice in these courts to take notes,' Ben replied. 'No judge can remember all the evidence in a case, especially in circumstances like this, and sometimes the small details turn out to be the most important.'

'Name me a witness,' the judge said suddenly.

'I beg your pardon?'

'Name me a witness.'

Ben looked inquiringly at Andrew.

'Mrs Pettifer,' Andrew replied.

Still smiling, Conrad nodded.

'Right. How's this? Mrs Pettifer is 67. She lives with her husband Fred, 69, at 36A Alwyne Street N1. They bought the house years ago, it was too big for them once the children were gone, so they divided it into two flats. Having been in the building trade all his life, Fred did the work himself, except for the electricity, because you can't take chances with that, can you? They live downstairs in 36A. A year or so ago, they leased 36B, the upstairs flat, to Henry and Susan Lang. Mrs Pettifer didn't really know Henry because he was at work the whole time, but she did get to know Susan because of their chats in the garden with the laundry, and over coffee in her kitchen. She heard some things about their marriage, but very properly, she was not asked what she heard. She babysat for the two girls on Fridays sometimes when the Langs went out to the pub and the Indian. Then Susan started getting dressed up rather smartly, and going out at night by herself two or three times a week, returning home after midnight. Mrs Pettifer heard her high heels on the stairs. Sometimes, she heard the Langs arguing. He would shout at her, and she thought she sometimes heard him hitting her. In February, Susan left without warning, taking the children with her.

'In a very nicely judged cross-examination, Miss Farrar got her to say that she really couldn't be sure who hit whom, and that she did smell a pungent odour coming from upstairs, which at the time she thought to be Turkish coffee – not that she has ever tasted Turkish coffee, but still – and which Miss Farrar almost got her to agree might have been the smell of someone smoking cannabis.

'I could go on...'

Andrew and Ben looked at each other. In his corner, Lewis was chuckling out loud.

'Not necessary, Judge,' Andrew replied.

'I may well need your help with the law on provocation,' Conrad said. 'I'll let you know if I do. Now, shall we get on with it?'

'How did it go?' Jess asked, as Ben and Andrew returned to the courtroom, Lewis, still chuckling, behind them. 'Are we going ahead?'

'He liked your cross of Mrs Pettifer,' Ben replied.

71

'Mr Lang, I want to ask you now about Wednesday 28 April. But before I get to the day itself, was there something that happened two days before, on Monday 26 April, which concerned you?'

'Yeah.'

'Tell the jury about that, please.'

'I was at work. It was about 10 o'clock, and this man came in and said he wanted to talk to me about getting his car serviced.'

'Was this man someone you had met before?'

'No, I'd never seen him before. He said he wanted a private chat, which usually means he wants to talk about how much it's going to cost, and whether we take cheques or accept instalment payments, and all the rest of it, so I took him into the office. But it turned out he wasn't interested in getting his car serviced.'

'What *was* he interested in?'

'He was interested in giving me a message. He said Danny Ice had sent him, and if I knew what was good for me, I would withdraw my custody application and let Susan keep the children.'

'Did you recognise the name "Danny Ice"?'

'Yeah, it was a name Louise had given me, as someone Susan had been associating with, someone involved in crime.'

'What kind of crime?'

'Well, we know that, don't we?' Mr Justice Rainer intervened.

'We know now, my Lord,' Ben agreed. 'But Mr Lang, my question is what you knew about Danny Ice when this man came to see you?'

'I only knew what Louise had told me, but she told me enough for me to believe that he was a serious bloke and he was up to no good. I didn't need any more convincing about that.'

'You took him seriously?'

'Yeah, I did.'

'Did the man who came to see you explain what he meant by if you "knew what was good for you"?'

'He didn't need to, did he? He opened his jacket, and I could see he was carrying a big knife – it looked like a hunting knife of some kind – and once he mentioned the name "Danny Ice", I knew exactly what he meant.'

'Yes, but we need to make sure that the jury are in no doubt about it. What did you think might happen to you if you didn't withdraw your custody application?'

'I believed that serious violence would be used against me.'

'Did this man give you his name?'

'No. He just said that Danny Ice had sent him.'

'Did you say anything to the man?'

'Yeah. I told him to get the hell out of my garage before I got my lads to throw him out.'

'How did he respond to that?'

'He just smiled – but he did get out.'

'Did you think about withdrawing your custody application?'

'What, and leave my children with Susan, when she was running around with people like that, and doing drugs? No, I didn't think about it; not even for a minute.'

'Let's come, then, to 28 April,' Ben said. 'Mr Justice Wesley had asked Mrs Cameron to report on the case, and she had asked you both to come to her house for a meeting at 12.30: is that right?'

'Yeah.'

'All right. I want to take things slightly out of chronological order. First of all, the jury have heard the medical evidence, which was that immediately after stabbing Susan, you experienced a form of shock, which lasted for two days. Is that right?'

'It is, yeah.'

'What effect, if any, did that shock have on your subsequent memory of the events of 28 April?'

Henry shook his head.

'I lost all memory of the events from leaving home in the morning to being in a cell at the police station when they brought me back from hospital two days later.'

'You remembered nothing at all?'

'It was a total blank.'

'Did there come a time when your memory of 28 April returned?'

'Yeah. Last Thursday evening, at about 8 o'clock.'

Ben paused.

'Mr Lang, you understand, I'm sure, that the prosecution will say it's just a bit too convenient that your memory comes back a few days before your trial begins, when you've been asked about it repeatedly, not only by the police, but also by Miss Farrar, Mr Davis and myself. What do you say about that?'

Henry nodded.

'Honestly? If it happened to somebody else, I would probably be saying the same thing as Mr Pilkington. All I can say is, that's what happened to me. It's not something you have any control over.'

'And you told us about it when we saw you the following afternoon?'

'I did, yeah.'

'How did it feel when it all came back to you?'

The tears were welling up again.

'It was horrible. I was physically sick. I didn't sleep. I lay awake all night, reliving it. If you want to know the truth, I wish it hadn't come back. If I could wipe the memory out forever, I would.'

'Even though you wouldn't be able to tell the jury what happened?'

'Despite that. Yeah.'

72

'At what time did you leave your flat on the morning of 28 April?' Ben asked.

'About 11.30.'

'How did you get to Mrs Cameron's house?'

'I walked.'

'Why didn't you drive? It's quite a walk, isn't it?'

'I just wanted to walk. You can't always park round there, and I didn't want to be worried about it. And I wanted to think about things. I wasn't sure what to do about the threat I'd received, whether to tell Mrs Cameron, you know, and I thought the walk might give me the chance to clear my head.'

'Let me ask you about that. The jury may want to know why you didn't tell someone about the threat immediately, either Mrs Cameron or the police.'

'I know. I should have done, but you have to understand: she had my children, and if I told anybody, Danny Ice knew where my children lived, and I wasn't sure any of us would be safe.'

'So what did you decide to do?'

'I decided not to tell anyone, and if Danny Ice tried anything, I would deal with it myself.'

'What do you mean, exactly, deal with it yourself?'

'Look after myself. My lads at the garage would deal with anything that happened there. They work with some pretty heavy duty tools, and it would be a stupid man that would try anything on at the garage. If it happened somewhere else, I would just have to look out for myself.'

'But if –'

'I know. Like I said, I should have told someone. But I didn't.'

Ben nodded.

'Did you take anything with you from the flat?'

Henry did not reply immediately.

'Mr Lang?'

'Yeah. I took a knife.'

'I needn't show it to you. Is that the knife the jury have seen, our Exhibit 2, one of the knives from the set in your kitchen?'

'Yeah.'

'How did you carry the knife?'

'I have a long jacket with a deep inside pocket.'

'I'm sure it's obvious to everyone,' Ben said, 'but was that a method of concealing the knife?'

'Yeah, obviously.'

'You didn't want Mrs Cameron to see it?'

'I didn't want her to see it, and I didn't want Susan to see it. We were having a meeting. I didn't need them to know that I was carrying the knife. I hoped I wouldn't need it.'

'So that the jury are clear about this, Mr Lang, did you take the knife with you on 28 April because you had already decided to kill Susan?'

'No. I would never have done that.'

'In that case, why did you take the knife?'

'Because I believed that Danny Ice was likely to use violence against me, and I needed the knife for self-defence.'

'Looking back today –'

'It was a stupid thing to do,' Henry said. 'I know that now, and if I could turn the clock back I would. But I can't.'

'How did the meeting go?' Ben asked.

'Just like I thought it would. It was a complete waste of time.'

'Why do you say that?'

'Mrs Cameron was trying her best to get us to come to some agreement, but Susan wasn't interested in agreeing, and, to be honest, neither was I. Mrs Cameron wanted to know what kind of accommodation we had for the children, how we were going to look after them, that kind of thing. She wasn't interested in the fact that they were being exposed to drugs and crime. She was more interested in whether I was working too hard, and who I was going to get to look after them when I worked late.'

'What was the atmosphere like?'

'It was all right. Susan and I were polite to each other, as much as we could be. She had the odd dig at me, but she could never resist that, and I didn't react. Most of the time, I just wanted to get out of there, so I'm sure I didn't make a great impression on Mrs Cameron, but I wanted to talk to her on her own, not with Susan there.'

'I take it that no agreement was reached, then?'

Henry shook his head.

'I would have been generous to her if she'd only agreed to let me keep my children. I would have let her see them whenever she wanted, and I would have offered her some money, maintenance, you know. But I didn't want to say that in case Mrs Cameron got the wrong idea…'

'You didn't want her thinking you were trying to buy custody of the children?'

'Yeah, and I wasn't. That wasn't my intention. It was just that I wanted Susan to see what she was doing to my children, and if she gave them back, that was all I would have asked of her. But that was the one thing she wouldn't agree to.'

73

'What happened when you left Mrs Cameron's house?' Ben asked.

Henry took a deep breath.

'We left together. I looked around. There was no sign of any trouble, no sign of any of her friends, so I thought I was all right. We were about to go our different ways, but we were still talking. We crossed over the street for some reason, towards that little mews area – I'm not sure why – and we were still talking.'

'Talking about what? What was said?'

'It was the same old stuff: I'm telling her all I want is custody; she's saying she will never give me custody; I'm saying her lifestyle is dangerous for the children; she's laughing at me, telling me to grow up. It's the same stuff we were saying to Mrs Cameron, except the gloves came off once we were on our own, and it developed into an argument.'

'How heated was it?'

'Very heated. We were both very angry, and we were both very loud. I remember thinking, someone's going to call the police if we go on like this. So I thought, this is pointless, I'm wasting my time, and I decided to leave and make my way back to work. And we had one last exchange of words.'

'I'll ask you in a moment about what was said in that last exchange of words, Mr Lang. I want to ask you this, first. Just answer yes or no. Did you say something to her, and did she say something to you?'

'Yeah.'

'After that exchange of words, what happened?'

He was silent for some time. Ben did not press him.

'I don't know what came over me. I lost all control. I wasn't aware of what I was doing. The next thing I was aware of was the knife in my hand, and there being blood everywhere, and her lying on the ground.'

'And then what?'

He shook his head.

'I slumped down to the ground and sat there, and I couldn't make my mind work, and I couldn't make my body work. I just sat there.'

'Did you intend to kill Susan?'

'I don't know what I intended. I had no control over what I was doing. One moment, she said something to me, and the next I was watching her bleeding to death.'

'Did you react to what she said to you?'

'Yeah.'

'Mr Lang, please tell the jury what was said in that last exchange of words between you.'

'I said: "Look, I can't do this any more. You can have all the men and drugs you want. Just give me my children."'

'How did she respond?'

'She said: "What makes you think they're yours?"'

74

'Mr Lang,' Andrew said, getting slowly to his feet, 'you had a visit at your place of work from this mysterious man who said he was giving you a message from Danny Ice: is that right?'

'Yeah.'

'You'd never seen this man before?'

'No.'

'And you'd never met Danny Ice, had you?'

'No.'

'And the message was: "if you know what's good for you, withdraw your custody application and let Susan keep the children?" Yes?'

'That's right, yeah.'

'So, as long as Susan got custody, you would be all right?'

'I presume so, yeah.'

'Well, that's what he's suggesting, isn't it?'

'I suppose so.'

'Did he suggest that there was a time frame involved?'

'Time frame? What do you mean?'

'Did he say you had to withdraw your application that same day, the next day, within a week, before the next hearing, or when? How long did he give you?'

'He didn't say anything about that.'

'How were you supposed to know what Danny Ice expected of you?'

'I don't know. I suppose he meant, do it as soon as possible.'

'I see. In any case, you weren't going to withdraw, however long he gave you, were you? You told us that.'

'I wasn't going to withdraw, no.'

'Did you think you were in immediate danger?'

'Immediate danger?'

'Yes. When the man left your garage, did you think to yourself, "Danny Ice could come for me at any time; I'd better take steps to protect myself immediately"?'

Henry hesitated.

'Well, let me help you,' Andrew said. 'When you left work that day, where did you go?'

'Home.'

'Did you go out anywhere after going home?'

'Yeah, I'd arranged to have a pint with the lads from the garage.'

'You went to the pub?'

'Yeah.'

'Did you take a knife with you?'

'No.'

'So, you didn't think Danny Ice was coming for you that evening, did you?'

'I don't know.'

'The next morning, 27 April, were you at work again?'

'Yeah.'

'Did you take a knife to work with you?'

'No.'

'You didn't think Danny Ice was coming for you that morning, did you?'

'I don't know.'

'And then –'

'I didn't feel the need at work. We have knives and a lot of other dangerous tools at the garage.'

'All right, fair enough, but what about on the way to work, what about on the way home?'

'I don't know.'

'But then we come to the morning of 28 April, when you're going to see Mrs Cameron, don't we?'

'Yeah.'

'Yes. And on that morning, you do take the knife with you, don't you?'

'I did, yeah.'

'Yes. And are you telling this jury that you thought Danny Ice might strike when you were going to meet your wife and the court welfare officer?'

'He might have, yeah. He knew where I would be, didn't he?'

'Two days after the man had given you the message?'

'Yeah. Why not?'

'Well, you hadn't really had much chance to withdraw, or do anything, had you?'

'I could have called my solicitor, couldn't I? That's all it would have taken.'

'Mr Lang, you're not seriously telling this jury that you thought you might be attacked in the street two days after being warned, are you? Even though the man didn't give you any time frame?'

'I did think I was in danger, yes.'

'Really?'

'Yes, really.'

'Why didn't you call the police?'

'I've already explained why not.'

'What, you thought Danny Ice might pose a danger to your children?'

'Yeah.'

'But Danny Ice's interest was in making sure Susan kept the children, wasn't it?'

'That's what the man said.'

'Yes. So there was no threat to the children, was there? The threat was to you?'

'Yeah, but –'

'The police could have solved that for you, couldn't they? They could have spoken to Danny Ice and told him they knew what was going on, couldn't they? If necessary, they could have arrested him.'

'Oh yeah, that's brilliant, that is. I would really have been for it then, wouldn't I, if I grassed him up?'

'Would you? Let's think about that for a moment, Mr Lang. You tell the police about Danny Ice, and then somebody attacks you.

It's not going to take the police long to work that one out, is it? Do you really think Danny Ice would be loyal enough to Susan to go inside as easily as that?'

'I don't know, do I?'

'Didn't it occur to you that if you told somebody that Danny Ice was threatening you, and word of that got back to Mr Justice Wesley, Susan would have some explaining to do in court?'

'I don't know.'

'Don't you? You'd already told the judge about her running around with drug dealers. You'd said that in your affidavit, hadn't you?'

'Yeah.'

'And you wanted to persuade the court that she wasn't a fit person to have custody?'

'I suppose so, yeah.'

'Yes, and this would have been proof positive, wouldn't it? It would have been just what you needed to persuade the court to trust you with the children rather than her, wouldn't it?'

'I don't know.'

'It's all nonsense, isn't it, Mr Lang? There never was a man sent by Danny Ice, was there?'

'There was.'

'Did the lads at work see him?'

Henry hesitated.

'They might have done. Like I said, he wanted to see me privately in the office.'

'But they might have seen him arrive or leave, might they?'

'Yeah, they very likely would have.'

'And no doubt we'll be hearing from the lads later, will we?'

Ben stood.

'That's not a proper question, my Lord.'

Mr Justice Rainer raised his head, but Andrew continued before he could say anything.

'My learned friend is quite right. You don't need to answer that, Mr Lang. What did this man look like?'

'Look like?'

'Yes, what did he look like? What was he wearing?'

Henry shook his head.

'I don't know. Average height, dark hair.'

'How old?'

'Thirties, forties? I don't know.'

'What was he wearing?'

'A dark jacket, I think; and blue jeans. I'm sorry. I can't remember exactly. It's been a while.'

'You never lost your memory of 26 April, the day when the man came, did you?'

'No.

'Just 28 April?'

'That's right.'

'It would have been an unusual event, wouldn't it? It's not every day someone calls on you at work and makes threats of violence, is it?'

'No.'

'You would remember exactly what he looked like, I suggest. Did he have facial hair, a beard or moustache?'

'No… no, not that I recall.'

'Was he white or black?'

'White. Yeah, white, but sort of swarthy.'

'What sort of build?'

'Average, I suppose.'

'Average, you suppose. Again, it's all nonsense, isn't it, Mr Lang?'

'No.'

'You took the knife with you because you intended to kill your wife that day, if you got the chance, isn't that right?'

'No. That's not right. I would never have done that.'

'Mr Justice Wesley had already given Susan interim custody of the children, and you were afraid you would lose them permanently because you were working too hard to look after them properly, weren't you?'

'I was concerned about that, yes. Of course I was.'

'She was running around with drug dealers, and taking drugs herself, and fooling around with other men – men involved in crime – and you'd had enough, hadn't you?'

'No.'

'You didn't trust the High Court to do it for you, and you decided to make sure that the children would come back to you. You decided to take matters into your own hands.'

'That's ridiculous.'

'Mrs Cameron thought you were obsessive about the children, didn't she?'

'I can't say what she thought.'

'They were your children, weren't they? Always *your* children?'

'They are my children, yeah.'

'And you weren't about to let this unfit mother take *your* children, were you?'

'That doesn't mean I wanted to kill her.'

'If you wanted to show the court what was going on, all you had to do was tell Mrs Cameron, or the police, about Danny Ice, wasn't it? You even had a witness – Louise – didn't you?'

Henry did not reply.

'You told the jury that you lost control because she suggested that you might not be the children's father, is that right?'

'Yeah.'

'Just that one remark made you lose all control?'

'Yeah.'

'There was nothing you could do to keep yourself from killing her?'

'I didn't intend to kill her, as far as I know. I just lost all control and lashed out, and she died.'

'She died because you stabbed her repeatedly and very violently with a knife, Mr Lang.'

'Yeah. I was holding the knife when I lashed out, yeah.'

'So at some point you must have taken the knife out of your jacket pocket. When did you do that?'

'I don't know.'

'Before she made the remark that made you lose control, or after?'

'I don't remember.'

'Do you not? Are you saying that you might have taken the knife out of your pocket even before she made the remark about the children?'

'Well, no... it must have been when I heard her say it.'

'Whenever you did it, it wasn't because Danny Ice was after you, was it? He wasn't there, was he?'

'No.'

'Mr Lang, this wasn't the first time Susan had taunted you, was it?'

'Taunted me?'

'Yes, taunted you, tried to wind you up. She was quite good at winding you up, wasn't she?'

'She was. Yeah.'

'I made a note of something you said to my learned friend Mr Schroeder, when he was asking you questions. You remember, Mr Schroeder was asking you questions about the meeting at Mrs Cameron's house, and you told him that you and Susan were polite to each other. Yes?'

'Yeah.'

'And then you said, and I made a note of this, "She had the odd dig at me, but she could never resist that, and I didn't react."'

'Yeah, that's true.'

'Well then, Mr Lang, if she was always having a dig at you, and it was something you had come to expect, and you could choose not to react, why would you lose control just because she made some stupid remark when you were in Harpur Mews?'

'It was because of what she said.'

'Really? Because of this one remark, after all the unpleasant things she had said to you over the years — and I accept that she said some very unpleasant things, Mr Lang, I'm not trying to defend her — but that one remark took away all your self-control, did it?'

'It did, yeah. You have to understand —'

'It's the jury who have to understand, Mr Lang. Why don't you explain it to them?'

Henry was silent for some time. He looked directly at the jury.

'I'd lost Susan a long time before. She'd gone off and chosen the life she wanted – away from me. I'd accepted that, and even if I hadn't, there was nothing I could have done about it. I just wanted my children, and I wanted to make sure I could keep them safe – that her way of life didn't put them in danger. My children are all I care about now. And for her to say they weren't even mine…'

He broke down and wept.

'Mr Lang,' Andrew said, 'I've almost finished. But if you need a break –'

With a huge effort, Henry recovered.

'I don't want a break. I just want you to understand what I'm saying. I didn't care what she said about me. But to suggest that they weren't even mine… the children were all I had left. That was the one thing I couldn't deal with. I can't deal with it now, and I couldn't then.'

'Mr Lang,' Andrew said, 'you took the knife with you because you wanted to finish it once and for all if you got the chance, isn't that right?'

'No. It's not right.'

'You didn't lose control over one obviously stupid remark, did you?'

'I did.'

'And when you realised what you'd done, you pretended to everyone – not only to the police, but even to your own solicitor and counsel – that you couldn't remember anything about it.'

'It was true. I couldn't remember.'

'And your memory conveniently returned four days before this trial began?'

'Yeah.'

'Thank you, Mr Lang.'

Andrew resumed his seat.

'Are you suggesting to the jury that it is not possible for a single remark to cause a man to lose self-control, Mr Pilkington?'

The judge's intervention took Andrew by surprise. He glanced at Ben, who seemed equally startled. For a second or two he found himself with no idea how to respond.

'No, my Lord,' he replied.

'That wouldn't accord with the law of provocation, would it?'

'No, my Lord, and I don't suggest that it could never happen. But I do suggest that it didn't happen in this case.'

'That's a matter for the jury to decide, isn't it?'

'It is, my Lord.'

'And they should take into account that a particularly wounding remark might well have that effect, shouldn't they?'

Andrew felt the heat rising under his collar.

'With all due respect, my Lord, it is for the jury to decide what points assist them, and what points do not assist. May I also point out that the defendant is very ably represented, and it is not for your Lordship to make points to the jury which I'm sure my learned friend will make very well when the time comes?'

'I'm merely trying to ensure that the jury doesn't overlook anything,' the judge replied. 'In the interests of fairness.'

'My Lord, I must protest in the strongest terms –'

'The court will rise for lunch,' Mr Justice Rainer said.

He left court abruptly. When he and the jury had gone, Andrew turned to Ben.

'I don't believe this man. Was I being unfair to Lang?'

'No,' Ben replied.

'Well, that's it. I'm going to ask him to discharge the jury.'

'Why? Because he said something that might possibly help the defence?' Ben smiled. 'I don't think so, Andrew.'

'It's not that –'

'Andrew: have lunch – and take a few deep breaths. I'll see you at two o'clock.'

75

When Mr Justice Rainer took his seat on the bench after lunch, Ben remained standing.

'Yes, Mr Schroeder,' the judge said.

'My Lord, I've asked for the jury to be kept out of court so that we can deal with a question of law.'

'Yes, very well.'

'My Lord, the point is this. Susan Lang was represented in the family proceedings in front of Mr Justice Wesley by a solicitor, Miss Turner, and counsel, Miss Fisk. Both Miss Turner and Miss Fisk have made witness statements, which my learned friend has seen. May I invite your Lordship to read them?'

Geoffrey took the statements from Ben and handed them to the clerk, who in turn passed them up to the judge. Ben did not sit down entirely, but leaned against the back of counsel's row while the judge read. It did not take him long. He nodded to indicate that he had finished.

'My Lord, this evidence is clearly relevant. Mr Lang says that he was threatened with violence by Daniel Cleary, and that was why he took the knife with him on 28 April. The prosecution dispute that. The independent evidence of Miss Fisk and Miss Turner is that Daniel Cleary was making threats against Mr Lang on behalf of Susan Lang. That is bound to assist the jury in deciding where the truth lies.

'The difficulty I face is that when Susan Lang said these things to Miss Turner and Miss Fisk, they were acting as her legal representatives, and on the face of it, whatever she said to them is privileged. I concede that the privilege between lawyer and client does not come to an end automatically if the client dies. But I submit that there are two reasons why your Lordship should rule that the privilege must be set aside in this case, to allow this evidence to go before the jury. I have handed up a copy of *Cross*, with the relevant passages flagged up. If I may take your Lordship through them –'

The judge shook his head.

'There's no need, Mr Schroeder. I did my homework during the lunch break. You say, firstly, that there can be no privilege because the statements Susan Lang made were in furtherance of a crime – namely threatening violence with the intention of improperly influencing the outcome of the family proceedings. Secondly, you say that I should make new law and hold that the privilege cannot be maintained where it would deprive a defendant accused of a serious crime of evidence relevant to his defence. Is that correct?'

Ben smiled. 'I couldn't have put it better, my Lord.'

'Yes,' the judge said. 'Well, I should have thought that both those arguments were plainly right. Let me hear what Mr Pilkington says about it.'

Andrew stood slowly.

'My Lord, the privilege between lawyer and client is a strong one, and there is no authority that a court can set it aside merely because it may be convenient to the parties in other proceedings.'

'Even when the evidence may be necessary in the interests of a fair trial for a man accused of murder?' the judge asked.

Andrew hesitated.

'There is no authority that allows the court to set the privilege aside.'

Mr Justice Rainer nodded.

'What do you say about the argument that the statements were made in furtherance of a crime?'

'The statements may have indicated that Mrs Lang was *involved* in a crime, my Lord, but the statements she made to her lawyers weren't in *furtherance* of a crime. In fact, quite the contrary. Telling the lawyers made it likely that something would be done to discourage her from continuing with her plan to commit the crime.'

Andrew sat down.

Ben was about to rise, but he saw the judge shake his head. It wasn't necessary for him to reply to what Andrew had said.

'I can deal with this question quite shortly,' the judge said. 'The prosecution say that I have no power to allow relevant evidence to go before the jury, even though it may make a decisive difference to the way in which the jury view the case. I would have to be given a very strong reason to keep from a jury evidence that may assist the defence in a case of murder, and I have been given no such reason.

'Mr Schroeder argues that the statements were made in furtherance of a crime, and therefore, are not privileged in the first place. Mr Pilkington agrees that the privilege would not arise if that were correct, but he says that for Mrs Lang to tell her lawyers what she had done would not have been in furtherance of the crime. Firstly, a crime was certainly involved. If the evidence is correct, it suggests that both Mrs Lang and Mr Cleary were committing the offence of blackmail and perhaps other offences, such as perverting the course of justice. Secondly, for Mrs Lang to take her lawyers into her confidence about it, perhaps hoping to persuade them to conduct the proceedings in a certain way, or perhaps to persuade them to cover up for her, seems to me to be clearly in furtherance of crime. For that reason, I do not need to set a privilege aside. There was no privilege to begin with.

'If I am wrong about that, Mr Schroeder argues that I should make new law and hold that the privilege must be set aside when it would prevent a jury from hearing evidence relevant to the defence of a man accused of a serious crime, such as murder. I am clearly of the opinion that, if that is not already the law – and it seems from a perusal of *Cross* and *Archbold* that there is at present no rule to that effect – it certainly should be the law. Professor Cross, an eminent authority on the law of evidence, seems to support that view.

'Quite apart from that, this man Daniel Cleary – or "Danny Ice", as he likes to call himself – has hung over this trial like a black cloud, and it is time to let some light back in. Cleary has an appalling criminal record for offences similar to the one he threatened to commit against Henry Lang, and it cannot be doubted that he is a wicked and dangerous man. It would be outrageous to prevent the jury from hearing independent evidence that Cleary drove Mr Lang to desperate measures at the instigation of his wife. It might very well lead to a miscarriage of justice.

'It is important to note that Mrs Lang – the client and the beneficiary of the privilege – is dead, and can have no continuing interest in the privilege. Whether the law should be the same where the client is still alive, I need not decide today, and I leave that question open. But in this case, I declare the law to be this: that, where privileged information is relevant to the defence of a man accused of a serious crime, and where it may make a difference to the jury's determination of the question of guilt or innocence, the legal privilege cannot be allowed to stand in the way of the evidence being presented to the jury. I will allow the defence to present the evidence. Let's have the jury back.'

'I'm much obliged,' Ben said.

Andrew stood again.

'My Lord, while the jury are still out, with some reluctance, I ask your Lordship to discharge the jury and order that this case begin again in front of a different judge.'

Mr Justice Rainer smiled.

'Why, Mr Pilkington? Because I have ruled against you?'

'No, my Lord. Before lunch, your Lordship intervened to question the points I was making to Mr Lang in cross-examination, in such a way as to suggest that your Lordship was taking sides. The prosecution is just as much entitled to an impartial judge as the defence.'

'I was simply drawing attention to the obvious,' the judge replied.

'Your Lordship was doing it in such a way as to discredit my cross-examination,' Andrew said. He paused. 'In addition, I am disturbed that your Lordship was able to anticipate, not only the application my learned friend Mr Schroeder was going to make this afternoon, but also the arguments he was going to present, to such an extent that your Lordship was able to research them over lunch.'

There was a silence.

'I am disturbed that your Lordship was able to do all that before he was even shown the witness statements in question. It implies that your Lordship has been receiving input into this case from some outside source, rather than relying on counsel, which, with respect, is improper.'

'Andrew...' Ben whispered.

Mr Justice Rainer did not reply immediately.

'Mr Pilkington,' he said, 'I am not going to be drawn into an unseemly argument with you. I strongly advise you to be cautious before you address a judge of the High Court in the manner in which you have addressed me. There is no basis for discharging the jury, and your application to do so is refused.'

Ben saw Andrew opening his mouth to respond.

'Andrew,' he repeated, this time loudly enough to make sure he was heard.

Andrew looked at him sharply.

Ben shook his head vigorously.

'No.'

Reluctantly, Andrew sat down.

'Jury, please,' the judge directed.

76

'Harriet still insists on giving evidence first,' Barratt whispered to Ben. 'She feels responsible.'

'But –'

'I've told her how you feel, but she's adamant.'

Ben nodded, and turned back towards the bench.

'My Lord, I call Harriet Fisk.'

Harriet seemed very composed. She was dressed in her best black suit, with a crisp white blouse and moderate heels, her hair up, held in place with an elegant silver pin. She took the New Testament from Geoffrey.

'I swear by Almighty God that the evidence I shall give shall be the truth, the whole truth, and nothing but the truth.'

'Are you Harriet Fisk, and are you a practising barrister with chambers at Two Wessex Buildings in the Temple?'

'I am, my Lord.'

Ben smiled.

'Miss Fisk, there is one matter I want to deal with straight away, so that the jury will be aware. Are you and I in fact members of the same set of chambers?'

She returned the smile. 'Yes.'

'Until her death, did you represent Susan Lang in the family proceedings in the High Court?'

'Yes, I did.'

'The jury may find it strange that you represented Susan in those proceedings, while I am representing Henry in this case. Can you confirm that it is in fact quite usual for members of the same chambers to be on opposite sides of a case?'

'Yes. Barristers are all independent practitioners, and only act on instructions from solicitors, and many firms of solicitors may retain barristers from the same set of chambers. It's quite common to have both sides of a case in chambers.'

She looked at the jury and smiled.

'We're honour bound not to sneak a look at each other's files.'

The jury chuckled.

'And I might add that your learned junior, Miss Farrar, represented Henry Lang in the family proceedings, although we're not in the same chambers.'

'Thank you. Was your instructing solicitor in the family proceedings a lady by the name of Val Turner?'

'Yes. That's correct.'

'Miss Fisk, has my instructing solicitor, Mr Davis, explained to you that his Lordship has ruled that you are no longer bound to Susan Lang by any legal privilege?'

'Yes, he has.'

'And with that assurance, are you willing to give evidence about something Susan Lang told you while you were still acting for her?'

'With that assurance, yes, I am.'

'I want to take you back to 21 April, a week before Susan Lang met her death. Do you remember that day?'

'Yes.'

'Did you do something in relation to the family proceedings on that day?'

'Yes. Miss Turner and I had a conference with Susan Lang in chambers.'

'At what time was that?'

'I recall it was just after lunch, about 2 o'clock. I wasn't in court that day.'

'Was there a particular purpose for that conference?'

'Yes. We were getting to the stage where Mrs Cameron, the court welfare officer, was making progress with her inquiries. Mr Justice Wesley had already indicated that Susan would not necessarily get permanent custody of the children, and Miss Turner and I were worried about some aspects of the case.'

'Tell the jury, please, what you were worried about.'

'Mr Lang was alleging that she was associating with criminals and taking drugs, and from our observation of Mrs Lang, we suspected that there might be some substance in those allegations. Miss Turner and I decided that we owed it to Mrs Lang to counsel her to change her behaviour if she was serious about having custody.'

'You were worried about the impression she was likely to make on Mrs Cameron?'

'Yes. And we had to tell her that if she lied to the court, as responsible legal representatives, Miss Turner and I might reach the position where we could no longer ethically ask the judge to award her custody.'

'How did Mrs Lang respond to your advice?'

'She became very defensive. She seemed to take on board what we said, but then she said that what she did in her spare time was her business, and not the court's, or ours. I concluded from this that she didn't intend to make any real changes.'

'Did Mrs Lang also say something else to you?'

'Yes. She said there was no need for us to worry, because Henry would give up his claim for custody and it would never come back before the court.'

'How did you react to that?'

Harriet shook her head.

'I remember that Val – Miss Turner – and I looked at each other. We both felt very anxious about what she had said. Giving up his claim for custody was the last thing we would have expected Mr Lang to do. It was clear from his affidavit that he was very serious about it. It didn't make sense, and it didn't sound good.'

'Did you ask Mrs Lang why she thought her husband would abandon his claim for custody?'

'Yes.'

'Please tell my Lord and the jury what she said.'

'She said that her friend, whom she called "Danny Ice", was going to warn Henry to abandon his claim for custody – or else.'

'Or else what?'

'She wasn't specific, but it was obvious what she meant. She was telling us that this man "Danny Ice" was going to threaten Mr Lang with violence.'

'No doubt you know now who "Danny Ice" is, but did you know at the time?'

'No, but the name said it all, really.'

'Miss Fisk, as responsible legal representatives, did you respond to what Mrs Lang had said?'

'Yes, we most certainly did. We told her in no uncertain terms that she was probably committing a criminal offence and could be prosecuted; not to mention that if anything like that got back to Mr Justice Wesley she could kiss any hope of custody goodbye. We also told her that we couldn't condone what she was doing, that we couldn't continue to act for her, and that we might even have a duty to inform the court.'

'What did she say to that?'

Harriet smiled grimly.

'She immediately tried to distance herself from it, saying that it was all Danny Ice's idea, and she had nothing to do with it.'

'How was the matter left?'

'Miss Turner and I didn't feel we could do any more at that stage, but obviously if Mr Lang had in fact withdrawn his application, we would have had to consider our position.'

Ben paused.

'Miss Fisk, on the first day of this trial, did you take advice from a senior member of the Bar, and did you subsequently tell myself, Miss Farrar, and Mr Davis what had happened?'

'Yes.'

'Before his Lordship had any opportunity to rule on the privilege question?'

'Yes. Obviously, I understood that the evidence I could give was relevant. I knew I was taking a risk, professionally speaking, to speak out before his Lordship ruled, but my conscience wouldn't allow me to keep quiet when I knew that Mr Lang was at risk of being convicted of murder.'

'You did the right thing, Miss Fisk,' Mr Justice Rainer said.

Harriet turned towards him.

'Thank you, my Lord.'

'Please wait there, Miss Fisk,' Ben said. 'There may be some further questions.'

'Miss Fisk,' Andrew said, 'you have no way of knowing whether Danny Ice ever did make a threat to Henry Lang, do you?'

'No. I can only say what Susan told me.'

'And she told you that he was *going* to make a threat, not that he had made one?'

'That's correct.'

'Thank you. I have nothing further.'

After Harriet had left the witness box, Andrew turned to the judge.

'My Lord, the jury will hear me say this. I have no reason to doubt the evidence given by Miss Fisk. If my learned friend wishes to call Miss Turner, of course he is free to do so, but I will have no questions for her; and I will not suggest that the jury should not accept Miss Fisk's evidence.'

Ben stood.

'My Lord, I am most obliged to my learned friend. In that case, I will not take up the court's time unnecessarily. May Miss Fisk and Miss Turner be released?'

'Yes,' Mr Justice Rainer said. 'Mr Pilkington, are you ready to make your closing speech?'

77

'May it please your Lordship, members of the jury, you've already heard from me once at the start of the trial, and I'm not going to keep you for very long now. You already know, and his Lordship will remind you when he sums up, that your choices in this case do not include a simple verdict of not guilty. Either Henry Lang is guilty of murder, or he is guilty of manslaughter by reason of provocation. Provocation means, not only that he was in fact provoked to lose his self-control by what his wife said, but also that a reasonable man in his position would have been provoked to lose his self-control. On behalf of the Crown I say that there are four very good reasons why you can be sure that the right verdict is one of guilty of murder.

'Firstly, Henry Lang had a clear motive for killing his wife. Secondly, his explanation for taking a knife with him to Mrs Cameron's house on 28 April is not credible. Thirdly, Mr Lang's suggestion that he lost his self-control because of the stupid remark he says Susan Lang made is not credible. Lastly, Mr Lang's story about losing his memory and recovering it so conveniently four days before this trial started is also not credible.

'First, the motive. Members of the jury, Henry Lang is a man who obsessed about his children, and who was obsessed with his children. You remember Mrs Cameron's evidence. It was always "his" children, wasn't it, never "our" children, or even "the" children? Mrs Cameron was worried about his obsession, so much so that she made a note of it after her very first meeting with him. She was right to be worried. Henry Lang was a man who was determined to have his children back at any cost. Mr Justice

Wesley had already awarded interim custody of the children to Susan. He simply couldn't take the risk that he might lose custody permanently, and he was ready to go to any lengths to prevent that. He wasn't going to leave the fate of his children up to the High Court, was he? He was going to take matters into his own hands. He was going to make sure that Susan Lang couldn't keep him from his children any longer.

'Members of the jury, I'm not going to pretend that Susan Lang was a perfect mother. I can't. You've heard the evidence, and you know better. Indeed, you may well have some sympathy for Mr Lang because of the way she treated him during the marriage. You may also think that it was very likely that Mr Justice Wesley would have given custody to Mr Lang if he had pursued his case. That's one of the things that make this case so tragic. Susan Lang was drinking and taking drugs, and she was associating with some very undesirable people. The prosecution don't seek to avoid that, and if the High Court had known about it, you may think that there could only have been one result. That's why we have courts, members of the jury, so that judges can make difficult decisions when people can't agree about sensitive matters such as child custody. Unfortunately, Mr Lang wasn't prepared to be patient and allow the High Court to do its work. But the law doesn't allow people to take matters into their own hands in the way he did.

'Second, his reason for taking the knife with him to Mrs Cameron's house. He told you that he had been threatened by a man who said he was speaking on behalf of Daniel Cleary. You've heard a good deal about Daniel Cleary in this trial, and you know that he is a man with a bad record, a man who might well have been capable of threatening someone. You've heard the evidence of Miss Fisk – which the prosecution don't challenge in any way – that Susan Lang said that Daniel Cleary was going to threaten Henry Lang, with the intention of getting him to give up his fight for his children. But Miss Fisk couldn't tell you that Daniel Cleary ever did such a thing, because she has no way of knowing whether he did or not. She also told you that when she and Miss Turner, quite rightly, challenged her about what she had said and pointed out the possible consequences, Susan Lang retreated very quickly and tried to talk her way out of it by saying that she had nothing to do with it and blaming it all on Daniel Cleary. But members of the jury, that doesn't make any sense, does it? Why would Cleary have threatened Henry Lang unless Susan had asked him to? Isn't it more likely that the whole Daniel Cleary story was simply made up for effect?

'Did Henry Lang really believe that he was in danger from Daniel Cleary on the morning of 28 April? He'd been out and about on the two previous days, and he hadn't taken a knife with him then, had he? What was so different about 28 April? Did he really think that Daniel Cleary would strike him down for not withdrawing his custody application only two days after he had been warned? Did he really think that Cleary would strike him down when he was meeting with his wife and Mrs Cameron? And if he did, why did he expose himself by walking the considerable distance from his home to hers, instead of driving? He said that there were sometimes parking problems in that area, but Susan managed to park there, didn't she?

'No, members of the jury: when Henry Lang carefully selected that knife from the set he kept in his kitchen, it wasn't because he was afraid of Daniel Cleary. Henry Lang had already decided to kill his wife if the chance presented itself. The chance did present itself, and he seized it with both hands – literally.

'Third, Mr Lang tells you that he lost his self-control because Susan uttered six words: "What makes you think they're yours?" A hurtful thing to say? Of course. To a man like Henry Lang it was a low blow, a disgusting thing for her to say, designed, you may think, to wound him as much as possible. If Susan Lang said that, there was no excuse for it. But, members of the jury, he told you himself, didn't he? She was good at winding him up, and he was used to it. He controlled himself during the meeting with Mrs Cameron, as he had controlled himself every day throughout the time when their marriage had begun to go wrong: when she went out at night; when she came home drunk; when she started smoking cannabis at home; and when she finally left, taking his children – *his* children – with her. Did that one remark in itself cause him to lose his self-control to such an extent that he made that frenzied attack on her? To stab her with that large knife seven times, with such severity that any one of his blows would have been fatal in itself? Or was this the opportunity he had hoped for when he carefully selected the knife before leaving home?

'Finally, Mr Lang's claim that he lost his memory of the critical events of 28 April, and recovered it only four days before trial. Members of the jury, if you're caught red-handed holding a knife covered with your wife's blood, and she's bleeding to death right in front of you, you're going to need a pretty good explanation to avoid a conviction for murder, aren't you? It takes time to concoct a story good enough to get you out of that. So Henry Lang did the sensible thing. He bought himself some time. He told the police, and he told his own lawyers, that he couldn't remember anything at all. They repeatedly confronted him with the facts, and still he said he couldn't remember.

'And then, four days before the trial, hey presto, his memory returns. It's simply not believable, is it, members of the jury? And the story he concocted during all those long days awaiting trial isn't believable. The truth is that he made use of the time to come up with a story he thinks will buy him some sympathy in your eyes. But that's all it is – a story.

'Members of the jury, the only verdict that makes sense is that Henry Lang is guilty of the brutal, premeditated murder of his wife, and it is your duty to say so by your verdict.'

When the judge and jury had left for the day, and the courtroom was quiet, Andrew approached Ben and Jess, who were gathering up their papers.

'Thank you,' he said to Ben.

Ben looked at him inquiringly.

'For stopping me when I was about to go too far with the judge.'

Ben smiled. 'I've never seen you in that mood before,' he said. 'You are always so calm and collected. Rainer is really getting to you, isn't he?'

'There's something wrong, Ben. I can't put my finger on it, but there's something not right.' He paused. 'Anyway, it's looking good for Mr Lang. I'm sure you are happy about that.'

'You think so?' Jess asked. 'I'm not so sure. That was a convincing closing speech.'

'Thank you,' Andrew replied. 'But I think the judge is going to do his best to row him out.'

'I'm not sure we want that,' Ben said. 'You know as well as I do: if a judge goes too far in one direction, it often drives the jury the other way.'

'Not in this case.'

'Why not?' Barratt asked.

'Sympathy,' Andrew replied. 'Some of the jurors are going to put themselves in Henry Lang's position, and say, "You know what? I might have done the same thing."'

78

Aubrey Smith-Gurney finished his tea and checked his watch: 4.30, time to leave for an appointment he was dreading.

Aubrey had a wide acquaintanceship at the Bar, but while he knew Stephen Phillips as an opponent in one or two cases, he did not know any of the three members of Phillips' chambers from whom Conrad Rainer had stolen so blatantly. Now he had to meet them on their home ground, and he had to ask a lot of them. What made it worse was that, in their position, he knew, he wouldn't agree to what he was going to propose. If he had not given Conrad Rainer his word he would have called it off, but it was too late for that now. Reluctantly, he picked up his briefcase, left his room, and made his way down the building's main staircase and out of chambers. Slowly, with the air of a man carrying a huge burden, he walked up Middle Temple Lane and turned right into the Inner Temple towards Crown Office Row.

The senior clerk greeted him when he arrived and took him to Stephen Phillips' room, where Frank Reilly, Jonathan Weatherall and Martin Cohn were already waiting with Phillips. He declined the offer of tea, and the clerk left discreetly. Phillips waved him into an armchair. Aubrey sat down and put his briefcase on the floor beside him.

'Do you know these fellows, Aubrey?' Phillips asked. 'Left to right, Martin, Jonathan and Frank.'

'No, I don't think so. I'm sure we've seen each other around the Temple, but not in court as far as I remember. Aubrey Smith-Gurney. I'm in Two Wessex Buildings, Gareth Morgan-Davies' set.'

'Bernard Wesley's set before he went on the bench?' Martin Cohn asked.

'Yes, that's right.'

'I thought so. I've had a long-running saga in the Family Division against Kenneth Gaskell. He's in your set, isn't he?'

'He is, indeed.'

'*Johnson v Lambeth Borough Council*, wasn't it, Aubrey?' Phillips asked. 'That was the last time we saw each other in court, I think. I thought the Court of Appeal had rather an off day myself, but I'm sure you were pleased with the result.'

'Pleased and rather surprised,' Aubrey smiled, 'an all-too rare experience for me, I'm afraid.'

'You always were too modest, Aubrey,' Phillips replied. 'Anyway, down to business: what can we do for you?'

Aubrey swallowed hard and took a deep breath.

'I'm here to ask for your help,' he replied, 'and I know it's not going to be easy. I have to tell you about something that has happened, and ask you to try to understand it. It involves Conrad Rainer, who is a very old and dear friend of mine.'

The mention of Rainer's name produced smiles.

'How is Conrad?' Jonathan Weatherall asked. 'We haven't seen him in chambers since he was appointed. Is he still the life and soul of every party in town?'

'Not every party in town, surely,' Frank Reilly insisted, 'only the fashionable ones – at Annabel's and the like.'

'He's well enough, physically,' Aubrey replied, 'but I'm afraid his lifestyle has rather caught up with him.'

There was some laughter.

'Well, that was only a matter of time,' Reilly said. 'There are only so many hangovers the body can take before it starts to fall apart.'

'It's not a matter of drink,' Aubrey said, 'or perhaps I should say, that's not the main problem. To be perfectly candid, he's got himself into a lot of trouble. Conrad has a gambling habit.'

Glances were exchanged around the room, but this time there was no laughter.

'We all know that,' Reilly said.

'I'm sure you do. What you probably don't know is that over the last year or two it's got worse; in fact, it's safe to say that it's become an addiction, and it's got out of control.'

'Are you saying he's lost money?' Phillips asked, after a silence.

'A great deal of money, I'm afraid,' Aubrey replied.

Weatherall shrugged.

'And this is our problem because...?'

Aubrey paused.

'That's quite a long story, Jonathan. I'll try to keep it as short as I can.'

'Take your time,' Phillips said.

Aubrey nodded.

'Conrad, shall we say, fell into bad company and started gambling on a regular basis at an establishment called the Clermont Club.'

Weatherall nodded. 'John Aspinall's place, upstairs from Annabel's.'

'Yes. He played a card game called *chemin de fer*. I won't go into detail about the game unless you want me to. Suffice it to say that it's a game of chance with not much skill involved, and you can lose a fair bit of money in an evening if your luck isn't good. Over the course of time, no one's luck is all that good, and Conrad was no exception. He lost money – a lot of money. To be perfectly frank, I'm not even sure of the exact amount. He didn't add it all up for me, and I didn't press him. But from what he has told me, I'm sure it must be at least £30,000, and it may be significantly more than that.'

'I'm still not seeing what that has to do with us,' Weatherall said.

'I'm coming to that,' Aubrey replied.

He made a massive effort to put the mortgage and Deborah's trust fund out of his mind.

'When you're addicted to gambling and your luck has deserted you, you look around for sources of funding to chase your losses. It's not a sensible thing to do, obviously. The sensible thing is to cut your losses and give it up, but when you're an addict, you don't think sensibly.

'So Conrad was looking around for a supply of money and he

was introduced to a man who offered to provide it. This man told Conrad that he was part of a syndicate that made loans to people in his position.'

'You're joking,' Reilly said.

'I'm afraid not. I need hardly add that this man has connections to organised crime, and in fact, I happen to know that he has a record for violence.'

There was a silence.

'What was he thinking?' Cohn asked.

'He wasn't thinking,' Aubrey replied, 'at least, not rationally. That's the point I'm trying to make. He was thinking like an addict. Obviously, someone with Conrad's experience of the law wouldn't touch a loan like that if he was in his right mind. The syndicate charges a massive amount of interest and, if you don't pay, they don't take you to court. They have more direct methods of debt collection.'

'How much did he borrow?' Phillips asked.

'He tells me £20,000.'

There were gasps around the room.

'In addition to what he had already lost?'

'Yes. Needless to say, although that kept him afloat for some time, his luck didn't get any better.'

'Has he lost it all?'

'No. I don't think so. He came to me for help earlier this week, and he still had some of that money left, though probably not very much. Of course, I told him that everything depended on his staying away from the Clermont Club, and away from the bad company he was in. That was a condition of my support. I think he understood and he promised me that he would stop immediately.'

'Do you believe him?' Reilly asked.

'Yes. I think he has finally come to terms with the position he's in. He realises that it's gambling that has brought him to that position, and I think he wants to do something about it. Well, he has to. He has no choice. It's destroying him.'

'This is terrible,' Phillips said.

Aubrey closed his eyes.

79

'I'm afraid there's worse to come,' he said.

'Oh?'

'Just before Conrad was appointed to the bench, he was in chambers one day. He was in the clerk's room, but the clerks were elsewhere.'

He paused.

'Stephen, I want to make it clear that I'm not defending what he's done. I'm trying to explain it to you – and to myself. As a matter of fact, I don't think Conrad would try to defend himself if he were here. Be that as it may, he was in the clerk's room and he noticed – I think your clerk puts the cheques for your fees into small brown envelopes: is that right?'

Phillips nodded. 'Yes, and leaves them in our pigeon-holes in the clerk's room.'

'He noticed that there were brown envelopes for Frank, Jonathan and Martin, and he took them.'

There was a shocked silence.

'What?' Phillips whispered eventually.

'The calculation he made seems to have been this: everyone knows it takes solicitors forever to pay our fees. It's the bane of all our lives. So we barristers don't question our clerks about fees unless the fee is outstanding for a very long time. It was a calculated risk, but it bought him some time for his luck to change. In the long run, it was madness, of course; he couldn't possibly have got away with it indefinitely. One of you was bound to ask your clerk about your fees at some point, and as soon as any one of you did that, the clerk would say that the cheque had been put in your pigeon-hole. He would then contact the solicitors, who would say that the cheque had been paid, and the game would be up. If his luck hadn't changed by then, it was over.'

'But in order to benefit from the cheques,' Weatherall said, 'he would have had to –'

'Forge your endorsements on the cheques so that he could pay them into his account,' Aubrey said. 'Yes. That's exactly what he did.'

Another silence.

'This is outrageous,' Reilly said. 'How did he ever think he could get away with it?'

'In the same way he thought he could get away with everything else. His luck would change, he would win the money back, and everything would be fine.'

'The man's a High Court judge,' Reilly said. 'It's insanity.'

'That's what I've been telling him,' Aubrey said. He smiled. 'Still, here I am today, several months later, and apparently none of you knew your cheques were missing until I told you.'

He reached for his briefcase, and took out several sheets of paper. He stood and handed them to Phillips.

'This will give you all the details – the cheque numbers, the amount of the fees, the dates of payment, and so on. If you ask your clerk to check his records, you will be able to reconstruct the whole thing.'

Phillips perused the papers and handed them to Martin Cohn.

'You said you wanted our help, Aubrey,' he said. 'What exactly are you asking us to do?'

'I'm asking you to work with me to make sure that Frank, Jonathan and Martin get their money back,' Aubrey replied.

'It doesn't sound as though there's much chance of that,' Reilly said. He sounded deflated. Everyone had now looked at the papers Aubrey had handed to Phillips.

'I think there is a chance. It will take some time, but I think it can be done. But I have to ask you to be patient, and I have to ask you to wait until he has paid back his loan to the syndicate.'

'Why should we wait?' Cohn asked indignantly.

'Because the syndicate won't wait,' Aubrey replied, 'and if they get to him first, you'll never get a penny.'

Cohn was shaking his head.

'Look. I understand how you must feel. I know how I would feel if it had happened to me. I would want to go straight to the police.'

'That's exactly what we should do,' Weatherall said.

'But if you do that, you will never see your money, I can promise you that. Conrad will face ruin and bankruptcy. He will be removed from the bench, and the chances are he will end up in prison. That doesn't do anyone any good.'

He took advantage of a hesitation as the barristers looked at each other grimly.

'I hope the reason I'm asking you to wait is obvious enough. If Conrad doesn't pay the syndicate immediately, they will take action. He's already received threats, and these people are very unpleasant. He will come to harm, probably serious harm. It's not inconceivable that he may end up dead. In any case, the whole thing will probably become public and, once again, he will be facing bankruptcy and ruin. He can't pay you all at the same time. The syndicate has to come first: that's a matter of survival.'

'How long do you think it will take him to pay off this so-called syndicate?' Phillips asked.

Aubrey shrugged. 'I wish I could give you an answer to that, Stephen, but I can't. I don't know the precise figures involved. If it's just a question of making regular payments, perhaps six months. I can't see it being less than six months, but then again, I don't know how much time the syndicate will give him. He can't control that.

'What I do ask you to accept is that he deeply regrets what he has done, and that he wants to make things right.'

'He wants to avoid the consequences, more like,' Reilly said.

'Those two goals are not incompatible,' Aubrey replied.

'We can't give you an answer now,' Phillips said, after some time. 'This is something we will have to discuss and think about carefully. Apart from anything else, it has repercussions for chambers. We will have to tell the solicitors concerned what has happened – hopefully before they find out for themselves – and it could do a good deal of harm to our reputation.'

'I understand that, Stephen,' Aubrey said. 'But the best news you can give the solicitors is that you are on top of the situation and that you are taking steps to bring it under control, to make sure such a thing never happens again.'

'How does it help Conrad, even if we agree to this?' Cohn asked. 'We can't avoid telling the solicitors who it was that stole from us and, even if we could, they could easily find out for themselves. So it's all going to become public anyway.'

Weatherall nodded. 'I agree. It can't remain a secret.'

'I disagree,' Aubrey replied. 'Any experienced clerk can explain what happened as an accounting error. Members of chambers often write each other cheques, or endorse cheques to each other, for work done on a case, and there's nothing surprising about Conrad continuing to receive fees for work he did before he became a judge. It can be done. The question is whether you are willing to do it.'

Phillips was nodding.

'If this becomes public,' Aubrey added, 'it won't be good for your chambers, any more than it will for Conrad.'

'We will think about it and let you know,' Phillips said.

'Thank you,' Aubrey said. 'There's one more thing. I don't have a lot of time. The syndicate is going to come calling any day now. I don't know how long Conrad can hold them off. Any delay at all, and it may be too late.'

Phillips sighed deeply.

'How late will you be in chambers tonight?' he asked.

'As late as necessary,' Aubrey replied.

80

When Aubrey called, just after 9.30, Conrad Rainer was in his kitchen. Nothing had changed. He had not yet brought himself to clean up the blood spatters, and Greta Thiemann's body was still in his storage area, competing for space with the vacuum cleaner and the brooms. He had once again fortified his front door using his sofa and coffee table. To his relief, he had seen no sign of anyone taking an interest in him on the way home from the Old Bailey, and tonight he had at least made arrangements for food. At lunchtime, when his court reporter had gone out for her sandwich, he had pressed money into her hand and asked her to buy one for him, plus a packet of crisps. He had lunched in the judges' mess, so a light supper would do him no harm, and he still had a small supply of chocolate biscuits. No one had tried to force their way into his flat, and he felt more composed than he had the previous evening as he sat nursing his glass of whisky.

All the same, something had to be done. He knew that. He had called Gerry Pole and they had had a lengthy conversation. Now, all that remained was to finish the trial of Henry Lang.

'Conrad,' Aubrey began, 'how are you? How are things going?'

'Oh, bearing up, Aubrey, bearing up.'

'Has there been any sign of…?'

'Cleary? No, none at all.'

'Good, good.'

There was a silence.

'Conrad, I need to talk to you. I saw the three members of your chambers this afternoon, and we need to talk about it.'

Conrad felt his stomach muscles tighten and tried to relax.

'How did it go?' he asked.

'Not over the phone, Conrad. I need to see you in person.'

He closed his eyes. The last thing he wanted was to leave the sanctuary of his flat at night, to expose himself in the darkness, without a rush-hour crowd to provide him with cover.

'Does it have to be tonight?' he asked.

'Yes.'

'It's just that I hadn't planned on going out again tonight, Aubrey. I'm not properly dressed and…'

'I can come to you if you prefer,' Aubrey suggested.

His heart skipped a beat.

'No. No.'

'It's no problem.'

'No. I'll meet you somewhere… let's go to… to the Club.'

'Yes. Yes, all right, if you prefer the Club.'

'I'll get a taxi; say about 40 to 45 minutes?'

'See you then,' Aubrey replied.

Conrad dressed hurriedly, and wrapped himself in a raincoat with a silk scarf over his mouth. He added an old trilby hat, pulled down over his eyes. He was nervous about standing still on the kerb, making an easy target of himself, but if he was to flag down a taxi he had no choice. Mercifully, he was able to hail one almost immediately. He looked around him as the driver sped away from his building. He saw nothing suspicious, but that did little to calm his nerves.

Dinner had ended and the Club was quiet. Luke was prowling around an empty lounge, and seemed relieved to have something to do when he brought their drinks, fussing unnecessarily about cleaning their table, and making sure they had mats and a clean ashtray. Aubrey had to encourage him gently to leave them alone.

'As I said, Conrad, I spoke to Frank, Jonathan and Martin this afternoon,' he said. 'Stephen was there as head of chambers. There was nothing I could do about that, but I doubt it made any difference. I gave them details of the cheques, and explained the situation you were in with Daniel Cleary – I didn't use names, of course, but I painted the picture – and I explained why you had to deal with Cleary before you could pay them back. They listened politely, and they told me that they would have to discuss it and get back to me. I waited in chambers, and they called just after 9.15.'

He paused.

'And…?'

Aubrey shook his head.

'I'm sorry, Conrad. In a nutshell: it's too much money; it's too great a breach of trust; and most of all, it's too much of a gamble with the reputation of chambers if they're seen to condone serious criminal offences to get their money back. They're not going for it. It was a reasonable strategy, but it didn't work. I'm sorry.'

Conrad nodded. He felt winded. He lit another cigarette and took a drink of his whisky.

'Not your fault, old boy. You tried, and I'm grateful to you.'

He was silent, smoking and inhaling deeply, for some time.

'So, what now?'

'It's likely that they will go to the police first thing tomorrow,' Aubrey replied. 'They have no reason to delay, especially as they're so worried about their reputation.'

He paused awkwardly.

'Conrad, as I said before, there are some things I can't know…'

'Understood.'

'But if you were, unbeknownst to me, contemplating any evasive action, you would have to do it tomorrow. If you leave it any longer, you may be too late. Stephen will give the police more than enough evidence to arrest you – certainly more than enough to take you in for questioning – and once that happens, everything falls apart.'

Conrad nodded.

'I can't do anything tomorrow.'

Aubrey stared at him. 'Why on earth not? Don't you understand what I'm saying to you?'

'Yes, I understand perfectly well. But I have a trial to finish, the trial of Henry Lang.'

Aubrey laughed out loud.

'Conrad, I hardly think the trial of Henry Lang is the most important thing here…'

'We've already had the prosecution speech. It will finish some time tomorrow.'

'It's still too much of a risk.'

'It's a risk I have to take.'

Aubrey stared again.

'You've lost me.'

'I know how ridiculous this is going to sound, Aubrey, after all I've told you about myself recently. But the fact is: I haven't lost all my professional pride. I'm a judge. I want to do what I took an oath to do. I want to do justice to Henry Lang, to make sure he gets a fair trial. Amid all the wreckage my life has been reduced to – entirely through my own fault – that's the one thing I still have left to cling on to. If I can prevent any injustice to Henry Lang, at least I will have done something useful in the short time I have left as a judge.'

'There will be no injustice, Conrad,' Aubrey insisted. 'Lang will be tried again before another judge, that's all. It happens all the time.'

'A retrial is not the same animal as a first trial, Aubrey. You know that as well as I do; and another judge won't understand the case in the same way I understand it.'

'Why does that matter? You're not deciding Lang's guilt or innocence. He is being tried by a jury.'

'A jury directed by a judge. In this case, the judge's summing-up will make a difference.'

Aubrey was shaking his head, frustrated. Conrad smiled.

'Aubrey, Henry Lang and I have a lot in common.'

'I seriously doubt that.'

'No, really, we do. For one thing, we've both been victims of Daniel Cleary, and in a strange way our lives have been running on parallel lines, both of us lurching from crisis to crisis. We have both called down the storm on to our heads, and now it has arrived, and it's about to obliterate us both. But there is one difference, one chance of salvation: I'm lost; no one can give me any shelter from the storm – not now – but I may just be able to shelter Lang and pull him to safety.'

Aubrey did not speak for some time.

'You won't be able to do that if they arrest you tomorrow morning,' he said, in due course.

Conrad smiled again.

'The police don't arrest people just because someone makes a complaint: especially in my case. One of the advantages of being a High Court judge is that I enjoy a heightened presumption of innocence. They will think very carefully before they come after me. They won't make a move without consulting the Director of Public Prosecutions, and the Director won't make a move without an opinion from Treasury Counsel, and they are going to dot all the Is and cross all the Ts. That's not going to happen overnight, is it? I don't think I will have any problem finishing the trial.'

He took a deep drink.

'And after that…'

'And after that…?' Aubrey asked.

'You can't know what happens after that.'

81

As Conrad walked down the stairs leading from the entrance to the Club, a taxi approached. He hailed it. He climbed into the back seat, and sat silently for several seconds.

'Where to, guv?' the driver asked cheerfully.

He looked at his watch. It was nearing midnight. He was on the brink of calling out his home address, when he stopped himself.

'The Clermont Club, 44 Berkeley Square.'

'Right you are, guv,' the driver replied, checking his side mirror as he pulled away from the kerb.

The drive was a short one, and within a few minutes, Conrad was walking hurriedly, compulsively, upstairs, to the cash desk. Vicente greeted him politely, but Conrad noticed a hesitation in his manner. He produced all he had left –£250 in crumpled notes – and laid them on the desk. Vicente looked at the notes, but did not pick them up.

'Could you give me one moment, Sir Conrad?' Vicente asked. 'I'll be right back.'

He left the cash desk and disappeared to Conrad's right into the Holland Room. A moment or two later, John Aspinall appeared from the same room.

'Conrad,' he said, extending his hand. 'They told me you were here. How are you?'

'I'm well, John, thank you. I've been at my Club. I'm not quite ready to go home, and I thought I'd call in and play a few hands.'

Aspinall nodded.

'Actually, Conrad, there's a bit of a problem with that.'

'A problem? What do you mean…?'

Aspinall took him by the arm.

'Not here. Come to my office.'

Together they climbed the short, but steep staircase behind the cash desk, which led to the top floor of the Club.

'Only exercise I get these days,' Aspinall smiled. 'Still, better than nothing, I suppose.'

He opened the door to the office, and ushered Conrad inside. The place was a mess, with papers lying haphazardly on the desk, chairs, the floor and every other available space, and a glossy calendar from a Soho Chinese Restaurant hanging crookedly from a hook on the wall. A croupier Conrad did not recognise was seated at the desk. Aspinall dismissed him with a single shake of the head. He wished Conrad good evening, and left the room. Aspinall waved Conrad into a chair.

'Throw the papers on the floor,' he said. 'God knows, it won't make any difference. How anyone ever gets any work done here, I'll never know.'

Once seated, Aspinall drew himself up and folded his arms in front of him.

'We're concerned, Conrad,' he said. 'You lost a lot of money the other night.'

Seeing that Conrad was about to reply, he held up a hand.

'No, let me finish. I have to tell you, we've had doubts for some time. I've never asked you for a deposit, Conrad. It's something I don't like to do. But as you know, we don't extend credit. The Club depends on members being good for their losses. Our reputation depends on it, as does our own solvency, for that matter. I'm afraid we're not convinced that you would be able to cover any further losses.'

'John, look –'

'I'm sorry, Conrad. It wouldn't be fair to us, or the other members. I'm afraid I've decided that you can't play here again unless you make a substantial cash deposit as a reserve. Shall we say £30,000? And you wouldn't be allowed to place wagers that would take you below that limit if you lose. If that's not a problem, then we will always be glad to see you. But otherwise, I must draw the line. I'm sorry, Conrad.'

Conrad stared at him for some time. He nodded.

'All right, John,' he replied quietly. 'It doesn't matter anyway.'

Aspinall stood.

'Look, take a taxi home on us. Vicente will give you enough.'

'No, thank you, John,' Conrad replied. 'I can find my own way.'

82

'Members of the jury,' Ben began, 'my learned friend Mr Pilkington gave you four reasons for returning a verdict of guilty of murder. I want to give you four reasons for returning a verdict of guilty of manslaughter by reason of provocation. And unlike Mr Pilkington, I don't have to prove my side of the case. The prosecution has the burden of proof, and unless you are sure they have proved that Henry Lang is guilty of murder, you must return a verdict of manslaughter. The learned judge will explain that to you when he sums up.

'My four reasons are these. First, Henry Lang had no reason to kill his wife. Second, Henry Lang certainly had no reason to kill his wife outside Mrs Cameron's house on 28 April. Third, Henry Lang's explanation for taking the knife with him to Mrs Cameron's house is not only credible, but is supported by independent evidence. Fourth and last, Henry Lang's account of what happened at Harpur Mews on 28 April is also credible, and is supported by independent evidence.

'First, he had no reason to kill Susan Lang. The very fact that he was the one who began divorce proceedings and made an application for custody of the children speaks for itself. If he intended to kill her, why would he do that? Why not just get on with it and kill her? Yes, Mr Justice Wesley had given interim custody to Susan, but it was *interim* custody, and the judge had made it clear that things could change at the final hearing. They would have changed, wouldn't they, almost certainly, you may think? Since the first hearing, Henry had built up a convincing case that

Susan was drinking too much, taking drugs, and associating with criminals like Daniel Cleary. Her own friend, Louise, told Henry as much, didn't she? Henry had every reason to think that he would be awarded custody once word of that reached Mr Justice Wesley, or even Mrs Cameron. And if he did try to kill her, what if something went wrong? What if he was arrested for it? Members of the jury, trying to kill Susan might have been the only way he could actually lose custody of his children.

'Second, he certainly had no reason to kill Susan Lang at Harpur Mews on 28 April. Let's assume for a moment that Henry had decided to kill Susan. Would he do it on a public street, outside the house of the court welfare officer, just after a meeting with her, just around the corner from a police station? If anything went wrong, if she screamed, or escaped, or survived the attempt, it would have been over for him, wouldn't it? Surely, members of the jury, a man who, according to the prosecution, was so intent on killing his wife would choose a better time and place. He knew where she lived, didn't he? He knew she came home late at night. You may think she would have been easy prey for anyone really determined to kill her.

'Third, his explanation for taking the knife with him. Let me make this clear, members of the jury: I don't condone his decision to carry a knife for one moment, and neither should you. It was a stupid thing to do. He knows that now, and he should have known at the time. He should have gone to the police, and reported it to Mrs Cameron immediately. Of course, he should. But that doesn't mean that he intended to kill his wife. The prosecution ridicule the idea that Henry was afraid of Daniel Cleary, but there is independent evidence that Cleary was a threat to him. First, you know about Cleary's criminal record, which includes convictions for violence and blackmail – making unwarranted demands with menaces – which is exactly what Henry says he did. It's not a huge leap, is it, to accept that when one of his drug clients asked him for a favour – leaning on Henry to drop his case – he would have been only too pleased to keep his client happy? Not only that, but you heard from Harriet Fisk, Susan's barrister, and you remember what she told you, I'm sure. Susan actually told her, in the presence of her solicitor, Miss Turner, that "Danny Ice" was going to put pressure on Henry to drop the case, to threaten him with violence. Mr Pilkington didn't dispute Miss Fisk's evidence at all; he accepted that evidence on behalf of the prosecution.

'Yes, it was a foolish thing to do, but Henry is not charged with illegally carrying an offensive weapon. If he were, he would have to plead guilty, but he's not. He is charged with murder, and if you're not sure that he took the knife with him with the premeditated intention of killing Susan that day at Harpur Mews, then there must be a reasonable doubt, mustn't there? I would suggest that, not only is there a reasonable doubt, but the evidence is very much in favour of Henry being afraid of "Danny Ice", and ill-advisedly taking the knife with him for self-defence in case Cleary decided to carry out his threat.

'Lastly, members of the jury, the prosecution pour scorn on the idea that six words could have caused Henry Lang to lose all self-control. But is that so unreasonable? Remind yourselves, please, when you are in your jury room, of those words. "What makes you think they're yours?" I will repeat them. "What makes you think they're yours?" Members of the jury, there's no doubt, is there, that Henry Lang is a man who cares on the deepest level about his children? Mrs Cameron thought he was a bit obsessive, and she was worried about that tendency in him, and you may well be inclined to agree with her. But surely that supports what Henry told you. This is a man who always talked about "my" children, never "our" children. The prosecution described Susan's words as stupid. But they weren't stupid; they were deliberately vicious words, the most cruel she could have spoken to him, carefully calculated to cause Henry as much pain as she could. Could there be anything more hurtful, anything more calculated to send this man into an uncontrollable rage, than to question the paternity of his children? If he wasn't their father, who was? One of the men she consorted with? Daniel Cleary? Is it so hard to believe that for a few moments – tragically, for long enough for him to take Susan's life – he lost all self-control?

'His loss of self-control is also shown, I suggest, by what happened after he stabbed her. Did he run away, try to hide, try to dispose of the weapon? No. He did none of those things, none of the things a man in possession of his reason, a man who had just successfully completed a premeditated plan to kill, would have done. Instead, he sat on the floor just a foot or two away from where she lay dying, knife in hand, until the police arrived, and when the police arrived, he did not resist them in any way.

'Henry tells you that he later had no memory of what had happened. Again, the prosecution pour scorn on the idea that he couldn't remember, and on the fact that his memory returned before the trial began. But, members of the jury, there is no dispute that when the police found Henry Lang, he was in trauma-induced clinical shock, and he remained in trauma-induced clinical shock for two days, during which period he was taken to Barts hospital for treatment. There's no dispute about that, is there? You heard about it from the police officers. You heard that the police surgeon, Dr Moynihan, diagnosed trauma-induced clinical shock, as did the doctors at Barts.

'The prosecution's own expert, Dr Harvey, told you that this man suffered trauma-induced clinical shock, and he told you that retrograde amnesia is a known symptom of that condition. Is it so surprising that this man of hitherto good character was traumatised by what he had done? Is it so surprising that the memory of what he had done was so painful that his mind took pity on him and spared him the agony of reliving it for as long as it could?

'Members of the jury, on any view, this is a tragic case. There is nothing you can do about the tragedy of Susan Lang's death. But there is one thing you can do. By your verdict, you can prevent a second tragedy – the tragedy of convicting Henry Lang of an offence he didn't commit, and taking him away from his children for ever.'

83

When Mr Justice Rainer began to sum up, Ben and Andrew exchanged nervous glances. Not only did he still look tired, pale and drawn, but he had not asked them for any guidance about the law of provocation. Both barristers knew that it was not an easy branch of the law for juries to understand, and any error in the summing-up could have a serious effect on the verdict. But to their considerable surprise, the judge delivered a textbook summing-up, not only getting the law exactly right, but also putting it in such simple terms that the jury could hardly fail to understand it. He then reviewed the evidence, of which he had taken hardly any notes, accurately and thoroughly, before reminding the jury briefly of the points Ben and Andrew had made in their closing speeches.

'Members of the jury,' he concluded, 'if there's anything you and I have learned from this case, it's surely that an evil man like Daniel Cleary can do irreparable damage to people's lives. He is, you may think, a man with a record for violence, apparently without conscience; a man who thinks nothing of threatening to destroy others for his own gain, willing apparently to destroy Henry Lang for nothing more than a chance of keeping a client, to whom he sold illegal drugs, happy.

'Members of the jury, it's a matter entirely for you, but you may think that Henry Lang may well have been so afraid that he took a knife with him for protection. You may also think, and again it's a matter entirely for you, but you may also think that when Susan Lang uttered those terrible, terrible words, calculated to destroy her husband as surely as Daniel Cleary intended to destroy him, he reacted in a blind rage and lost all self-control. You may think that the justice of this case lies in what I have just said, and while, I say again, it is a matter entirely for you, if that's the view you take, you would be entitled to reflect that view in a verdict of manslaughter.

'Wait for the jury bailiff to take his oath, and you may then retire to consider your verdict.'

The jury retired just after midday.

'Which way do you think the judge is leaning?' Andrew asked, approaching once the jury had retired and the judge had left the bench. 'Difficult to tell, wasn't it?'

They all laughed.

'I think I can guess,' Ben replied. 'He wasn't particularly subtle about it, was he? I only hope he hasn't turned the jury against us.'

'I don't think so,' Andrew said. 'My money's on manslaughter, but I wish I knew what this man's obsession with Daniel Cleary is about.'

'He does seem to have it in for old Danny Ice, doesn't he?' Barratt said. 'I'm surprised he hasn't had him arrested.'

'There's something about that side of the story that disturbs him,' Jess said, 'that's for sure. He kept bringing him up, time and time again, didn't he?'

'Well, there you go,' Andrew said. 'Nothing we can do about it. At least he got the law right. That's something.'

As Andrew turned away, he saw DI Webb approaching.

'Sorry to disturb you, Mr Pilkington, but could I have a word?'

'Yes, of course,' Andrew replied.

'Outside court, sir, if you don't mind.'

84

'If you wouldn't mind coming with me, sir,' Webb said as they left court, 'we've got a quiet corner in the hall over here. We shouldn't be disturbed.'

Looking towards the corner, Andrew saw a uniformed officer, by his appearance an officer of high rank, and another man whom he recognised as John Caswell, a senior lawyer in the office of the Director of Public Prosecutions, with whom he had often had dealings.

'Mr Pilkington,' Webb said, 'this is Assistant Commissioner Lawton.'

'Brian Lawton,' the officer said, extending his hand.

'Commissioner,' Andrew replied, taking his hand. 'John, how are you?'

'Well, Andrew, thank you,' Caswell replied.

'What can I do for you?' Andrew asked.

'It's a sensitive matter, Andrew, and an urgent one. We have a very difficult situation on our hands, on which the Commissioner and I would like your advice.'

'Of course.'

'Earlier this morning, the police received a complaint against Mr Justice Rainer.'

'A complaint against the judge?' Andrew asked, taken aback. 'A complaint about what?'

'Three of the barristers in his former chambers say that Rainer stole cheques from them, forged their signatures to make it appear that they had endorsed the cheques in his favour, and deposited them in his own bank account.'

Andrew was speechless for some time.

'How much money is involved?' he asked.

'A little more than £16,000,' Caswell replied.

Andrew paused again to allow it all to sink in.

'When is this supposed to have happened?'

'Shortly before he was appointed to the bench.'

'Fortunately,' Lawton said, 'the officers who took the complaint realised immediately how sensitive it was, and referred it to my office without delay. Because DI Webb has been involved in this case, I have asked him to take charge of the investigation, and I have instructed him to interview Rainer as soon as possible.

'I also contacted Mr Caswell to discuss how to proceed. On his advice, I have already obtained a search warrant for Rainer's address in London. He has a flat at the Barbican. He also has a house, a family home, down in Guildford. I've asked the Chief Constable of Surrey, on a confidential basis, to stand by to get a warrant down there if needed.'

'It's a bit early in the investigation to apply for a search warrant, isn't it?' Andrew asked. 'Do you know what you're looking for at this stage?'

'They have the evidence, Andrew,' Caswell replied. 'The head of chambers and the senior clerk brought the paperwork with them. They have all the details, and we're taking steps to get copies of the cancelled cheques, which should confirm what we know already. The solicitors who issued the cheques will also have records.'

'But what do you hope to find if you search his flat?'

'We have reasonable grounds for believing that there may be further evidence to support the allegations,' Lawton replied, 'and there's every reason to believe that we may find evidence of further offences. According to the head of chambers, Rainer has a serious gambling problem, and is very heavily in debt. It appears that he resorted to stealing the cheques to buy himself time to win some of the money back, but it didn't work. It may be that these three barristers are not his only victims. The senior clerk is checking his records.'

Andrew took off his wig and ran a hand through his hair.

'This is incredible,' he said.

'Did you notice anything strange about the judge during the trial?' Lawton asked. 'I mean, was there anything about his behaviour that seemed unusual?'

Andrew nodded.

'Yes. As a matter of fact I'd been in touch with the Director's office about it. He handled the trial competently enough, certainly given that it was his first criminal trial. The summing-up was sound – a little too defence-minded for my taste, but nothing I can really complain about. But he was obviously very stressed. He looked as though he hadn't been sleeping well. His behaviour in court was erratic, and when we called him on it, he admitted that he wasn't feeling well.'

'It's a stressful job,' Caswell suggested.

'Yes,' Andrew agreed. 'But there were a couple of other things that concerned me.'

'Go on,' Caswell encouraged, as Andrew hesitated.

'One thing was that he seemed to have an obsession with a man called Daniel Cleary. Cleary has a record for violence and blackmail, and it was part of the defence case that he had threatened the defendant to get him to drop his child custody proceedings. So he was a significant figure in the trial, but not to the extent the judge seemed to think. He was continually reminding us all what an evil fellow Cleary was. It was out of all proportion to his actual importance.'

'We could look into whether there has been any connection between Rainer and Cleary,' Lawton suggested.

'Perhaps you should,' Andrew agreed.

'What was the second thing?' Caswell asked.

'The defence made an application to admit some evidence which, on the face of it, was privileged. Rainer held that it wasn't privileged and allowed it in. I opposed it, but actually I think he was probably right on the law. That's not what concerns me. What concerns me is that he knew that the application was going to be made, and what it was about, before the defence mentioned it in court.'

'Perhaps the defence nobbled him out of court,' Webb suggested.

'No,' Andrew replied firmly. 'Ben Schroeder and Barratt Davis are straight arrows. There's no question of that.'

'So, the judge had input from someone else?' Lawton asked.

'I think that's very likely,' Andrew replied.

'That's not necessarily suspicious, is it?' Caswell asked. 'You said it was his first criminal trial. He may well have approached someone to help him behind the scenes. There's nothing wrong with his taking advice as long as he makes his own decisions.'

'Except that whoever he approached seemed to know all about what the defence was planning,' Andrew pointed out.

'Well,' Lawton said, 'we can look into those things, but they don't seem to have any bearing on the matters we're investigating now.'

'There may be a connection to his gambling,' Andrew suggested. 'I didn't know about that before you told me.'

'Perhaps,' Lawton agreed. 'But the question is: what do we do now? From my point of view, the sooner DI Webb interviews him, the better.'

'Not yet,' Andrew said.

'Why not? What's he doing at the moment, other than sitting in his chambers waiting for the jury's verdict?'

'No,' Andrew insisted. 'He's presiding over a murder trial. If DI Webb interviews him before the trial finishes, he may take the view that he has to withdraw from the case. I may even have to ask him to withdraw myself.'

'It's looking like a defence verdict,' Webb grinned. 'Would we necessarily object to a retrial at this stage?'

'Yes, we would,' Andrew replied sharply. 'We have a duty to ensure fairness. The defendant is always at risk of disadvantage in a retrial. I am advising in the strongest terms that you wait until the jury has returned a verdict and Lang has been sentenced.'

'In any case,' he added, after a pause, 'you can't conduct a formal interview with a High Court judge in his chambers. You would have to take him to a police station – and do it very discreetly.'

'I have to agree,' Caswell said.

'When will the trial be finished?' Lawton asked.

'Some time later today.'

'And would he be sentenced today?'

'There's no reason to delay. If Lang is convicted of murder, it's life imprisonment, and if he's convicted of manslaughter the tariff in this kind of case is about four years. That's not going to change. If he delays at all, it wouldn't be later than Monday morning.'

'I don't like having to wait that long.'

'In that case I could have officers keeping him under surveillance over the weekend, sir,' Webb volunteered.

Lawton nodded reluctantly.

'All right, but I want this dealt with as soon as he's passed sentence,' he said.

'Right you are, sir,' Webb replied.

'Just be careful, Inspector,' Andrew cautioned. 'You're dealing with a High Court judge. Don't go jumping in before you're sure of your ground.'

'Amen to that,' Caswell agreed.

'All I'm going to do, sir, is show him the paperwork,' Webb said, 'and ask him what he has to say about it. Unless I'm missing something, I don't see that there's anything he *can* say. I don't think he's going to argue with us. I think he'll put his hands up.'

'Just be careful,' Andrew repeated.

85

The hours of waiting dragged on, seemingly interminably. In the bar mess, Ben and Jess made endless cups of coffee and talked about anything but the case. Barratt spent two hours in the cells with Henry Lang, but by then his nerves were getting the better of him. Henry was subdued and uncommunicative, and in any case there was nothing more to say; nothing left but small talk. Barratt had no appetite for that, and rather than risk conveying his anxiety to his client, he eventually came back upstairs. He used a public phone box to call his wife, Suzie, and tell her he would be late home. The rest of the time he sat in the dim evening light of the hall outside court, pretending to be interested in *The Times*.

It was 11 o'clock at night before Geoffrey, somehow managing to look pristine in his gown, dark suit and white shirt despite the lateness of the hour, made the rounds and told everyone that the jury was ready to return a verdict.

Ben glanced round as Henry was brought into the dock by the prison officers, and offered a smile, but Henry was looking down, as ever, and did not respond. When Mr Justice Rainer had taken his seat, the jury were brought in. They looked exhausted, the men with ties hanging loosely around their necks, their faces suggesting that the verdict had not been agreed without a hard-fought, if not angry, debate. Juror number ten, a woman, looked displeased. The clerk, without undue haste, picked up the indictment and turned to the judge.

'My Lord, 11 hours and 20 minutes have elapsed since the jury retired.'

The judge nodded. The clerk turned towards the dock.

'Will the defendant please stand?'

Henry complied slowly.

The foreman turned to the jury.

'Members of the jury, who shall speak as your foreman?'

The foreman sat nearest to the bench in the front row. He was a short rotund man, his shirt crumpled and his hair out of place. He stood. He was holding a folded sheet of paper in his hand.

'Members of the jury, have you reached a verdict on which you are all agreed?'

'Yes,' the foreman replied, with a nervous look around him.

'On this indictment, charging the defendant Henry Lang with the wilful murder of Susan Lang, do you find the defendant guilty or not guilty of murder?'

The foreman raised his sheet of paper to eye level, unfolded it, and having glanced around him again, read aloud from it.

'We find the defendant Henry Lang not guilty of murder, but guilty of manslaughter by reason of provocation,' he said.

'Well done,' Ben heard Andrew whisper. He nodded in return.

'You find the defendant not guilty of murder, but guilty of manslaughter by reason of provocation; and is that the verdict of you all?'

'Yes.'

'Thank you, members of the jury,' Mr Justice Rainer said. 'It's obvious from the length of time for which you have been out that you have given this case the greatest possible care, and I wish to say that I agree entirely with the verdict you have returned.'

He looked down at Ben.

'Mr Schroeder, it appears to me that the usual sentence in a case of this kind is of the order of four years imprisonment. In this particular case, with its unusual circumstances, it is my view that a sentence of two and a half years would amply meet the justice of the case. Would you wish to address me?'

Ben gasped. This would be an extraordinarily light sentence for taking a life under any circumstances.

'No, my Lord,' he replied quietly.

'Very well.'

The judge looked towards the dock, where Henry remained

standing, expressionless, still looking down.

'Mr Lang, the jury have found by their verdict that you killed your wife, Susan Lang, when you had temporarily lost your self-control because of a remark she made questioning the paternity of your children. I cannot and do not condone what you did, but I do understand it. I am also convinced, even though I have no means of knowing what view the jury took, that Daniel Cleary played a crucial role in your decision to carry a knife with you on that fateful day. Again, I cannot and do not condone what you did, but I understand it.

'You are a man of previous excellent character, and I do not think for a moment that you will ever trouble the courts again. In the circumstances, I think it right to impose a sentence which some may think to be lenient, but I do so because it seems to me to meet the justice of this tragic case. You will go to prison for two and a half years. The time you have spent in custody awaiting trial will be deducted from the sentence, and you will be eligible for release when you have served two thirds of the sentence. You may go down.'

Andrew turned to DI Webb who was sitting behind him, and they both shook their heads.

As the prison officers led Henry from the court, the judge turned back towards the jury.

'Members of the jury, I'm sure that this must have been a very distressing case for you. But you should understand that unless men and women such as yourselves give us your time for this vital work, the criminal courts could not function. In recognition of your service, I will discharge you from further jury service for a period of ten years.'

He suddenly looked down to counsel's row.

'I have the power to do that, don't I, Mr Pilkington?'

Andrew could not help smiling.

'Yes, my Lord.'

'I see Detective Inspector Webb in court. Inspector Webb, would you stand, please? The jury and I heard the evidence of the conduct of the police officers who attended the scene under your command, and it is my opinion that you all showed bravery of a

high order. I shall be writing to the Commissioner of Metropolitan
Police with my recommendation that each of you should be highly
commended for your courage. You also have the thanks of the
court.'

Webb bowed his head. 'Thank you, my Lord.'

As the judge rose and the courtroom began to clear, Barratt leaned
forward and slapped Ben on the shoulder.

'Brilliant result,' he said. 'Absolutely bloody brilliant.'

Ben smiled and took Jess's hand. She squeezed hard.

'I suppose we should go down to see Henry,' Barratt said, 'late
though it is. What are you two going to do when you get home? Do
you have plans for the weekend?'

'Sleep until Monday morning,' Jess replied, smiling. 'How
about you?'

'Oh, Suzie and I will have our usual late-night verdict session.'

'I'm not sure I dare ask,' Ben laughed.

'Soup and a grilled cheese sandwich, with a bottle of Beaujolais,'
Barratt replied. 'A long-standing tradition.'

Outside court, DI Webb shook hands with Andrew, who took his
leave. DS Phil Raymond was waiting for Webb, wearing a suit and
tie, and looking none too pleased about it.

'You do know it's almost midnight on a Friday night, sir, don't
you?' he asked. 'Not to mention that I've been here since 2 o'clock?'

'Yes, I know, Phil,' Webb replied. 'I'm sorry about that. It wasn't
my idea, believe me. Mr Assistant bloody Commissioner Lawton
said he wanted Rainer interviewed as soon as possible, so I thought
I'd better have you here. No one thought the jury would be out as
long as they were. I mean, it was Friday afternoon and they all
have homes to go to, don't they? I was expecting to have Rainer all
to ourselves by 5 o'clock at the latest.'

Raymond nodded.

'So, what do you want to do, sir? Go into his chambers and nab
him now, before he goes home?'

'No,' Webb replied. 'He looks absolutely exhausted. If we
interview him now, whatever he says won't be much use in court.

The defence would have a field day slagging us off for interviewing a man who looks like he's about to drop dead from fatigue. To be honest, I'm not much better myself. My brain's about to shut down for the day.'

'Mr Assistant Commissioner Lawton's not going to like it, sir.'

'Mr Assistant Commissioner Lawton isn't here, is he? He's probably fast asleep in bed, sleeping the sleep of the righteous. And he's not going to be the one having his head kicked in by defence counsel if Rainer is charged and it comes to trial, is he?'

He pondered for a few moments.

'All right, this is what we do. Meet me at Rainer's building at 8 o'clock tomorrow morning. I'll contact the management there and tell them about the warrant, so we can make sure of getting access. Bring uniform with you to help with the search. We'll have it all wrapped up in time for lunch.'

86

Mr Ensley, the managing director of the property management company responsible for the building containing Conrad Rainer's flat, met DI Webb and DS Raymond, and the two uniformed constables they had brought with them, at the front door just before 8 o'clock. Webb showed him the search warrant. He admitted them reluctantly, shaking his head and muttering to himself, but escorted them to the lift. He continued to talk to himself under his breath as they rode, otherwise in silence, up to the fourth floor.

'I don't know about this, Inspector,' he said as they arrived at the flat. 'I don't know about this at all. This *is* the Barbican, you know. We don't expect this sort of thing – not with the class of tenant we have here.'

Webb and Raymond exchanged tired smiles.

'We'll behave ourselves, sir,' Webb promised. 'We'll be nice and quiet. We just need to have a chat with Sir Conrad about one or two things; shouldn't take long.'

'Police! Open up, Sir Conrad, please!' Raymond called out, banging loudly several times on the door.

There was no response. He tried again, with the same result. Suddenly, he bent down and put his head against the door. He pulled away and turned to Webb.

'There's a bit of a funny smell, sir.'

Webb swore under his breath.

'Open the door,' he ordered Ensley brusquely. 'Now.' His tone of voice made clear that he expected to be obeyed, without any further references to this sort of thing not happening in the Barbican.

Ensley complied and stepped back. Raymond entered first. The source of the smell was immediately obvious. Gingerly he opened the door of the storage area. He recoiled violently.

'Oh, Jesus,' he spluttered hoarsely. He turned away abruptly, pulled out a handkerchief to hold over his mouth, and leaned against the wall by the door, fighting for breath.

Webb gestured to the two constables with a nod of his head. They entered the flat. Raymond had left the door of the storage area open, and they had a clear view of what was inside. The younger of the two constables turned pale and walked slowly back out into the corridor. Ensley was hovering by the door, trying his best to catch a glimpse of what they had found. Webb pushed him away.

'Please go back downstairs, Mr Ensley, and keep the front door unlocked. Some colleagues will be joining us.'

'What's happening?' he asked.

'Please do as I say, sir.'

Ensley walked away towards the lift, shaking his head.

Webb looked around him. He took in the haphazard arrangement of the furniture, a sofa and a table obviously out of place and at unnatural angles to the other furniture. He registered the blood stains on the floor, the sofa, and on the bust of Mozart.

'You all right, Phil?'

Raymond turned back from the wall and put the handkerchief back in his pocket. He nodded.

'I'll be fine, sir.'

The younger constable had not returned. Webb turned to the older officer.

'Take a quick walk through the flat, just to make sure there's no one here. Keep your eyes open for evidence, and stay away from the area in the middle there, where the blood stains are. Call me if you find anything.'

'Yes, sir.'

'Phil, you'd better borrow the phone and get the pathologist and the scenes of crime officers here.'

'I thought this was supposed to be a theft case,' Raymond complained.

'So did I,' Webb replied.

Treading as lightly as he could, doing his utmost not to step on anything that might interest the scenes of crime officers, Raymond made his way to the small circular table on which Conrad Rainer kept his phone, and dialled a number. He began to talk quietly. Webb forced himself to look more closely at the body of Greta Thiemann and noted the wound on her head. He looked again at the bust of Mozart.

'Interesting choice of weapon,' he mused to himself. 'He couldn't do it with a candlestick or a bottle, could he? Couldn't have that kind of vulgarity, could we, Mr Ensley? Not in the Barbican.'

The older constable returned, shaking his head.

'Nothing, sir, except a big pile of clothes on the bed, and all the drawers open. It looks as if he may have packed and left in a hurry.'

'He killed her and ran,' Raymond said. He had finished on the phone. 'But who is she, and what's she got to do with stealing cheques from barristers?'

Webb shook his head.

'He didn't kill her last night, Phil. We don't need the pathologist to tell us that, do we? Just look at her. She's been dead for some time.'

He looked around him again.

'Get on the phone again and put out an alert to all ports and airports. Rainer is to be apprehended on sight on suspicion of murder.'

Raymond nodded.

'I can't help thinking… you know, sir, last night… if we'd.'

Webb pointed a finger at him.

'Don't say a word,' he ordered. 'Not a bloody word.'

87

Aubrey Smith-Gurney passed the clerk's room with no more than a quick wave to Merlin, and made his way hurriedly to his room. It was not yet 9 o'clock. He took off his coat and hung it up on the stand by his door. He sat down behind his desk and took his copy of *The Times* from his briefcase. The headlines in all the morning newspapers dealt with the same sensational story, and they had grabbed his attention like a slap in the face when he emerged from Temple underground station and approached the nearby news stand. He had almost torn *The Times* from the vendor's hand, flinging the coins into the man's palm, before virtually running to chambers and racing up the staircase. His heart was pounding. He forced himself to breathe more slowly and tried to make his mind focus on the article on the paper's front page.

TOP JUDGE MISSING AS WOMAN'S
BODY IS FOUND IN HIS FLAT

Police make gruesome discovery in the Barbican
One of the country's leading judges is believed to have disappeared in mysterious circumstances, leaving the body of a woman in his expensive Barbican flat. High Court Judge Sir Conrad Rainer has not been seen since Friday night, and was not at his flat when police visited it on Saturday morning and discovered the body of a woman. The woman appeared to have been dead for several days. A police spokeswoman told The Times that the body has not yet been formally identified, but is believed to be that of Greta

Thiemann, 35, a citizen of the German Democratic Republic who had lived in London for more than seven years, and was a West End socialite with no known employment. The cause of her death has not yet been established, but the spokeswoman said that the case is being treated as one of murder.

Sir Conrad was last seen by court staff leaving the Old Bailey after 11 o'clock on Friday night, after a jury had returned a verdict in the murder case he had tried during the week. Staff said that the judge appeared to be behaving normally when he left the court, apparently to return to his flat in the Barbican. Sir Conrad, who is 55, was a highly respected QC with an extensive commercial practice before being appointed a High Court judge in May of this year. He was knighted on his appointment to the bench.

Police believe that the judge may be able to help them with their inquiries, and are anxious to talk to him, but despite extensive investigation over the weekend, their efforts to find him have so far been unsuccessful. The judge's wife, Lady Rainer, told police that she had expected him to return to their home in Guildford on Friday night, but that he never arrived. Lady Rainer has not heard from her husband, and has not seen him for more than a week. According to the police spokeswoman, Lady Rainer confirmed that Sir Conrad had a supply of clothing and personal effects at his Barbican flat, and that he had his passport and driving licence in his possession.

At a hastily-convened press conference on Sunday morning, the officer in charge of the investigation, Detective Inspector John Webb, appealed to the judge to report to the nearest police station. 'We are concerned for Sir Conrad's safety,' Inspector Webb told reporters, 'as is his wife. Lady Rainer is particularly distressed and anxious for any news of her husband. We are asking Sir Conrad to contact us immediately, and we are asking any members of the public who may have any knowledge of his whereabouts to contact their nearest police station without delay. In particular, we believe that Sir Conrad had a few close friends in the legal fraternity in London, and we would be very pleased to hear from them.'

Answering a question from the Times correspondent, Inspector

Webb said that the police visit to the judge's Barbican flat on Saturday morning was in connection with other matters, and that there is presently no evidence that those matters have any connection with the murder of Greta Thiemann. 'The discovery of her body was a complete surprise,' Inspector Webb said. 'We don't know of any link to the other matters we are investigating, but obviously, that may change as the investigation continues.'

Aubrey threw the newspaper down on his desk and stared at the far wall. He could not even begin to sort out the flood of different emotions flowing through him, but they certainly included fear, anger, and a sense of betrayal. He knew too much. He had allowed Conrad to tell him too much, believing that he had appealed for his help. He knew, even if the police didn't, who Greta Thiemann was, and what part she had played in Conrad Rainer's life. He also knew – or thought he knew – all about the 'other matters' into which the police were inquiring, and he knew that it would not take them long to identify him as one of the close friends Conrad had in the 'legal fraternity' in London.

He didn't know how or why Greta Thiemann had died, and he didn't know where Conrad Rainer had gone: although that was only a partial truth. The way out that Conrad had chosen was, as they had agreed, something he couldn't know. But he had every reason to believe that Conrad's route would have included the Isle of Wight. If he was honest with himself, he had helped to set it up; and now it had linked him to a murder.

How long he sat there without moving, he could not have said. But he was suddenly aware of Merlin standing in front of his desk. He had not heard him knock, or seen him enter the room.

'I'm sorry to disturb you, sir,' the senior clerk said, 'but we've had a call from the police, a DI Webb. He would like to speak to you, and wonders if 2 o'clock would be convenient.'

Aubrey did not respond immediately.

'Mr Smith-Gurney?'

'Yes. Yes. I suppose 2 o'clock would be as good as any other time.'

'I'll let him know, sir.' Merlin paused. 'Isn't DI Webb the officer in charge of that case that's in all the papers this morning, the one about the murder – ?'

'Yes, he is,' Aubrey replied abruptly. 'Is Mr Morgan-Davies in chambers?'

Merlin looked at Aubrey carefully for some seconds.

'I believe so, sir. He's reading some papers for a case next week. Shall I tell him you would like to see him?'

'No, that's all right, Merlin,' Aubrey replied. 'I'll tell him myself.

'Very good, sir.'

Merlin turned and left the room.

Aubrey sat for a few seconds more before making his way to see his head of chambers.

88

'Come in, Aubrey,' Gareth Morgan-Davies said cheerfully, as Aubrey put his head around the door.

'Do you have a minute, Gareth?'

'Of course. Sit down.'

Aubrey walked slowly forward, sat in a chair in front of Gareth's desk, and pushed *The Times* across to him.

'Have you seen this?'

Gareth laughed. 'Yes, I was reading about it on the train on the way in: highly entertaining. The press must think it's Christmas come early. It's not often a story like this falls into their laps, is it? High Court judges on the run from the police, the bodies of exotic ladies found in their flats? Whatever next? What's the world coming to? All we need to add is a touch of drugs or the Church and Bob's your uncle – we'll end up with one of the great scandals of our time; and what's the betting that one or other will show up before too long?'

Aubrey did not laugh.

'The thing is, Gareth… I'm involved, or at least I think I might be.'

Merlin showed the officers into Gareth's room, and left discreetly, hanging an 'in conference' sign on the door before making his way back to the clerk's room.

'I'm Gareth Morgan-Davies, head of chambers, and this is Aubrey Smith-Gurney,' Gareth said, extending his hand.

'How do you do, sir? I'm DI Webb and this is DS Raymond.'

They all shook hands and took seats, Aubrey to Gareth's right behind his desk, the officers in chairs in front of it. Raymond produced a notebook and pencil from his pocket.

'Do I detect a Welsh accent, sir?' he asked.

'You do indeed,' Gareth replied. 'Cardiff. What about you?'

'I was born in England, sir, but my family was from Llanelli originally. I never had the accent unfortunately, but I recognise it when I hear it.'

'I'm sure you do,' Gareth said.

There was an awkward silence.

'Actually,' Webb said, 'it's Mr Smith-Gurney we wanted to talk to.'

'Yes, I know,' Gareth replied, 'but I'm his head of chambers, and he wants me to be present: just for moral support and to see fair play, you know? I hope that's not a problem. He's not a suspect, is he?'

Webb sat back in his chair and looked at Gareth thoughtfully.

'A suspect in what, sir?'

Gareth shrugged. 'I don't know: whatever you're investigating, I suppose.'

Webb nodded. 'I see you have this morning's paper on your desk, sir, so I'm going to assume you know why we're here.'

He turned towards Aubrey.

'We're just looking for information, Mr Smith-Gurney. Some barristers in his former chambers told us that you knew him well. In fact, they had the impression that you and he were good friends.'

'That's quite true,' Aubrey replied. 'I've known Conrad for almost my whole life. We went to school together, we went to Cambridge together, and we came to the Bar together. We've always been close.'

'Then perhaps you won't mind helping us to find him, sir. Candidly, we're worried about him. We know he's had serious financial problems, and obviously now there's a suspicion that he may have had something to do with the death of this lady, Greta Thiemann. He's a man who has a high profile, and I'm afraid we can't rule out the possibility that he might take his own life. We haven't told his wife that, or the press, for obvious reasons, but it's a concern; and if he is still alive, we would like to find him before he does anything stupid.'

'If I knew where he was, I would tell you,' Aubrey replied. 'I don't. But I'm pretty sure he hasn't killed himself.'

'Why do you say that? After all, he's got himself into a lot of trouble, hasn't he? He's probably feeling desperate. I'm sure I would be, in his position.'

'I know the man,' Aubrey replied. 'He won't kill himself. He's taken off; that's what's happened. But I don't know where. He wouldn't tell me. He wouldn't tell anybody.'

'Except whoever helped him escape,' Raymond said.

'What?'

'Well, he must have had help from somewhere. Stands to reason, doesn't it?' Raymond continued. 'We know he was at the Old Bailey until after 11 o'clock on Friday night because we were there as well. We were the investigating officers in the murder he was trying. By 8 o'clock the next morning he's vanished into thin air. We've had every police officer in the country looking for him and we've put out alerts to all the ports and airports, and there's no sign of him. I can't see how he could have done that without help from somebody. When did you last see him, Mr Smith-Gurney?'

'Last Thursday evening, at our Club. We had a drink; quite late, 9.30 to 10, I would think.'

Raymond offered his notebook.

'Could we have the Club's details, please sir?'

Aubrey wrote them down.

'Can anyone confirm that, sir?'

'Yes. The person you would want to talk to is a young man called Luke, who's the steward in the main lounge.'

'What did you and Sir Conrad talk about at that meeting?' Webb asked.

Aubrey thought for some time.

'All right. You're going to find all this out sooner or later,' he replied, 'so I might as well tell you the whole story.'

89

'Conrad had confided in me several days before, just as he was starting the Henry Lang trial. He told me he had been gambling far too much, and he had lost a lot of money.'

'Where was he doing his gambling?' Webb asked.

'At the Clermont Club in Berkeley Square.'

'Blimey. You'd need a few bob to play in a place like that, I should think,' Raymond commented.

'Conrad wasn't short of money,' Aubrey replied, 'at least, not at first. He was doing well at the Bar, and there was some family money on his wife's side. The problem was that he got out of his depth. Greta Thiemann was his mistress. She encouraged him to play for higher and higher stakes because she liked the thrill of it all – as long as it was his money they were gambling with, rather than hers. Of course, his luck eventually deserted him and he lost a great deal of money.'

'How much money?' Webb asked.

Aubrey shrugged. 'I'm not sure he told me the whole story. It couldn't have been less than £30,000 to £40,000.'

'Did his wife know anything about all this?'

'No. I don't think so.'

'If Greta lost him that much money,' Raymond said, 'it sounds to me like he had an obvious motive for killing her.'

Aubrey shook his head. 'No. If Conrad killed her, it would have been a sudden loss of temper, a loss of self-control. He wouldn't kill anyone in cold blood. I've known Conrad for many years. I'm sure of that.'

Webb smiled grimly.

'Oh, please don't tell me that, sir. We've just finished one provocation case. I'm not sure I could take another.'

'I'm not saying he did kill her,' Aubrey replied quickly. 'I don't know whether he did or not. All I'm saying is, if he did, it wasn't premeditated.'

Webb nodded.

'Well, let's get back to the gambling. Had he managed to pay off his debts, or did he owe money to anyone?'

'He owed money.'

'Who to? The Clermont Club, or some people there?'

'No. He borrowed money to pay for what he lost at cards. You have to, if you want to go on playing, especially somewhere like the Clermont. You can't default on your gambling debts; and of course you have to have funds to keep playing so that you can chase your losses.'

'Borrowed from whom?'

Aubrey hesitated.

'From a man who claimed to represent what he called a "syndicate". He told me that Greta had introduced them.'

Raymond scoffed.

'Oh, here we go. How much?'

'£20,000, at a ruinous rate of interest, needless to say, and regular payments. He would have ended up paying half of what he borrowed in interest, in addition to the amount itself. And the man made very clear to him what would happen if he failed to pay. I'm sure I don't have to spell it out for you.'

'No, you don't, sir,' Webb replied. 'We've come across people like that before, obviously. Any chance of a name?'

'Daniel Cleary. Conrad said he was known as "Danny Ice".'

Both officers sat back in their chairs. It was some time before either spoke.

'Can I make sure I've got this right, sir? Sir Conrad told you that he had borrowed from Daniel Cleary? Are you sure about that?'

'Yes. That's what he told me.'

Webb shook his head.

'Well, that's quite a coincidence, isn't it? Daniel Cleary turned

PETER MURPHY

up in our murder case – the one Sir Conrad tried just before he disappeared. The defendant in that case claimed that Cleary had threatened him, and scared him so much that he carried a knife with him – the knife he had on him when he was provoked to kill his wife. So, I'm to believe that the judge was sitting there, trying my case, listening to evidence about Daniel Cleary, while he was in debt to Cleary and receiving threats from Cleary himself, am I? Is that what you're telling me?'

'I can only tell you what Conrad told me, Inspector.'

The officers looked at each other.

'So now we have another possible theory, sir, don't we?' Raymond suggested. 'It's possible that Cleary could have been involved in Sir Conrad's disappearance.'

'Let's hope you're wrong,' Webb replied. 'But if you're right, Cleary might be on the hook for killing Greta Thiemann as well.'

'With his record, I wouldn't put it past him,' Raymond replied.

Webb breathed out sharply.

'I want scenes of crime to go over Rainer's flat again with a fine-tooth comb, and this time they're looking for evidence that Cleary was there, fingerprints, anything.'

'Right you are, sir.'

'All right,' Webb said to Aubrey. 'There's just one more thing. The reason we went to the flat on Saturday morning was that we had received a complaint from three barristers in his former chambers, claiming that Sir Conrad had stolen money from them, in the form of cheques, presumably to cover his debts. But you know all about that, don't you, Mr Smith-Gurney?'

Gareth had been sitting quietly beside Aubrey, saying nothing. But now he stirred and put a hand on Aubrey's arm.

'I'm not quite sure what you mean by that, Inspector.'

'I don't think Mr Smith-Gurney will deny it, sir. My information is that he attended a meeting with these three barristers and their head of chambers, and tried to reach a compromise with them, in return for their not telling us about it. Isn't that true, Mr Smith-Gurney?'

'Conrad felt very badly about what he'd done. They were

colleagues and friends, and he had stolen from them, and he hated himself for it. He was anxious to repay them, but he couldn't do that until he'd repaid Cleary – not if he wanted to stay alive and well. So I asked them to give him time to make good the loss.'

'Some might call that being an accessory after the fact to theft,' Webb said.

Gareth sat up in his chair.

'This stops here' he said decisively. 'All that was going on was an attempt to resolve a situation so that no one lost out. The barristers would commit no offence simply by not referring the matter to the police, so Mr Smith-Gurney was entirely within his rights to act as he did. If you want to go down that road, you will have to caution him, and he will need a solicitor, and this meeting is at an end. Your choice.'

Webb sat back with a smile.

'I have too much work to do to mess around with that, Mr Morgan-Davies. My priority is to find Conrad Rainer, and my next priority after that is to find out who murdered Greta Thiemann, and both of those things now seem far more complicated than they did on Saturday morning. So no, I'm not going to waste my time on a doubtful accessory to theft.'

He turned back to Aubrey.

'Are you sure you don't know where he is?'

'I don't know where he is. If I did, I would tell you.'

'And if he contacts you…?'

'I will tell you.'

'Do you believe him, sir?' Raymond asked, as they made their way out of chambers into Middle Temple Lane.

'No,' Webb replied.

90

The annual Christmas party at Two Wessex Buildings tended to follow a familiar pattern. Members of chambers were expected to be punctual and to entertain the numerous guests until 8.30, at which time the guests, with a few favoured exceptions, were expected to leave. Most members of chambers left shortly after, but there were a few who stayed on to enjoy a quiet drink or two afterwards. Bernard Wesley had started the tradition of inviting anyone who was still there at 9.30 into his room for a brandy. Gareth Morgan-Davies had continued the tradition. On this occasion, the cold and rain had driven most of the members of chambers and their guests away early, in the hope of getting home before the weather took the forecast turn for the worse. By 9.30, when Gareth Morgan-Davies produced his bottle of brandy, only Ben and Jess, Harriet, and Aubrey remained.

'Well, I must say, you're a dark horse, Harriet,' Gareth said, toasting everyone. 'We didn't know about this man of yours. You've been keeping him up your sleeve, have you?'

'She certainly has,' Ben grinned. 'We share a room in chambers, and I didn't have a clue.'

'Nor did your pupil-master,' Aubrey added.

Harriet blushed.

'When you grow up with a father who's an ambassador, you get addicted to keeping secrets. I've been seeing Monty for about a year. He's been keen to meet some of you, so I thought tonight I would take the plunge.'

'I'm so glad you did,' Jess said. 'He's charming.'

'Thank you.'

'And he's a fellow in your father's college?'

'College fellow and University lecturer in anthropology.'

'Well, it was a pleasure to meet him,' Gareth said. 'I'm sorry he had to rush off.'

'Yes. He had to get back up to Cambridge for some faculty thing tomorrow morning. I'm going up there to spend Christmas, so he'll have to endure Christmas dinner with my parents. Poor man. If he survives that, he can survive anything.'

'I'm sure your father is delighted,' Aubrey said.

She smiled. 'If he is, he probably won't tell me. I'll find out about it from my mother.'

She saw the newspaper on Gareth's desk and saw her chance to change the subject.

'Did you see the *Standard* this evening?' She stood, picked the paper up and turned to the page she wanted. 'Here's a name we all remember.' She began to read aloud.

BERMONDSEY MAN SENTENCED
FOR BLACKMAIL AND ASSAULT

A Bermondsey man who threatened a West End art dealer with violence, and assaulted him with a crowbar over an alleged gambling debt, was jailed at the Old Bailey today for seven years. Daniel Cleary, 38, also known as 'Danny Ice', was described by Judge Milton Janner as 'an exceptionally vicious and ruthless man who preyed on vulnerable men and women in need of money'. Passing sentence, the judge added that a long prison sentence was needed to protect the community from Cleary and to deter others who might be tempted to commit similar offences. The judge cautioned members of the public to resist the temptation to borrow money from people they did not know.

Ben glanced at Jess.

'Any mention of Henry Lang?'

Harriet scanned the article again.

'No, not a word. The victim's name is Evans.'

'Barratt would have told us if Henry's case had been brought up, surely,' Jess said.

Harriet continued reading.

Virginia Castle, defending, told the court that Cleary had a long history of drug addiction, and had given in to the temptation to act as an enforcer for men involved with organised crime, to make money to fund his addiction. She added that Cleary hoped to get help for his addiction while serving his sentence.

Jess laughed.

'Good for Ginny. I'm sure Danny Ice will emerge from prison totally rehabilitated.'

'I'll bet Ginny will be representing him again within six months of his release,' Ben said.

'You are such a cynic, Ben, aren't you?' Gareth said. 'I'm sure he'll be a model citizen.'

'For six months, yes, he probably will.'

'Talking of names, Harriet,' Gareth continued, 'is there any mention of Conrad Rainer, by any chance?'

Aubrey frowned and looked down at his shoes.

Harriet shook her head. 'No. It only deals with this one case. Why do you ask?'

'The *Sunday Times* mentioned him last week,' Gareth replied. 'There was a reported sighting of him in Brazil – São Paulo, if I remember rightly. Hearing about Daniel Cleary again reminded me of it.'

'If you're going on the run, Brazil is as good a place as any,' Ben commented. 'No extradition treaty with the UK.'

'It's all speculation,' Aubrey said quietly. 'There have been a lot of so-called sightings, but none of them has been verified, or anything close to it.'

There was a silence.

'It was a strange business, Aubrey, wasn't it?' Ben asked.

'In what way?'

'Well, Rainer was being threatened by Cleary while he was

trying a man who was also being threatened by Cleary. That's quite a coincidence, isn't it?'

'Yes, I suppose you could look at it in that way.'

'How else could you look at it? And he went through the whole trial without telling anyone, did he?'

'Would you really expect him to, Ben? In the circumstances?'

'I think he might have told Andrew Pilkington in confidence. Andrew is Treasury Counsel. He could have arranged protection for him.'

Aubrey shook his head.

'But the whole story would probably have come out. He would have been taking a terrible risk.'

'Perhaps so. But Cleary wasn't just a personal problem, was he? He was also highly relevant to the case he was trying. Surely, at the very least, he should have – ?'

'Recused himself?' Aubrey laughed. 'Yes, technically he should have, of course. But judicial propriety wasn't the main consideration by then, was it? Conrad knew this was going to be his last case. If he'd told Andrew – or you – why he needed to hand the case over to someone else, that would have been the end of him, there and then.'

'He could have found some reason, other than telling them that he was involved with Cleary,' Ben replied. 'A judge can always find a way out of trying a criminal case if he really wants to.'

'But he *didn't* want to,' Aubrey said. 'He thought that Henry Lang was provoked to kill his wife, and he thought a conviction for murder would have been a miscarriage of justice. He wanted to do everything he could to prevent that.'

'In which he was successful,' Gareth pointed out, 'with a certain amount of help from Ben and Jess, of course.'

'Yes, and I'm sure that the verdict would have eased his mind.'

'Are you saying that Conrad was deliberately trying to steer the case towards manslaughter?' Harriet asked.

'That was obvious,' Ben interjected, before Aubrey could reply. 'Andrew Pilkington wasn't pleased about it, and Jess and I were concerned that he was going too far, and that he might push the jury the other way. He had no criminal experience at all. It was sheer good luck that the jury came back with the right verdict.'

'I don't think that's fair,' Aubrey said morosely. 'Conrad could have coped with any criminal trial, with help from the Bar. But he was under tremendous pressure. Even so, he did his best to get a just result. Some of us think that's what judges are there for. I think you might at least give him some credit for that.'

'And while we're on that subject,' Ben said, 'Rainer knew all about the application we were going to make to admit Harriet's evidence – the privilege question – because you had tipped him off about it.'

Aubrey smiled.

'I believe I admitted that when you bearded me in my den at the time.'

'Yes, but I didn't know the whole story then, did I?'

'Conrad may have consulted me about it and asked for my views, Ben. Judges are allowed to consult before making a decision, you know. If he hadn't asked me, he would have asked one of the Old Bailey judges over lunch. It happens all the time.'

'But you'd spoken to us about it before you spoke to Conrad,' Ben replied. 'There are rules, Aubrey, and the rules are there for a purpose.'

'Are you going to shop me to the Bar Council, Ben?'

Ben shook his head. 'No, of course not.'

'Well, then…'

Gareth held up a hand.

'All right. Let's remember this is supposed to be a party. Everyone have another brandy.'

He refilled the glasses, and the tension slowly eased.

'I have a different question,' Gareth said, as they raised their glasses in a silent toast.

'Off the record, Aubrey, you really don't know where Conrad Rainer is?'

'I honestly have no idea,' Aubrey replied.

'And you didn't help him on his way?'

'No comment.'

Gareth laughed.

'I take it that you don't think he was done in by Daniel Cleary?'
'No.'
'Or that Daniel Cleary murdered Greta Thiemann?'
'No.'

'Are the police ever going to find Conrad Rainer?'
'No.'

They were silent for some time.

'So what happened to Conrad Rainer, Aubrey?' Gareth asked. 'He'd been successful all his life: doing well at the Bar, nice home in the country, a wife with money. What on earth went so wrong for him?'

'It wasn't enough,' Aubrey replied. 'He wanted more. He wanted excitement, the thrill of gambling; and he found a woman who not only encouraged him, but made it all a lot more exciting – and a lot more dangerous – than he ever expected.'

He was silent for some moments.

'But it was more than that,' he added. 'He wasn't afraid of the danger. He courted it. He loved it. He loved every minute of it. He loved it so much that finally, he called down the storm, and he stood right in its path and faced it. And it carried him away.'

Author's Note

In the course of my research for this book I took the fortunate decision to contact the Clermont Club to ask for their help. I told them that I was writing a novel, and that I wanted to set some of the scenes in the Club, and that I would very much like the chance to see the place for myself. I assured them that this was not another book about Lord Lucan, the Club's most notorious member, but that he would play a peripheral role in the story. I didn't have much confidence that they would be very keen on the idea. I couldn't have been more wrong.

I received a friendly, welcoming reply from Alison Sullivan, the Clermont's general manager, inviting my wife Chris and myself to visit the Club and spend some time. Alison also offered to have members of her staff answer any questions I might have. Needless to say, I took full advantage.

Chris and I were made very welcome. Melodie Triffaux, the Clermont's marketing executive, gave us a guided tour of William Kent's magnificent town house at 44 Berkeley Square. As befits an important listed building, Kent's design, including the famous staircase, has been carefully and lovingly preserved, but the Club has done far more than legally required to ensure its continuity and the Club's presence there is almost inconspicuous. The house is one of the architectural glories of London and, regardless of the book, it was well worth the trip just to see it.

The casino manager, Marcello Benelli, was able to help me to reconstruct what the Club had looked like in 1970 and 1971, as the John Aspinall era was drawing to a close, but still three years before Lucan's disappearance. He had some photographs from the period, and was able to tell me how the use of various rooms in the Club had changed since then – surprisingly little, as it turned out, but these are valuable details for an author. Marcello also took me through the mechanics of *chemin de fer*, a game which is no longer played commercially at the Club, but which had been a staple in its day. I had learned the basics from online sources, but there are many details that Marcello, with his long experience of casinos, brought to life for me.

As a parting gift, they gave me a copy of John Pearson's *The Gamblers* (Arrow Books, London, 2007). I had already read Pearson's book on Kindle, but it was nice, and very useful, to have it in hard copy. Pearson provides a penetrating insight into the group that frequented the Clermont at the time – not only Lucan, but also Dominick Elwes, James Goldsmith, Ian and Susie Maxwell-Scott, and others – and into the world of high-stakes gaming generally. It was a valuable resource.

As ever, my thanks to Ion and Claire at No Exit Press, my agent Annette Crossland, and my editor, Irene Goodacre. Thanks also to Chris, for whom the visit to 44 Berkeley Square, though enjoyable, must have been poor compensation for having a husband who spends so much time at his computer.

About Us

In addition to No Exit Press, Oldcastle Books has a number of other imprints, including Kamera Books, Creative Essentials, Pulp! The Classics, Pocket Essentials and High Stakes Publishing > oldcastlebooks.co.uk

For more information about Crime Books to go > crimetime.co.uk

Check out the kamera film salon for independent, arthouse and world cinema > kamera.co.uk

For more information, media enquiries and review copies please contact marketing > marketing@oldcastlebooks.co.uk